THE QUIET AFTER

FOLIANT
BOOK 1

MIKE KRAUS

MUONIC
PRESS

THE QUIET AFTER
FOLIANT: ONE

By
Mike Kraus

MUONIC
P R E S S

© 2025 Muonic Press Inc
www.muonic.com

www.MikeKrausBooks.com
hello@mikeKrausBooks.com
www.facebook.com/MikeKrausBooks

CONTENTS

WANT MORE AWESOME BOOKS?

Find more fantastic tales at books.to/readmorepa.

If you're new to reading Mike Kraus, consider visiting his website (www.mikekrausbooks.com) and signing up for his free newsletter. You'll receive several free books and a sample of his audiobooks, too, just for signing up, you can unsubscribe at any time and you will receive absolutely *no* spam.

SPECIAL THANKS

Special thanks to my awesome beta team, without whom this book wouldn't be nearly as great.

Thank you!

READ THE NEXT BOOK IN THE SERIES

Foliant Book 2

Available Here
books.to/foliant2

CHAPTER ONE

The O'Brian Family
Los Angeles, California

Jason O'Brian leaned forward in the driver's seat, pressing his chest close to the steering wheel, both hands coiled around the contoured leather. Grunting, he rotated one shoulder as the incessant chorus of bleating horns barraged the RV from outside, like being caught in a war between several species of geese.

"You know," he said with a firm shake of his head, "I still remember when your parents agreed to loan us this beast," He slapped the steering wheel with the palm of his right hand, glancing toward his wife Samantha in the passenger seat. "We had plans. Long, winding dirt roads, nothing but the trees, the ocean and maybe the occasional campground."

Jason took a breath and straightened his arms, leaning back from the wheel.

"We made lists, Sam, remember? National parks, landmarks up and down the west coast. I remember very, very clearly."

"Don't say it, Jason." Samantha lifted a single eyebrow into a peaked arch above one narrowed, ice-blue eye.

He made an exaggerated motion to peer through the front slope of the RV's windshield.

"I swear, downtown L.A. must be nature's best-kept secret."

"You're full of jokes today, aren't you? How do you propose we drive down the west coast without going through Los Angeles?"

"What about you, kids? You remember those lists?" Jason looked up into the rear-view mirror, catching the attention of Elijah and Sarah in the back seat where they were both looking out the windows while absentmindedly stroking the family German Shepherd, Kale. "Pretty sure the only natural thing I've seen all day is Kale back there, and those whole-wheat chips your mom bought at the stop 'n rob."

"This is between you and Mom," Elijah was quick to respond. "Leave us out of it!" He thumbed the earbuds back in his ears, exchanging an exaggeratedly wide-eyed look with his twin sister next to him.

"I see how it is." Jason tapped the brakes and turned the wheel, fighting with the large RV to make its way around a slow-moving truck that filled the lane ahead.

"It would help if you knew how to drive this thing," Sam remarked with a half-hearted smile. "I could always take over if you want."

"Excuse me? I don't remember 'bumper-to-bumper traffic in a seven-ton box navigation' being in the list of training exercises, do you?"

"No, but I did learn how to handle stress." Sam laughed and Jason joined in with her, the two sharing in their exchange of good humor. She passed a quick glance at her rear-view mirror, the laugh dying on her lips.

"And I learned what a convoy looks like." She leaned toward her mirror, craning her neck for a better angle. "Jason?" Her voice drew taut, a thin, gasping whisper as she clawed at the vinyl dashboard separating them from the windshield. "Check your mirror."

Her husband jolted to attention, leaning to look into the driver's side mirror. While the traffic around them was nearly at a standstill, the group of armored transports surged forward, charging at a rapid pace as they wove through traffic, horns blaring, cutting through the line of civilian vehicles. Jason's mouth dropped open, his grip around the wheel tightening, drawing his skin into pale whiteness around the knuckles.

Sparks exploded in the mirror, the crunch of metal-on-metal deafening as the lead vehicle barreled into a space between cars too tight to fit. The front side panel of a box truck folded inward, crumpling as a twenty-ton transport hammered into it, knocking it aside to make room for the rest of the convoy. The other vehicles were concealed behind the lead transport, but the sounds of grinding metal and shattering glass flooded forward in a constant stream. As the transport lurched left, slamming hard into a small hatchback, a smaller, but equally determined Humvee was revealed behind it, trying to follow in its wake.

The mirror of a large-sized SUV burst apart as the transport struck it, scraping broadside, forcing the vehicle away as it did its best to speed forward. The almost deafening storm of honking horns intensified, growing in frequency and volume, complemented by the screams and shouts of displaced motorists. Second by second, the speeding convoy barreled its way through, carving a ragged, broken path through the traffic, parting the vehicles in an uneven thunder of colliding bumpers.

"Jason!" Samantha shouted, but Jason was already snapping into motion.

His grip tight around the wheel, he cranked it right and pumped the gas, grinding the RV's bumper against a car in front of him, shoving it out of the way. Another vehicle slammed on its brakes, rubber squealing as it tried desperately to stop, leaving a sparse gap for the RV to work its way through. Mere seconds later, the convoy screamed past, the vehicle ahead of the RV thrown up and forward by the armored transport's impact. Wheels left the pavement, spinning wildly, a chain-reaction of vehicular destruction tangling into a winding mass of crumpled metal ahead of them.

Jason battled with the RV, navigating it into the next lane, forcing another line of cars to slam on their brakes, hammering horns shouting their displeasure. Voices followed the horns, the exact words muffled, but their intent and general meaning more than clear. He tracked the speeding convoy as he transitioned to the other lane, each car passing by in a mottled green blur of armor, glass and rubber tires. Jason didn't bother to count them, too focused on keeping the RV out of their way, cranking the wheel back left again to correct his angular path to the right.

"Dad, what's going on?" Elijah yanked the earbuds out of his ears, eyes widening in the rearview mirror, his sister mirroring his movements as the pair became aware of the rapid change in scenery. Sarah clung tight to Kale as she rocked back and forth, nearly falling to the floor.

"Stay buckled up, Eli! You, too, Sarah! Just hold on tight, okay? Try to get Kale in her crate if you can!"

Samantha clicked the volume knob of the radio, twisting it right as Jason broadsided another car, jolting it sideways against a guardrail.

"—while the President has yet to speak at his rally at the Convention Center, there are reports coming through of some sort of disturbance in downtown Los Angeles. Uh, in fact, reports are coming through now of some sort of..." the voice trailed off as Jason shot a concerned look toward his wife, receiving only a shrug of her shoulders in response.

Jason hammered the brake pedal and steered left, scraping alongside a mid-sized passenger van. A shower of sparks erupted from the point of impact as the RV slewed left, grinding past another car, punching a wider gap within traffic ahead. Slowly the road rose ahead as they approached an onramp, lifting at an angle, the gaps widening between tightly clutched vehicles. Through the static of the radio speakers, the newscaster cleared his throat as he came back on the air.

"Reports are coming in from eyewitness accounts in downtown Los Angeles that there appears to be some sort of biological event. We repeat, a biological event appears to be occurring throughout downtown Los Angeles. If you are in or around the Los Angeles Convention Center, please seek alternate routes. Our phone lines are flooded with—"

The newscaster's voice abruptly cut out, replaced with dead air as the RV crunched its way between two more cars, slapping them aside and charging up the onramp toward the elevated freeway standing a hundred yards above the streets of downtown LA. Shouts began to come from behind, filtering through the aluminum and glass sides of the vehicle, and a surge of foot traffic swept behind them along the sidewalks and roads. Far in the distance, barely visible in the side mirrors, pedestrians and motorists were clawing at their throats, dropping to their knees, exiting their vehicles and convulsing on the ground.

"How far are we?" Jason asked through clenched teeth, his foot hammering harder on the gas.

Samantha was already checking her side mirror, sharpened nails digging into her palms. "Not far enough. Keep driving."

"Mom? Dad? What's going on?" Eli twisted around to try and peer through the back windshield, an entire RV length behind him. Sarah huddled close to her window, palms pressed to the glass, watching the swarming traffic and the wave of death that was drawing ever closer.

"We don't know yet," Jason replied, easing down on the accelerator.

"People out there – Mom, they're—"

"I know – just hush, let your father drive. Jason! Look out!"

There was another jolting slam as he broadsided the front

5

panel of an SUV. The impact sent the smaller vehicle skidding away and Jason corrected his over-steer, once more bringing the RV straight, trying to push them farther up the onramp. The engine gunned and roared, accented by a chortling growl of other high-powered motors and the distant shouts of confused, panicking pedestrians. Beneath them, the military caravan careened its way through the traffic, continuing to batter its way between vehicles, the lead vehicle forcing spaces wide enough for the following ones to fit through.

As he watched, a large tractor trailer slewed through the gap made by the caravan, then slammed headlong into one of the support columns holding the elevated freeway aloft. A massive bang of crushed metal erupted from the point of impact, glass exploding outward. Two other vehicles swerved around the suddenly halted truck, angling toward the road ahead. Each of them struck another support, one right after the next, the first car folding like an accordion as the second slammed into its rear end at high speed. The onramp banked sharply left and Jason refocused on the road as traffic began to move again. Up ahead, a pickup swerved diagonally before them, brakes squealing before it struck the guardrail with enough momentum to buckle metal and rip the barricade from its moorings.

Jason stared wide-eyed as the truck tore through the mangled remains of the rail and plunged over the edge, vanishing from the elevated onramp and smashing hard onto the pavement below. Somewhere in the distance an explosion roared, the street beneath their tires shaking with the deep rumble of the detonation. The RV followed the gradual lefthand turn, two cars in their wake slamming together into a tangle of wreckage. As they followed the upward bend, Jason glanced out through his driver's side window at the streets far below.

Traffic congealed like a week-old scab, vehicles clotting the road, creating a barricade of buckled metal in the wake of the military convoy's passing. Littered throughout stopped cars and trucks, people opened their doors and stepped out only to slump to the ground, motionless, joining the throngs of pedestrians that were no longer running, but strewn about on the sidewalks and crossings. They were too far away from the RV for Jason to make out the details, but no one was moving, and even the honking and jostling of the traffic had gone eerily silent and still.

"Jason? Are you seeing this?" Samantha pointed out the opposite window as Kale barked furiously in the background. "Everyone's just..."

"I know."

"Something's going on down there. We need to get *higher*, get away from it!"

"I know, I'm trying!"

Vehicles no longer moved on the surface streets, the bustling traffic turned to an ocean of stalled motorists, the narrow gaps between cars filled by collapsed, motionless figures. Smoke rose both from the crashes beneath the overpass and in the distance, twisting in wide spirals, fueled by a base of glowing oranges and reds. The onramp made one more gradual bend, which Jason followed, using the RV's bulk to push his way through until they pulled up onto the elevated freeway, several stories above the pavement below. More cloying smoke boiled at the base of the support columns, a thickening cloud obscuring the horrors beneath them. Up ahead, other vehicles stopped along the freeway shoulder, people standing outside their cars and trucks, staring back toward the downtown congestion.

Jason braked the RV, bringing it to a shuddering halt and gripped the handle of the driver's side door. "Jason!" Samantha grabbed at his arm, stopping him. "What are you doing?"

"They're okay." He nodded toward the others standing on the elevated freeway.

"We don't even know what's going on!"

"That's what I'm going to try to find out." He looked into the mirror at his twins, both of whom were staring out their windows. "You all stay here, keep the doors locked. I'll be back in a flash."

Jason tugged the handle of the door and pushed it open before Samantha could stop him, stepping out from the RV and down onto the pavement of the freeway. The ground was firm, yet swayed slightly as he stood there, like walking the deck of a cruise ship on unsteady seas. An overpowering smell of gas and smoke rolled over him, swirling upward through the gaps in the roadway. Reaching behind him, he closed the door of the RV and stepped to the edge of the overpass, staring out at the carnage.

A vast sea of stalled traffic and dead bodies filled the distance between where he stood and the area surrounding the Los Angeles Convention Center, a massive carpet of glittering metal, starred glass and slumped corpses. Even within his limited field of vision there had to have been thousands dead, if not tens of thousands. His eyes stung with the stink of fuel and lingering smoke, his swimming head causing him to sway in slow circles. The opposite door slammed, and Samantha swept around the front of the RV, face pale and eyes wide.

"Jason! Are you—"

"I'm okay," he blurted out. "I just feel a little dizzy is all." Jason swayed gently again, moving uneasily from one side to the next.

"It's not you." Sam pressed her hands to his arms and squeezed tightly. "It's the freeway *moving*! Get in the RV. Get in *right now*!"

CHAPTER TWO

The O'Brian Family
Los Angeles, California

Jason stared wide-eyed across the sea of carnage beneath the elevated highway. Traffic was a patchwork quilt of stalled and smoking vehicles, a ragged gouge dug by the military convoy terminating at the support structure holding the roadway above a vast sea of death. His throat burned raw with the thickening smoke, tears streaming free from his stinging, blinking eyes. Shock drove a stake through his spine, sticking his feet to the underlying pavement, his body rigid and fixed like a stone statue.

"Jason!" Samantha shouted, staying close to the RV. "Did you hear me?"

He took a single step back from the edge, still hypnotized by the wreckage spread out beneath them. Downtown Los Angeles pushed out to the north, little more than a smoking wasteland of stalled cars, trucks and tractor trailers. The square blockade of the convention center fell within his view far in the distance, a short way to the left of the circular sports arena famous for hosting football games and musical venues. There was no sense of revelry, no anticipation of an entertaining show, just the smoldering wreckage of a city, once vibrant with life.

Buildings were clustered one on top of the next, just like the stopped vehicles blocking the roads, a relentless, claustrophobic barrage of concrete, stone and glass shrapnel. Smoke twisted from the equally gray façade of tightly grouped buildings, the glitter of glass windows gleaming beneath the gaze of the late morning sun. Bodies littered the sidewalk and shoulders, some draped over the hoods of cars, others slumped out from barely opened doors, filling the narrow empty spaces between stopped vehicles. The ever-present smoke formed an acrid, throat-burning reek that soured Jason's stomach.

Helicopter rotors swept the air above them and he craned his neck, staring up into the sunbaked sky. At least three pale-colored copters fell into view, a swirling trio of newscasters, each fighting for a better angle. A short distance away, another group of bystanders on the overpass lifted their hands, shouting at the helicopters, begging for an attempted rescue. However, they made no attempt to come closer, instead circling for a better angle, far more concerned with the headlines than with actually saving lives.

"They're dead," he gasped, turning toward his wife, making his way directly to the RV's driver's side.

"Who?"

"Everyone." The word was bitter in his mouth.

"If they're all dead there isn't much we can do. But first things first. Get back in the RV, Jason. That dizzy feeling isn't you, it's the whole highway!"

As if on cue, the road shifted beneath Jason's feet, his forward stride jostling as the pavement threatened to swing out from under him. A whining groan of strain bellowed from the supports beneath the multi-lane freeway and, from somewhere nearby, a shrill voice screamed in abject terror. Jason wheeled toward the scream, the same group of bystanders focusing their attention on the bridge beneath them instead of the helicopters above.

"Kids!" Samantha shouted, her voice echoing above the backdrop of wailing sirens, far into the distance. "Get strapped in! We need to move right now! Jason, I need you here with me, *now*!"

She bolted toward the passenger door, disappearing beyond the front of the RV. Jason swung up the steps and pulled the driver's side door open, even as the road shifted again, a sudden sideways lurch that threatened to knock him off the stairs and back onto its cracked surface. Lunging into the driver's side, he jerked himself into the seat, gripping the steering wheel for purchase as the RV leaned sharply left. A ragged, uneven crack formed in the pavement, the roadway buckling as a dark line of fracture split its surface. Undulating snapping tore from the cracked and buckled concrete, a sudden whiplash whine of something critical giving way. Jason stared out his window as the guardrail to his left dipped sharply down, a massive chunk of the road breaking off and tumbling from view.

Up ahead, a throng of traffic clotted the road, people darting frantically, a few other survivors fortunate to have made it to the higher altitude that had apparently protected them from death below. Those same bystanders who had been begging a helicopter for rescue scattered, trying to make it to their vehicles, as if there was anywhere for them to go. A woman sprinted toward a green hatchback, but the road shuddered violently, slowing her sprint. Seconds later, a slab of elevated freeway jerked downward, a crack widening, and then broke away, her hatchback vanishing into the void. She leaped to her feet and screamed a wild, feral sound, leaping toward the falling car as if she might grab it and drag it back up, single-handedly. Instead, another violent crack smashed the road like a hammer, and a chunk of pavement beneath her gave way, swallowing her screams down to the blistered roadway far below.

"Onramp!" Samantha shouted, clutching Jason's right arm. "Behind us! There! Reverse, get us onto that ramp!"

Jason swallowed a thick lump of tension down his throat, leaning over his wife to get a look through her window. His rearview mirror was useless, snapped off and reduced to jagged metal, leaving him no view.

"Just trust me! I'll navigate."

Jason nodded, twisting the key and gunning the ignition. Ahead of them, the road collapsed, one side of the freeway lunging up like a drawbridge, a sudden upward slam that sent a young man cartwheeling down into the abyss. Jason ground the gears, finally finding reverse, his fingers gripping tight around the wheel.

"Go! Straight back! Just drive!" Samantha leaned toward the mirror and Jason followed her instructions.

His foot hammered the gas and the RV lurched, even as the cracks spread like spider webs on the road before them. More chunks of elevated freeway snapped off and fell, exposing blunt bones of rebar. A violent shudder shook the road just ahead, a chunk of pavement nearly disintegrating by the front tires of the RV. Thick clumps of it broke apart and away, the front tires dipping suddenly forward as the RV teetered, sliding toward the empty air. Jason slammed the accelerator, the gear already punched into reverse, the back tires whirling wildly, elevated just enough to not grip pavement. They slid, scraping against the road as they moved toward the collapsed freeway before them, larger chunks of ragged rock breaking loose.

"Back!" Jason screamed so loud his smoke-seared throat burned even more. "Sam! Kids! Get in the back, we need some weight!"

Samantha understood, unclasping her seatbelt and throwing herself backwards over the rear seat. The twins tore their own belts loose, scrambling to their feet, the three of them pushing through the narrow space into the living quarters of the RV, Kale barking and whining from inside her crate where it sat on the floor near the sofa. Metal scraped on pavement as the RV inched forward, more road shattered into fragments, spilling away. Every one of the bystanders who had been huddled around their vehicles were gone and what remained of the elevated highway was jigsaw puzzle fragments barely held together by fraying strands.

"We're here!" Samantha shouted, the three of them surging toward the rear and the RV gently eased back, the weight shifting.

Jason slammed the gas, the rear tires spinning wildly until finally rubber squealed a shrill scream, striking pavement and taking hold. The RV lurched back, screaming away from the collapsing road, barely avoiding another large section of crumbling asphalt as it vanished from view. The RV backtracked, striking a car with a muffled crunch, though at a shallow enough angle that it pushed the vehicle away and kept moving.

"Turn left, turn the wheel left, point the backside that way!" Samantha furiously shouted her instructions as she peered through a narrow window in the rear of the vehicle. Jason followed her guidance, cranking the wheel as he accelerated, bringing the RV sharply around as they reversed. Sam shouted in surprise, tumbling to the left, Eli and Sarah desperately grasping for a handhold.

"Sorry!" Jason shouted absently as his family tried to claw themselves upright.

Another massive chunk of the overpass buckled and folded inward, the spider web cracks shattering the foundation that had held them up just moments before. The rear of the RV tipped upward as they met the sloped onramp in the ornate cloverleaf of crossing interstates. The rear bumper thumped and scraped the upward pavement, but the RV ground backwards, still moving from the collapsing road ahead.

"Keep turning that wheel! Sharper! Sharper!" Samantha's voice echoed throughout the RV's interior.

Cupboards swung open as he swerved the vehicle, dishes

spilling out, clattering throughout the living spaces of the camper. Sarah shrieked briefly, though it was cut off by a clamp of her teeth.

"Everyone okay?" Jason called, unable to see their status in the rearview mirror.

"Worry about the RV! I've got the kids!" Samantha screamed back.

The vehicle scraped along the sharply bent guardrail, the rear of the RV bouncing as it struck metal. Jason used that momentum to keep twisting the camper around the bend in the onramp, trying not to focus his attention on the rapidly deteriorating interstate overpass they were barely leaving behind. A large section of road where the onramp met the cloverleaf shattered apart, breaking into jagged fragments then tumbled away, leaving sparse, empty air in its wake. Through the chasm that had opened up, the mass of broken and burning vehicles collected below, somewhat obscured by smoke.

Sections of pavement tumbled down and hammered the roofs of the vehicles below, slamming into them with an echoing orchestra of metallic impacts. Dark smoke coagulated beneath the shattering freeway, blissfully obscuring the worst of the carnage below. He cranked the wheel, bringing the RV back around, smashing aside another smaller vehicle before they hit the crest at the upper section of the ramp. Jason hit the brakes, halting the RV on the breach, his rapid breathing filling the silence of the RV's front half while Samantha gripped a shelf near the rear of the vehicle, her muscles taut with the effort of her squeeze.

"Mom? Dad? Are we safe?" Elijah inched forward, his voice a quiet, fearful whisper from the rear, a silhouette of his head barely visible in Jason's mirror.

Jason and Samantha exchanged a brief glance, worry lining the corners of their eyes, lips pinched into flattened grimaces, mirror images of each other, sharing in a common concern. Samantha cleared her throat, then turned to the twins.

"Sarah? Elijah? Are you both okay?"

"I'm all right," Elijah replied.

"M—me, too," Sarah echoed, though her voice was thin and frail.

"Come on. Let's head back to the front, all right? Are you two with me?"

Jason's back remained rigid; his fingers tightly twisted around the wheel. Both arms were as straight and firm as rebar, his elbows aching from the straightness of his arms and the tight grip of his hands. Using various handholds, Samantha guided the children back through the RV, its floor littered with spilled dishes, various cabinets opened. She picked her way forward, closing cabinets as she did, though she left the discarded dishes where they lay.

"Stay with me. Okay? Sarah, come on." Samantha patiently urged the twins onward. She turned and once more met Jason's eyes in the rear-view mirror. "You okay, Jason?"

"Yeah," he replied through an exhalation. "I think so, anyway. Once my heart crawls down from my throat I'll give you a better answer."

Samantha threaded her way into the second-row seat, then crawled through and took her place in the passenger seat, finally letting out a breath she'd been holding once she was settled in place. Eli and Sarah did the same, finding their spots in the next row back. For a time, the only sound within the RV was the uneven inhalations and exhalations of their breathing and the quiet hum of the engine. Helicopter rotors continued sweeping overhead, though still at a high distance, the only exterior sounds throughout the suddenly broken cityscape that surrounded them.

"What's going on down there? Dad, did you say everyone was dead?" Sarah's worried voice asked the question as she leaned forward.

"Try to stay calm, okay? We're safe for the moment, but...." Samantha angled her head, looking back behind her. "Street level is a no-go. Whatever killed those people could still be down there. Right now, it seems our only protection is our elevation."

"So, they are dead? Like—really dead?" Eli's eyes glistened.

"I think so, buddy," Jason replied. His desire to protect his children was just barely overridden by his desire to keep them informed.

The RV rested at an angle; the windshield pointed toward the vast chasm of broken pavement ahead. Smoke clouded the sky, and even the very distant sirens from earlier had ceased their wailing. Jason engaged the emergency brake and settled into the driver's seat, forcing his stabbing breath to regulate. He reached toward the radio again, turning it on and listening. The station that had broadcast a few moments before was nothing but static, the rustling hiss of dead air coming from the speakers. Samantha reached over before Jason could, adjusting the dial, tracking through the various stations.

"—out of Sacramento, California. Reports from Los Angeles —" static broke in, hissing over the man's words. "—dead. Passage in and out of the city remains at a standstill, making it very difficult to—" the voice crackled into broken static again. "FEMA advises caution—" more static ripped apart the man's stuttering speech.

Samantha sighed audibly and tracked the dial a bit more, finally landing on another squelch of whispered, interrupted words.

"—as far south as Irvine and as far east as San Bernadino. There's still no word on the President who was expected to speak at a rally ahead of his re-election campaign. Fears are mounting that the... among the thousands of dead on the city streets. Domestic and international air travel in... LAX is being re-routed while we await word—" more static broke into the man's restless speech.

Samantha's jaw clenched, her steel eyes focusing on the radio. Pink lips parted slightly, revealing the clenched fence of her teeth. Jason had seen that look before, and as frayed as his nerves were, it settled him, if only a little.

"--WBKF out of Bakersfield. We've been attempting to connect with our sister station in Los Angeles for the past thirty minutes but have been unable to reach them since the crisis began. Witness testimony from a news helicopter reports that traffic is at a standstill downtown by the convention center with evidence of a potential biological incident. Rumors of streets filled with corpses are as of yet unvalidated, however—" Samantha snapped the radio to another station, withdrawing her fingers as though she'd touched something hot.

"Useless," she muttered. "Nobody knows anything."

"Word is coming through," a voice piped up, from another station, "what happened in Los Angeles may not be an isolated incident. We are hearing word from a station outside Las Vegas, Nevada that—" static overrode the voice, drowning it out in a metallic hiss of noise.

Jason once more dialed into some closer frequencies, but every Los Angeles station was masked in silence and static.

"Okay. Clearly, we need to rely on ourselves to figure this out." Jason curled his fingers once more around the vinyl steering wheel. "What do we know?"

"What do we know? Nothing." Samantha shrugged. "But apparently it's not isolated to Los Angeles if that last transmission is to be believed. We need to make a few educated guesses."

"I'm listening." Jason peered into the back seat, both Elijah and Sarah huddled together, inched forward, also clinging to every word their mother might say.

"The way that convoy came flying through, they were responding to something." Samantha's voice changed as she leaned across to look out the driver's side window. "That leads me to believe this might have been some sort of attack. Most likely biological, based on what the radio was saying right when everything went to hell in a bobsled."

"But why are we okay up here?"

"Without knowing exactly what it might be, I can't make any judgments one way or the other. What I will say is that we cannot assume anything. I don't need to remind anyone what assumptions do." She shot a look toward the back seat, both children nodding their understanding.

"Do you think this had something to do with the President?" Jason asked. He stared toward the north, trying to make out the vague shape of the Los Angeles Convention Center in the distance. A low-hanging haze filled the air, further fueled by fire and smoke, shrouding downtown L.A. in a choking mask.

"Seems like a major coincidence that it coincided with his speech, that's for sure. That doesn't necessarily explain what might be happening in Las Vegas, but we have to consider that information unconfirmed."

"If they were responding to something, where do you suppose they were headed?" Jason's attention focused on the wide lane of vehicular damage left in the wake of the frantic convoy. "I mean, they were obviously responding to *something*. They wouldn't be tearing through downtown LA for no reason."

"Who knows." Samantha looked out her window. Dark smoke billowed from beneath them, a roiling churn of grays and black, the place where the massive overpass used to exist nothing more than a cloud of dust and dirt slowly expanding in the breeze. "I don't know the layout of the city well enough to even guess. Maybe the convention center?"

"Just use the map on your phone," Sarah said from the back seat, leaning forward, presenting her cellphone resting on the palm of her hand. "If you really want to see where they were going."

Samantha withdrew her phone from her pocket, holding it in her hand, staring down at the dimly lit screen.

"That's not a bad idea, but there's something more important we need to do first."

Samantha navigated to the contacts section of her phone, swiping through a short list of familiar names. She settled on the entry for 'Mom and Dad Home' and stared down at the image that looked back at her. The square-shaped image stood stark against the white backdrop on her screen, her mother and father looking back at her. In the background, the sprawling landscape of their 200-acre vineyard in Oregon filled the rest of the image, rolling green hills and the immaculate twist and curls of richly colored vines.

She'd taken the picture herself only a few days earlier. After finishing a two-week long training course a short distance from their vineyard, she'd met her family there and borrowed her parents' RV, planning on a nice, leisurely trip down the west coast. They'd already made a few stops along the way but had hoped to continue on for a short distance before heading east for another week. After dropping the RV back off, they were scheduled to catch a flight back home to Grand Rapids.

"I'm sure they're okay," Jason said, resting a hand on his wife's knee. "Even if this hit Las Vegas and Los Angeles, I have to think coastal Oregon wasn't in anyone's crosshairs."

"We don't even know if this was an attack. It could have been almost anything." Samantha continued looking at the phone in her hand. She swallowed and tapped the number beneath the profile image, placing the phone on speaker.

No sound came out. There was no rapid busy signal, no hiss of distortion, no operator warning of circuits being busy. Just a deep, unsettled silence, a void of sound from the other side of the line. Anxious eyes lifted toward Jason, and he met those eyes with his own, lined with a similar anxiety. Los Angeles was consumed by smoke in all directions, thick and acrid, a wasteland of choked traffic and dead bodies. They were trapped on an isolated onramp, the freeway collapsed around them with nowhere to go and no way to tell how to get there.

Samantha hung up and tried again, but only got the same empty response. Jason withdrew his own phone and located the same contact, typing out a swift text message and pressing send. His message hovered there, showing no sign of delivery.

"Kids? Jason? Turn them off." Samantha nodded to her husband and children. "Turn them all off, okay? They're not doing us any good here and we need to conserve the batteries."

She leaned forward and uncoiled a length of cable from beneath the radio of the RV. Slotting it into her phone, she leaned back as the battery indicator lit, showing a tiny lightning bolt as proof of its charge. Jason and the kids listened to her directions, each of them holding down their power buttons until the screens winked to blackness, then stashed the slabs away.

Samantha tapped the call icon again, and again no sound came back.

"Please," she whispered, her eyes settling closed. "Please." She tried again and again, but as with the previous attempts, the only response she got was silence.

CHAPTER THREE

The Tills Family
Silverpine, Oregon

Sheila Tills jostled within the driver's seat of the Kubota UTV as it rolled over the uneven, grass covered pasture. Along each side of the wide, rolling path, vineyards grew thick and long, a seemingly endless sprawl of wooden frames, twisting vines and plump, rich smelling fruit. There was nothing Sheila loved more than rolling around beneath the late morning Pacific coast sun, sheltered by the canopy above the driver's seat of the UTV. Up ahead, in a small clearing to the right, she spotted Doug, her husband, as he chatted with a younger man, a sunhat covering his eyes, his hand gripping a clipboard firmly between clamped fingers.

Doug turned and waved, and Sheila waved back, slowing the UTV and easing it toward the side of the freshly mown path.

"Sheila! This is Gary with the Clatsop County Inspector's office. He was just signing off on our solar panels, weren't you, Gary?" Doug nodded, glancing at the young man above his narrow spectacles. His mouth eased into a crooked grin, framed within the neatly trimmed gray beard that covered his face.

"You know how it is, Mr. Tills. Gotta dot those I's and cross those t's."

"Gotta make sure the county is getting the money they believe they're owed is more like it. And how did that work out? Those panels kicking back the right kilowatt hours?"

"Everything looks top shape, sir." Gary nodded, then turned toward Sheila.

"Sheila Tills." She stepped free of the Kubota and shook the younger man's hand. "Pleasure to meet you."

"Pleasure's mine." Gary tipped his hat, then tucked his clip-board under his arm. "We're all set here, Mr. Tills. Thank you for your time." He turned and walked away, his work boots collecting dark mud from the path leading back to a nearby parking lot. The vineyards ended in a sharp corner, allowing the mown passage to lead out toward the front of the large building that stood nearby.

"Immaculate timing as always," Sheila said, a hand resting on her husband's shoulder. "Word travels fast around here, even when we try to keep things a secret."

Doug grunted good-naturedly. "Mhm. Figured they'd be out sooner rather than later what with everything we've been doing. Can't fault the man for doing his job, but still."

Sheila patted the seat next to her. "Hop in. I want to get back to the office, see if we got the stuff from Will."

"Oh boy. You in that big of a rush to get another bill from the accountant?" Doug gripped the rollbar of the UTV and started to hoist himself into the passenger seat as Sheila rounded the vehicle.

"Oh come on, now, be nice. It's supposed to be *good* news this time."

Doug grunted again. "Uh huh. I'll believe it when I see it." Doug crossed his arms and rested back in the seat as Sheila slowly accelerated.

Ahead of them, the building loomed large, a two-story structure with north-facing windows that gleamed in the light of the afternoon sun. Grassy hills sloped down along each side of the circular building, so that only one story was visible from the front. At the rear of the structure, loading dock doors were closed, a concrete slab jutting out over the grass. A meandering gravel path wound up the hill to the right, allowing trucks to make necessary deliveries right to the basement-level storage area.

"Mr. Tills!" A man strode forward, hand raised, cheeks flushed red with the exertion of running. "Sorry! Mr. Tills, can I grab you for a second?" Sheila coasted the UTV to a halt and Doug stepped out to intercept the man who jogged toward him.

"What can I do for you, Avery?" Doug asked.

The red-faced man wore dirt-stained overalls and a wide-brimmed hat, which he fumbled to peel off his head. Sweat-shined skin rode the curve of his skull, with tufts of hair bunched above his ears.

"One of the straddle harvesters blew a few bearings." Avery gestured toward the vineyards on the right side they'd passed moments before. "Fool thing is throttling those grapes instead of picking them, we've had to shut her down."

"That could be a problem. We still have a belt down, too, right?"

"Yes, sir. Belt number three is waiting for a new gear. It's already slowing down grape collection for the Chardonnay we're trying to get ready." Avery glanced apologetically toward Sheila and cleared his throat.

Doug shook his head, chewing his lower lip. "And which straddle harvester blew the bearings?"

"Number four."

"Can you grab the straddle from belt three and swap it out? At least put the two broken things together so we can get four up and running again?"

Avery considered that suggestion, his thick, gray eyebrows

clenching like crawling caterpillars. He was close to Doug's age and, after years of outdoor work, was finally slowing just a bit in the last few years as the vineyard prepared for its upcoming expansion. "That might take some work, but it should be manageable. We could lose a few hours of harvest this afternoon."

"I'll help you with it." Doug glanced at Sheila, who shook her head and leaned over in her seat.

"We've got a big dinner rush tonight, Doug. I need you inside."

"Son of a... well, we have to get production moving again somehow." Doug turned back toward Avery. "My wife's the boss, though. Make that happen, if you can. Swap the straddles, get one harvester and belt combo back running again, see if any of the field workers want a little overtime tonight to help build a bit more backlog. A few hours, maybe?"

"Yes, sir, Mr. Tills! Consider it done." Avery nodded and took a step away.

"Then get McHenry's on the phone." Doug looked at Sheila again, and she nodded. "Tell them we want a repair guy out tomorrow, first thing. If he can get here tonight, I'll pay extra. As long as we've got a couple of folks working OT who can supervise."

"You got it, sir!" Avery bowed his head again then spun away and jogged back toward the vineyards at a much slower pace than he'd run earlier.

Doug dabbed at his sweat-glistened head and slotted himself back into the passenger seat as Sheila gently accelerated. "You sure about all of this? Sure we're not expanding further than we can handle? That's a lot of cash we just flashed around."

"It's tough now," Sheila acknowledged. "But I think it's the right move. You know, Avery wouldn't turn down you putting him in charge of more things. Get him a manager title, put these decisions in his hands instead of yours. I think the only reason he asks you so many questions is because he feels like he has to."

"What about you? You still need an office manager. Anyone you trust?"

"A few, maybe. Let's kick that can down the road for just a little longer. I want to make sure the finances support it." She pulled the UTV alongside the concrete loading dock and cut the engine, stepping out onto the grass.

Doug vacated the passenger seat, the two of them walking to the bay doors of the loading dock side-by-side. Stepping to the side, Doug pressed a small doorbell and moments later the door eased open, a young man staring out at them.

"Mr. and Mrs. Tills! Come on in." He gripped one door and hauled it open, giving them room to enter. "Sorry, we're still categorizing last night's delivery. You weren't kidding when you said it was going to be big!"

They both stepped into the warehouse, which was little more than a carved-out section of the lower basement level, a concrete floor laid down and shelves lining several of the sparse walls. Industrial sized freezers had been dug into the eastern walls, meant as overflow capacity while stacks of boxes filled most of the empty space on the lower level. A couple handfuls of employees were busy opening boxes and transferring contents to shelves or the freezers themselves.

"You've got quite the team going here," Sheila said, surveying the hustle and bustle of the gathered employees.

"They work hard. Though, as you know, they're still mostly waitstaff doing double duty as warehouse clerks. I don't mean to pry, Mrs. Tills, but if this is going to become an every week occurrence—"

"We might want to look to hire a few dedicated full-time employees. I can read your mind."

"You always could."

"We're expecting some news today, and I'll let you know as soon as I have info for you. Keep up the great work." Sheila patted the man on the shoulder as they walked past, crossing the concrete floor and heading toward a nearby stairwell.

"More full-time employees? With benefits, do you have any idea what that would cost?" Doug leaned close, whispering his concerns into his wife's ear.

"You don't have to remind me, Doug. Let's just wait to see what Will sent over and we can talk more about it after that."

They navigated the upward staircase, coming out into a second level hallway. A surge of four women stopped their forward progress, stepping back to make room for Sheila and Doug.

"Mrs. Tills—" a woman raised her hand.

"I hear you, Wendy, and I promise I'll be with you in just a few minutes, okay? I need to have a quick pow-wow with Doug first." She pressed a hand to Doug's back and gently guided him forward. "Can it wait just a minute?"

"Of course." Wendy's smile faltered somewhat, but she nodded and swept a length of long hair from her forehead, turning toward the other people around her.

Sheila punched a keycode into the pad mounted to the wall alongside their office, the door clicking as she struck the final number. Angling the handle downward, she opened one of the double doors wide enough for her and her husband to squeeze through. The office was wide and curved, following the bend of the north-facing windows that overlooked the vineyards. Hardwood polished with a bright shine was mostly concealed by a large area rug, ornately decorated with a meandering patchwork of curled vines and grapes. Several posters hung on the wall, encased in thick, straight frames. Various brands of wines stood beneath paintings of colored bottles, thick bunches of grapes adorning elaborate cursive text on others.

Perched on the far wall, just between two outward sheets of full windows was a map of Italy, a few key locations marked by hand-stitched stars. A large desk was perched near the back half of the luxurious, yet functional office, a high-backed swivel chair slotted into its mahogany well. Sheila slipped the chair out and glanced at her husband.

"There's room in here for one for you, too."

Doug shook his head. "My place is out there." He pointed through the glass. "You're the office maven. Always have been."

"Mhm. If we get too much bigger, I won't be able to do this alone. You're going to have to be a manager with me, like it or not."

"Don't remind me." Doug stood just to her left as she slid the chair in and focused her attention on the computer screen.

She clutched at an adding machine to the left and dragged it over, tugging it across the blotter so it was within arm's reach. As she did so, she tapped the keyboard of the computer, then used the mouse to navigate, quickly accessing their email client, the window folding up from the bottom of the screen. Their accountant's words echoed within her mind, the unspoken promises of the financial results they would soon see with their own eyes. He'd been hesitant to give her actual numbers over the phone, but his implication had been as clear as the sun which shone over the vineyards.

Sheila swept to the attachment on the email coming from their accountant and double-clicked to open the document. Sheila and Doug stared at the numbers, Sheila's lips moving slightly as she recited the data contained on the screen. The fingers of her right hand danced over the keys of the adding machine, the soft clicking of impact soothing the frayed surge of her nerves. Staring at the screen for another moment, she leaned over and lifted the paper from the adding machine, comparing the two sets of numbers. She ran her fingers through the tangled curls of dark hair, which had just started showing the briefest hints of gray at the edges.

"Are you sure you're adding that up correctly?" Doug leaned against the desk, his arms ramrod straight as he drew close to the computer monitor. He squinted at the tiny text on the screen, his own close-cropped hair already a stark sheet of pale gray, almost shifted to white.

"Yes, I added them correctly, Doug. Put your bifocals on and look again." She tapped the numbers on the screen, then tugged on the curl of white paper coming from the adding machine. "They match."

Doug sighed and fished his glasses from the chest pocket of his button-up shirt, then snapped the arms out and perched them over his scrunched nose. He mouthed silent words as he tracked his gaze left-to-right, reciting the numbers staring back at him from the screen.

"Well, I'll be a chimp's cousin." He shook his head. "This is for the month?" He drew back and gestured toward the numbers.

"For the month. The restaurant is doing far better than we projected, Doug. Far, far better."

"He forgot to subtract payroll." Doug stabbed a finger toward the numbers. "I knew it. They can't be right, he forgot—"

"He subtracted it here, Doug. Right here." Sheila pressed her own index finger to another line on the sheet. "This is accurate." Sheila leaned back in the chair, which squeaked under her shifting weight. "I mean we all saw the dollars coming in. I think we felt like good things were happening. But I just assumed payroll, benefits, that huge food order we made, I figured that would wipe it out."

Doug blew out a gust of air and stood upright. "All these fool tourists who like to toss their money away, I suppose. Figured most of these people would just go to Portland."

"Those fool tourists are paying our bills, dear." Sheila slipped out of her chair and stood, tearing the strip of paper from the adding machine to get a better look. "I wouldn't be so quick to insult them. Portland has become so commercialized; these people want to remember what small-town Oregon used to be like. That's what we give them. Besides, as close as we are to the Pacific, it only makes sense to expand beyond the vineyard."

Doug walked around the desk, approaching one of the huge windows overlooking the sprawling backyard. A stark blue, cloudless sky perched overhead, the sun bringing out the richness of greens throughout the vineyards outside. He moved slowly and cautiously, as if navigating a very thin beam beneath his feet.

"The vineyard was - *is* - our dream, Sheila. It's everything we wanted." He stood at the window, pressing a palm to the glass as he stared outside. "Is expansion really what we want?"

"We won't forget our roots." Sheila stepped up next to Doug, pressing a hand to his back. "This is just the obvious next step. We're growing."

"Bigger isn't always better."

"Are you having second thoughts? I hope not, because we just got that huge delivery."

"No, no, no second thoughts." Doug offered a soothing, wry smile. "I just figured at our age, maybe we'd be slowing down a little. But I'm glad we're not." He pressed his hands to his wife's shoulders, then drew her in, gently kissing her cheek. "There's no one I'd rather do this with than you."

"Well, I'm happy to hear that, dear. But we're still going to need to hire more full-time employees." She patted his cheek. "Just think," she continued as she walked away, waving a hand toward the windows, "not just wine and a small restaurant. A wedding destination and food catering. The bed and breakfast. Maybe even all three meals instead of only lunch and dinner."

Doug continued staring out the window as a tractor rumbled in front of and below him, turning lazily down a broad path of flattened grass separating rows of vines. Three other workers gathered together in a spontaneous trio, one of them gesturing toward a nearby section of land, the other two captivated by whatever directions were being given.

"This was just you and me at one point. Now look at us."

Doug laughed with a soft shake of his head, then approached his wife, locking his fingers in hers, drawing her close. "You know I'm just being my crotchety old self. I couldn't be prouder of what you've built here."

"What *we've* built here, Doug. This has been a team effort."

"A team effort born of the ideas in your head. Based on your family's experiences living in Europe." They released each other's hands and walked across the ornate patterned rug that lined the floor of their spacious office. "When we first started out, I was a glorified handyman."

"Don't be ridiculous. Yes, you used your hands to help build this place, but you used your smarts, too, just like me. Don't undersell your contributions, Douglas."

"I love it when you call me Douglas."

Sheila rolled her eyes and picked up her pace, walking toward the double oak doors that led to the rest of the vineyard offices. Pushing open the doors, they both stepped into a frenzy of activity, a dozen people moving about, gliding from one duty to the next, a few hushed whispers ceasing as heads turned toward them. Sheila softly clapped her hands to get their attention, and the rest of the background conversation silenced, everyone turning to face them.

"Good morning," she said gleefully, her voice bright and chipper. The echoes of her clap still fading, voices eased into whispers and then silence, all eyes turning toward them. "We've gotten some very early numbers from our first foray into this new future."

Everyone stood captivated by what she might say next.

"The results, I am happy to say, have been very, very good. And it's thanks to all of your hard work. We could not have done this without you."

Excited whispers passed throughout the gathered crowd, heads turning, small pats of encouragement passing between fellow employees. A soft chorus of applause broke out, everyone coming together to share the joy of early sales reports.

"But the work's not over," Sheila continued, "there's still so much to do." She directed her attention toward a middle-aged man, flanked by four younger employees, two men and two women. "Bradley, how is the sorting of that food going? We saw them working through the deliveries downstairs; are we going to be okay for the dinner rush?"

"Not everything is put away, but enough to get us ready for dinner tonight. We've been getting the tables set, as much as we can without disrupting a few of our late lunch guests."

"Who's on staff for tonight? Do we have a hostess as well as waitstaff? I think we're anticipating a pretty big crowd."

"Of course." The man turned and placed a hand on the shoulder of a young, well-groomed man to his left. "Bruce is our host for dinner. Jody and Paula will be the lead waitresses, and Carlos is one of our waiters. We have at least a dozen more coming in."

"Arriving early, I hope?"

"Absolutely. We're giving them a thirty-minute crash course on what the night is going to look like. Kitchen staff will be even earlier than that."

"How is the kitchen looking?"

"Clean and well-organized. Thanks to Wendy." The middle-aged man pointed toward a somewhat younger woman, who nodded her appreciation. "She's got that kitchen staff whipped into shape. Already stocking the freezers, the dry goods are all prepared and ready."

"Special for tonight?"

"Pan-seared salmon with lemon dill sauce and asparagus risotto. We were planning on pairing it with our house Chardonnay, but we're nearly out."

Doug cleared his throat and glanced away, a wash of heat warming his cheeks.

"Instead we're offering a wonderful Sauvignon Blanc. Bright acidity and herbaceous notes pair very well with the dill and asparagus. It's quite nicely balanced. I can provide a plate for you if you'd like to sample everything?"

"I trust you," Sheila replied with a smile, "but thank you, Bradley." She angled her neck a bit, looking toward a nearby table. "Are those the menus?"

Bradley reached over and plucked a menu from a stack nearby, handing it off to Sheila, who accepted it gratefully and opened the cover.

"Mrs. Tills?" An older woman stepped apart from the surrounding group. "If you don't mind, we need to get back to work. Is there anything you needed us for beforehand?"

Sheila remained focused on the menu, her gaze still fixed on the rows of text and well-placed images. "How is that batch of Merlot?"

"We've got forty bottles already labeled, and should have another forty ready for you by dinnertime."

"Excellent." Sheila traced her finger along a specific line of text, her lips moving silently as she recited the meals back to herself. "What about the Chardonnay? I know we've had some struggles, but it was in high demand at the tasting last week. Are we simply out of luck?"

"No, ma'am. We've got... thirty bottles ready, I believe. I can promise you another two dozen after that. The next batch should be fermented within the next few days. It's coming along very nicely; I think you'll be quite pleased."

Sheila gently closed the menu, gave Bradley a wide, approving smile, then passed the menu back to him. Relieved, Bradley nodded his thanks and backed away, joining the others and heading back toward the dining area.

"We had that issue with the soil earlier. If I remember right, it was impacting some of the plants?"

"That got sorted out," the woman replied, eyes darting toward

Doug. "The vines are responding well, and the fruit is looking promising. We'll begin the harvest next week."

Sheila nodded, somewhat disapprovingly. "So, we're looking at several weeks out from there? Or more?"

"That is a possibility. We have three barrels already prepared, but that's always been a popular choice and we're having trouble keeping up with demand. The online sales are crazy right now."

"Well, things can't be perfect." Sheila gave the woman a gentle forward nod of approval, then placed a comforting hand on her arm. "You're doing very well, Isabella. Very, very well."

"Thank you, Mrs. Tills." Despite her age, Isabella's cheeks flushed red with pride as she stepped away to hurry back to the wine cellar.

"I'm sorry about that soil problem," Doug said quietly. "That's on me and my crew. The harvester, too. Machinery is helpful when it works, but when it doesn't—"

"It's not on anyone, Doug. Stuff happens. It's how we respond to it that matters. You know that better than I do."

"Point taken." Doug stared at the barely controlled chaos that surged all around them, people dashing from room to room, pockets of several different conversations happening, a whirlwind of activity with him and Sheila at its eye. "You were asking about office manager. What about Bradley?"

"Took the words out of my mouth. And maybe Wendy for kitchen supervisor?"

"All I can see is those nice numbers we got in our email shrinking second by second." Doug stuffed his hands in his pocket. "The price of expanding, I guess."

"Don't tell me you don't live for this, Doug. I can see it in your eyes."

Doug shrugged. "Maybe a little."

The door suddenly burst open, a crash of impact as a waitress spilled out, running at a swift sprint. Her face was drawn taut, cheeks sunken and eyes wide, her face the color of pale ivory. She clutched bunches of silverware in each hand, her apron stained dark with some sort of spilled liquid.

"Mr. and Mrs. Tills! You have to come see this! Something's happening!" Her voice spilled from one frantic word to the next, her lips barely keeping up with the flurry of her voice. The door behind her swung back, sweeping through the doorway before settling into place.

"What?" Doug strode forward, automatically stepping into the fray, driven by instinct.

"The dining room! We have the televisions on!" The young woman wheeled back toward the door and shouldered through, banging it back open the other way. She paused for a moment, dumping the silverware in a nearby plastic tub by one of the wait stations. Doug followed with Sheila close behind, the two of them moving into the dining room.

While the basement and the back were the engine room of the restaurant, the dining room was its expansive cabin. Squared off, with over a dozen large windows spaced evenly apart, the distinctly European flair was evident throughout its design and décor. Sculpted columns rose along the walls' perimeter, meeting a sweeping intersection of ornate support beams, from which hung a half dozen decorative chandeliers. The staff had clearly been busy preparing for what was sure to be a frenetic dinner hour. Several of them stood, gathered in a tight cluster, huddled around a nearby flat-screen television.

Sheila had never wanted the televisions installed in the first place; she thought it ruined the ambiance. Guests were there to eat and celebrate, not to be glued to large screens perched equidistant throughout the interior of the dining room. In the end, Doug had won that argument when an especially captivating World Cup soccer tournament filled the dining room for six days straight.

A few late lunch customers were scattered about as well, taking up two of the dozens of tables evenly spaced throughout the ornate dining room. The chairs around those tables were askew and empty, the customers joining the wait staff in their silent absorption of the images on the television screen.

"What the devil—" Sheila shook her head as they entered.

On one of the tables, a glass of wine had been upended, its dark liquid staining the white tablecloth, seeping toward the curved edge. Silverware lay scattered, dropped from loose hands as people had immediately headed to the televisions for a better look. Sheila picked up her pace, stepping past her husband as Doug did his best to keep up. They joined the crowd of onlookers, gathering into a cluster of wide eyes, staring in disbelief.

Helicopter footage filled the screen, a high-altitude sweeping shot of a broad cityscape below. The ticker labeled the location as Chicago, Illinois, a city that Sheila had never visited, nor ever desired to. The sideways motion of the elevated camera scanned myriad streets and roadways crisscrossed throughout tightly stacked buildings. Skyscrapers thrust upward, punching through the gathered clusters of smaller buildings, thick spires of glass and steel.

Sheila barely saw them. Instead of staring at the buildings and city streets, clotted with traffic, she focused intently on the sidewalks lining the streets, the pedestrian walkways draped in the darkened shadows of tall monoliths. Nothing moved anywhere throughout the sweeping images of the city. All traffic had stopped, all vehicles wedged into a tight conglomeration of steel and glass, an immobile gridlock of traffic. But it wasn't even the traffic that drew her rapt gaze or drew her lips into a tight "o" - it was the bodies that filled the sidewalks, the motionless corpses draped across hoods and trunks, or wedged within the narrow spaces between vehicles. Limbs were slung over limbs, bodies on top of bodies, a sea of death caught within the frame of the sweeping news copter's camera.

Wherever the helicopter moved, whatever different angles of footage it shot, corpses were splayed side-to-side and atop each other, a thick field of the dead. Her mouth went dry and she reached out instinctively, clutching Doug's hand and squeezing it within the clasp of her own.

"Chicago, Illinois is but one major city seemingly impacted by what FEMA is calling a biological incident," the newscaster reported. Footage shifted slightly on the television, though the ticker remained Chicago. A scene of Millenium Park came into view, the chrome jellybean-shaped statue perched within its courtyard.

"We once again must reiterate the warning—the images you are seeing may be disturbing to younger or more sensitive viewers." The newscaster voiceover paused momentarily, clearing his throat. "Our news office has made the executive decision to show these images in their entirety to ensure that our viewers grasp the gravity of this situation."

Bodies filled the park around the chrome statue, so thick and congested there wasn't even room to maneuver through them. The young waitress gasped, pressing a hand to her mouth, stepping clumsily backwards. Her ankle struck a chair leg, and she nearly went over, but a lunch customer swept toward her, catching her before she could fall. The screen shifted once more, to a handheld device in a restaurant high above a sprawling cityscape below. With a line of static, the ticker changed to Seattle, Washington and the camera jostled as it moved closer to the rounded window.

"Is that the restaurant on top of the Space Needle?" Sheila squeezed Doug's hand again, even harder.

Through the glass, the cell phone video recorded the chaos on the street of the city below. Like Chicago, cars were wedged into spaces too tight, many of them smashed together, windshields starred and broken. Columns of twisting smoke curled up from within the thick mass of vehicles, pale fingers grasping upward for something they'd never hold. The sidewalks, as much as they could be seen, were equally filled, but not with cars, with lifeless bodies instead, many face down, a few face up, a congestion of flesh, bone and blood. The camera on the phone swung around again, turning toward the person recording, a young, pale-faced woman, her mascara streaked with flowing tears. She gasped and tried to speak, though the newscast wasn't broadcasting her actual words.

"Video uploaded to social media shows customers within the restaurant at the top of the Space Needle witnessing the catastrophe down below. Our attempts to reach out to those users have gone unanswered and, in fact, the cellular network nationwide appears to be suffering severe problems, and is down entirely in some regions, though we don't know what relation that may or may not have to the disasters unfolding before us." The screen switched briefly to the newscaster, a haggard, fifty-something looking man who fumbled through a sheet of paper before him. His breathing came deep and unsteady, his gripping fingers white with pressure.

The screen shifted once more, ticker changing to New York City, but the scene on the ground was alarmingly similar. Alongside stalled vehicles and clogged city streets were countless dead bodies, sprawled and lying motionless atop each other or next to each other, a flesh and blood barricade. Helicopter footage swung swiftly west, drifting over the Hudson, a ferry floating aimlessly against the darkened water. Dead bodies were scattered throughout the ferry and bobbed in the water around it, the camera passing swiftly over them as the helicopter angled for a better view of the carnage.

"New York." The newscaster came back, blinking his thick eyelashes as he tried to focus on the papers in his hand. "Seattle. Chicago." He coughed, pressing a tight fist to his lips. "We've received more footage from Boston, Houston and elsewhere. The reports continue to flood in, one after the next, cities all throughout the United States, all showing the same grisly scenes." The newscaster's voice was a tearing sound as he stopped to clear his throat, his palms pressing the thick stack of papers to the desk's surface.

The scene shifted again, the ticker reading Houston, Texas, and just like the others, it was filled with streets of the dead. In every single instance not a single person moved within view, the news helicopters recording what appeared to be the final gasps of humanity at large. Sheila wrapped her arm around her husband's waist, the two of them clinging to each other as the screen flickered, lined with static, then shifted again.

The ticker changed to Los Angeles, California, and a smoldering highway fell into view, portions of an upper level of road collapsed into the throngs of traffic below. Fires churned within the city streets, smoke rising, the thick shadow of the Los Angeles Convention Center barely visible in the background.

"Still no word from the President of the United States," the newscaster continued, "who was expected to give a speech at a campaign rally in Los Angeles. Like most others, the news out of L.A. isn't good, reports of thousands of dead throughout the downtown area and even into the vast network of outlying suburbs. Our attempts to reach our boots on the ground in these cities have gone unanswered, and we're left to only assume the absolute worst—"

Doug and Sheila's grip around each other tightened, both of them turning to look deep into the other's eyes, equally drawn wide by shock.

"Samantha," they both whispered, too afraid to say the name aloud for fear of bringing their worst nightmares to life.

Sheila pushed away from Doug in a rush, wheeling apart, shoving her hand into her inside pocket. She clamped her fingers around the cell phone there and ripped it free, nearly tearing the fabric at its seam. Her grip clasped around the phone as she desperately hunted for her daughter's contact, finger trembling as it hovered near the entry. She forced her breathing to steady as she tapped the mobile number and immediately pressed the phone to her ear. An undulating buzz within the speaker indicated the ringing of the phone on the far end, but after four such buzzes, it fell to voicemail.

"Come on." Sheila lowered the phone again and punched the contact info, then lifted the phone, but only a rapid, uneven buzzing of broken circuits came back through the speakers. Her eyes pressed tightly closed, tears pinched at the corners, stinging with salt as she tried once more. Stabbing the call button, she lifted the phone again, but on the third attempt, all she heard was a vast and sickening silence.

CHAPTER FOUR

The O'Brian Family
Los Angeles, California

Samantha sat on the smooth roof of the RV, legs bent and staring south across the broken city. The elevated freeway, once a river of endless traffic, was a jagged spine of broken concrete, partially collapsed in various sections. The RV stood parked on a section of intact onramp near the highest elevation, just wide enough to keep them from plunging into the chaos below. It no longer shuddered or swayed, the thick, cylindrical concrete columns keeping it upright and stoic. The altitude provided Samantha with a unique perspective on the City of Angels, spread out before her beneath a lingering haze of pollution, fog and smoke. From where she sat, the city resembled a dying animal, its wounds festering under the weight of whatever had rolled through its streets a few hours earlier. She and Jason had both suspected the same thing, though she was hesitant to say it too loudly for fear of making it real.

The skyline, which once defined L.A.'s sprawling pride, was barely visible through the haze, the tops of skyscrapers little more than dark silhouettes, silent and cold. Whatever life had surged through the veins of the L.A. city streets had come to a screeching halt just like the vehicles themselves that clotted the streets beneath them. The freeways were littered with the wreckage of vehicles, smashed and scattered like forgotten toys. A ragged trench had formed in the midst of the vehicles as the military convoy had desperately plowed their way through, only to fall victim to the same mysterious phenomenon as everyone else farther down the road. Near the pathway, cars were piled up along each side, crumpled forms blocking any clear trajectory through the ruins. Some vehicles had driven straight into nearby barriers, or into each other, speeding desperately away from the wave of death that consumed them despite their efforts. The silence was the worst part to Samantha; there were no honking horns, no angry drivers or music blaring from open windows. Just the vast, relentless stillness of death.

Bodies lay twisted among the wreckage, some slumped over their steering wheels in their cars, others flung onto the road in unnatural positions. Many of them had fallen in and around their vehicles as they'd thrown themselves from their seats and attempted to flee, only to be overcome. Samantha's gaze caught on a figure lying face down, barely visible through the creeping smoke, not far from the edge of the elevated freeway. He wore a business suit, his dark jacket spread over him like a thousand-dollar funeral shroud, face somewhat turned, cheek pressed into the street. Above her, the sky was a sickly orange, the sun struggling to break through the layers of smog and pollution. It cast long shadows over the city, deepening a sense of dread that hung in the air. Somewhere, far off in the distance, an explosion had sounded a short time before, its rippling echo rolling to her across the miles, sounding endlessly through the city like some final groan of expired life.

A dark column of smoke rose from the direction of downtown beyond the Los Angeles Convention Center. The banners that had once waved proudly were still and limp, barely recognizable. One of those banners had advertised the President's campaign rally; Samantha had recalled seeing the vibrant red, white and blue flag as they'd driven past a few hours earlier. President McDouglas was leading what appeared to be a monumentally victorious re-election campaign, the rally in Los Angeles a massive celebration of his seemingly inevitable victory. It was difficult to use the word victory when soaking in the city spread out before her, and Samantha couldn't fight the feeling that something larger was at play. She and Jason had turned on the radio, hearing static and panic-filled reports about incidents in other areas of the country. Every instinct Samantha had told her the country was under attack and Los Angeles was little more than a blistered skeleton, its once life-rich flesh burned and bleached from its bones, the remains laid bare in the hot summer sun.

The RV shifted as someone scaled the ladder toward the rear, making their way up to the roof. Samantha didn't have to turn to know who it was, she could just feel her husband's presence even when her back was turned. Jason made his way up onto the RV roof and carefully walked along its smooth surface, settling down into place to the left of his wife.

"You all right?"

"Just trying to wrap my head around it, I guess." She planted her palm on the roof and turned toward Jason. "How are the kids?"

"Okay. They're playing cards for the first time in years. Eli wanted to bust out his video game, but I talked him out of it. Said we didn't want to waste the batteries this soon." Jason joined her in looking across the city.

"They must be getting hungry."

"Eli mentioned it. I told them both to eat their sandwiches from the cooler, I didn't want them going to waste."

"Do we have anything in the refrigerator?"

"We did. Milk and yogurt, the leftovers from dinner last night. Sarah and I moved as much of it to the cooler as possible, hoping the ice packs would hold out a little bit. The longer we sit without the engine running, the less the batteries are going to charge and the shorter lifespan the appliances will have. Last I checked, the fridge still felt a bit cool. It's just a small twelve-volt model, so it might keep running for a bit, but not forever."

"What about the microwave and air conditioner? Those aren't just twelve volts, are they?"

"No, they're 120. I opened the circuit breaker and cut the power to those appliances, though, so the fridge at least will last longer."

Samantha pulled out her phone and held it before her, staring at the screen.

"I came up here to see if reception would be any better, but it's not. I still can't get through to Mom and Dad."

"I'm sure there are a few million people trying the same thing. Probably more than that if you venture outside of Los Angeles itself."

Samantha leaned a bit, trying to get a better view of the mass of vehicles and freeway below. Nobody moved through the wreckage of cars or bodies; it was little more than an ocean of death and they were barely above its deadly waves.

"Doesn't look like a few million people trying to use their phones down there."

"Do you think it's safe? Maybe it was localized to where we are." Jason asked.

"Safe? To go down there?" Samantha shook her head. "I'm not sure, but I've been wondering the same thing. Whatever caused this was invisible, as far as I could tell. I sure don't remember seeing anything, so it might be tough to tell whether it's still down there or not."

"I don't suppose you've seen any survivors?"

"None." Samantha's response was curt and short. "But we can't stay up here forever. Eventually we need to find our way out of this city." She stood on the roof, spreading her arms slightly as if standing on a surfboard.

There was a slight jostle of movement beneath her spread feet as the RV swayed gently, but it settled quickly into stillness. She stepped behind Jason, who was pushing himself upright as well, and walked the roof, looking down past the edge of the top of the RV.

"We can't keep following the freeway," Samantha said, gesturing toward the jagged ruins of the road ahead of them. "The only direction we really have to go is down." Jason joined her at the rear edge of the roof, both of them looking toward the ramp that had taken them to where they were, safe above the chaos and death below.

"We can't take the risk of going down until we know for sure that it's safe." Jason stared down the winding slope of the ramp that plunged back toward the mass of vehicles and dead bodies. "You still think this was an attack of some kind?"

"Seems that way to me. Especially within spitting distance of the campaign rally." Samantha looked again at the large silhouette of the Los Angeles Convention Center, the roof of the RV giving her a unique vantage point. "That's certainly where the convoy was heading. All signs point to an attack in my opinion."

"Who'd want to use bioweapons on big cities?"

Samantha took another tentative step, snorting at him. "You know the players as well as I do. Could be anyone. C'mon, let's get down from here." She moved toward the ladder and scaled it, rung-by-rung, crawling down from the roof and onto the cracked pavement of the elevated freeway.

Jason followed her, standing along the edge of the road next to her as she stared off into the distance, squinting through the surrounding smog, darkened with hints of smoke from crashed vehicles below.

"What are you looking for?"

"See those birds over there?" She pointed toward the roof of a nearby building, rising above even the upper altitude of the elevated highway where a group of birds were chirping excitedly at one another.

"Yeah, I see them. They don't seem to be affected by whatever's going on, though they're at a higher altitude like we are." Jason's brow furrowed as he took another step forward, moving in for a closer look. "Actually, that's a good thought."

"What's a good thought?"

"If we can lure the birds down from the perch, maybe we can see if it's still safe down on street level." Jason took a step back from the edge of the road and walked toward the front door of the RV.

Samantha followed him as he opened the door and stepped up into the vehicle, threading his way into the narrow cabin of the living quarters. Eli and Sarah were seated around the rectangular surface of a fold-out table, cards clutched tightly in their hands. Kale rested on a nearby couch, lifting her head as Jason and Samantha approached, her tail thumping the cushion behind her.

"Everything okay, Dad?" Eli asked, his voice trembling a bit as he set his cards down, anxiety widening his eyes and pinching his lips into a thin, straight line.

"It's okay, Eli. We're still okay."

"Nothing about this is okay," Sarah said with a shake of her head. "I'm sick of being cramped in here. I swear I can feel the RV shaking still."

"I know," Samantha replied, moving past Jason to place a calming hand on her daughter's shoulder. "That's what we're trying to figure out right now."

Jason had opened one of the cabinets in the RV's kitchen, standing on his tiptoes as he pushed boxes away, searching through the contents.

"What are you looking for, Dad?" Eli stood.

"Didn't we have a box of crackers or something in here somewhere? I thought we got them yesterday at the store."

"Yeah, when Eli was hangry," Sarah replied.

"I was not hangry," Elijah protested.

Sarah eyed Samantha and lifted her eyebrows. Samantha pressed a finger playfully to her lips, encouraging the girl to remain quiet.

"Where are they?" Jason looked over his shoulder and Eli's cheeks blushed.

"They're by my bed." He darted away, moving through the narrow gap and into the rear section of the RV where the makeshift bedrooms were found.

The rear bedroom compartment had a single fold-out bed where Jason and Samantha typically slept as well as a built-in set of bunk beds for the twins. It was tight, but surprisingly comfortable and had only generated a few heated discussions about not having enough room. Eli returned a moment later, a red box of crackers in his hand, holding them out for his father.

"Are you hungry?"

"No. It's for the birds." Jason took the crackers and made his way toward the front of the RV again.

"For the... what?" Eli stared inquisitively at his mother.

"Come on outside," Samantha said, "just... don't look that way." She pointed to the south, through the wall of the RV.

If things were as bad as she thought they were, her children would be growing up very quickly. Despite that, she was going to do whatever she could to keep them as isolated as possible from the horrors of the world. Kale dropped off the couch, took a moment to stretch, then trotted after the rest of them. Exiting the door on the passenger's side, Samantha quickly led the children around the RV and to the opposite side of the street, keeping the vehicle between them and the worst of the death and destruction. Jason was already opening the box of crackers, reaching into it to lift out a few of the crispy wafers.

"Is Dad going crazy?" Eli asked in a whisper as Jason pulled out a cracker, broke it into pieces, then held it into the air.

Jason whistled sharply at the nearby birds, who all remained huddled near the ledge of the nearby roof, paying him no mind. Samantha looked at the birds, the dark feathers of crows, their wings twitching, and a shiver ran along the base of her spine. Soon enough the birds would be descending to feed on the dead. Jason tossed a section of cracker toward the roof and shouted nonsensically at the birds, though they seemed to pay him no mind.

"He's not crazy," Samantha replied quietly. "He's trying to lure the birds down to the street below. To see if it's safe to go down there again."

"Come on, you stupid birds!" Jason shouted and threw another section of cracker.

It dropped down off the edge of the roadway and dusted a section of pavement below.

"Rats with wings." Jason shook his head.

"Those are pigeons," Sarah corrected. "Not crows."

"Do you know what they call a family of crows?" Eli asked, prodding his sister in the ribs. "A *murder*. How cool is that?"

"It's not cool at all," Sarah replied with a trademark teenage-girl eye roll.

Samantha couldn't help but smile faintly, appreciating the good-natured exchange from the twins, who seemed to be keeping their heads on straight despite the chaos that surrounded them.

"Caw! Caw!" Jason made ridiculous bird sounds and tossed another fistful of crackers into the air, scattering them down toward the road.

Finally, one of the birds reacted, fluttering its wings as it hopped up on two legs and turned. The others on the ledge responded to the first, the whole group of them suddenly moving, twisting around in curiosity.

"There we go," Jason said and tossed more crackers, aiming high in hopes of catching the crows' attention.

As the shards of food sprinkled down, one of the crows hopped to the edge of the roof and peered down, wings slightly spread. It balanced precariously on its talons, then propelled itself off the roof and swarmed down toward the road below. Two of its friends followed suit and moments later, the entire flock swept down from their elevated perch.

"Stay back." Jason turned and held a hand toward his children. "You don't want to see what's down there."

"Yes, I do." Eli took a step forward, but Samantha gently held his arm and kept him from moving.

"Please," she said quietly, "just stay here with your sister and Kale."

Eli seemed to notice the German Shepherd for the first time and nodded reluctantly, remaining where he was as his mother joined his father at the edge of the elevated roadway. Together, Samantha and Jason peered over the edge, down several feet to the choked highway below. Several cars were jammed nose-to-nose and side-by-side, with several dead bodies visible, slung to the pavement in and around the stopped vehicles. The fragments of thrown cracker had landed on the roof of a blue Ford pickup down below, which was parked at an angle across a lane of traffic. A Volkswagen had slammed into its passenger side, the windshield starred by the impact of someone's skull within the smaller vehicle.

The birds were scattered about the roof, pecking eagerly at its metal surface, the *clackclackclack* of their beaks faintly audible below where the O'Brians stood. As Jason and Samantha watched, two of them separated from the group and fluttered down to the pavement itself, digging on the road for the sparse sections of broken crackers.

"They seem okay," Jason said, his attention still focused on the birds below.

Samantha nodded in agreement, watching the flock of crows as even more descended from seemingly nowhere. Soon there were dozens of the black birds, all searching for a morsel of food to eat. She stepped back from the edge, her eyes narrowed in focused concentration.

"What's on your mind?" Jason asked joining her in taking a step back from the precipice.

"The birds are alive," she said quietly, "but is that enough? Does that really give you comfort?"

Jason sighed reluctantly. "They're pretty different biologically from us. It could be a bit of a leap of faith, but they did use canaries in mines."

"That was for dangerous gases or lack of oxygen, not some kind of attack vector that kills people in seconds."

"Still." Jason shrugged. "We can't stay up here forever."

They stood near the edge of the road, both of them looking back toward their children. Kale sat between Eli and Sarah, studying them with her dark, penetrating eyes. Her black nose twitched gently, the nostrils flaring a bit as she sniffed the air. Samantha looked into the dog's dark eyes; the animal might as well have been an extended member of their family. Samantha had plenty of experience with German Shepherds in her previous life and Kale had been a rescue dog from a military training program. She had, apparently, been difficult to train and too eager to please. Not disciplined enough for military service, but fine for a family dog.

Somehow, though, Samantha had succeeded where the military trainers had failed, shaping Kale into a very disciplined, well-behaved animal who could be an eager plaything and a fierce protector, all within the span of a few seconds. She hadn't been convinced adding a dog to the family was something they could manage but had been more than happy to be proven wrong.

Jason gently touched her hand, his fingers brushing hers. "You're thinking it, too. I can tell."

"Thinking what?" Her eyes darted toward her husband, reading the same thoughts in his eyes that she had in her own mind.

"We need to test the air down there with someone more biologically similar to human beings. Birds are one thing, but we need a mammal."

Samantha shook her head, her gaze fixed on Kale, who tilted her head inquisitively as if trying to read their minds. Her fur-covered brow furrowed in confusion, her tail halting its sideways wag in mid-stream.

"I don't know if I can do that," she whispered, keeping her voice low so the kids wouldn't hear. "She's not just a dog, Jason, she's a member of our family."

"Believe me, I know. And I agree. I'm just not sure what our other options are. We can't sit up here forever, but I'm not willing to just take our kids down there with us, hoping that everything is okay."

"Believe me, I'm not either."

They stood next to each other for a moment, silently considering their next move. Eli watched them, his own inquisition sharpening the slant of his eyes.

"What are you guys talking about?" He finally asked.

"Just trying to figure out what comes next," Samantha replied, cupping her chin between her fingers.

Eli looked at them for a moment longer, then glanced down at the dog, then over to his sister Sarah. "You want to send Kale down there," he said quietly, leaning a bit to scratch the dog's head. "To see if it's safe."

Samantha and Jason exchanged a brief look, then Samantha looked back at Eli. "I don't think we can risk going down there until we know for sure the air is clear."

"The birds were okay," Sarah said, joining her brother in scratching Kale's brown fur.

"Birds are built a little differently." Jason joined his wife, both of them facing the children. "Kale, at least, is a mammal, like humans are. We'd feel a lot better knowing for sure that mammals can survive down there."

"But we don't want to put Kale in harm's way," Samantha said in a rush, shaking her head. "We wouldn't do that to her."

"Why not?" Eli asked bluntly. "Isn't that kinda what she's for? She's our protector, that's what she's always been. "

"True," Samantha replied.

"Well, what you'd be asking her to do is protection. Protecting the entire family."

"But she's also a part of this family."

"You and dad would risk your lives protecting us," Eli shrugged his narrow shoulders. "And I'd do the same for Sarah, much as I hate to admit it."

"Right back at you," Sarah replied.

"Of course—" Samantha started to answer before Elijah interjected again.

"Then I think it's okay for Kale to do the same thing. Protect her family."

Samantha swallowed down a sudden lump that had formed in her throat. She leaned forward and cupped Eli's cheeks in her palms. He blushed deeply, drawing away, though a lingering smile lifted the corner of his lips.

"Sarah? What about you?" Samantha turned slightly to look at Eli's twin sister. "Are you okay with this?"

Sarah's throat tightened, but she jerked her head into a fierce nod, refusing to let Elijah be the only brave one. Still slightly bent in front of Eli, Samantha turned and looked at Jason, whose own thin lips betrayed his conflicted emotions. He started to speak, but before he could, a sudden preening groan sounded from beneath them, a lingering strain of buckling metal and frail concrete. The road suddenly shivered, as though the earth itself got a sudden chill. Starting soft and quiet, the groan lifted, rising in volume as the elevated freeway shifted in a nauseating lurch.

Samantha stood bolt upright, twisting toward the RV to sprint back to the vehicle, but just as she took her first step, the groan halted into an unsettled creak beneath her feet and the freeway halted its rocking movement.

"We're running out of time," Jason said. "We need to do this now."

"So, what are we going to do?" Sarah's voice elevated to a higher pitch, an expression of sudden concern. She crouched next to Kale and wrapped her arms around the dog's neck. "Are we just... sending her down there alone?"

"No." Jason made his way to the RV and stepped inside as Samantha joined her daughter in standing next to the dog.

"It's okay, sweetheart," she said, gently gripping her daughter's shoulder. "The birds were fine. I'm sure it'll be okay."

Jason exited the RV with Kale's leash bound in a loose loop, gripped in his right hand. Spotting the leash, the dog immediately stood and wheeled toward her master, her tail thrashing wildly in anticipation. She let out a little woof and squirmed free of Sarah, excited to see what Jason held in his hand.

"I'll take her down part way."

"What?" Samantha shook her head. "That defeats the entire point of her going down there for us."

"We can't just shoo her along on her own. She's a good girl, but someone has to guide her down there." Jason crouched next to the dog and stroked her head, clipping the leash to a small, metal clasp on her powder blue collar. "I'll stop halfway and tell her to go the rest of the way on her own.

Samantha bit her lower lip to keep from arguing. They'd bought a full carload of dog supplies before they'd even met Kale, not even knowing if the dog they inevitably got would be male or female. Samantha herself had chosen the powder blue color because it could work for either gender. The minute they'd met Kale, she'd sprinted forward, squirming and jerking around too enthusiastically for them to even put the collar on. They'd gone up a few sizes since they'd had her, but Samantha had always stuck with that powder blue color. It just seemed like "her".

After fumbling a bit with the collar, Jason managed to get the clasp closed through the loop and stood, gripping the leash in his hand. Kale darted right, then left, lowered her head, tail wagging eagerly, as she let out a plaintive, pleading whine. As Jason took a single step forward, she leaped up on her hind legs, did a half-pirouette and came down with a thud, landing with both front paws. It was her typical walk time happy dance, though against the backdrop of the shattered skyline of desolate Los Angeles, Samantha struggled to contrast the two different images. A ruined city, clad in yellow smog and smoke and death; an enthusiastic dog, out of her mind with excitement to be going for a walk, despite the circumstances that surrounded her. In a way, Samantha envied Kale's exuberant ignorance.

"Are you sure about this?" She approached Jason and clasped a hand on his forearm.

"Yeah. I'm sure. I've got it."

"Be careful. If you get even the slightest sense that something's wrong—"

"I'll come running right back, I promise."

Samantha gripped his arm even more tightly and pulled, drawing him close to her. She leaned forward and gave him a gentle kiss on the corner of his mouth, and he returned it, quick, but filled with emotion.

"Good luck, dad." Elijah called out from behind, and Samantha turned to give her son a brave smile. She looked back to wish Jason good luck herself, but he'd already advanced down the ramp, navigating the slope carefully as Kale tugged at the leash.

"Easy girl," Jason said, gently pulling back.

Kale obeyed, slowing her forward progress, responding to the gentle tug with a slower movement. She turned her head, looking back at him patiently, but with a glimmer of eagerness in her eyes.

"I know, Kale. It's walkie time. I'm coming."

Thick cracks etched their way along the downward slope of the ramp, leading back to the road. A thick slab of pavement had fallen away to Jason's left, revealing the exposed bones of rebar thrust out from the meat of the road's insides. The world at large remained disturbingly quiet, a vast sea of silence that all but consumed them. To the left, the flock of crows called mournfully as they pecked at the pavement, eating the crackers Jason had tossed them.

"Hopefully they're *only* eating crackers," he whispered, and Kale twisted back around in his direction. "Keep going, girl." They walked a bit longer, reaching almost the halfway point between the elevated freeway platform and the road below.

More veins of thick fractures littered the surface of the road at his feet, one of them thick enough that he was compelled to step over it. To his right, one of the guardrails was bent left, peeled away from its moorings, crumpled by the hood of a passenger van that had collided into it. The doors of the van stood open, the vehicle itself empty. The driver and passengers had likely panicked and sprinted down the ramp, straight to their own deaths. A brisk shiver ran down the length of his spine as he held fast, pulling the leash taut, hesitating to release Kale even once they'd gotten so close. Bunching the leash in his hand, he walked his way along its tight tug until he reached Kale, who had obediently sat down, patiently waiting. Jason took a breath, trying to taste the air on his tongue, but only tasted the typical hint of acrid smoke that stained the Los Angeles skyline.

"You ready, girl?" He spoke quietly into her ear, bending to one knee next to her.

Kale wagged her tail back and forth, her head tilting slightly in inquiry.

"See the bottom of the ramp there?" Jason leaned forward and pointed to the spot where the ramp met the road.

Although Kale couldn't possibly understand English, she stood up on all fours, her tail thrust bolt outright behind her.

"I need you to go there and wait."

Kale turned, head tilted once more.

"Go," Jason repeated and reluctantly thumbed the clasp of the leash open as he continued pointing at the spot with his other hand.

It was less the word that propelled Kale into action and more the familiar click of the opening leash. She broke free of Jason's grip and sprinted down the ramp, claws clicking on pavement, Jason holding his breath all the way until she reached the bottom. He remained in a kneeling posture, gripping the leash tightly, his bent knuckles whitening, and his ligaments aching.

"Wait!" He shouted the word and stood, extending one hand, showing his palm.

Kale hit the bottom of the ramp and trotted onto the street, then turned at the sound of her master's voice.

"Stay!" Jason ordered again, thrusting outward with his palm.

Kale stood at the base of the ramp, tail wagging, looking back at him with her head cocked. For a long moment, Jason just held his pose, silently communicating to the dog across several dozen feet of empty space. Kale stood stoic and straight, ears twitching and tail moving, seemingly feeling no ill effects of the lower altitude.

"Jason?" Samantha's voice called down from above. "Jason, is she okay?"

Jason twisted and looked over his shoulder. "I think she's fine!" He turned back around and inched his way forward.

Tipping gently backwards to counterbalance the slope, he took another step, then another, heading down with a cautious, practiced gait. Glancing back once more, he spotted Samantha turning away, talking to Sarah and Eli, oblivious to his movements.

"Don't get mad," he whispered in a voice that Samantha couldn't hear, then he moved more quickly, breaking into a jog, approaching the spot where Kale stood.

His chest ached with the rapid-fire force of his heart's steady acceleration, and it wasn't until he reached the bottom of the ramp that he realized he was holding his breath the whole way. Kale was excited to see him, lunging forward and intercepting him, smashing his thighs with her head, tail slashing diagonally behind her. Jason gathered himself, taking in his surroundings. Only about ten yards away, on a nearby sidewalk, dead bodies were sprawled, face down, face up and some on their sides, a mass of corpses within a stone's throw of where he stood.

Vacant eyes stared out from one particular body, an elderly woman who wore a shawl draped over her shoulders, a handbag that had to be fifty years old resting on the sidewalk from her outstretched fingers. Blood had pooled on the ground, coming from her mouth and nose, and her face was twisted in a mask of agony carried over from life into death. He took a cautious, gentle breath in, once more tasting the air. That same metallic, somewhat bitter tang prickled his tongue, but it wasn't poison – at least not whatever had killed the people who surrounded him. Taking another breath and then another, he eventually drew more air into his lungs through shallow inhalations until he was finally satisfied that the air was clear. Kale woofed from where she stood, eager to continue their walk, but Jason softly shook his head as he approached her.

"Sorry, Kaley-girl, your job is done." He crouched and ran his fingers along the slope of her fur-covered skull.

Kale's tail drooped, her black lips seemingly turning down into an almost comical frown.

"I know, girl, I'm sorry." Jason gave her one more pat, but before he hooked the leash, he turned to look back to the elevated freeway.

He grinned at his family and lifted his hand into a wave, signaling that both he and the dog were okay. Samantha waved back, though it didn't seem to be a wave of greeting. In fact, her lips were pursed into a circular shape, her eyes wide and her mouth moving. She almost seemed to be— shouting at him.

"We're okay!" he screamed back, but then Samantha's second hand went up and began sweeping back and forth more frantically.

Jason's already rapidly beating heart managed to pick up the pace, fluttering in his chest like the wings of the nearby crows. He took an uncertain step forward, Kale tagging along just to his right as the entire world roared in anguish, the elevated onramp suddenly bucking left and right several inches in each direction, sending the RV swaying as it shook.

"Oh crap..." He stumbled backwards, still on street level, the shaking happening before him, not beneath him.

Kale had eased her way past him, sensing that her family was in danger, then turned and looked back at Jason, her dark eyes searching for instruction. From where he stood, he could see the thick concrete pillars supporting the onramp and the ragged fractures that etched their winding path up the curved surface. Thick, dark cracks splintered the concrete, carving dark lines of separation through the support pillars as the ramp groaned in protest and buckled. The pillar that had already partially broken away lurched and snapped, another section of the asphalt and concrete separating, breaking apart, and slamming down to the roadway below.

The crows screamed in panic and bolted skyward as an avalanche of debris from a piece of the onramp pounded down to street level, slamming into a median between the surface streets. It showered vehicles and corpses, burying them in a sudden wash of dirt, rock and other debris, the entire onramp starting an uneven list to one side. Kale lowered her head slightly and coiled her legs, preparing to spring into action back up the ramp.

"Kale!" Jason shouted loudly, stopping the dog in her tracks. "Stay!" He sprinted forward, moving past her at speed.

Kale jerked as he passed, barely overcoming her compulsion to join him.

"I said *stay!*" he shouted even louder, thrusting his palm back in her direction.

Kale let out a pathetic yelping bark of protest, but held her ground, not following him toward the onramp. Jason leaped above a broad crack in the pavement and hit the ramp, then lowered himself and sprinted forward as fast as he could, given the sharp incline.

"Come down!" His throat burned raw with the force of his scream. "Samantha! Grab the kids and come down!" He was shouting as he ran, hoping his voice would carry over the groans of the teetering structure.

Samantha seemed to understand, spreading her arms out and guiding Eli and Sarah forward into a loping, somewhat clumsy run. They jogged forward, trying not to run too fast to avoid spilling over as Jason made his way back toward them, his legs burning with the effort of the uphill run. They met about halfway, Eli and Sarah running past him as Samantha released them, holding up for a second.

"Come on," she said, jerking her head toward the bottom of the ramp.

"I have to get the RV." Jason gasped through staggered breaths, pointing up at the vehicle.

"No, you don't. Leave it!"

"I can't leave it! All of our stuff is in there!"

"Our stuff doesn't mean anything. We need you, not our stuff!"

"I've got time!"

"Jason—"

"I've got time!" He charged up the ramp, twisting away from Samantha as he picked up the pace, leaving her caught between her children and her husband.

For a moment, a swell of anger burned in her chest, but she forced it away, shaking her head and lunging forward in the wake of her sprinting children. They'd already reached the base of the ramp, Sarah ducking low and throwing her arms around Kale's neck, squeezing the dog tight to her chest. Elijah wheeled toward his parents, eyes widening when he realized that only one of them was following.

"Where's Dad?" He took a long step forward as Samantha reached the bottom of the ramp. "Mom, where's Dad?"

Samantha gasped, catching her breath, a fist pressed tight to her sternum. Through the smoke and the yellow smog, Jason was already racing up the steps to the RV and disappearing inside.

"It's okay. He'll be okay." Samantha choked out the words, gripping her son's shoulder and gently pulling him away from the base of the ramp. "Come on, kids. We need to keep moving!"

Sarah took a step with her, then froze, eyes fixed on the sprawled corpses on the sidewalk several yards ahead. The road was a jumbled mass of stopped vehicles, many of them crushed into each other by the hastily speeding military caravan. From street level, Samantha made out the crumpled, twisted wreckage of one of the armored transports, which had slammed headlong into a support column after getting separated from its brethren. Pale smoke drifted in the air around the various vehicles that had converged into a tangled mass of armor and metal, creating a chain reaction that only further blocked the road.

A shuddering roar came from the elevated onramp again, one of the support columns shattering, chunks of concrete falling away like flecks of plaster from a sheet rock wall. Exposed rebar came visible, then before Samantha's eyes, buckled and bent, the roadway starting to fall apart. The RV screamed to life, barely audible above the undulating vibrations of the collapsing overpass. As another ragged chunk of street broke off, the RV lurched backwards, maneuvering down the ramp in reverse. It clipped a vehicle along the right side, metal scraping on metal, then pushed it into the chasm created by the crumbling asphalt. The car tipped for a second, lifted up, then spilled off, slamming hard, roof-to-roof on another vehicle below.

Angling slightly, Jason continued in reverse, moving the RV toward them, slamming into an empty passenger van, crunching past it and continuing on. Samantha led her kids backwards, pulling them and the dog away from the base of the ramp, gently turning Sarah's face from the grisly scene on the sidewalk.

"Let's give him some room— he's coming, okay, he's coming!" They backpedaled as another sudden jolt of sound and movement rocketed the earth itself.

A sound both alien and frighteningly familiar erupted from the onramp, the concrete lurching left, then right, a massive, fractured splinter of sound splitting the air in a guttural snarl. Immediately the road began to break away, sections of cracked and blistered pavement crumbling apart. Two of the support columns folded in upon themselves, dropping the onramp in a sudden downward rush of debris.

As the RV neared the base of the ramp, everything collapsed before and around it and a billowing explosion of smoke and dirt roiled around them, crashing over the O'Brians like a cresting ocean wave, forcing them to turn away from the sound and the sight as the outward cloud of debris swallowed the RV whole, with Jason still trapped inside.

CHAPTER FIVE

Jane Simmons, Speaker of the House of Representatives
Hurricane, West Virginia

Located approximately 350 miles west of Washington, D.C., Hurricane, West Virginia is an emerging small town near Interstate 64. Known for its charm, its privacy and its proximity to the nation's capital, Hurricane is a growing community with a rural backdrop but easy access to more urban amenities. With a population of approximately 7,000, the small town sits approximately forty-five minutes from nearby Yeager Airport in Charleston, making travel to and from the nation's capital relatively easy.

Jane Simmons considers all of these factors as she stands in her kitchen, looking out through the window over her sink and into the darkened trees that line her backyard. She is accustomed to the frenetic pace of Washington life and is at home in those surroundings, though she also appreciates the quieter, simpler times. As the Speaker of the House, it would almost be expected for her to have a million-dollar brownstone near Georgetown, or an equally expensive home alongside the Potomac River, but she prefers her quiet corner of the world. Far enough away from Washington so she momentarily forgets the chaos that consumes her, but close enough that she can return to it if needed.

There are plenty of times when it's needed and as she hovers by the kitchen counter alongside her husband, she wonders when that next time might be. She doesn't linger too long on that subject; she instead focuses on her children, particularly Ramona, her twenty-year-old college junior who, for the first time since coming home from Georgetown, has asked her to cook for her.

Her husband opens the stove, a wash of heat radiating from inside, forcing him to step back with a laugh. It's a hearty laugh from his belly, a welcome sound, and Jane puts a hand on his back and grabs a pair of potholders, lifting the chicken pot pie from the oven and setting it on the kitchen counter. She steps back toward the sink and lifts open the window facing the backyard, letting in a soft breeze of cool air and releasing some of the pent-up heat from the kitchen.

Her children chatter from around the dining room table, sixteen-year-old Lucille leaning across the table and begging Ramona for tips on getting her driver's license on the first try. Even young Pearl, three years Lucille's junior, is participating instead of being glued to her phone wedged in the corner of the living room on her favorite plush chair.

It's only too easy for Jane to forget the virtues of quiet, family life during the unbridled chaos of her political career, but she remembers it tonight, when things seem to be going better than they have in a long, long time. She leans into the feeling as she places the pie plate on a ceramic warmer on the table, Ramona taking a deep breath before she closes her eyes and sighs.

"They don't serve food like this at college," she says and presses her palms together.

"How many innocent birds died to make that?" Pearl doesn't seem too impressed about the meal choice.

"It's Ramona's favorite," Jane's husband, Charles, reminds their thirteen-year-old as he places a gentle hand on her shoulder and navigates to his dining room chair.

Ramona has already used a pie server to scrape a ragged triangle of dinner out of the pie plate and heaps it on her own, staring longingly at the crust, gravy, meat and vegetables.

"And that makes it okay to slaughter animals?" Pearl crosses her arms, and that familiar teenage stoicism settles in.

Her older sister has managed to wrestle her way free of that, but Pearl is caught in the throes of it and Jane tries to remind herself of that before she scolds her.

"Let's just focus on dinner, Pearl, okay? We can discuss the morality and immorality of the American food industry another time."

"Can't you do something about it?" Pearl asks. "You're an important person in Washington."

"Less important than you think." Jane lifts one thick, dark eyebrow and retrieves the pie server from Ramona, carving out a chunk and dropping it on Pearl's plate. "Certainly not important enough to take on the poultry industry."

Despite her younger daughter's misgivings, Pearl licks her lips as she stares down at her dinner hungrily. Pearl isn't the only one looking at dinner hungrily as claws click on the hardwood floor, Jane's two dogs making their way into the dining room as the smell carries through the house. Their three cats appear as well, roaming the perimeter of the expansive dining room, tails lifted upright, smelling the rich fragrance in the air.

"When do you take your test?" Ramona asks her younger sister as she uses a fork to scoop up a heap of the chicken pot pie.

"Not for another couple of weeks," Lucille replies with her mouth full. "I need to have the stupid learner's permit for six months first."

"Biggest piece of advice I can offer you," Romana points a fork at Lucille, preparing to bestow the endless wisdom that only a twenty-year-old can. "Don't mess with the red lights. Even if it's yellow, you stop. Those instructors have no patience for skating through an orange light."

"There's no such thing as an orange light, Ramona," Charles advises. "If it's yellow you should be stopping."

"Yes, sir, Mister Law Abiding citizen," Ramona replies.

Jane smiles at the good-humored exchange. It's a return to a life she had before, a life before Ramona went to Georgetown and a life before the gears of the Washington machine ground so quick and so hard.

"Who sitting around this table got a speeding ticket most recently?" Ramona asks, focusing her attention on the chicken pot pie, but lifting her eyes upward to look at her father.

"Did you tell her about that?" Charles glowers at Jane, though a slight smile betrays his inner humor.

"I might have vented a little bit." Jane shrugs, using her fork to push around the dinner on her plate. "If I can't vent about my husband – the Speaker of the House's husband – getting a speeding ticket to my oldest daughter, who can I vent to?"

"I'm trying to be a role model here." Charles shoves a forkful of pie in his mouth.

Jane sees the humor in his expression, even as he chews. Since becoming Speaker of the House, Charles has taken on more and more parental responsibilities and he's taken them in stride. Jane can't help but dwell on just how fortunate she is to be sharing her dining room table with her entire family, even with all of its warts. Life is good, and it serves her well to stop and remember that every once in a while.

She hasn't even touched her dinner, preferring to just sit there and enjoy the time with her loved ones. The dining room is a large, square section of their house, a nice upper middle-class Colonial, set outside of downtown Hurricane, their three-acre backyard consumed mostly by trees. The house is filled with love, the rich after-smell of chicken pot pie, the heat that continues to float from the direction of the kitchen, and the voices of her husband and daughters. This is what life is, and not for the first time, Jane holds on to the tiniest of wishes that life would perhaps slow down and allow her more opportunities to appreciate that.

As Jane finally decides she's ready to eat, a sound draws her attention back toward the kitchen she'd left moments before. It's a somewhat foreign sound, a strange, repeated rush of noise that stands apart from the quaint, rural township where she and her husband bought their house many years ago, when she first began her political career. While the sound is foreign it is also familiar, but in a wrong context and one that confuses her at first. She sets down her fork and pushes the chair back from the table, standing and taking a step toward the kitchen.

"Jane?" Charles looks up at his wife, eyes narrowed in inquiry.

"Do you hear that?" Jane asks the room itself, already halfway back to the kitchen door.

Heat still fills the room, thickening the air and gathering the smell of chicken, vegetables and gravy. It's a pleasing smell, but she pushes her way through it, walks to the sink, and tries to peer out of the window which she'd cracked open to let out the heat. The sound is louder there, a dull repeated thud of noise getting closer and closer, and not just one source, but multiple. She hears these sounds frequently while on the White House grounds or while visiting military bases, but she doesn't hear them at home. Not in her kitchen, not staring through a window into her backyard.

"What is it?" Charles stands framed in the kitchen door, a pinched look on his face.

"Helicopters."

True to her word, it's not a single helicopter, but multiple helicopters, and the rotors are beating loud enough to tell Jane that they very well might be coming directly to her house. Jane's chest squeezes tightly, a vice is closing in around it, trapping her suddenly racing heart inside a tighter cavity. Outside, through the windows, the leaves on the trees are rustling wildly as a downward force of wind slices through the foliage running along the edge of Jane's backyard. The engines are even louder, almost screaming now and Ramona stands next to her father, staring out past him, trying to get an angle of the window.

"Stay here, okay?" Jane leaves the kitchen and walks back out into the dining room.

"What's going on?" Lucille wears a concerned look that young Pearl mirrors, both uncertain about what might be happening.

"I'm... not sure," she says, sounding even less comfortable than she feels. "But just stay here. I'm going to run outside for a minute." Jane propels herself through a second door which connects the dining room to the expansive living room, which faces the front yard of the house instead of the back.

Just like the backyard, there are trees running along the edge of the road leading to her driveway, and those trees shake and thrash, their leaves twisting under a barrage of wind. Jane moves even more quickly, fueled by the pistons of her legs which are pumping wildly. She reaches the front door and throws it open, stepping outside and her entire world comes to a crashing, sudden halt, slamming upon her with such unexpected and blunt force that she nearly stumbles.

Two aircraft approach from the near distance, flying in low and getting lower with each passing moment, clearly headed toward her property. As their rotors continue their tilt upward she can see that they're a pair of V-22 Ospreys, grey in color, with the Marine Corps emblem emblazoned on both. A third Osprey hovers directly above the Simmons house, its angular tail coming around as it searches for an effective landing place on the sprawling front lawn or perhaps even the roadway itself. The aircraft are large before her, looming broad and dark against the pale light of dusk, stark against the small town backdrop of her quiet, rural residence.

The aircraft directly above her draws downward, its brushed

metal exterior clearly visible in the low light of approaching evening. The tilt rotor aircraft had been used from time to time to transport White House staff and other government personnel, but seeing one hovering over her house, with another pair of them coming in for a landing, takes the air from Jane's lungs.

Downdrafts batter her on her front stoop, flattening the grass as the aircraft hovers downward. In the short distance, the other two aircraft are angling toward them, the tilt-rotor mechanisms swiveling, bringing them around to land. Sand kicks up from the well-manicured lawn, a swirling vortex of grit that fills the air. The two support aircraft are closer, one of them banking down, preparing to land alongside the first while the third coasts over the roof of her house, making its way toward the backyard.

"Holy—" Ramona gasps from behind Jane, having followed her mother to the front door. "What are those?"

"I asked you to stay inside."

"I am inside." She gestures toward her feet which are about a foot inside the opened front door. "Is that the President?"

"Can't be. He's in Los Angeles right now." That fact sends a bitter chill through Jane's entire body, and she checks her phone. There's no sign of messages, but also no signal. *Not good,* she thinks.

She stands on the stoop as the lead Osprey slowly lowers, its tires touching down on the grass, supports buckling slightly with the weight of the aircraft. Swirling winds buffet the house and Jane herself and she holds up a hand to try and block it from hitting her eyes. Grit coats her face, rotor wind slashing at the slacks and button-up dress shirt she wears. The remaining two aircraft also set down, their rotors whipping into a more gradual deceleration, the slicing wind easing, allowing her to step off her front porch and start to approach.

Rotors still spinning, the rear hatches of both aircraft tilt downward, opening the interior holds. At once, a cadre of Secret Service agents and Marines swarm from both Ospreys, the Secret

Service sprinting across the yard in her direction while the Marines take up a defensive formation around the aircraft. The agents are wearing their typical neatly pressed shirts and slacks, the trademark white coil of communication devices twisting from their ears. What Jane notices most of all, however, is that the agents are all wearing tactical vests, bulky, pouch-laden military gear covering their torsos. A few of the agents grip rifles in two hands while others sweep across the yard, converging on the house at speed.

They move in a strangely well-orchestrated chaos, an oncoming wave of highly trained operatives. One man seems to be directing traffic, shouting into his upturned wrist, gesturing wildly with the fingers of his right hand as several agents take position around the perimeter of Jane's property. She approaches an agent, but before she can ask her question, another figure steps from the first Osprey, a stoic, bald-headed man, his broad shoulders filling out the military dress uniform he wears.

His eyes meet hers and she doesn't bother asking the agent the question. With several quick, efficient strides, the man in dress greens comes toward her, even as more Marines dressed in camouflage disembark from the Osprey, weapons ready.

"Madame Speaker, forgive the intrusion," the man says in an elevated voice, almost shouting to be heard above the din of the aircraft. "I'm Colonel William Drake, and we need to move you and your family to a secure location!"

"What?" Jane takes an uncertain step backwards. "I don't understand!"

"We believe the United States has come under attack. Biological or chemical weapons have been deployed in several cities and your safety is now our top priority!"

The rotors of the aircraft continue their oscillation, which makes it somewhat difficult to make out the colonel's words.

"Did you say an attack?" Jane's throat is sore, her mouth dry, the blistering wind from the rotors lifting all moisture from her lips.

"Madame Speaker, we believe the President of the United States and the Vice President are both deceased. These attacks are active and ongoing, and we need to move you and your family to a secure location immediately!"

Jane blinks back at the man in the Service A uniform. Over a dozen Secret Service and a handful of Marines take up strategic positions across her front yard, the two Ospreys perched, blades still spinning at nearly full speed.

"If you'll excuse me, Ma'am," the colonel continues, moving forward, forcing Jane to retreat back into the house.

Her family scatters as she comes back inside, the Colonel joining them, a trio of Secret Service riding close to his coattails.

"I apologize for the abruptness, but we need to get you all to pack bags and come with us ASAP. This is not a drill, this is not a test."

One of the agents lifts his wrist to his mouth, then lowers it, peering at Jane. "Can someone unlock the back sliding glass door, please?"

"Charles?" Jane turns to her husband, who nods and is already moving back through the house.

"Mom, what's going on?" For the first time in a very long time, Ramona actually looks afraid.

"We need to do what these men say, Ramona, okay? Can you go talk to your sisters? Get them to start packing?"

"Essentials only, please," Colonel Drake suggests, a mild edge to his voice. "We only have a few moments."

Other voices raise from deeper in the house, and another surge of Secret Service sweeps through, moving in careful coordination, propelled by their training and preparation. Everywhere Jane looks, a man in black slacks, a white shirt and tactical vest is standing while others are helping her family pack for an unexpected trip.

"I don't understand," Jane says. "I don't know what you expect me to do."

"I expect you to follow our requests, get packed up and move to a secure location with your family. That's my first and only concern right now, Madame Speaker."

Jane nods as the reality of the situation settles in. Her house has become a whirlwind of Secret Service activity, her family huddled together as the agents sprint throughout the home, lugging out suitcases and backpacks. One agent has both dogs on their leashes, guiding the two petrified animals toward the sliding glass door at the rear of the house.

"Charles!" Jane goes to her husband, who is standing near their three daughters, all gathered together as the hurricane of activity sweeps through. "They're going to very likely take you on a separate aircraft. You and the girls, okay? I'll have to go on the other one."

"What's happening?"

"I'm not exactly sure. I'm going to try to get more information on the way. Just— take care of our girls, okay? Take care of our daughters?"

"Of course."

"Mom, I don't like this." Pearl hugs herself with her arms.

Two agents sweep past, each of them carrying a cat in their arms.

"Molly!" Pearl reaches toward a black and white tabby cat, its eyes wide, claws dug into the white-clad arm of the agent gripping her.

"You'll see Molly again. They're here to protect us. That's their only responsibility, so there's no reason to be afraid."

Jane stands before her family, her three daughters and her husband, each of them doing their best to put on a brave face, though they all understand the gravity of the situation. She's been in politics for most of her adult life, her children have been exposed to that world, though their current experience is anything but typical exposure.

"Just do what the agents say. Listen to them and follow what they tell you. I'll meet you as soon as I'm able."

"Madame Speaker, we need to go. *Now*." Colonel Drake stands just behind her, close enough to gently grasp her arm as two Secret Service agents flank her on both sides.

Jane ignores him at first, stepping forward to give each of her children a brief, but strong embrace, one at a time. She reaches Charles last, cups his cheeks and kisses him before allowing herself to be pulled away. Secret Service come from seemingly nowhere and gather around her in a tightly formed quartet, ushering her toward the front door. As a singular organism, they move through the front door and out onto the lawn where the primary gunmetal-gray Osprey's engines begin to whine, the rotors spinning even faster.

Another slash of wind brackets Jane, forcing her to lower her head and lead with her shoulder to soften the blow of the whipping rotor wash. The hatch at the rear of the Osprey remains open as Drake leads her to it, a camouflage-garbed Marine standing just inside at the top of the ramp formed by the lowered door. Jane allows herself to be led up into the Osprey's belly, but its interior is like nothing she expects.

Where harsh, bare metal jump seats would normally be located, there instead stands a VIP seating area with several soft, leather seats taking up a section of the body, the seats facing each other, though they are all empty. Monitors are mounted discretely near the windows, an array of other communications equipment strategically spread throughout the surrounding real estate. A section of wall between the cabin and the cockpit carries a wide array of technical equipment, including several flat-panel monitors, fold-out computer keyboards and communications gear.

"Uhh... I've never been in one of these before, but this doesn't look standard issue." Jane looks at the Colonel.

"Nothing about this situation is standard," Drake says as he gestures toward the seats.

The murmur of secure communications fills the space, punctuated by the whispered voices of Secret Service agents who have followed her into the aircraft, along with Colonel Drake. Men are gathering headsets and tugging them over their ears, several of them moving to accompanying seats as Jane herself is ushered toward her own. Voices are soon drowned out by the increasing pitch of the rotors and even as Jane just barely secures her safety harness, the aircraft begins its sweeping ascent. Her stomach lurches with the unexpected upward drift, but she swallows her nausea down and takes a deep breath in a desperate attempt to retain some frail grasp of her composure.

Jane peers through the rounded window beside her, watching as the landscape falls away, trees replaced by a curtain of dusk sky, littered with clouds. From where she sits, everything appears amazingly normal. The quiet, bustling town of Hurricane spreads out below her as the V-22 angles upward and gains altitude, flanked by a pair of converging Ospreys. Colonel Drake settles into one of the seats across from her, separated by a small desk, and leans forward.

"I need you to do something for me." The request is simple and straightforward but carries connotations too numerous to consider.

Jane nods without speaking, a boiling suspicion already building in her gut. Colonel Drake twists in his chair, nodding toward a nearby Secret Service agent.

"Initiate the secure video call."

Jane clears her throat and folds her hands in her lap, lacing her fingers together. It takes all of her strength to keep her posture firm and upright, and her legs press tight together, formed to the contours of the leather chair. The Secret Service agent folds out a keyboard from the interior wall of the cabin, his fingers dancing along the keyboard. A screen above the keyboard flickers and fades from dark to dim, then more swiftly illuminates. Framed within the monitor screen is an older man with a neatly trimmed layer of gray hair, his eyes narrow. His chin is sloped to a narrow point, the rigid lines of his jaw clench with a firm tautness that mirrors the tension in Jane's own limbs.

"In a perfect situation," Colonel Drake says after clearing his throat, "we would have the Chief Justice of the Supreme Court on this call, but we've been unable to reach him this evening."

The tone of the Colonel's voice tells Jane all she needs to know. Quite a few people are suddenly hard to reach.

"If you don't recognize the man on the screen, it's the Honorable Gordon Tilton, Chief Judge of the U.S. Court of Appeals for the Fourth Circuit. He is the highest-ranking federal judge we were able to contact on such short notice, but the gravity of the situation has forced us to make some unconventional decisions."

Jane clears her throat, remaining bolt upright. Colonel Drake stands briefly and takes a step toward a nearby set of drawers, built in to the interior wall of Marine One. He pulls a drawer out and retrieves a thick book, which Jane identifies even before she sees it. Drake returns to the seating area and sits across from Jane, placing the Bible on the small table that separates them.

"If this is what I think it is—" she starts to say, her voice showing the slightest hint of a tremble.

"It is. We can answer questions later. We have to do this now."

"I don't—"

"Chief Judge Tilton, if you would." Colonel Drake turns toward the monitor and the man in the screen nods, a restless sigh metallic through the wall-mounted speakers.

"Place your right hand on the bible, if you would, please, Madame Speaker." Tilton nods toward her and though Jane nearly protests, she instead does as requested and flattens her right hand on the surface of the leather-bound bible. Tilton clears his throat and draws himself straighter on the other side of the two-way secure call.

"Please repeat after me."

Jane nods her head, her teeth clenching so tightly they ache.

"I do solemnly swear that I will faithfully execute the Office of President of the United States, and will to the best of my ability, preserve, protect and defend the Constitution of the United States." His voice cuts to silence, the aircraft's interior drifting into an unsettled quiet.

All eyes fix on Jane, breaths are held and even the slightest motion freezes. The interior of the Osprey is put on pause as they all await her next words.

"Madame Speaker," Colonel Drake says.

"I do solemnly swear that I will faithfully execute the Office of—" she hesitates for a moment, steadies herself, and exhales. "That I will faithfully execute the Office of the President of the United States, and will to the best of my ability, preserve, protect and defend the Constitution of the United States." The words tumble from her mouth almost by pure reflex, somehow snaking through the gritted fence of her teeth.

"Congratulations, Madame President." Chief Judge Tilton nods curtly as if this is just another day in his long and storied career.

The Secret Service agent clicks a key and the call cuts off, the screen once more snapping into blackness. For a moment, she just sits in her seat, back pressed against the leather, the world outside swimming past her window. The sky darkens as the sun passes behind cloud cover, Mother Nature continuing on, unconcerned with the trials and tribulations of mankind. Jane peers through the window at a sprawling city that appears below, a broad expanse of urban territory hammered into the West Virginia wilderness.

Vehicles clog Interstate 64 beneath her, an immobile mass of metal filling both lanes of travel, bumper-to-bumper. Grid works of roadways cross between and around tight clusters of buildings downtown, vehicles stopped everywhere Jane looks, the entire city transformed into a thirty-square mile parking lot. For a brief snippet of time, Jane thinks she sees dead bodies sprawled about the green grass of a park just north of the congested area of the city center. The Kanawha River to the south is dotted with boats that float aimlessly without purpose or movement, an entire city brought to a complete and total standstill.

"Charleston," Colonel Drake says quietly, leaning over to peer out the window. "Unconfirmed reports say they were attacked as well. We've been trying to get in touch with anyone, but all we get is static."

"What in the world is happening, Colonel Drake?"

"That's what I'm hoping we can figure out, Madame President."

"Stop calling me that."

"That's what you are."

Jane closes her eyes, her back teeth clenching even more tightly together, threatening to grind ivory into powder.

"Trust me, we all know it's a bad situation. But it is our reality, and we need to navigate through it." Once more, he turns to the Secret Service agent, who is still positioned near the monitors, one hand against the wall for balance as Marine One sways gently around them.

Colonel Drake clears his throat and gives the Secret Service agent another backwards look. "How are we coming?"

"Almost there, Colonel."

Instead of just a single monitor screen showing the faint light of illumination, four separate screens do, all of them mounted in a tightly formed quartet on the interior of the cabin wall. The first face appears in the upper left, a round-faced, clean-shaven man, his lips pinched in a firm, horizontal line. Two other faces coalesce into view, all three of them showing the hint of a military uniform over their shoulders, hair and faces neat and trimmed. Finally, the fourth face appears in the lower right corner, huddled close to the camera, showing some slight discomfort at the method for communicating.

Colonel Drake stands as the fourth face emerges, then snaps off a straight-backed salute, one of the crispest and cleanest military greetings Jane has ever seen.

"Madame President, joining us from their secure locations are the remaining Joint Chiefs of Staff."

"Wait— remaining?" Jane lifts a hand in inquiry.

"Washington, D.C. was among the targets struck today. The other four members of the Joint Chiefs, including the Chairman himself, are currently unaccounted for."

"My word." Jane leans back in her chair, the crushing news forcing her back against her will. "How many lives—"

"If you'll excuse me, Madame President, we are hoping to make everything clear momentarily. If I can finish introductions."

"Of course." Jane pulls herself up in her chair, once more folding her hands in her lap, attention focused on the four monitors ahead.

Colonel Drake points to the upper left monitor. "Vice Chairman of the Joint Chiefs of Staff, Admiral Dean Austin, Chief of Naval Operations." The man nods curtly, and Drake gestures toward the second screen. "General Orson Bradley, Commandant of the Marine Corps." There is no nod, no acknowledgement, just a rigid, fixed glower from across the miles. "General Wilmot Massy," Drake continues, "Chief of the National Guard Bureau." He turns slightly and waves a hand toward the final screen. "General Kingsley Poole, Chief of Staff of the Army. Gentlemen, let me introduce President of the United States Jane Simmons."

A gruff, uneven greeting comes from each screen, visually, though not verbally, the men in the cameras only interested in getting down to business. Jane is grateful for that.

"Gentlemen, I thank you for making yourselves available during such trying times."

"Madame President," they collectively reply, their voices twisting together.

For an extended moment she sits there, leaning slightly, anticipating what the four men might say. But none of them say anything, they all sit just as still as if awaiting her. The silence stretches long enough to become uncomfortable before Colonel Drake steps in.

"Gentlemen," he says, "the President is completely in the dark. Please bring her up to speed."

The men stare back, all in silence at first, though the Vice Chairman inches forward in his seat, coming a bit closer to the camera.

"Intelligence is limited, I'm afraid to say, Madame President. We're hearing reports of attacks from various locations across the country. Initially we believed that perhaps they were isolated incidents, but as time has gone on, they are occurring more frequently and with greater intensity."

"What sorts of incidents are you talking about?" Jane shifts in her seat. "You'll have to forgive me, Vice Chairman, I was sitting down to dinner when all this happened. I've got a blank slate here."

"Cities across the country appear to have suffered biological or chemical attacks. It seems to have started in Los Angeles and Las Vegas and has spilled over to several larger cities throughout the United States. As was already mentioned, Washington, D.C. fell victim a very short time after L.A. It was quick enough and things are still developing at such a rapid pace that we haven't yet formulated a response."

"And how are we being attacked? Did you say chemical or biological?"

"That is what we believe, yes, though we have not yet gotten specifics. We have not yet determined whether the threat is domestic or international, but based on the scope and complexity, it would seem to be a targeted attack on our nation, most likely from abroad. There's a litany of countries that could be responsible, but we haven't yet begun to dive into the true scale and scope of what we're dealing with."

"What are we hearing from locals?" Jane asks.

"Well, that's sort of the problem, Madame President." General Massy, representing the National Guard, answers that question. "We haven't been able to communicate effectively with boots on the ground. This attack, whatever it is, is remarkably potent. It seems to kill anyone and everything within a certain radius of its deployment, and the vast majority of observers who were close enough to tell us what happened are dead."

"And the current death toll?"

"Impossible to say. While the attacks began with larger, more major cities, they have now begun to spread to several smaller ones as well. As you no doubt noticed, Charleston, West Virginia fell victim a short time ago. Lexington, Kentucky, Cleveland, Ohio, countless more that we haven't yet heard from."

"So, what you're saying is our entire nation is under attack – maybe from foreign threat actors or maybe not – and that we have no idea what the nature of the attack is? Or even who initiated it?"

"I'm afraid that is exactly what we're saying, Madame President. The speed and efficiency of this whatever is being used is making it difficult to—"

"And how exactly *did* this happen, Vice Chairman? How exactly did an attack of this scale hit us without us even knowing it was coming?" Jane's voice is elevated, loud and echoing within the confines of the aircraft as the shock of her whole situation begins to wear off, her responsibility and focus taking over her whole being. "Where the hell is the intel community?"

There is an uncomfortable silence in the wake of her elevated voice, an unsettled uncertainty throughout the four men broadcast through their secure channels.

"We are still investigating that, Madame President," Admiral Austin replies, his voice low and couched.

"See that you do."

"With all due respect," General Bradley interjects, "our concern right now is trying to hold together our nation. There will be plenty of time to point fingers later, but for now we need to survive this onslaught."

Jane almost shouts back, to cast blame and point fingers, but she restrains herself. "Of course," she replies, relaxing a bit in her seat. "I want more information, and I want it fast. We've got enough spies inside and outside this country that we should have known what our attackers were doing before they knew it themselves."

"I wish we had more information for you," Admiral Austin says. "We'll get it to you soon, though, President Simmons."

Jane blinks, those two words pressed together still making no sense in her own ears.

"What are our next steps?" Jane asks.

"We are all reaching out to everyone we can," the admiral responds. "We have to know exactly what we're dealing with before we can decide how we deal with it. I'm afraid we're still in the information gathering stages."

"While thousands of our citizens die by the hour, if what you're saying is true."

"By the minute. Time is certainly of the essence, Madame President."

"I'm glad we're on the same page." It takes all of Jane's strength not to bury her face in her hands as that responsibility and focus bleeds away in the face of the stark numbers. "Continue what you're doing," the newly minted president says. "As expediently as humanly possible. We need to stop the bleeding, and we need to formulate a response. But most importantly, we need to find out how to save some lives."

"Understood, Madame President." Admiral Austin nods curtly.

The four men stand in frame, staring at her expectantly, as if awaiting their next command. Jane leans over slightly, releases a breath and lifts both hands to press to her temples.

"Madame President?"

She jerks her head up, surprised to see the faces still staring back at her.

"Are they dismissed?" Colonel Drake asks.

"Yes. Of course. Dismissed." She waves a hand and the four monitors snap into blackness. The faces vanishing, she finally presses the palms of her hands to her temples and applies gentle pressure. A headache builds, a forceful swelling in her skull, and her grip does little to hold it at bay.

"Do you have ibuprofen in this place? Or whisky. Or both."

"Of course." Colonel Drake simply passes a look to a Secret Service agent and he's on the move, walking toward the rear of the aircraft.

"What am I supposed to do?" Jane glances up, hands still clasped together in her lap.

"Your job, Madame President."

"You know," Jane smirks despite herself. "Nobody ever actually thinks that the Speaker of the House will ever need to be sworn in. I'm not exactly up to speed like the President is." Her expression drops. "Was."

"We're all struggling at the moment, ma'am. This is unprecedented in the history... of the *world*."

"Of course." Jane shakes her head and rests back against the chair. "But this is an unprecedented intelligence failure as well. This will make 9/11 look like... I can't even imagine."

"Yes ma'am."

Jane leans over and stares once more through her nearby window. Sprawling sections of wilderness pass below, separated here and there by the urban arteries of highways and small towns.

Once more it occurs to her how absolutely normal everything looks from so high up. In the distance, the silhouette of a large plane approaches, moving slowly across the horizon like some large whale passing silently through the ocean's depths.

"In a perfect world, we'd be in the White House situation room," Colonel Drake continues, "hashing this out in person with all of our resources at our disposal." He leans toward the window himself, hesitating. "We are no longer in a perfect world. Frankly, we're still trying to decide what location even constitutes as 'secure' for you and your family."

"Colonel... William."

"Yes, ma'am?"

"Do me one favor. Speak to me frankly, please. I may be a politician, but you just spirited me away from my family's dinner and swore me in as President. If I need to know something, don't wrap it up with a bow. Give it to me raw. Understand?"

"Yes, ma'am." Drake's whole body seems to release the slightest bit of tension at her words.

The large plane draws closer, lumbering toward them, its path altering slightly as it comes closer. A shuddering roar consumes the entire Osprey and Jane grips the armrests of her seat, arms bulging with the tight flex of her muscles. A darkened shadow passes over the aircraft as the larger plane sweeps above them, and Jane follows the sound, though only sees as far as the front bulkhead.

"We're refueling," Drake says, anticipating her question. "Have to do it in mid-air, we can't risk setting down."

"Is my family safe?"

"Your family is safe. They're following us to the secure location. As soon as we figure out where we're going, you'll see them as soon as we land."

"Thank you."

The Osprey jostles softly as the refueling takes place, but Jane settles into the seat for the ride, regaining her grip on her composure. As strange as it is, there's some comfort in the fact that everyone else is as clueless as she is. After several minutes pass, the shadow moves back across the Osprey, the plane moving to the next aircraft in line. They're flying north, that much Jane can tell by the position of the sun, but the destination is unknown, as is how long it'll take to get there.

Sprawling wilderness passes beneath her, the soft glow of the setting sun shining through her opposite window, thick, bright and orange. Colonel Drake has stopped talking and pulls out a tablet, scrolling through the data on the screen, gently chewing his lower lip. Jane settles back into the silence, allows the temporary reprieve from chaos to wash over her and stares out the window at the nation she once knew.

CHAPTER SIX

The Tills Family
Silverpine, Oregon

Static filled the television screen as it continued to cycle through the horrific images across America. Seattle's Space Needle looming large above a city of the dead. New York's trademark gridwork of streets teeming with stopped cars and fallen bodies, a vast sea of stillness and death within the busiest city on the planet. Millenium Park in Chicago and the famous Cloud Gate statue, the huddled corpses and sprawled bodies reflected in its trademark chrome-plated sheen.

Most major cities of the United States were stricken by the mysterious attacks and the television relentlessly cycled through each one as if to further reinforce the fact that every one of their viewers was doomed. Typical shock value mass media hysteria, though perhaps deserved for once instead of overblown. Sheila's grip tightened around her phone and Doug's grip tightened around her arm as they began to turn away from the screens.

The already somewhat distorted images were being overwhelmed by digital noise, streaks and smears of color and sound scraping away the background imagery, even the newscaster's voice no longer audible beneath the squeal of interference. The group gathered before the television screens in the vast dining room of the vineyard had expanded since the broadcast had started, nearly three dozen customers, diners and employees converged along the east-facing windows.

"She won't answer." Sheila lowered the phone, staring down at the screen. "Samantha won't answer."

Through the group, voices escalated and rippled, a collective surge of panic pulsing through the people gathered there. Heads turned toward each other, strangers asking strangers whether what they were viewing was real.

"Do we even know where she is?" Doug asked. "When did we last hear from her?"

"She called this morning after they'd left Yosemite National Park." Sheila swiped away her daughter's contact card and revealed the time on the screen of her phone. "Doug, if they were driving since they left Yosemite, they could have been close to L.A."

"We can't jump to conclusions. Keep trying to reach her. Meanwhile—" He lifted his head back toward the group gathered around the television.

"They're all dead!" Someone in the group shouted, pointing toward the screens. "That's thousands of people!"

"We need to go!"

"What if it happens here?"

The crowd separated, voices rising in chaotic concern as people began to scatter away. A young, well-dressed man and his equally young and well-dressed wife gripped each other's hands as they swept across the dining room.

"We left Benson with the sitter— what if something happened?" The wife turned toward the husband, tears streaking her eyes, the two of them running past.

"My parents live near Seattle! I can't reach them!" A middle-aged woman stared down at her phone as she and her two girl-friends shoved past an elderly couple and bolted toward the door.

Doug stepped away from Sheila's side and moved to grab the old man, who had nearly been knocked to the ground. He placed both hands on the man's arms and held him upright.

"Are you okay?"

He nodded meekly, turning to look over his shoulder as the crowd continued to surge from the dining room in a wild panic.

A slightly younger woman gripped the old man's arm and wrenched it away from Doug's grasp. "We need to go. We need to get back to the children. We need to make sure they're okay."

"I was just trying to help—" Before Doug could finish, the woman was practically dragging the older man away, ushering him clumsily across the floor.

"Someone call 9-1-1!" another voice cried out among the din.

"What are they going to do?" someone else snapped back sardonically.

"We're being attacked! It's Russia! I know it's Russia!"

"It's China! North Korea!"

Doug moved back toward Sheila's side, huddling close to her as people rushed to leave.

"I'm sorry!" A breathless young man wearing an apron approached them both, narrow-eyed, a pleading look in his eyes, his hands outstretched. "I have to go. I know I'm supposed to be here until eight, but I have to go." He lifted the apron strap over his head and dropped it on the floor, then bolted past the two of them before they could say a word.

"This is it— this is really it?" Someone else stood in the center of the room as the crowd rushed away, staring aimlessly around him. "This is the end." He turned and stared out of the windows, looking for answers in the sprawling vineyard outside.

"Come on, Dad!" A young woman grabbed the hypnotized man by the wrist and dragged him away.

"We need to pay for our meal—"

"No, we don't, we need to go!" As a pair, they sprinted back toward the door, alongside everyone else.

Caught within the group of desperate people, Doug spotted a couple of their waiters and waitresses hurrying out the door who hadn't even told them they were leaving, though he couldn't blame them. "We need to stay calm," Doug said as he strode forward, toward the group. "Please, everyone, we don't do any good by losing our cool!"

"Mr. Tills? I don't— can I—" A sheepish young man's gaze darted out the windows, then back toward Doug, his head swiveling. "I know my shift is— but— I want to—"

"Rollie, please." Doug pressed a firm hand to the young man's arm. "If you need to go, you need to go. Just be safe, that's all I ask. Drive carefully, okay?"

The young man nodded jerkily, then made his way toward the exit in a trance. Sheila was conversing with a couple of vineyard office workers dressed in business casual wear. One a woman and one a man, the woman's long, dark hair was swept across her face, her exposed left eye shimmering with tears. The man's jaw worked in a frenzy grinding of teeth, his pale face stricken with concern.

"Do you have a ride home?" Sheila asked the woman, leaning a bit. "Didn't James drop you off at work today?"

"He did." The woman nodded and lifted her phone. "I've tried calling him three times, but he won't answer. I can't even get through."

"I know. The phones aren't working at the moment. I've tried, too."

"I can give you a ride." The man whispered to her. "Don't you live just off Elkhorn Drive?"

"Yeah."

"It's on my way."

"Are you sure?" The woman wiped the tears from her eyes with the back of one hand and tugged the hair from her face.

"It's fine. I'm going that way, anyway." His gaze drifted toward Sheila's. "If that's okay, anyway. There are still two hours left in my shift, and—"

"Go. Both of you can go. Just get somewhere safe and drive carefully."

The man nodded and the two of them hurried away as Doug approached, the chaos continuing to unfold around them.

"I told Rollie he could go home, too. As far as I'm concerned, we can close up for the day."

"I wouldn't be able to focus on work anyway." Sheila lifted her phone from her pocket again and once more tapped to try Samantha. "And I doubt we're going to get that dinner rush."

She lifted the phone to her ear, but only listened for a moment before slipping it back into her pocket. Near the wall of windows overlooking the vineyard, the television screens had all gone dark.

"Mr. and Mrs. Tills?" Another pair of office workers approached them, a small clutch of waitstaff lingering around behind them. "What— what should we do?"

"We're going to close for the day," Sheila replied, and the group visibly relaxed.

"Should we come back?" One of the men in a business suit asked. "I was in the middle of working on the schedule for next week, I don't want to—"

Sheila and Doug exchanged a brief look of concern.

"Are we opening tomorrow?" A young waiter piped up from the back. "I don't know if I can come in. My sister goes to UCLA and my parents are going to be freaking out."

Collectively, the group began talking all at once, barraging Sheila and Doug with questions. A screech of tires came from in front of the vineyard as harried customers left the parking lot. Doug braced himself for an inevitable slam of impact, but it never came, just more engines growling to life as people urgently sped away.

"Focus on getting back to your homes safely," Doug said, raising his voice to overwhelm theirs. "That is all you should be worried about right now. It's impossible to know what tomorrow will bring but get home safely and stay home. Under no circumstances should you worry about coming back to work unless we call you or you otherwise hear from us."

"But the phones are down."

"We have a landline," Doug replied. "Do all of you have—"

Eyes gaped back at him. Three people nodded, but the others in the group just stared at him incredulously, as if he were speaking a foreign language.

"Okay. We can worry about that later. I'm sure things will be back to normal soon. Those of you who can go home, please go home. Do you all have rides or cars?"

Every head in the group nodded, then the group dispersed, everyone walking briskly toward the exit. The large group of customers and the earlier throng of employees had all managed to file through the doors already, leaving the majority of the dining room empty.

Doug strode after the last group of employees and Sheila joined him, the two of them leaving the dining room, making their way through a squat corridor and into a small entryway where the host station stood. Employees pushed their way through the doors leading to the front parking lot. A few of them hadn't spoken to Doug or Sheila first and glanced back at them, faces contorted in a brief expression of guilt, though said guilt didn't stop them from pushing their way through the doors and into the parking lot outside. A car pulled swiftly from a parking space, firing in reverse, screeching on their brakes and then accelerating. It sped forward, forcing two bystanders to recoil, stumbling out of its way to avoid getting mowed down. The car swerved wildly toward the exit, but a throng of vehicles were waiting in line. It slotted into its place at a slightly askew angle and revved the engine, as if that might help things move faster.

A larger group filed to the right, making their way down to the employee parking lot near the back of the restaurant. The customer lot was already almost empty, though a black-colored Cadillac was just gunning its engine. It had parked backwards, so when it accelerated, it surged forward, and Doug recognized the faces of the elderly couple in the seats. The old man huddled in the passenger seat while his slightly younger wife gripped the wheel, steering the large car out of the lot and back toward the line trying to exit the parking area.

Wind blew softly through the nearby trees, a natural, gentle breeze in stark contrast to the revving, impatient engines of the customers and guests trying to depart. There were still a few cars in the customer parking lot and Doug approached them, leaning a bit to peer into the windows. The cars were empty, and he crouched alongside one for a better look, then glanced toward his wife.

"Do you recognize these vehicles?"

Sheila shook her head as she walked closer. "I'm not sure who —" her eyes widened slightly. "Wait! The tour!"

"The what?"

"Jackie was giving a group the wagon ride tour."

Doug shot upright and reached to the small of his back, grasping for a radio he had clipped to his belt. He tugged it free and turned it on, the static immediately coming from the speaker.

"Jackie, are you there?" He pressed the talk button, interrupting the static for a moment as he spoke.

The button released, the static returned, and he held the radio near, waiting to hear some acknowledgement of his call. Time dragged on, a few seconds of static-filled silence that seemed interminable. They both stepped aside as more cars angled up the slope from the employee parking lot and made their way toward the exit. Slowly, the line leading back to the road was dwindling, but as more employees tried to leave, it thickened and grew once more. Someone in the line even honked their horn with an aggressive, fist-pounded bleat of frustration.

"Mr. Tills? Is that you?" Jackie's voice came back through the radio.

"Yes, it's me. Where are you right now?"

"On our way back. We stopped mid-tour, I'm driving the tractor as fast as I can. People started getting notifications about —" Jackie's voice trailed off, swallowed by static.

Doug gave her another moment to continue. Just as he was about to thumb the button again, her voice interrupted him.

"Is it true? What they're saying? People got all these notifications about some sort of attack? But now the phones won't connect, and these groups are— well, they're freaking out a little." Her voice lowered at the end of the statement, shifting into a static-filled whisper.

"Just get back as soon as you can, okay?"

"I see you now," Jackie replied and Doug lifted his head.

Near the far edge of the employee parking lot, the tractor had emerged, rolling its way along the grass at the edge of the vine-yard. A large wagon was towed behind it, filled with nearly a dozen people in back. Jackie was forced to steer the tractor toward the edge of the lot as two vehicles sped from their spaces, frantic employees desperately trying to leave. Doug gave them a moment to cruise by, then led Sheila across the parking lot to intercept the tractor as it neared. Jackie sat on the bucket seat of the modern machine and cut the engine. Immediately, the people in back began scrambling toward the rear gate, even crawling up over the sides of the wagon so they could get out.

"Everyone calm down! Please go to your cars and leave in an orderly fashion." Sheila lifted her hands and stepped away from Doug, facing the last remaining group of guests.

"Is it true?" a white-haired woman frantically asked. "Is what they were saying true? Are we under attack?"

"I'm afraid we don't know the details," Doug replied. "We know as much as you do, the phones are down and it looks like we aren't getting a satellite signal on the TV, either. But we're telling all of our guests and our employees to go home. We're closing for the day; we just want everyone to be safe."

A man who had crawled over the wall of the wagon turned and lifted his hands so his wife could pass their child down to him. As he pulled the child to his chest, his wife clambered over the wall and dropped down, landing next to him. Exasperated, Doug walked past them and toward the rear of the wagon, unlatching the rear gate and dropping it down to make it easier for the people inside to leave. Jackie dropped from the seat of the tractor and joined him back there, the two of them working together to help the people get down from the high wagon.

"Sorry," Jackie said to the white-haired woman, "usually we park down there. We've got a little step ladder."

"It's okay, dear," the woman said, her wrinkled face glistening moist with tears. "I'm just worried is all."

"We're all worried," Doug replied in a gentle tenor. "It'll be okay. We just need to get everyone home safe and things will be okay."

"They said Seattle was hit by some chemical attack." The woman placed her hand to her chest. "Mustard gas or something?"

"I— don't know about that," Doug replied, turning his attention to the woman's husband, who was trying to navigate the long drop to the pavement.

He and Jackie helped him down as well, then walked alongside the older couple, who were making their way toward the blue sedan in one of the parking spaces.

"But it's true? That Seattle was attacked?"

"It seems that way, yes. It was on the news when the television was still working." Sheila did her best to soothe her own voice.

"Are you two both okay to get home? Do you need any help? Is there anyone we should call?"

"We're okay. Walter has been trying to call our son ever since we first saw the reports. But not only does the phone internet not work, we can't make a call either."

"Try a text message. It takes less bandwidth, which might get through." Doug guided the woman toward the passenger side of the sedan while her husband went to the driver's side.

She stared at him in focused confusion, but he decided not to bother elaborating. Fumbling for his keys for a moment, the man opened his door, slid into his seat, then reached over and unlocked the passenger side. The line by the exit was dwindling once more, people starting to file back out, making room for more cars to join. A few yards away, the SUV pulled out of its spot, driven by the younger man who had helped his wife get their child down from the wagon. It swept ahead, filing in behind the last of the employee cars struggling to depart. Another couple, closer to middle-age, had descended the wagon unassisted, and were getting into their own vehicle, a late-model pickup truck. Doug and Sheila stepped back, giving the elderly couple some space.

"What else did you hear? On the news?" The white-haired woman left the door open, staring up at Doug expectantly.

"Nobody seems to know what's going on. Just a lot of people dying in a lot of places. Big cities, from the sound of it." Doug purposefully didn't add any more details about Chicago, New York or Los Angeles. "Drive safe, okay?"

"Thank you," the woman said with an affable nod, then slammed the door.

Doug and Sheila stepped back as the engine growled to life. The pickup truck was already on its way toward the exit line and walking back to the tractor, Doug peered over his shoulder to see the sedan joining it there.

"Thanks, Jackie," Sheila was saying in a low voice when Doug approached. "Appreciate you keeping your head. You could have panicked."

"I'll be honest, Mrs. T.," Jackie replied, "I am panicking. But there's nothing I can do." She turned and looked toward the employee parking lot. "Everyone bolted, huh?"

"Mostly everyone, yeah. I still see Benjamin's car down there, but something tells me he's around here somewhere. We'll have to take a walk around and see." Doug turned his attention back to Jackie. "Are you okay? You have somewhere to go, I assume?"

"Sure. Yeah. I've got a place I'm splitting with two friends. It's not far from here. Are you sure you don't want me to stick around and help?"

"You need to get back home and be safe." Sheila gently touched her arm.

"Is there somewhere safe?" Jackie bit her lower lip.

Her hair was mostly pulled back into a ponytail beneath the straw hat she wore, but strands of that hair swept across her face, which was layered in sweat and a bit of dirt.

"Of course." Doug did his best to sound reassuring. "We just need to give it a little time. Eventually we'll figure out what's going on. It looks like this is in the big cities from what the news said, and we're far from those, so I'm sure we'll be okay. "

"It doesn't seem okay." Jackie lifted her phone from the pocket of her overalls and stared down at it. Her eyes lifted back toward Doug. "I didn't tell the people in the wagon, but I don't think it's just Seattle. I got a text from my cousin, who lives in Los Angeles. She said something was happening there, too, but then she stopped messaging me. I'm not sure if it's because the phones went down, or...."

Doug nodded, glancing toward Sheila, who winced slightly at the mention of Los Angeles.

"The news reports mentioned Chicago, New York and Los Angeles." Doug kept his voice to a whisper, although there was no one else around to hear him. "I didn't want to say anything in front of the guests, but yes, it's happening in other places besides Seattle."

Jackie blew out a breath.

"Go home, okay? Get back to your roommates. Just hang tight, I'm sure we'll get some directions soon."

"Sure. Yeah. Soon." Jackie forced a smile on her pinched lips, then walked down toward the employee parking lot.

Sheila lifted her phone again and tapped out a brief text, then tapped the send button, staring down at her screen.

"Anything?" Doug was almost afraid to ask.

"Nothing," Sheila replied.

They stood together, staring out at the wide expanse of pavement that surrounded them. The line of traffic had cleared out again, just in time for Jackie to drive by in her pickup. Without other vehicles blocking her way, she cruised to the entrance, honked her horn briefly, then vanished behind the trees and onto the roadway outside.

"What on Earth are we going to do, Doug?"

"Try to get some information? I'm not really sure." He turned back toward the employee lot just in time to see a broad-shouldered man step around the corner, walking over the grass and onto the pavement.

"Benjamin," Doug said and the two of them walked toward him as he scaled the gradual incline. "Where've you been?"

"Where did everyone go?" His voice was a rasping growl. "You closing up early? Thought you and the missus had a big crowd tonight?"

"Haven't you heard?" Doug asked, the three of them gathering together.

"Heard what? I've been out on the mower. Grass was getting pretty gnarly out there." He removed the hat from his head, fished a bandana from the pocket of his denim work pants and wiped away a sheen of sweat.

"There's been an incident," Doug replied, pausing before he

said the word, unsure how to phrase it. "Several incidents, actually."

"Incident? The hell are you talking about, 'incident?'"

"You don't have a phone? It's been all over the news."

Benjamin shoved his fingers into his pocket and retrieved an old school flip-phone which he turned over in his weathered hands.

"I don't get along with those big screen things. This one's damn near indestructible. I got no time for those fancy, shiny new things. All I ever do is make and receive calls, mostly from you two."

"Somehow that doesn't surprise me." Doug shook his head, patting Benjamin on the shoulder. "We sent most of our people home. Come inside for a moment, we can get you some water and fill you in."

"I've still got a lot of work to do."

"You can get to that later. This is a pretty big deal. C'mon." Doug and Sheila made their way back toward the restaurant with Benjamin following along, grumbling about the work that still needed doing.

In his sixties, Benjamin had been working for the Tills since day one, the first employee they'd ever hired. Running a vineyard, it had made sense to hire the groundskeeper first, and so they had, and they couldn't have asked for a better one. He knew the land as if it was his own living room and had done impressive things with the property, despite the limited resources they'd started with. He even owned a tiny house on the property that they'd bought for him, one of the perks of being their groundskeeper, so unlike most of the employees he had no reason to rush off and go anywhere.

They made their way up the slope of pavement and back toward the entrance to the restaurant and Benjamin scowled. "You going to fill me in or what? Just keeping me on pins and needles here?"

"We don't know much," Doug replied, turning and walking carefully backwards as he spoke. "But it sounds like there have been some attacks. Possibly biological in nature. A lot of people've died."

"Attacks?" Benjamin stopped short. "Like— actual *attacks*? From someone?"

"We don't really know. Several major cities have been hit. There's no death toll yet, and I'm not sure anyone really knows what's going on."

Benjamin studied them both and used his bandana to wipe more sweat from his forehead. He was a widower and he and his wife had never had children, as far as Doug was aware, so Benjamin had no family to speak of, at least none that he'd spoken about in all the years they'd known him.

"Do you... have anyone you want to reach out to?" Doug asked, phrasing the question carefully.

"Nah." Benjamin shook his head. "What about you? Been able to connect with Samantha and her family?" There was a note of concern buried within the gravel of his voice.

Sheila cleared her throat, her head shaking. "Not yet." She dropped her eyes to her phone. "But I'm sure they're fine."

Doug looked over her shoulder, down at the screen, the text message still caught in a sort of limbo between sending and not sending. They stood just outside the restaurant, staring collectively at the empty parking lot.

"I'll go get a bottle of water for Benjamin." Sheila stuffed the phone back in her pocket and swept away. "Be back in a minute."

"There's still a car down in the employee parking lot." Benjamin stabbed a thumb over his shoulder. "Some old rusted out camper van. I think it belongs to Darryl."

"Did you see Darryl out in the vineyard when you were on your way back?"

"Nope. I know one of the straddle harvesters went boots-up.

That's not really in Darryl's wheelhouse, but I think he was pitching in to help."

"We'll have to search the grounds at some point, make sure everyone's gone. There are no customer cars left, but you never know how people might have gotten here or if someone got left behind." Doug glanced back toward the restaurant, then looked at Benjamin again. "You sure you don't have somewhere you want to go?"

"I've been living in that house for years, Mr. Tills. It's fine for me and a whole lot cheaper than trying to buy property in this state. Cost of living these days, I'll tell you, through the roof."

"Well, we're glad to have you. Just want to be sure you're okay."

"When have you ever known me not to be okay? Takes a lot to faze me and the work still needs to get done, no matter what's happening in big cities. This place doesn't take care of itself."

"No, it doesn't." Doug took his own phone from his pocket to check the notifications.

He tapped out a text to Samantha, too, but had the same result as his wife, the message stuck without delivering. Hastily, he shoved the phone back in his pocket.

"We've come a long way, Ben. The three of us - I mean, you, me and Sheila. You were with us since day one. No matter what we threw at you—"

"Doesn't matter, Doug. Long as the grass is green, and the grapes are juicy." He shrugged and looked away, shifting his stance awkwardly.

The door to the restaurant opened and Sheila came back out, two bottles of water pinched between the fingers of her right hand. She gave one to Benjamin, who accepted the gift eagerly, cracking the top and taking a drink. Sheila opened the second bottle, sipped some water and handed it to Doug, who took another drink.

"Hope you don't mind sharing. Some nagging voice just told me it was better to drink in moderation."

"How many cases of bottled water do we have on the loading dock?"

"I know. I'm sure it's just me being paranoid."

"No such thing as paranoid, Mrs. T." Benjamin pointed the bottle in her direction. "The people in Seattle and Los Angeles might tell you the same thing."

Sheila winced slightly but recovered before Benjamin really noticed. Without another word, the groundskeeper swallowed down the rest of his bottle and Sheila held her hand out so he could give it to her. Benjamin placed it in her hand, took another swipe across his forehead with his bandana, then tucked it back into a pants pocket.

"I'm going to go for a walk around the grounds. Make sure there's nobody lurking around anywhere. Last thing we need are some squatters."

Sheila and Doug exchanged a humorous look as Benjamin headed back in the direction of the fields. Benjamin stopped short at the top of the downward slope.

"Mr. and Mrs. Tills?" A quiet voice carried from the direction of the parking lot and Sheila separated from Doug, walking briskly toward it.

A young woman approached, one of the waitresses who'd recently started at the restaurant, Brandi. Benjamin took a step back to give her some space. Her cheeks were red, and her dark hair was swept in a tousled tangle across her face and down her back. She wore a black t-shirt and dress slacks, carrying a set of heels in her left hand, her bare feet moving gingerly across the pavement.

"I'm sorry. I'm so sorry."

"Brandi?" Sheila came a few steps closer. "No reason to apologize. What's wrong?"

"My car... it won't start." Brandi's cheeks grew redder as she looked at the ground.

"Is that your car down there?" Benjamin asked, nodding toward the aforementioned old camper van.

"No, I think that belongs to Darryl."

"I'm confused." Benjamin crossed his arms. "You say your car won't start, but I only see one car down there."

"It's— it's parked in one of the rear lots. Over by the vineyard, where the trucks come to load and unload." Brandi's cheeks flushed an even deeper shade.

"Why on Earth do you park way over there?" Doug asked. "We've got this employee lot for a reason, Brandi, you're welcome to use it."

"I know. I appreciate that, I really do, it's just—" Brandi's cheeks reddened further and she turned away from the Tills.

"Brandi, what's going on?"

She exhaled, shaking her head, the tangle of her hair sweeping across her shoulders. "I'm so sorry," she repeated.

"Why do you keep apologizing?" Sheila placed a comforting hand on her back.

"My car hasn't actually started for a few days now. I think something is really wrong with it."

"What?" Sheila dropped her hand. "I don't understand. How have you been getting home?"

Brandi started to reply, her lips quivering. She bit down and closed her eyes, which only served to force a twin trickle of tears down her cheeks. Benjamin cleared his throat before quietly retreating and continuing toward the parking lot.

"I've been staying in my car." Brandi finally managed to squeak the words out. "Just for a couple of days. Just so I can save up enough money to call the tow truck and get it taken care of."

"Brandi!" Sheila drew back in surprise.

"I'm sorry, Mrs. Tills, I'm so sorry! I wasn't trying to take advantage of you, I wasn't—"

"Don't be ridiculous, I'm not worried about that." Sheila shook her head. "You should have told us! We could have advanced you a couple of paychecks. Or at the very least let you use a spare bedroom. You didn't have to stay in your car."

"I wasn't sure what else to do. My parents live in Portland, and I didn't want to bother you or speak out of turn—" her voice choked, and she tried to swallow through a sudden sob that surged in her throat. "The news, it didn't say anything about Portland, did it?"

"Not that we heard," Sheila replied.

"Okay. Good. I've been calling my parents, but nobody answers."

"The phones haven't been working for us, either. Where do you live now? With your parents all the way in Portland?"

"Oh gosh, no. I split an apartment with a few other friends. None of us could really afford one on our own, but we found a place near Young's Bay that we could afford. I've tried calling and texting them, too, but it's not happening. I'm really, really sorry."

"Okay. Well, please, dear, stop apologizing." Sheila wrapped her arms around Brandi, giving her a hug before holding her by the shoulders at arm's length. "As long as you're stuck here, we'll find you a place to sleep. You've worked so hard for us in the short time you've been here and I really wish you'd told us how you were struggling."

"I didn't want to burden you, honestly. My issues are my issues." She rolled her shimmering eyes. "And I didn't want to risk getting fired, either, not when you guys are so awesome and this job is everything I wanted and... yeah. I'm sorry. I'll stop."

"Well, you're stuck with us now," Sheila replied, giving her a smile and a wink. "Sorry to say, your issues are now our issues whether you like it or not, at least until all this gets sorted out." She waved a hand in the general direction of the universe.

"Do you think it will?"

"What? Get sorted out?" A flicker of uncertainty passed

across Sheila's face, but she nodded. "I'm sure it will. Do you want something to eat, dear? You look famished." Sheila started to guide Brandi back toward the restaurant door again.

"I skipped lunch because we were so busy. I figured I'd just grab it later, but then all this happened."

The three of them went back into the restaurant, moving through the host station and back into the dining room where several tables were still littered in food and half-filled glasses of water, wine and other drinks. Doug shook his head as he absorbed the condition of the place in the wake of their guests' hasty departure.

"What a mess."

"We can deal with the mess later, Doug. Let's see about getting Brandi some food." She turned and looked at the young woman as they headed through the empty dining room and back toward the kitchen. "What have you been eating the last few days?"

"The chef's been taking care of me," Brandi replied with a sniff. "He fixes me a plate when I need it. I've been paying for it, honest."

"Oh, hon. Stop worrying about all that. You're not getting fired." Sheila looked at Doug, who nodded in agreement.

"It's us who should be getting fired, for not noticing what was going on and helping you out," he added.

"I couldn't agree more." Sheila nodded. "And I'm glad to hear you've eaten well at least." Sheila stopped just inside the double doors and held them open for Brandi and Doug to follow.

The kitchen was in a mild state of disrepair, the people working inside having hastily vacated upon watching the news. Large saucepans remained on the stove, though the stove itself had at least been turned off before the workers ran out. Lids stood slightly askew on the pans and Sheila made her way around a free-standing table and lifted one, peering inside.

"We've got some pasta in here. Should still be relatively fresh;

they were preparing it for dinner tonight." She stepped to the left and lifted another lid. Sheila smiled as she bent slightly, sniffing the aroma from its contents. "Braised short rib ragu," she said with a thin smile. "The perfect sort of meat sauce for the ziti. Doug, grab me a plate."

"Really, Mrs. Tills, you don't have to—"

"Of course I do. Who else is going to eat all of this?"

Doug opened a cabinet and retrieved a plate and Sheila began to spoon some of the ziti from the first pan. She heaped it onto the plate, took it from him, then layered on the braised short rib sauce. A rich fragrance filled the air of the kitchen: rich meats, tomatoes and a hint of red wine.

Sheila handed the plate to Brandi, who took it eagerly, gripping it in two hands as she marched back out to the dining room, with Sheila and Doug following behind. As they pushed through the door, Sheila checked her phone again, shook her head softly, sighed, and thrust it back into her pocket.

"Mr. and Mrs. Tills?" A voice called out from the entrance of the restaurant and Doug froze, turning toward Benjamin's voice.

"Stay here, I got this." Doug held out a hand to Sheila and Brandi, who were standing next to one of the few empty tables.

The door opened as he approached, Benjamin standing there alongside Darryl, a younger man and the owner of the camper van parked in the employee parking lot.

"Darryl!" Doug said, walking closer. "Looks like Benjamin found a stray after all."

"Found him by the straddle harvester, like I thought." Benjamin nodded in affirmation. "Apparently didn't get the memo that everyone was clearing out for the day."

"Is something going on?" Darryl rubbed one exposed forearm with a gloved hand, massaging some feeling back into it. "Sorry, I get absorbed in my work sometimes."

"I saw Avery leave with the rest of the group." Doug gestured with his thumb back toward the road. "Did he leave you out there on your own?"

"I had to step away and use the restroom. When I came back, Avery was gone, but I just figured he'd come in for a late lunch or something. Then I noticed that everybody was gone. I wasn't sure what happened and was just about to come back here when Benjamin flagged me down."

"You don't have a phone or anything on you?"

"It was in my van. I don't like carrying it if I can help it. Too distracting. Plus, it was almost out of juice. I forgot to plug it into the car charger last night, and—"

"Wait, car charger?"

"Yeah. Sometimes when I pull a couple of doubles in a row, I just snooze in the camper van. Avery and Benjamin know all about it, I assumed one of them cleared it with you guys first." Darryl nodded toward them, one eyebrow arched higher than the other.

Doug and Sheila exchanged looks and Sheila shrugged her shoulders noncommittally.

"It's okay, we'll talk to Avery and Benjamin about that later." Doug gave Benjamin a brief, narrowed glance and the older man shrugged his shoulders casually, no sign of apology or acquiescence appearing. "So that camper van is yours?"

"Sure is. Not a lot of space, but enough for me and it's easier than trekking back to the campsite."

"You're staying at a campsite?" Benjamin shook his head. "Doesn't anyone just have a normal house anymore?"

"Don't you live in that little cottage at the edge of the property?" Darryl chuckled. "Thing's got, like, twelve square feet in it. You practically have to sleep standing up!"

"Have you priced out houses lately?" Benjamin snorted.

"I have. That's why I'm staying at the campsite. It's a semi-permanent set up; I know the owners and they float me a decent deal." He once more focused his attention on the Tills. "So, what's going on? Where did everyone go and why is the place such a mess?"

"Something's happened," Doug replied. "Something bad, though nobody seems to know the true scale of it."

"What do you mean."

"Do... you have any family nearby, Darryl?"

Darryl shook his head. "Parents live in the Midwest. I came out here to find myself when I was a dumb teenager and, well, I guess I haven't found myself yet because I'm still here."

"There's been a series of attacks," Doug said, still struggling to find the right words to describe what was happening. "Several major cities have been hit. Los Angeles, Seattle, Chicago and New York among others. We caught a bit of a newscast a short while ago, but we can't get anything on the TV anymore, and our phones are down, too."

"Attacks? Not... nuclear?"

"No. Chemical or biological is what they were saying. But it sure seems like nobody really knows anything beyond a *lot* of people have died, all in a very short period of time."

Darryl stood in stunned silence, his gaze roaming the room, staring toward the windows, then back at the Tills as if taking it all in.

"How... how many dead?"

"We don't know. We don't know anything, really." Doug lifted his cell phone from his pocket. "These things have been all but useless. We haven't even gotten an emergency broadcast notification or anything."

"Did you try the local stations?" Darryl took a few steps toward one of the TVs mounted on the wall.

"Everything cut out," Sheila edged her way closer to a nearby table, where a remote rested on the pale-colored tablecloth. "But maybe we should try again to see."

"Listen," Doug said, gently interrupting the conversation. "I appreciate we all want to know what's going on, but I think we really need to check out the grounds. There are hundreds of acres here and we don't know who left and who might still be lurking around. I'd just feel better knowing everyone who wanted to leave, did leave."

"You're right." Sheila stuffed her phone back in her pocket. "Let's help Benjamin finish checking everywhere. We can speculate more and try to find a working broadcast after that."

"Do you want to stick around?" Doug asked Darryl. "If you've got somewhere to be—"

"I don't. Just that campground, and to be honest, I'm not wild about trying to make my way there right now with all this going on."

"You're welcome to stay as long as you need. We've got plenty of space."

"While this warms the cockles of my heart," Benjamin said, "I've got work that needs doing. Attacks or missing people notwithstanding, this place doesn't have a pause button. Come grab me when you get to searching." Benjamin stalked off, grumbling in his trademark tone while Doug watched, bemused.

"I think he needs a few minutes alone." Doug looked at Sheila, who nodded. "That's fine, we'll grab him on our way. Let's divide into a couple of groups and make the rounds, verify that things are clear."

"I think that's a good idea," Sheila agreed, touching the phone in her pocket. "Whatever we can do to keep our minds occupied."

Brandi returned from the kitchen, where she'd gone to drop off her dirty dishes. "That was *amazing*. Thank you."

"You'll need the energy," Doug said. "Darryl, you're with me. Brandi, you and Sheila take the side-by-side. We'll cover more ground that way and we can meet up here after we're done. Be sure to check everywhere – all the nooks and crannies."

With a series of nods and affirmative grunts, they headed out to begin their search.

CHAPTER SEVEN

The O'Brian Family
Los Angeles, California

"Dad?" Sarah's whisper was barely audible as the deafening roar faded from the collapse of the elevated freeway.

Samantha waved at the dust that surrounded her and moved forward, heading to the spot where the RV had been a moment earlier. Before she'd taken two steps, there was another throttling roar, a scream of mechanical rage and the RV appeared out of the gloom. It started as a huge, rectangular silhouette, then it burst through the smoke, twisting contrails in its wake as it continued its backwards trajectory. Samantha lurched to the left, dragging Eli and Sarah with her, Kale scrambling hurriedly after them.

The RV plowed through the smoke, brakes squealing as it roared down the final length of the on-ramp. With a scraping smash, the rear of the RV hammered into a parked car, battering it forward, lifting it onto a nearby sidewalk. Somehow it steered out of the collision, slamming into another pair of stopped vehicles, wedging its way through as it continued its reverse.

It scraped along a delivery truck, pushing it up on two wheels as it forced its way through a gap just a little too narrow. Trundling for another few seconds, it crunched and scraped past two more vehicles before it ground to a squealing, shuddering halt a few hundred feet away from where Samantha and the kids stood, staring in wide-eyed amazement. The snarling engine rose in pitch, then drifted into a gasping wheeze before finally silencing, the vast quiet of the world around them descending once more.

That quiet was momentarily punctuated by the mournful call of a nearby crow, its head lifting as it brayed its anger at the manmade battering ram that had disrupted its meal. Samantha stayed where she was, hugging her children to her, the German Shepherd clinging to her leg, showing no interest in separating from her beloved family members.

"Jason?" Gently, Samantha released her arms from around the shoulders of her children and tentatively stepped forward.

The road was littered, not just with the acres of stalled vehicles, but with chunks of the elevated freeway, thick slabs of broken rock filling the empty space between them and the stopped RV. She navigated the uneven terrain carefully, stepping up and walking forward, unsure of what she might find. On the other side of the RV, which had backed its way down the ramp, the squeal of hinges sounded as the passenger's side door opened.

Samantha continued carefully, one step at a time, though as she covered half the distance to the stopped recreational vehicle, Jason's silhouette emerged from the smoke and dust, a hand outstretched and pressed to the grill of the vehicle, helping him stay standing. He wavered slightly, looked as though he might fall over, but then regained his balance, pushing himself forward.

"Sorry," he gasped. "Didn't mean to scare you. That was a little too close for comfort." His labored stride carried him another few paces, where Samantha intercepted him, the kids and the dog just behind her.

"Yes, it was!" Samantha wrapped her arms around him, the two kids converging as well. "I thought we might have lost you."

"You won't get rid of me that easily." He looked back toward where the onramp used to be, but there was just an empty section of air, the concrete, steel and asphalt construction little more than a shattered pile of broken rubble.

The remains of a few support columns remained standing, exposed rebar thrust from the once-smooth concrete surface. Each of them ended in jagged fragments, piles of crumbled debris gathered around their bases. They could no longer see the vehicles that had caused the collapse in the first place, each of them buried beneath the avalanche of broken pavement, twisted metal guardrails and other assorted wreckage. Dust still clung to the air, a swirling mist that obscured the road ahead, not that they could continue north anyway, with the pile of broken road in the way.

"Come on," Jason said, taking a step back toward the RV. "Let's get back inside out of this dust, figure out what to do next. Maybe call a mesothelioma lawyer while we're at it."

"Is the RV still alive?" Samantha asked. "It looks like it took quite a beating."

"She's a workhorse." They'd already reached the RV and Jason whacked the exterior with a flattened palm as if slapping the flank of a large animal. "The backside took the brunt of it but I don't think I lost a single window in all that nonsense."

They followed along the driver's side, circled the front and made their way around to the open passenger's side door, all four of them, plus Kale, filing inside. Jason ushered them in, then closed the door and leaned back against the expansive dashboard of the vehicle. He released a breath he'd been holding, letting the events of the past hour wash over him in a sudden, rocking rush that nearly knocked him over.

"We should all get cleaned up," Samantha said, holding out her arms and looking at her dust-caked hands. "We're filthy and don't want to spend any more time inhaling this concrete dust."

"Can we use the bathroom?" Sarah asked, already taking a few steps toward the rear of the RV.

"Should be able to. We've got a hundred gallon tank of water and the house batteries should have enough power. But don't shower, okay? Just change your clothes and bring your dirty ones up here."

Sarah sighed, retrieved her clothes from the compact dresser in the bedroom, then disappeared into the narrow alcove that served as their bathroom.

"Eli, go grab some clothes. I'll get ours, hon." Jason and Eli walked together toward the rear, leaving Samantha alone near the front of the RV.

She glanced through the windshield, though dust still clouded the air, swirling with the traces of smoke, preventing her from making out a whole lot of detail. Jason returned only a moment later, wearing a fresh pair of jeans and a button-up flannel shirt. He held Eli's clothes and his own in his hands and made his way past Samantha and to the front door. Grabbing a black trash bag out of a cabinet near the door, he put the clothes into it. The bathroom door opened, and Sarah appeared, carrying her old clothes under her arm.

"Throw 'em in the bag with ours." Jason thumbed toward the bag lying on the floor next to the door.

Samantha grabbed spare clothes and went into the bathroom next, appearing a moment later with her own dirty clothes bunched in a pile which she added to the trash bag. Jason took the bag and tied it up, then shoved it into a cabinet in the back of the RV to be cleaned at some unknown opportunity in the future.

They each took turns running just a little bit of water in the sink, washing their hands, their face and their hair just to make sure the lingering traces of concrete dust were as removed as possible. Samantha playfully scratched Kale's head while they had her somewhat maneuvered into the shower, Jason doing his best to fill his hands with water and pat down the dog's dusty fur. The shower was tiny, way too small for an entire German Shepherd to fit, so it was a frustrating game of maneuvering while Samantha and Jason tried not to get too wet.

Once all that was done and Kale had calmed down, Jason retrieved a bottle of water from the refrigerator and set it on the small, makeshift dining room table, while everyone took their seats around it. He cracked the bottle and took a sip, then handed it to Samantha, who took her own sip and then handed it around the circle.

"Still cold," Sarah said as she lowered the three-quarters empty bottle.

"Mini fridge is running off the same battery that powers the water pumps." Jason took the bottle from Sarah, stood, and poured some into Kale's water bowl, which rested on the kitchen floor.

Kale immediately began to slurp, her enthusiastic tongue spraying water over the cabinets and the faux-tile floor. Samantha studied the various appliances in the kitchen, making a few mental notes to watch out for. Jason was correct, the twelve-volt house batteries would power things like the water pumps and the refrigerator, and as long as they could start their engines once in a while, those batteries would charge and be ready when they needed them next. Larger items that required dedicated 120-volt power would be unusable, however, unless they were hooked up to an external power source.

"Okay, so, we need to talk." Jason said, shifting a bit in his seat. "First of all, we've been through a lot today already. How is everyone holding up?" He leaned over, looking intently at Elijah first, then Sarah. "And be honest."

"I'm okay." Eli shrugged, though he wouldn't meet his father's eyes.

"Me, too," Sarah replied. "I mean it was scary, sure. But we're alive, aren't we?" Her voice dropped. "Unlike all those people out there...."

"You took the words out of my mouth. Thank heaven we were in the right place at the right time. Keeping our heads on straight is going to be very important to staying that way. Do the two of you understand?"

"Yeah, Dad, we understand." Eli nodded firmly.

"Your father's right. Whatever's going on is *big*, but we can handle it as long as we pay attention like we've already been doing." Samantha had a hardness in her voice.

"The four of us right here—" Jason gestured toward the family.

"Five," Sarah interrupted. She leaned over and scratched Kale's head, her ears perking up.

"The five of us, thank you." Jason allowed himself the slightest of grins. "The five of us are all we've got right now, as far as we're aware. We need to be careful. Observant. Protective. We need to watch each other's backs."

Sarah's eyes narrowed. "This isn't a combat zone, Dad."

"Don't be so sure," Jason replied. "Treating it like one might be our best course of action." Old instincts sharpened, clarifying the bustling thoughts that jumbled through Jason's already busy mind.

"While I don't disagree with your father," Samantha gently took his hand in hers, smiling at him. "We should keep some perspective. We still don't know what's going on, and jumping to conclusions and being *too* paranoid might hurt us more than it helps."

Jason's jaw worked back and forth a few times before he let out breath. "Fair enough. We'll balance it?"

"Perfect." Samantha patted his hand and turned her attention back to Elijah and Sarah. "Any questions?"

"Yeah, we get it, Mom." Eli turned to his twin sister. "We get it, don't we?"

"Yeah, we get it."

"Good. Don't be afraid to ask us questions. Don't be afraid to come to us with anything you think seems out of place or a little weird. That's what we're here for."

"This whole thing is a little weird." Elijah leaned back in his chair.

"It's more than a little weird." Samantha rested her hands on the table between them.

"Do you have any idea what we're dealing with out there, Sam?" Jason leaned on his left elbow, turning toward his wife. "You'd be able to make a better educated guess than I could. It seems safe to assume we're clear of whatever did all of... *that*, eh?"

"I would think so, considering, we're, you know, still alive and everything."

"Do you have some idea what it might be, Mom?" Sarah inched forward a bit in her seat.

"It's tough to tell. It could be biological, but it could even be something chemical, like a nerve agent of some kind. I could examine a few of the bodies, maybe form a better educated opinion, but if it *is* biological I don't want to risk an infection."

"Ew," Sarah replied with a scowl. "Examine the bodies?"

"It's not the first time Mom has examined a dead body, Sarah," Eli said.

"Let's not talk about that now." Samantha reached across the table and gently touched her son's hand. "We need to focus on what's important, and right now what's most important is staying alive."

"Are there biological or chemical things that would have done all of *that*?"

"Dozens. Hundreds, maybe." Samantha mused. "Though, now that I think about it, it can't be biological. Those take time to infect and grow in the body... they can kill in several hours, in rare cases, but not instantly. Plus, I can't think of a method of dispersion that could have covered such a wide area and, again, killed so quickly. There are some neurotoxins that can kill fast, like Botu-linum, which is one of the more lethal neurotoxins known to man, but the way these people died, that just doesn't ring true. Any sort of explosive dispersal would require that the toxin is turned to aerosol before it's dispersed. Not impossible, but—"

Sarah and Eli stared at each other, then looked back at their mother as she continued rambling, words tumbling out faster.

"Something like mustard gas could be turned into aerosol and spread as well, but it's not immediately lethal. It often takes some time and there would be trademark skin blisters, which I don't recall seeing, but again, I haven't closely examined a body." Samantha crossed her arms, leaning back. "I'm sorry. These are wild guesses."

Leaning forward again, Samantha used the table to push herself upright, then stepped away from the table and walked through the aisle of the RV, heading toward the front windshield. Jason and the kids followed her lead, the entire group converging near the front. Without speaking, Samantha slid into the driver's seat, staring through the settling dust outside while Jason perched in the passenger seat, huddled near the edge, leaning over to get a better look at the road ahead.

"Eli and Sarah, if you don't want to see this, you can head back to the kitchen," Samantha said.

"No. I want to see. I feel like I need to see." Eli's voice dropped an octave, sounding a few years older than he was.

He took a step forward and Sarah followed his lead, the two of them standing between their parents, looking through the wind-shield. The city before them was coated in a layer of concrete dust and soot, a faint, pale haze filling the air. In the past few moments, much of the dust had settled into grit on the stalled cars and dead bodies, making it look like the scene of a volcanic eruption, the landscape shrouded in a layer of ash. With the dust clearing, the military transport that had crashed was just barely visible beneath a heaping pile of stone, its trademark riveted exterior clad in olive drab, standing out against the ragged, pale back-drop of fallen rubble.

Debris-buried vehicles were a barren landscape of ragged terrain, almost like the surface of an alien planet. While the fallen wreckage from the overpass blocked their path, its collapse had revealed a better view of the city beyond. Crows had settled on an SUV a block ahead, lurking along the edge of its roof, staring down at something Samantha couldn't see from where they sat. However, from their vantage point, there were still plenty of horrors within view. The sidewalk to their right was littered with corpses. Concrete dust had settled thick upon them, but the outlines of their sprawled bodies were clearly visible. Arms spread askew, legs twisted and tangled, many of their faces coated in white soot and hiding the bloody details of their deaths, a small favor.

The door to a brickwork building stood ajar and a pile of bodies were stacked like a cord of wood in its rectangular open-ing. A rush to escape the building had only resulted in the bodies tumbling upon each other, a heaping pile of lifeless forms. A passenger van was partially buried by another layer of debris, its door sitting open, two people who'd been trying to get out of it crushed by fallen sections of the overpass, their broken limbs extending out from beyond large chunks of concrete.

In every single direction, death filled their view, bodies either inside vehicles or outside, a massive graveyard spread out in all directions. Samantha leaned a bit and stared into the rearview mirror, the large silhouette of distant buildings caught within its rectangular frame, including the vague profile of the Los Angeles Convention Center that was in the same general direction as the military convoy had been traveling.

"Do you think the president was the target?" she asked, though the question wasn't directed at any one person.

"Seems pretty coincidental if he wasn't." Jason agreed. "They weren't stopping for *anything*. You don't see that kind of driving stateside."

"Mhm." Samantha nodded, continuing to look through the windows, mind churning through possibilities.

The cars stretched out behind her and the layer of dust continued to thin, revealing the details of the vehicles, many of which had been crushed and pushed aside by the military convoy. Samantha got a clear view through the windshield of a vehicle just behind them and found herself staring into the wide-open, vacant eyes of a corpse, still sitting at the steering wheel. The vehicle had been crushed so severely that the driver had been trapped inside with nowhere to go as the city's killer slowly infiltrated through the cracks in the windows and sucked the life from their lungs. Twisting back around to face front, she pulled her phone from her pocket once more and clutched it in both hands, staring at the screen.

"Are your phones still charging?" She glanced at Jason.

He reached toward the floor and lifted his phone up, still tethered to the charging cable. "Eli's is back by the bedroom. Still plugged in."

"Good."

"Did your mom and dad tell you where the battery in this thing is? Just in case we need to change it out if we drain it by going too long without firing up the engine?"

"There's a side compartment along the passenger's side. I think we'll be okay for a bit, though it's a good thing to watch out for." She reached over and patted her husband's thigh. "We're gonna get through this, Jason."

"Oh of course we will. We're a great team - I'm the brains and you're the brawn."

Samantha chuckled, her eyes settling closed as she slowly shook her head. "I think maybe I'm the brains *and* the brawn. You're just the guy who does what he's told."

"I'm pretty sure you put that in our wedding vows. Am I remembering that right?"

"Sounds right to me." Samantha leaned over and kissed him on the corner of his mouth, and he returned the gesture.

"Oh come *on*!" Elijah protested, making a gagging noise, then turned and stomped away.

"So, our son can stand up here and stare at a city filled with dead bodies without flinching, but his parents kiss and it's gag-city."

Jason shrugged. "Go figure."

They sat in their seats and stared out into the swirling grit of downtown Los Angeles. Traffic snarling all around them, the sun, little more than an orange smudge within the choking clouds of smoke and dust, continued to make its way across the sky, above a sea of wreckage and death surrounding them in all directions.

"What's on your mind?" Samantha asked, both of them still looking forward.

"This was supposed to be a relaxing family vacation. We'd been looking forward to this for weeks."

"Everyone has a plan until they get punched in the mouth."

"Who gave *that* motivational speech?"

"Mike Tyson."

Jason laughed and eased back in his seat while Samantha leaned forward and picked up a stray charging cable that rested on the floorboard, then plugged her phone into it while she looked at the screen. Jason glanced over as she opened her photos app and accessed an album of recent pictures. Their visit to Yosemite replayed through a series of images as Samantha slowly scrolled through them, her fingers tightening around the perimeter of her phone.

"That was a great day."

She glanced sideways up at him. "They've all been great days."

"They have been, haven't they?"

Samantha nodded again and scrolled through a few more

photos. It didn't take long until a picture of her parents appeared, standing near each other, engaged in some conversation. The sprawling wilderness of their Oregon vineyard spread out beyond, though the candid image of them standing close, Sheila's hand touching Doug's arm as they talked was almost more beautiful.

"I'm sure they're okay."

"The only thing I cling to right now is that hopefully Oregon wasn't affected by this." Samantha shook her head. "Whatever 'this' is."

"How far are they from Portland? This whole trip has been a blur, I can't remember."

"Little less than a hundred miles. They're a lot closer to the coast. Maybe two hundred miles to Seattle, though. If both Portland and Seattle got hit, they could be caught in the middle."

"Don't think about that, okay? It's not worth stressing about what we don't know. There's plenty to stress about already."

"How can I not stress, Jason? We've got to figure out something to do here and I'm grasping at straws."

"We'll figure it out. A few minutes to catch our breath won't kill us."

Samantha, still leaned over, glanced past her left arm and deeper into the RV's cabin, smiling as her gaze landed on the children. "No," she echoed with a slight shake of her head, "it won't." With a sigh she navigated from the photos app back to her text messages and stared down at the phantom message caught somewhere in no man's land. "Text messages are supposed to go out even when you can't make calls. What is going on with this?"

"The towers are probably down. Though they are supposed to have generator or battery backups." Jason scratched his chin. "Maybe they're overloaded, and this is more isolated than we think?"

"Who knows."

For another moment they both sat in silence, taking a

moment to relish the small breather nestled within the pocket of chaos that had consumed their lives.

Finally, Jason blew out a breath. "We can't just stay here," he said, turning toward Samantha. "Let's make a plan and execute it."

"No argument here."

Jason stood and walked through the front seats back into the cabin area of the RV. Samantha took his lead and followed. Kale lifted her head as they entered, tail sweeping across the floor, ears perked and awaiting her next instructions.

"Okay, O'Brians, listen up." He stood near the front cabin and leaned against one nearby wall. "We need to set a plan in motion."

The two children, seated back in their chairs, the table between them, rounded toward him in anticipation.

"We're all alive and we're grateful for that, as we should be. But our first priority has to be getting out of this city."

"Where can we go?" Sarah asked.

"We'll have to figure that out on the way, but I think we need to get on the move sooner rather than later. Now we only have half a tank of gas, so we'll need to get some more of that first and foremost. There are gas stations all over the place throughout downtown. Power still seems to be on throughout the city, so our first priority should be getting to a gas station and filling up the tank, then we need to chart our course out of here."

"What about emergency responders? FEMA or some other kind of government assistance? They have to be doing something right?" Elijah looked around the room. "They can't just let the city sit here, all these dead bodies everywhere."

"In normal circumstances waiting for help is the best idea," Samantha said, "but your father is right. This time, we have to move quickly. We have to get out of here. Los Angeles has already been attacked once, for all we know, more could be planned. This could have just been the opening salvo."

Eli and Sarah looked anxiously at each other.

"We're not trying to scare you," Samantha continued, "but we need to know that you understand the sense of urgency. We're in the middle of a kill zone here and we need to get out of the bulls-eye... to mangle a metaphor, sorry."

"What can we do to help?" Sarah asked.

"Just do what you're doing. Stay calm, listen to our instructions, be observant. That's the best I can tell you right now. If you can do that and we all work together then we'll make it through this okay."

Silence filled the cabin of the RV as Jason and Samantha stood near the door, the children seated several feet away, attention focused on every word she said.

"Are you guys on board?" Jason asked.

Both heads nodded, the twins doing their best to conceal their natural fear and uncertainty. Samantha stepped around Jason and walked toward them. Kale stood as she approached, moving to intercept her and Samantha dragged her fingers across the dog's head, giving her a good scratch on the ears.

"I know this is hard," she said as she neared the table where the twins sat. "I know this isn't anything we were expecting or planning for." They both kept their eyes locked on their mother. "I'm very proud of how you've both handled this so far. You've done really well. I just need you to keep doing well."

"We will." Eli nodded. "But we haven't really done anything."

"You've listened, stayed calm and kept your wits about you. That's the best possible thing you can do in an emergency situation. And if you need something— anything at all, tell us. If something is bothering you or you need to share your fears, talk to us. We're here for you. It might seem like we're mostly focused on getting us out of here, and we are. But we're still your mom and dad, okay?"

Sarah stood and wrapped her arms around Samantha's neck. Samantha returned the embrace, linking her fingers around Sarah's shoulders and holding her to her. They stood like that for a moment, then pulled apart, Sarah easing her way back into the seat. Samantha waited for a moment, anticipating Elijah doing the same thing, but he managed to hold himself in the chair, trying as hard as he could to keep his emotions in check.

"Do you think they attacked Grand Rapids?" he asked.

"I have no idea. Grand Rapids is tiny compared to places like Seattle and Los Angeles, so I'd hope it wouldn't be on their radar, but I don't know that for sure."

"What about grandma and grandpa? Do you think they're okay?" Sarah's voice trembled slightly.

"I've been trying to reach them." Samantha twisted the phone in her hands, looking at the screen. "I haven't been able to get through, but I'll keep trying, though, and I promise we'll let you know as soon as we hear something." She waited for a moment, trying to anticipate any other questions, but when they didn't come, she walked back toward Jason.

"I'll drive," he said with a soft smile. Samantha drew close and he looped a hand around the small of her back, then drew her in for another kiss. "I'm glad to have you here for this."

"You and me both." They separated again and she moved to the passenger seat while Jason maneuvered back into the driver's seat.

He stared again at the ocean of debris and carnage before him, a choking sea of death and wreckage. Heaping piles of collapsed stone buried the road and would have made it impassable, even if the vehicles hadn't been there. They were swallowed in an ocean of death, perhaps the only living souls in the city. The weight of that filled the cabin of the motorhome like a thick summer humidity, making the air itself heavier and denser.

Jason pushed the key into the ignition and started the RV, the engine growling to a bellow of life all around them. The dashboard illuminated with its array of indicator lights, the fuel gauge hovering at just about halfway, as Jason had remembered. Lights flickered briefly and then settled and he twisted back toward the kids.

"Everyone ready? Might want to buckle up. Not sure how rough this is going to be."

"We're good," the voices came back, the same words coming from both mouths.

Jason shifted into drive. He typically preferred a manual transmission when he drove, but the ease of use with an automatic in navigating the RV was a blessing. As he'd backed down the ramp, he'd turned the large behemoth of a vehicle, trying to angle it so it could be easier to drive forward. Vehicles still littered the roadway all around him, many of them pushed up against each other from the force of the military convoy.

"Are you ready?" Jason asked, looking toward Samantha.

"Let's do it."

Jason blew out a breath and eased on the accelerator, inching the RV forward. It scraped loudly along the side of a nearby truck, pushing it out of the way as he turned the wheel and angled the massive vehicle toward the gap in the traffic the convoy had created. The vehicle shuddered as he moved along another clutch of cars, Jason wincing as he heard the trademark sound of metal scraping metal.

"I really hope your parents aren't going to be too mad when I return their RV and it's beaten up one side and down the other." He gritted his teeth as they pushed through, grinding against a toppled over delivery truck.

"Oh, Dad is going to kill you," Samantha replied, a deadly serious look on her face. "But I'll see what I can do to smooth things over." A glint returned to her eye, and she allowed the faintest hint of a smile.

"My hero." Jason rolled his eyes and tapped the accelerator again, guiding the RV into the thick of things.

CHAPTER EIGHT

The Tills Family
Silverpine, Oregon

Sheila led the way down the road heading toward the employee parking lot, keeping herself tight to Brandi who moved with an almost hypnotic rhythm. She drifted a pace or two behind Sheila, letting her lead the way, head slightly dipped, her dark hair swept across the length of her right cheek. Doug and Darryl had moved further to the left, making their way toward a walking path along the western perimeter of the property line while Sheila and Brandi headed for the Kubota side-by-side which was parked nearby. Doug stopped short of the edge of the grass and turned toward the converted camper van that was parked in the employee lot, the only vehicle there.

"I still can't believe you live in that thing." Doug's statement was just loud enough for Sheila to hear and she grinned in spite of herself.

"Works for me." Darryl shrugged as the two of them began

walking again. "Cheaper than even the cheapest shoebox apartment downtown, that's for sure. And out at the campground I don't need to worry about waking my neighbors."

"That's what I mean," Doug laughed, voice beginning to fade as the two men continued on. "I would have *killed* to live in a van when I was your age. You're living the dream."

Sheila and Brandi stopped at the side-by-side. It was dark blue in color with thick, knobby tires and two seats for a driver and passenger. The rear of the vehicle extended into a large flatbed for carrying things, and a homemade rollbar ran over the top above the passengers to add a measure of protection.

"Doug! What's the plan?" Sheila asked, elevating her voice a bit to carry the distance between them. "You want us to go around back the long way?"

"Yup, that'd be perfect. We're going to hit up all the outbuildings." He shouted back. "We'll loop around back, pick up Benjamin and drag his grumpy butt along with us."

"Sounds good." Sheila gave Doug a thumbs up.

"We may check with the neighbors, too. Marcus has that bum hip. Plus, we can see if they've got any more information than we do."

"Are you sure about that?" she asked. "That development has a lot of houses, not just the Chancellors. We don't really know them all that well."

"I think I want to stop over anyway."

Sheila nodded. "Just be careful. Let us know how things look out there and how the neighbors are." Sheila turned and pointed toward the gravel road that extended beyond the restaurant and moved toward the other edge of the vineyard. "We're going to take the main road with the side-by-side, check out the tasting stations, the access road and the back parking lots. Just make sure there are no stragglers."

"You be careful, you hear me? Eyes open."

"You know I will."

Moments later, Doug and Darryl made their way down the walking path, moving through the recently groomed grass and vanishing from sight and sound.

"Have you ridden in one of these before?" Sheila guided Brandi over to the utility vehicle, and the younger woman stared at it, shaking her head. "Hop on in, it's safe, don't worry."

Sheila walked around the front side of the vehicle and stepped up into the driver's seat, wedging herself in behind the steering wheel. Doug had always been the primary operator of the UTV during the first days of the vineyard, but Sheila had taken to it after tiring of walking everywhere and had gotten far more comfortable with it than she had been at the start. Fishing a set of keys from the pocket of her pants, she slipped the smallest one into the ignition and twisted, firing up the diesel engine.

Once Brandi was settled into the passenger seat, Sheila accelerated, pulling the side-by-side away from the parking lot, its knobbed tires crunching along the gravel roadway. Almost immediately, the sprawling vineyards came into view on their left, an extravagant expanse of greenery spilling out across the terrain. As the utility vehicle rumbled along the curve of the gravel road, the vineyards stretched out like rows of green soldiers, their vines heavy with ripe clusters of grapes. The sun filtered through the neatly trellised canopies, casting dappled light on the rich, dark soil below. Each row ran with military precision, undulating gently over the rolling hills, fading into the hazy distance where the hills met the sky. Between the rows, patches of wildflowers and tall grasses swayed in the breeze, their colors vivid against the lush green leaves. The air was thick with the earthy scent of soil and the sweet promise of ripening fruit, mingled with the faint tang of fermenting grapes from the nearby winery. In the near distance, one of the straddle harvesters stood stoic among the winding vines and splayed grass, its metal, utilitarian silhouette in stark contrast to the natural unevenness of foliage surrounding it.

"Thank you for this, Mrs. Tills," Brandi said softly, her stiffened shoulders relaxing, if only slightly.

"Call me Sheila, dear, please. I think we've moved past the Mrs. Tills stage."

"That might be hard, but I'll try." A blush of red shaded the young woman's cheeks.

"I can't believe you were sleeping in your car."

"I didn't want to bother you or Mr. Tills. You've done so much for me. Gave me a job when nobody else would. The only waitressing experience I had was that run-down diner in town, which was more about playing self-defense with the rowdy old men than actually waitressing." Brandi rolled her eyes, the crimson in her cheeks deepening as she turned away.

"Waitressing can be taught." Sheila gripped the steering wheel, guiding the utility vehicle along the slightly meandering gravel path. "We look more at work ethic and sense of responsibility. You seemed to have that in spades. We haven't regretted that decision once."

"Thank you."

They drove in silence for a few more moments until the tasting stations appeared along the right side of the gravel road. Small sections of empty ground appeared, trees cut back to create open squares. Wooden booths had been constructed within the squares of empty space, a layer of gravel creating the angular shape that the booth was built upon. Wooden posts were hammered into the ground with small power boxes bolted to them, and mini-fridges were held in self-contained cabinets behind the booths to keep the wine chilled during extended tastings. In front of the booth was an elongated table with a handful of stools evenly spaced before it so people could sit and sample their drinks. Sheila slowed a touch, leaning over the steering wheel to check the empty section behind the booths.

"I still remember when we first set up these tasting stations. Doug wasn't convinced. Said the more wine we gave away, the less we'd sell." Sheila shrugged with a soft chuckle. "I'm never one to celebrate my husband's ill-formed opinions, but he was wrong on that count. Wine sales increased twenty-two percent the moment we started doing these tasting events. It was like night and day."

"So, you're the business mastermind, then."

"Don't let Doug hear you say that." Sheila guided the utility vehicle past the second tasting station, once more angling her neck to peer around the booth. "In all seriousness, it really is a team effort. It was his idea to open the restaurant in the first place. We were selling all this wine via mail order to start, and then started doing these tastings in person. We ended up having dozens of people just sort of milling around, wondering what to do next. Doug thought maybe we should set up a small little cafe, a place where they could get a quick meal. It escalated from there."

The utility vehicle drifted left as she spoke, its front tire riding up a grass-covered slope. It began to tilt gently, and Brandi gasped, clutching the roll bar and bracing herself in her seat.

"Don't worry, it's okay." Sheila steered back onto the gravel. "That's why we installed the rollbar when we repainted it." She chuckled and nodded upward to the metal cage that extended above their heads. "First time I ever drove one of these things, I came *this* close to rolling it down the hill by the cabernet block. Could have broken both of our necks."

"The cabernet block." Brandi nodded her head. "You know, all the time I've worked here, I don't know if I've ever really gotten a tour of the vineyards." She stared across the seat, toward the rows of twisting vines, many of them dotted with plump, ripe grapes. "They really are beautiful."

"That they are." Sheila's voice swelled with a hint of pride.

They'd spent a large chunk of the last two decades of their life building the vineyards and watching them evolve. It had helped keep their minds and their instincts sharp, helped them focus as they grew older. In many ways, the vineyards were extending their life, day by day, giving them purpose and drive that might have otherwise been lost. Samantha often asked them about retirement and Sheila always politely deferred, but as she rode along the gravel road, eyeing the sprawling greenery of her life's work, it was more obvious than ever that she was exactly where she wanted to be.

As she thought of Samantha, her bright mood darkened. Her phone was still in her pocket, pressing against the side of her thigh, a heavy weight that she had to resist looking at every few seconds. Unable to fight it any longer, Sheila pulled the phone from her pocket and glanced at the messages app again, once more seeing her attempted text. Instead of caught in that strange middle ground, it had changed to *Failed to Send*. She moved her thumb to the word *Retry?* and tapped it, then watched for just a moment to see what happened. It remained caught in the net of intermittent cell service and she pushed the phone back into her pocket, returning her other hand to the wheel to better guide the utility vehicle.

They passed three more tasting sessions, each one standing empty. As the final tasting station fell away, a secondary road curled in from the right, wider and smoother than the gravel path they traveled on. Thick tire tracks dug ruts in the ground, a sign of heavier, larger vehicles traversing that roadway. Sheila tapped the brakes, leaning forward to stare down the side road. Easing the steering wheel to the right, she followed the curve of gravel and trundled over the uneven terrain. A moment later they came to a secondary parking lot, lined with crushed stone, a small set of gas pumps sitting near the back side of the squared-off section.

"Is that gas?" Brandi asked.

"Diesel, yes. We've got an underground tank there, two hundred gallons worth. We use it for our tractors and other farm equipment. The straddle harvesters use it, too. We've got regularly scheduled refueling once every six weeks, although...." Sheila trailed off, leaving the implication hanging.

Pulling away from the parking lot, she drove down the access road for a bit, the shadows from surrounding trees casting a deeper darkness across the side-by-side. Sheila drove on for a moment until they reached the end of the access road where a gate was closed across the broad expanse of gravel ahead. It wasn't a very secure gate, but it was down and locked, which eased her mind, if only a little.

Sheila cranked the wheel all the way to the left and accelerated again, moving back down the road, then took one last look at the lot to make sure there were no other cars or people lingering around. As she followed the wider road to the narrower gravel path, instead of turning left to return to the restaurant, she turned right. They approached a hill, the path angling up into a gradual slope, the diesel-powered utility vehicle handling the incline with relative ease. It only took a few seconds to reach the crest of the upward hill and Sheila eased the vehicle to a stop, looking toward the vineyards below.

From the higher slope of the hill, the vineyards unfolded like a patchwork quilt of green squares, each section stretching in neat, parallel lines. Vines clung to the gentle curves of the earth, their leaves glistening under the setting sun. The blocks of the vineyard were separated by thin dirt paths, weaving through the rows like veins of soil. A pair of straddle harvesters stood dormant within view, their towering frames perched on each side of a row of vines, paused in mid-function. Seeing the harvesters made Sheila realize just how silent the world was, the normal background metallic hum of machinery non-existent. Farther down, the vines rippled with the breeze, their tendrils swaying in unison as if stirred by an unseen hand. In the distance, a scattering of oak trees framed the far edge of the vineyard, their dark silhouettes contrasting against the soft, rolling hills. The air smelled of sunwarmed earth and the faint sweetness of grapes just beginning to ripen, filling the space with the subtle promise of the coming harvest.

Taking it all in, the realization that things in the outside world were in such turmoil hit her like a physical impact in the chest, and she gripped the steering wheel hard to steady herself. Everything was so perfect from their perch, so solemn, serene and silent that it was easy to forget what was happening throughout other parts of the country. If she hadn't seen the news reports with her own eyes, she might not have believed it was happening, her small pocket of life an almost too perfect insulation from actual reality.

"Sheila?" Brandi's voice carried a tremor and Sheila glanced back toward her.

She'd stepped out of the seat and had taken a few steps across the grass, staring off toward the southeast, flattening her hand above her eyes. The sun shone brightly at their backs, a vibrant, orange glow coloring the sky and brightening the green of the surrounding trees. Sliding across the front seats, Shelia removed herself from the utility vehicle. From the top of the hill, to the east, she spotted small pockets of houses nestled within the green of the Oregon wilderness. Small gatherings of homes circled around a meandering paved road, sheltered by a canopy of trees in one area. In another, a winding river of dirt separated a few other small houses in a neighboring village. Their view was an expansive canvas, a perfect painting with nature's expert brush strokes.

But Brandi wasn't looking in the direction of either town. Her gaze was directed more southeast, across miles of trees and rolling hills. Far off, far enough away that Sheila couldn't estimate the distance, thick columns of smoke twisted up into the air, a fist of coiled gray and black at its base. Pale clouds floated amongst a sea of blue sky, yet just below, the horizon darkened, shrouded by the rising smoke from unseen fires.

"Is that... Portland?" Brandi was afraid to say the final word.

"I think it might be. The direction seems right."

"Is it on fire?"

Acid burned in Sheila's throat, her stomach churning with a

scalding boil of nausea. She'd seen the news reports, she'd heard the frantic edge in the newscasters' voices, but somehow, looking toward the horizon and seeing the rising smoke for herself brought everything into a crystal-clear reality. An American city was burning close enough for them to see and although it was many miles from where they stood, it hit home for Sheila. Someone had chosen Oregon as a place to attack, for some unfathomable reason. Danger had come as close to her front door as it ever had since World War II, when a firebomb was dropped by a submarine-based Japanese aircraft.

"Have you heard anything from your parents?" Sheila almost didn't ask.

Brandi shook her head and reached into her back pocket, slipping out her phone. She thumbed it on and stared down at its screen, flicking over to her text messages. Like Sheila herself there were messages caught in some invisible queue, not fully delivering, caught in some sort of limbo.

Mom? Just checking in. I know we haven't talked in a while. I've seen things on the news that don't look good. Wanted to make sure you were okay.

Sheila gently placed a hand on the young woman's shoulder. She didn't know Brandi well – the young woman had only been working at the vineyard for a short time – but there was a connection there, a traumatic experience shared between them. Brandi's eyes remained transfixed on the spiraling smoke in the distance, and together they stood facing it, both of them bracing themselves for the darkness likely still to come.

Half a vineyard away, Doug picked up his pace, walking a bit faster toward the pickup truck that was parked in a section of flattened grass alongside the walking path. Pulling his keys from his pocket, he stabbed the key fob and unlocked the truck, then opened the passenger side door.

"Sun's nice and bright," he said, leaning into the vehicle. A moment later, he withdrew from the truck's cab, clutching a flashlight in each hand. "But there are some dark corners in these barns. Still haven't got power out to them quite yet."

One was a larger, thick handled light with grid-work metal texture, the other was a much smaller, hand-sized instrument, resting comfortably in Doug's palm. He handed the larger flashlight to Darryl, who pressed the on switch to make sure the light worked as Doug closed and locked the door.

"How long have you been living in that camper?" Doug gestured toward the path, the two men continuing their walk.

"A few years, give or take. Had a run of hard luck, went from job to job for a bit. Seemed like the easiest way to keep a roof over my head and not end up on the streets. It helped that my buddy owns the campground I've been staying at."

"There's something appealing about being able to bring your house wherever you go. Sheila and I bought a beautiful RV a couple of years back. Planned a few nice, summer vacations. Never got a chance to use it this year, but our kids—" his voice trailed off, even just thinking about Samantha, Jason and their grandchildren.

"I am sorry about staying here with it," Darryl said, "I swear I thought it was cleared through the two of you."

Doug waved him off. "It's fine, I don't mind. I feel bad for your generation, both you and Brandi. Times are tough."

"Times are going to get a whole lot tougher, you ask me. If this is as bad as what you heard."

They continued along the walking path, moving just west of the twisting blocks of sprawling vineyards. The air was rich with the fruity scent of ripening grapes, though also tinged with a hint of metallics. To their right, one of the straddle harvesters rose above a row of coiled vines and fruit.

"Is that the one you were working on?" Doug sniffed the air. "I can still smell the burned rubber."

"Yeah, belt went bad. We were swapping some parts around to try and make one functional one out of the two broken ones. Never got the chance to finish."

"Avery works you pretty hard, does he?"

"I don't mind a little hard work. Between him and Benjamin, I keep pretty busy."

"One of those Jack of All Trades?"

"Master of none." Darryl shrugged. "Story of my life. But, y'know, whatever pays the bills."

There was a downward tenor to his voice and his gaze shifted away with a sigh, an unspoken statement in the slightest of gestures. Doug knew Darryl superficially, as well as he knew any of his few dozen employees, but he rarely had the time to have long, extended conversations with them. There was that recent project he'd been working on with Benjamin and Darryl both, over by one of the back parking lots. But even working alongside him for a time, there hadn't exactly been the opportunity for small talk. Guys like Avery and Benjamin who had been around for a long time were like family. But as much as Doug would have loved to get to know everyone who worked for him, things were just too busy for that. Avery and Benjamin both had the power to hire or fire their subordinates, just as long as they kept him and Sheila in the loop, which meant a lot of personnel decisions happened without being fully informed.

"You know that's not the full saying, right?"

"Huh?" Darryl gave Doug a quizzical side eye.

"Your 'a jack of all trades' one."

"What is it?"

"A jack of all trades is a master of none, but oftentimes better than a master of one."

"Oh." Darryl's brow furrowed for a second, then he smiled. "I like that, Mr. Tills.

"I think it suits you better than the shortened version." Doug patted Darryl's shoulder. "Here, let's check this out." Doug pointed toward a large, looming barn in the distance, just off the walking path to their left.

It was a broad, rust-colored structure, its shingled roof rising to a peak above the square block of its exterior walls. From the outside it looked like any normal barn, a place where animals might be kept, but they used it more for storage and supplies than as an animal shelter. They had their hands full with grapes, wines, and restaurants, so adding farm animals to that mixture wasn't something either of them had the capacity to deal with. The two men moved through the grass, which was a bit longer, though still well-groomed so far out into the vineyard thanks largely to Benjamin's ceaseless work.

The front doors of the barn were closed and secured with a lock, which Doug quickly unlocked thanks to the keychain he carried in his pocket at seemingly all times. Together they pulled the doors open, rolling them along the newly greased rails until the dark opening of the barn spread out before them, exposing its deeply shadowed insides. Doug turned his small but powerful LED flashlight on first, its bright beam cutting through the dark, shining across the rows of shelves that evenly lined the interior of the large structure.

Shelves were both built into the wall and in free-standing rows, though the main section of the barn was clear enough to pull in a tractor or other utility vehicle if it needed repairs. Various pieces of equipment filled the numerous shelves within the barn, everything from gardening tools and bags of soil to tractor parts, arrays of bolts, screws, and nails. There was a full workbench near the back side of the barn, large enough to stack pieces of heavy equipment on with a pair of tall toolboxes on wheels that could be maneuvered around for easy access to what might be needed.

The barn had been Doug's pet project, with Sheila ceding full control to him over what went inside, the layout and how it might be used. It still brought a sense of accomplishment as he stood in the shadows, passing his flashlight throughout the cavernous interior. Over their heads, a loft filled with hay and straw encircled the upper section, twin ladders leading up to the upper level. Double doors were set into the barn's exterior as well so the straw could be easily thrown out into a cart. They used straw liberally in the vineyards as mulch to control weeds, retain moisture and regulate soil temperature.

Walking along the left side of the barn, Doug followed the beam of his flashlight, passing it toward the rear of a nearby row of shelves, probing the various darkened corners of the barn. Behind him, Darryl followed suit, though his light roamed somewhat absently and unfocused. As Doug circled a shelf and brought brightness to the far corner of the barn, Darryl walked along the center, turning lazily at the waist as his light drifted around.

"Are you sure this is really necessary? Do you think there are actually people lurking around in here, trying to hide?"

"I don't think anything, really, but I'm also not going to leave anything to chance. People behave strangely when faced with crisis, and if someone is still around here somewhere, we either need to help them or encourage them to be on their way. I'd rather be a little more diligent than necessary and be sure, rather than leave anything to chance."

Darryl chuckled dryly. "Sounds like Avery and Benjamin learned from you."

"Nothing wrong with measuring twice and cutting once." Doug walked along the rear of the barn, passing the light through more corners and shelves. "And someone getting stuck in here and starving would be *terrible* for future business."

Darrly laughed, standing at the base of the ladder and pointing his light upwards, searching the piles of straw in the loft. "Pretty sure Avery measures eight times before he even thinks about cutting."

"As the man who has to pay for whatever he's cutting, that sounds good to me." Doug scaled the ladder, one rung at a time, holding the light in one hand as he pulled himself up with the other.

Perched at the top rung, he probed the straw with the light but saw no signs of anyone trying to bury themselves within it. Turning, he shone the light across the barn at the other loft, but again, he saw nothing but straw there as well. Crawling back down the ladder, he and Darryl finished searching the barn, then walked out, pulled the doors closed and locked them up again.

They stood just outside the large barn, the grass-covered hills sloping off into the distance. There was one more outbuilding just beyond the slope of a hill, the walking path making its way through a growth of somewhat longer grass. Shadows crept throughout the tangles of meadow, the afternoon sun casting a faint, orange glow throughout the previously blue sky.

"Tough to get my head around it, Mr. Tills. What you said about those newscasts?" Darryl peered at the sky beneath the canopy of his flattened hand. "Everything seems so normal here."

"Saw it with my own eyes. Otherwise, I'd be right there with you."

"We should check the set again when we get back in, see if we can pick up any local stations. I've got a digital antenna in my van we can use, if you don't have one."

"We've got one, and yeah, we should." Doug squinted as he thought. "I think I've got a radio in the basement somewhere, too. Haven't used it in years but if the TV's not working I bet something's on the radio."

"Good call." Darryl motioned at the outbuilding up ahead. "If you want I can check this one myself, it's not as big as the barn."

"That might not be a bad idea. I want to catch up to Benjamin, get him to come with us to visit our neighbors."

"Are you talking about that development just beyond the trees? Those neighbors?"

"Exactly."

"It looks calm from here."

"Yeah, but what kinds of neighbors would we be if we didn't go see how things are?"

"Fair enough." Darryl continued making his way toward the last outbuilding.

Doug stood on the gradual slope of the hill for a moment, watching Darryl as he walked toward the building. As Doug had done at the barn, Darryl fished some keys from his pocket and unlocked then opened the door. For a brief moment, through a wide expanse of empty meadow beyond the vines and grapes, Doug spotted the brief blur of the Kubota side-by-side as it traversed the gravel road on an upward slope. He started to raise his hand in greeting, but it disappeared behind the trees, its engine fading.

Oak trees grew thicker and more congested near the backside of the vineyard's property line, spilling out into tangles of additional foliage. Green leaves created a natural barrier between the vineyard and the houses beyond, the longer grass transitioning into a rear wall of forest. Just ahead, a large section of that long grass had been flattened and covered under a mix of crushed stone and gravel, large enough for a tractor to be parked. It was a Kioti, a compact tractor with a low profile, perfect for traversing the narrow paths between rows of vines. Its low-profile body helped it to navigate the slopes and hills of the vineyards as well, and it contained specialized attachments which were adapted to fit tillers, trimmers, sprayers, and in an emergency, harvesters.

Their primary method of grape harvesting was the straddlers, but when equipment broke down, as it so often did, the compact tractor could fill in, though it made the work much harder and longer than it would have otherwise been. Alongside the compact tractor were three standalone tillers as well. Like the tractor itself, the tillers were built narrow with in-row tilling, designed to work close to the vines without damaging them. The tillers were equipped with depth control settings to allow them to work the soil without disturbing the grapevine roots, which had a tendency to grow shallow, just beneath the surface.

The barn they'd searched for a few moments earlier was more than large enough to accommodate any of the large equipment so they could either store it inside or repair it. With how fast business had been growing, Doug and Sheila had been discussing the need to perhaps buy another tractor or tiller, though they hadn't pulled that trigger quite yet. He continued walking, passing the tractor storage area and moving on to a broad clearing of long, open meadow.

Rounding the slight bend of the walking path, Doug came upon an even wider clearing, a single small house standing in the center of the sprawling grassland. It looked almost impossibly small from a distance, to the point where Doug was pretty sure his RV had more room than the house that Benjamin called home. An old, rust-littered tractor stood in the grass in front of the tiny house and Benjamin knelt by it, huddled over the engine, which he had removed from the ancient piece of equipment. He clutched a wrench in one hand and cranked at an old bolt with all of his strength.

"Benjamin!" Doug announced his approach before getting too close.

Benjamin turned quickly, the hand with the wrench dropping to one side.

"What on earth are you doing?" Doug diverged from the walking path, crossing the grass at a swift clip. "Is that old piece of junk even worth repairing?"

Benjamin rested back on his knees, removing a handkerchief from his pocket and wiping the sweat from his brow.

"Everything is worth repairing. That's the problem with the world these days, they make everything disposable."

"We've got a brand new tractor you know, right? Tillers, too.

You really don't need to put the extra effort into fixing up this one."

"With all due respect, Mr. Tills, I disagree. Everything should be kept in working order. Never know when you might need it." He grunted and grabbed onto the tractor parked to his right, then used it to help him stand. "But I'm a little old school that way."

"I'm no spring chicken." Doug gestured toward himself. "You don't have to tell me about old school."

Bejamin wiped his hands on his pants. "Where's the kid?"

"Darryl? He's checking that last outbuilding." Doug turned around to be sure the young man wasn't close by. "What do you know about him?"

"Darryl? Why do you ask?"

"I haven't had a chance to get to know him – obviously, since he's been living here and I didn't even know."

"Not much to know. He had a rough go of it a little while ago, but he's a hard worker and a pretty happy one at that. Splits time between Avery and me. Does some odd jobs, handyman, but knows his way around a lawn mower, too. A bit odd in the head occasionally but then again, who isn't?"

"Alright." Doug crossed his arms. "You're a good judge of character. I just want to make sure anyone who's here with us during this nonsense isn't going to be... flakey."

"If you're asking if I trust him, then yeah, I do. Trust him enough to let him spend the night here in his camper van. Trust him enough to let him work on his own with those expensive tractors you and Mrs. Tills keep buying. He's a good kid, Mr. Tills."

Doug placed his hands on his hips and squared off to face Benjamin.

"Can I ask you a question?"

"Sure."

"When are you going to agree to call me Doug?"

"Probably never. I was raised to respect my seniors."

"Respect your—" Doug dropped his hands, then laughed with a casual shake of his head. "I see what you did there."

Benjamin refused to smile, once more turning his attention to the engine he was repairing.

"Listen, Benjamin," Doug continued, "why don't you put down that wrench?"

"You got something better for me to do?"

"I do – I'd like you to tag along while we go check on a few of our neighbors. That development that's just over there."

"That new place with all the McMansions?" Benjamin was down on one knee, lifting his eyes toward Doug.

"They're not *all* McMansions," Doug replied. "Just most of them. You remember Reginald and Patti, right?"

"Yeah, I remember. They helped with the basement back when."

"Yep. I want to check in on them and a few others, see if they're okay and if they have any information we don't. Maybe they've gotten word from friends or family."

"Doubtful." Benjamin tugged his old flip phone from his pocket. "I don't have one of your fancy pants smart phones, but I can't even make a text or call with this thing. It's D.O.A."

Reflexively, Doug pulled out his phone as well, giving the screen a passing glance. It was in the same status it had been since the crisis had started hours earlier. "I know. I'm seeing the same thing with mine." He swiped through the screen, checked the text messages, then examined the battery indicator.

Holding his thumb on the power button, he shut down the phone to preserve the battery and slipped it back into his pocket. Doug looked back in the direction of the restaurant, several hundred meters away, on the opposite side of the vineyard, hidden by the slope of the land, trees and vines.

"We still have power back at the restaurant, at least we did when we left. Who really knows how long that might last."

"Not long, I'd wager."

"Anyway – I'd feel better if we check on the neighbors."

"You looking for a third wheel?"

"The more the merrier."

"That last outbuilding's clear!" Darryl shouted over as he walked along the path in their direction.

"Thanks, Darryl." He waited for the younger man to come join them. Benjamin shoved his wrench in a toolbox on the ground nearby, then stood as well, the three of them coming together.

"Let's take a walk," Doug said, moving past the engine and heading toward Benjamin's tiny house.

For being so small, the structure was remarkably well-engineered and well-designed. Much like Doug's own RV, they managed to build it out in such a way that it had all the essentials one could ever need, just organized into a smaller space.

Doug hadn't spent much time in Benjamin's house, but the few times he had, he always came away impressed. Upon entering, the front door opened into a small living area with a worn-out sofa pressed against the left wall beneath a wide window, offering a view of the surrounding landscape. Directly opposite the sofa, a wall-mounted shelf doubled as both storage and a television stand, though the screen was small and outdated. It was a flat screen just for the sake of taking better use of space, otherwise Doug suspected Benjamin would have still clung to an old school CRT.

To the right of the living area, a narrow staircase led up to a loft-style sleeping area, where a queen-sized mattress sat on the floor, leaving just enough room to crawl in and out. A skylight above the bed provided natural light during the day and a view of the stars at night. Doug had often wondered how much longer Benjamin would be able to crawl in and out of the mattress on the floor, given his advanced age and his constant complaints about pain and stiffness.

Below the loft, tucked in the corner near the stairs, was the compact kitchen. It had a small sink, a two-burner stovetop, and a mini-fridge, all nestled along a single countertop. Open shelving above the counter held a few mismatched dishes, while a tiny microwave was squeezed in next to a toaster. The kitchen also had a small fold-out table that could serve as both a dining surface and extra counter space when needed. At the far end of the house was the bathroom, separated from the main space by a sliding door. Inside, there was a narrow shower stall, a composting toilet, and a slim countertop sink with just enough room for a toothbrush and soap. Storage cabinets were built into the walls, offering some space for towels and toiletries. Despite its size, the house felt well-designed, with hidden compartments for additional storage beneath the sofa and a fold-out desk built into the wall for occasional work. Solar panels on the roof powered the essentials, and the overall aesthetic was simple, functional, and made for easy living in a small space.

Doug had spoken to Benjamin about running an underground power line that he could run off of in the event he started to exceed the power his solar panels could provide, but they hadn't gotten to that step yet. They did, however, have solar-powered wireless repeaters that stretched to the far reaches of the vineyard, both to allow more seamless communication and so that Benjamin could piggy-back off their connection for his own use inside the tiny house. Equipment was getting more and more modern every day and there would come a time when perhaps even the harvesting gear would need an active internet connection.

Doug led Benjamin and Darryl out through the back reaches of the meadow along the rear of the vineyard. Tall grass clung to their lower legs as they moved through the meadow, making their way toward the forest of oak, pine and maple that separated them from the housing development on the other side.

"Just for the record," Benjamin said as they stepped into the trees and started making their way through, "I'm still not all that sold on this idea."

"What are you afraid of?" Doug asked.

"Afraid of? Nothing I'm afraid of. Just not sure how a village full of flatlanders and city imports are going to help us. The only thing I can see that comes out of this little visit is more trouble for us."

"How long has this been going on?" Doug ducked beneath a branch and stepped through a narrow gap separating a pair of old, weathered tree trunks. "A few hours? For all we know there are already some recovery operations in place, or it's not as bad as it sounded. That's what I'm hoping to find out."

"Mr. Tills, I hate to be the one to break it to you, but if major American cities are under attack, there's not going to be any kind of happy, quick resolution. Even if just one took the brunt of whatever happened, we're all going to be up a creek without a paddle for months, if not years."

"That's the sort of wild-eyed optimism I like to hear." Doug pushed aside a pair of thinner, younger saplings, making room for them to squeeze through. "What about you, Darryl? What's your take on all this?"

"I mean," Darryl shrugged, "I don't know these neighbors, but I'm all about helping folks as best as we can." Benjamin snorted as Darryl continued. "Going over to check on them is a good call."

"How long have you been here?" Doug smiled at Darryl's response.

The trees thinned, bleeding into another section of grass, more closely mowed than the last field they'd walked through. Shadowed structures lined the edge of the lawn ahead, spaced evenly apart, a collection of house-shaped silhouettes filling the near horizon.

"Eighteen months. Something like that. Maybe two years?"

"You remember those rainstorms we got last year? Four full

days' worth - we had to scramble to make sure the grapes didn't drown. "

"Sure, I remember. I was being pulled between Avery and Benjamin for four days straight. Pretty sure I didn't leave the grounds that whole week."

"I don't know if you remember, but our basement darn near flooded. The drainage system wasn't working, and we found out the hard way."

"Oh yeah, I heard about that after the fact. I was out in the fields most of the time trying to help keep the vines from all floating away."

"Well, Reginald and Patti Brigbee came over to check on us, discovered us up to our knees in water and stayed by our side the whole time, using buckets to bail out water, helping to keep our stock from soaking through." Doug winked at Benjamin. "This old codger doesn't like to admit it, but our neighbors were a big help during that disaster."

"All the more reason to check on them, then," Darryl replied. "They sound like good people"

"That they are." Doug lifted his arm and pointed toward the rectangular shape of a house to his right. It stood a ways away, a pair of other houses a bit closer to them. "That's their house right over there. They didn't have to help us out, but they did, and I figure the least I can do is make sure they're okay. If we can get a little more information out of them and others while we're at it, that's icing on the cake."

"You're a good egg yourself, Mr. Tills." Darryl smiled at the older man.

"Okay, okay, jeez," Benjamin lifted his hands in mock surrender. "You two can quit ganging up on an old man. Just lead the way, we'll follow."

They took a step forward, walking onto the backyard, but Doug stopped, staring at the houses spread out before him. He tilted his head slightly, angling his left ear a bit upward as his eyes narrowed in concentration.

"What's wrong, boss?" Darryl asked.

"I've been here a few times," Doug said softly. "There are families here. Lots of families, always a hustle and bustle of activity."

"Just another reason why I'd stay away," Benjamin said. "Damn noisy kids."

"Exactly. Do you hear that?" Doug angled his head again, turning toward the two men.

"I don't hear... anything." Benjamin shook his head.

"Me neither," Darryl said.

"Exactly. Things here are too quiet. Way, way too quiet."

CHAPTER NINE

The O'Brian Family
Los Angeles, California

Jason floored the accelerator, the pedal pushing down to the floor, an undulating roar of raw power snarling from the rear of the RV. For all the sound and surge, though, when the broad, blunt grill of the vehicle crunched against a pair of cars, it barely scraped them along the pavement, moving inch by frustrating inch. Jason steered into the grinding crush of metal at first, then cranked the wheel right, trying to work the large mobile home free of the tangle of stalled traffic.

Finally, gouging along the exterior box of a delivery truck, they pushed it diagonally and bumped up onto the nearby sidewalk. Scraping past the dislodged vehicle, Jason ground his teeth, the RV crushing a parking meter beneath its front wheels as he desperately tried to navigate it around and through the impassable dam of metal and glass. Half a mile in an hour had been his last estimate, the slow, sluggish progress excruciating as they tried to extricate themselves from the supposed kill zone.

"Sarah and Eli... put your headphones in, would you?" Jason turned slightly, calling back deeper into the RV. "We've got to go back on the sidewalk again."

The twins had their phones resting on the table between them in the makeshift kitchen, both of them tethered to outlets which piggy backed off the twelve-volt batteries. Eli clawed at his pocket, retrieving a set of earbuds while Sarah rolled her eyes, doing the same, both kids thumbing them into their ears.

"What are you trying to protect them from? They can feel it, even with the earbuds in."

"Feel it, sure. They don't need to hear it." Jason didn't especially want to hear it either, his throat burning with the acid reflux of his unsettled stomach.

The only reason they'd even made it a half mile was because they'd used sidewalks to get there, and the sidewalks had been clogged with corpses. Jason had been able to roll over the corpses much more easily than he'd been able to push aside the cars, so that was the path he'd chosen, much to his own dismay. Every time the RV ran over one of the bodies, the sound of cracking bones and squelching flesh was just barely audible inside the vehicle. The sounds made him wince, his shoulders already tense and starting to hurt from the stress, and he rolled them, trying to find some calm to center himself.

"They're just meat and bones now." Jason whispered to himself. "Don't let it bother you. Don't let it bother you." He eased off the accelerator and steered over another parking meter, straddling the sidewalk.

The RV ambled forward, the driver's side scraping paint from the vehicles to their left while the passenger side thudded against bent and twisted light posts as they forced their way along the Los Angeles sidewalk. Dead bodies were strewn about before them, more than Jason even cared to count. As the tires rolled over them, there was the slightest jostle of resistance, followed by a wet crunch of popping bone and flesh.

The uneven up-and-down jostling was more or less like riding a rut-littered dirt road. However, the sound the bodies made when the tires crushed them beneath their weight was unsettling, and he adjusted the volume of the radio, scanning through stations, hoping to land on something other than static. Since catching the final snippets of a newscast an hour earlier, they hadn't found a working station, so they'd been forced to listen to the crunching bones beneath their tires.

The twins, at least, had playlists of music already downloaded onto the phones, so even without a working internet connection they were able to block the outside. It was a small favor, but a welcome one for his children even though he had no similar blocking mechanism for himself. Tension gripped everyone inside the vehicle, the horrors of their actions drowning the O'Brian family into uneasy, unpleasant silence.

To the right and up ahead, a large office building stood tall, a glass-encased structure of at least thirty or forty stories. The front doors and front windows had been shattered open, a spray of glass glittering on the sidewalk from dozens of people that had surged from the building in their desperation to escape, resulting in a dam of death on the sidewalk before them. Bodies were piled on top of bodies, three high and deeper than Jason cared to count.

"I don't think we can make it over that," Samantha said quietly.

Already the RV was struggling to continue, tires spinning over the slick gore on the sidewalk, a gathering of multiple corpses beneath them clinging to the axles like fresh spring mud. Tires spun, humming as they tried to gain purchase on the blood and organ-soaked sidewalk.

"What are you stuck on?"

"Don't ask." Jason steered left to avoid the sprawl of piled bodies ahead, eyeing a crosswalk that angled across the street ahead, miraculously separating the lines of vehicles.

Alongside the southern edge of the crosswalk, a car had stopped, causing a multi-vehicle pile-up. One sideways sedan blocked a pair of angled pickups, which had, in turn piled up an SUV, two cars, a van and another larger truck. Jason slowed a bit, steered away from the bodies, then accelerated again, the tires slipping, spinning, then finally catching. It lumbered forward, bumping off the curb of the sidewalk and pressed through a gap between cars just a little too small for its broad body. Just beyond the passenger's side of the RV a car fell into view, its roof fully caved in, a broken body enveloped within the fist of buckled metal. Someone had thrown themselves from one of the upper floors of the skyscraper rather than battle the crowds trying to flee down the stairs.

A few other car roofs were in a similar state confirming that it was not an isolated person that had plummeted to their death. In one case, a van roof had nearly folded in upon itself from the sheer force of the body's impact, and in another, two people had landed on the same sedan, crumpling the hood and roof. The RV pressed onward, tires rolling across the fallen corpses that were strewn about the crosswalk, moving from one section of cars to the next before the attack had claimed them.

"I've seen a lot," Samantha whispered, lifting her eyes toward the ceiling, "I'm not sure I've seen anything like this."

Jason reached over and placed a comforting hand on her leg as he steered with the other and eased the accelerator further down. They ground forward, inch by gruesome inch, making slow progress. One tire rolled up and over a particularly large body, the RV actually leaning slightly to the left before it suddenly thudded back down again, the body beneath the wheel being crushed by the force of their movement. Seconds stretched on as they went through the same arduous, rocky motion, rolling over and through the litany of bodies that separated them from the next sidewalk where they might be able to pick up just a little bit of speed. Even Kale sat quietly in the main cabin of the RV, tail unmoving, ears perked, as if in silent contemplation of the horrific things they were experiencing.

Finally, they reached the other side of the long crosswalk and Jason maneuvered the RV again, steering around a truck which had been upended by a broadside collision. The front corner of the RV creaked as it hit the already buckled hood of the vehicle, pushing it aside as Jason started angling back around toward the next sidewalk.

"We can't keep doing this." Samantha shook her head, leaning over a bit to brace herself on the dash with an outstretched hand. "Not just because of the bodies, though that's a big reason."

Jason tapped the brakes and brought the RV to an unsteady halt, one tire starting to bump up onto the next curb.

"I don't disagree. The way we've been bumping along, I'm a little worried something might get damaged. I don't even want to think what the undercarriage of the RV looks like right now."

"Mom? Dad?" Eli plucked the earbuds out of his ears.

The sound of the young man's voice drew Kale's attention, and the German Shepherd stood, then trotted toward where the twins were sitting.

"Why did you stop?"

"We're just thinking out loud," Jason replied. "Trying to decide what to do. We've been at this for an hour now, and we've barely moved. Traveling this way doesn't seem practical."

Eli lifted his phone and tapped, then swiped, turning the phone around to show his parents. "Why not just use GPS to see if you can find a different route."

Jason's eyes widened a bit, then he shook his head and groaned.

"What?" Samantha asked.

"GPS." Jason pointed at Elijah. "I can't believe we forgot about that."

"*I* didn't forget." Samantha tapped her phone. "We would've had to download the local maps for it to be of any use, and the internet's down too, so...."

Jason leaned toward the console of the RV. "But did you remember *this?*"

"What are you two talking about?" Eli asked as, next to him, Sarah also pulled out her earbuds.

"The RV has its own built-in satellite navigation system." Jason grinned. "And, the best part is, all of the maps are saved on the computer, not streamed over the internet like on our phones."

"Say, that's right!" Samantha activated a touch screen control panel, then scrolled through a few different options. "They'll be a few years out of date, but who cares. Won't make a lick of difference to us."

On the central screen, a satellite-based image of their immediate area came into view, along with colored markings overlaid on roads along with their names and numbers. Several rectangular shapes representing buildings clarified, the patchwork of city streets colored in a darker gray against the paler, almost neon backdrop.

"Bingo. Zoom out a bit." He reached toward the console, but Samantha was already doing it, tapping a minus sign that drew the artificial camera higher from their point of view. A colorful, superficial rendition of the city spread out beneath the satellite imagery.

"This is where the overpass collapsed," Samantha said, pointing to a section of the map. "And this is the onramp we were on."

"Looks even closer than it feels."

"Look. Over here. The Los Angeles drain system. You thinking what I'm thinking?"

"Oh, that's clever. I like it."

The Los Angeles drainage system was one of the city's familiar landmarks. At one point in California's history, it had been the

Los Angeles River, though the constant development of the city had drained the river of most water. After a flood in the early part of the twentieth century, the local government had applied thick layers of reinforced concrete to prevent that from happening again. When the river lost its water, all that remained were the concrete channels that carved their way through various sections of Los Angeles' downtown.

Samantha leaned down even further, using her fingertip to scroll through the digital map on the screen. She zoomed in on a section of dark lines that ran alongside what had once been the Los Angeles River. "See these? They look like service roads that run alongside the drain. It's probably how maintenance and public works vehicles travel up and down that area without getting caught in L.A. traffic."

"We could use some of that." Jason once more risked a look out into the world beyond the windshield.

It was a vast ocean of cars and trucks, a choppy sea of metal, plastic and glass. Here and there, a body was strewn across a hood or a roof, though the tight clusters of vehicles thankfully did their part to conceal the worst of the carnage, though what was visible was beyond ghoulish. The deaths of those on the ground had been bloody, with crimson pooling from mouths and noses, though they appeared to be undergoing an accelerated rate of decomposition as well. Stomachs were distended and flesh was beginning to tear at tight spots, drawing scavengers from the sky in larger, more diverse groups. Crows had already thickened throughout the vehicles, the birds huddled in tight clouds of black feathers, either airborne or closer to the ground, the occasional caw loud enough that they could hear it inside of the RV's front cabin.

"If we can make our way to these service roads, we can probably follow along the drainage system. The only issue is that this route takes us deeper into the city instead of out of it, at least at first." Samantha scrolled the map along. "But I think we can get out of here if we go this way. It's just going to take longer than we had hoped, assuming this level of chaos is everywhere."

Jason let out a breath. "Longer doesn't sound great, but progress is progress."

"Yeah, but look, even if we go deeper into the city," Samantha continued scrolling as she spoke, "it opens up other options. See all these bridges? Following the drain system could lead us toward sections of the city that are easier to travel. It might open up routes we can't get to from here."

"Okay. I think I'm convinced." Jason settled back into the driver's seat.

"If I'm reading this map correctly," Samantha scrolled for another moment, then zoomed in on their location, "we can squeeze through that side street there to move to an area that may not be quite as congested." She pointed through the windshield. "It'll get us closer to the drains, too."

There was a gap between a small Spanish language convenience store on the right and an electronics store on the left with metal bars covering every window. Three cars were visible further down the side street, but the larger concern was the dead bodies sprawled about the road between the two buildings. Pedestrians had been crossing the street when the attack came through, and their bodies were blocking it.

"I don't know if we can crush our way through there." Jason drummed his fingers on the steering wheel. "And the last thing I want to do is get the RV stuck high and dry on... people."

"We could move them."

"What?"

"We can move the bodies."

"Weren't you saying before about how it wouldn't be safe to go near them if this was biological?"

"Yeah, but the more I've considered it, the less I think that. Besides, there are some gloves and masks in the glove compartment. "Samantha clicked open the glove compartment and folded it open, showing Jason what she was referring to.

"I think Kale has to go out." Sarah nodded toward the dog, who was up and moving again, sniffing along the baseboards of the built-in kitchen cabinets as she softly whined.

Samantha recognized that look anywhere. Kale was very good about not going in the house - she was exceptionally well house-broken - but they hadn't given her the opportunity to do her business when they exited the onramp, and it had been a few hours since she last went out.

"Okay." Samantha stood from her seat, pulling a mask and a pair of sterile gloves from the glove compartment. "Eli and Sarah, the two of you need to stay inside. That's not optional, so don't even argue."

Eli's lips parted, but he knew well enough to listen to his mother when she used that tone of voice. Instead, he gave an exaggerated sigh and slumped back down into the chair, arms crossed.

"Why are you mad about it?" Sarah asked. "Do you actually want to go out there with all those dead bodies?" A disgusted look pinched her lips and drew a deep furrow above her eyes.

"Anything's better than being cooped up in here."

"Well, keep yourself occupied doing something different. Both of you get up front while we're out, and keep an eye on us. Honk the horn if you see anything weird." Jason joined Samantha, grabbing his own mask and gloves. "Come on, Kale."

The shepherd lifted her head eagerly, tail wagging as she pulled her attention away from the baseboards and trotted toward them. Samantha strapped on her mask, securing it over her nose and mouth, then stretched the gloves over her hands. Jason mirrored her movements, then they made their way through the front door and closed it behind them.

Stepping out into the city was like stepping out into another world. From several feet away, a faint crow call began a chorus of them, but beyond that, the city was still and silent. Throngs of stalled and smashed vehicles spread out along the city streets to their right, the sidewalk ahead clotted with dead bodies. The masks partially helped with the smell, but it was still piercingly strong, a cloying mix of crimson copper and the tang of rotting meat.

Kale took a few steps forward into a narrow median of grass running in the middle of the sidewalk, then squatted and did what she had to, though her gaze darted around at the gruesome surroundings. She stood and stepped cautiously forward, her nostrils twitching relentlessly, sniffing the spoiled air, her ears perked in a permanent state of alertness.

Together, Samantha and Jason walked with minor trepidation toward the clogged side street between the two businesses. Kale jogged forward, moving past them, darting toward the bodies ahead.

"Kale!" Jason lurched forward as the dog swept toward the first sprawled dead body.

It was a young man, face-down on the sidewalk, arms splayed. Kale nosed the corpse's left hand, probing it. Her previously wagging tail dipped a bit, her ears lowering in concern. She whined softly, nudging the body's hand a little more aggressively as if trying to wake a sleeping child.

"Kale, come on, girl," Jason placed a calming hand on her hunched back, urging her to come a little closer.

Kale whined softly in his direction, eyes narrowed in deeper, conflicting emotions.

"Take her back to the RV," Samantha said, crouching down and petting the dog. "I don't think she knows what to make of this."

Jason took a few steps back, whistling for Kale and patting his leg. Almost reluctantly, Kale took a step back, glancing toward the dead body, then finally followed her master back to the vehicle.

Jason opened the door and ushered the German Shepherd back up the stairs and into the RV.

"Kale's back with you guys," he shouted into the vehicle.

"Okay, Dad," Eli replied.

"Come here, girl!" Sarah chimed in and Kale scaled the steps and disappeared into the RV as Jason closed the door.

Samantha already had her hands beneath the arms of one of the dead bodies and back-pedaled, tugging the lifeless concrete across the concrete. Jason hustled toward her, grabbing the young man's ankles and helping to move him across the pavement.

"How do you think they're handling this?" They worked together to set down the body.

"The kids?" Jason shook his head. "I have no idea. It's killing me a little bit, though. Kids these days already grow up too fast. Something like this just hammers on that accelerator."

The two of them moved toward another body, a young, tattoo-covered woman, who was curled in a fetal position. She wore leggings and a loose-fitting tank top.

"You see anything that clues you in on what might have caused this?"

Samantha shook her head as she clutched the woman beneath her arms. Once more, they worked together to move the body out of the way and rest it against the wall of the electronics store. "Not really. No lingering film or discolored skin that might make me think mustard gas or anything similar. But there are plenty of toxins that can do whatever this did without leaving a trace. The bleeding from their noses and mouths seems to be ubiquitous — that's got to be a clue."

They walked to a third body, a heavyset man on his back, his open eyes staring up toward the smog-shrouded sky. His mouth was slightly open, a string of colored bile seeping out through his lips, along with a trail of mostly-dried blood. Jason walked toward Samantha, pointing toward the large man's feet.

"I'll take the shoulders. This guy has a bit more mass than the others."

"Are you saying I'm weaker than you?" There was a shift in the mask covering her face that indicated a sardonic grin.

"Oh and here I thought I was just being nice." Jason gripped the large man's armpits then pushed off with a grunt, heaving him into the air.

Samantha grasped his lower legs, the two of them struggling to heft and move him out of the way. They dumped him somewhat unceremoniously at the edge of the building, dropping him more abruptly than intended. It took them nearly ten minutes to clear the rest of the side street working together, speaking very little, just focusing on the grisly work at hand. After dragging the last body away they stood together, looking up and down the connecting road. Another stretch of two-lane pavement ran perpendicular to the side road, a trio of cars parked askew at the intersection.

Jason walked down the road, wiping sweat from his forehead, the sun glowing down upon the desolate city like a heat lamp over an incubator. The heat rose from the pavement around them, slowly baking beneath the sun, which continued to shine through a mix of low-hanging smog and smoke. Jason reached the intersection, silently measuring the gap between the cars to make sure the RV could make it through. Samantha came up next to him, wiping her sweat away with the back of her hand.

"This city is going to turn into a petri dish." She turned and looked over her shoulder at the piled-up bodies they'd just spent several minutes moving. "All this death, all this heat... bacteria is going to start becoming a problem *real* fast."

"Let's make sure we're not here to see it." Jason stared at the empty section of pavement where one road met the next. "Do you think the RV can fit through here?"

"Looks good to me." Samantha already started to walk away,

her pace increasing as she angled back toward the RV. "A few more dents and dings won't matter."

"Oh gee, thanks," Jason mumbled, following behind her. "Hey - whatever you do," Jason called at her as she strode toward the RV, "don't look at the underside, okay? Just— don't."

Samantha stopped walking for a moment, her head tilting upwards, staring beyond the large vehicle's roof. Her shoulders tensed then relaxed, and she approached the front door, swung it open and stepped inside. Keeping his attention focused on his wife so he wouldn't stare beneath the RV either, Jason caught the door before it closed, hot on Samantha's heels. She seemed to be moving faster than before, rushing to peel the gloves from her hands and the mask from her face.

"Samantha?" Jason reached the front seats, but she was already stalking back through the RV, the twins watching her with an intense, narrow-eyed confusion.

They turned their gaze to Jason and he shrugged as she swept into the narrow alcove of the bathroom in the back of the vehicle and slammed the door behind her. Jason lifted a calming hand to the kids and continued walking past, reaching the door a moment later.

"You okay?"

"Fine." Her voice was a strangled, hoarse croak.

"Sam. You can talk to me." Jason stood just outside the door, trying to maintain a smile as he looked back toward the twins.

"I *am* talking to you."

Jason slowly tapped on the door to the bathroom with one knuckle. There was a ragged sigh on the other end, then it eased open, and Samantha stood framed within it, looking at him.

"It's going to be okay," Jason said.

"I know," she replied. "It's just— it's a lot, is all. Stuff like this, I can handle on my own, no problem. This isn't the first time. But when I think of Eli and Sarah, when I look at this entire city and see all these innocent people..."

"You get upset."

"I'm not upset," she replied through gritted teeth. "I'm really, *really* angry."

"You have every right to be."

Samantha stepped out of the bathroom and took a deep breath, her jaw flexing back and forth for a moment before she forced a smile. "Sorry, guys," she said, walking toward Eli and Sarah. "Mom just had a little moment."

"It's okay," Elijah replied.

"Is it bad out there?" Sarah bit her lip nervously.

"You know I won't lie to you." Samantha lowered into a crouch, looking over at her two children, who remained seated in their chairs. "It's pretty bad. I'm glad the two of you were in here."

"We can handle it." Elijah looked at his sister, who nodded back at him. "We can see how bad it is through the windows, y'know."

"I know. But trust me when I tell you that it's *way* worse outside." Samantha reached over and tussled his hair. "Just for now, let's try and make sure you don't have to handle it, okay? I know you can... but I'd rather wait to cross that bridge."

Elijah nodded and Kale made her way over, pushing her head into Samantha's hip. Scratching the dog behind the ears, she once more glanced at both of her children.

"It may be bad out there, but that doesn't mean it's bad everywhere. We're going to get out of this." She leaned a bit, and Jason was already sitting into the driver's seat.

Samantha stood and planted a gentle kiss on Elijah's forehead, then did the same for Sarah. Eli's nose scrunched up and Sarah's faltering smile returned, then Samantha walked back toward the front driver and passenger's seats where Jason had already gone and was waiting for her.

"Sorry about that," she whispered.

"Don't be." Jason shook his head. "You're still human and we just spent fifteen minutes dragging dead bodies out of the way after driving over them for the last hour. That isn't normal. Not by a long shot."

Jason slid the key into the ignition, then started the RV. It growled swiftly to life, the engine noise breaking the pervasive silence. Pushing down on the accelerator, Jason guided the RV toward the side street they'd just cleared. There was an unsteady moment as it began to move forward, tires catching on corpses already gathered beneath the large vehicle. But they rolled forward, jostling back and forth as the bodies were dislodged, then finally bumping over the sidewalk and transitioning to the street separating the convenience store from the electronics store. It was just wide enough for the RV to pass through and with the pavement clear, Jason leaned into the accelerator, picking up speed.

With a snarl of engine, the RV screamed down the side street, then Jason cranked the wheel, cutting the turn of the intersection at an angle. The front corner of the RV clipped one of the three stalled vehicles and battered it aside, but barely slowed as they transitioned to another street. It wasn't empty by any stretch, but there was just enough space between vehicles and around bodies that Jason could actually navigate, weaving a path through the potential obstacles, rather than pushing them out of the way or crushing them beneath their wheels.

Samantha glanced at the console's GPS display, which slowly scrolled along with their movements, following the path of the alternate route. Jason slowed as he swerved around a corpse splayed in the road, then wound around a stopped delivery truck near the sidewalk along a small, run-down restaurant. Cars were wedged into spaces on the sidewalk, leaving the road narrower than it would have been otherwise. Jason was forced to push aside a small hatchback with the nose of the RV before accelerating again, picking up speed a bit.

Shifting her attention from the satellite tracker, Samantha

adjusted the dial of the radio, scrolling through a hiss of static, her head shaking. Tiny snippets of voices came and went, though no matter how hard she tried she couldn't seem to bring them into focus or volume. She was just about to give up, when the station indicator passed a certain frequency, and a voice finally broke through.

"— this message repeats."

Samantha stopped scrolling, offering a sideways glance in Jason's direction. They waited for a long moment, listening to the faded background hiss before the voice began again. It started with a long, solemn tone.

"This is the Emergency Broadcast System. This is not a test."

Samantha huddled over, one ear turned toward the speaker.

"Multiple attacks have been reported in major cities across the country. At this time the cause of these attacks remains unknown. The Federal Emergency Management Agency is advising all citizens to shelter in place and await further instructions."

Jason blew out a breath, steering the RV around another sprawl of bodies which seemed to have gathered just outside a sporting goods store. The message continued its solemn report.

"If you are inside, stay inside. Lock all doors and windows. Avoid unnecessary travel, and do not leave your location unless directed by local authorities. Remain tuned to this station or another designated Emergency Broadcast System station for updates and further instructions. Ensure you have enough food, water, and essential supplies for at least 72 hours."

"Seventy-two hours?" Samantha shook her head. "There's nothing they're going to do in seventy-two hours."

"Stay off the roads to allow emergency personnel to respond. If you are outdoors, find shelter immediately. Take cover in the nearest secure building. Authorities are working to identify the threat and restore order. Please remain calm. Further information will be provided as it becomes available."

Jason slowed as they approached another intersection, more vehicles barricading their way, leaving no gap for the large RV to squeeze through. He moved his foot from the gas to the brake, slowing a bit as they approached.

"Stay tuned to official channels for updates. This is the Emergency Broadcast System. This message repeats—"

Samantha twisted the dial and killed the radio, the voice choking into static-filled silence. Jason braked again, stopping the RV completely in the middle of the road as they faced the congested intersection.

"We're going to have to move those cars, I think. Even if we just move a couple of them, we should have a clearer path through."

Samantha checked the satellite navigation system again, scrolling through the various streets and clusters of buildings around them.

"I think you're right. I'm not seeing any good alternate routes."

"You want to give me a hand?"

Samantha was already twisting in her seat, opening her mouth to speak when Sarah interrupted. "We know, Mom. Stay in here."

As Samantha stood, Kale sensed an impending adventure and stood as well, taking a step toward them.

"Not this time, Kale," Samantha replied. "You're staying here with the kids."

Kale whimpered softly, still in a half-step stance, tail slightly drooped. They removed another pair of masks and two sets of gloves from the glove compartment and exited the RV once more, stepping out onto the city street. They both stood for a moment just outside the RV, Samantha slowly turning as she stared at their surroundings. Buildings rose tall to the north, thick, sprawling fingers of skyscrapers trying to grasp the smog-yellowed clouds from the sky. Once more the penetrating silence of the world staggered them both, a sense of total and complete isolation.

Since the moment they'd crossed into the city, it had been a chaotic frenzy of noise and activity. The noise had stopped, the activity halted in a sudden freeze-frame of destruction.

"It can't be like this everywhere, can it?" Jason asked. "The kind of coordination it would take for that sort of mass attack—there have to be cities that haven't been hit."

"Doesn't much matter. People will be losing their minds, Jason, even if it was just a handful of big cities. They'll be going crazy wondering if they might be next. And with this much death, it's inevitable that the supply chain collapses. Think of everything that comes into the Port of Los Angeles... if that was hit, too, it's going to be a nightmare scenario."

"Look!" Jason pointed toward the clouds, his hand perched above his eyes to shield the sun.

Samantha stepped up next to him, standing shoulder-to-shoulder. For a brief moment, the outline of a faraway passenger plane walked a path across the sky above so high they couldn't hear its engine. It was visible for just a brief snatch of time before vanishing once more behind a fist of thickening clouds.

"Well that's surprisingly heartening." Samantha said. "They're headed north, it looks like. Wonder where they're going to land."

"No idea. Portland?" Samantha winced at the mention of the closest major city near where her parents lived. "Sorry. Maybe they weren't hit?"

"It's going to be worse, in a way, if they weren't. Millions of panicked people fighting for resources. We might be better off surrounded by corpses than by the living."

"Well, that's a morbid thought."

"It's the truth." Samantha broke away from Jason's side and walked toward the cars that had barricaded the intersection.

Jason trailed along behind her. They reached the cluster of vehicles together, one of them a dark blue SUV. Slowly, he made his way around the back of the vehicle, leaning a bit to stare through the side windows. The silhouette of a head was visible behind the wheel, though there only seemed to be one person inside. Jason reached the driver's side door and pulled it open, stepping back as the driver tumbled out and hit the ground with a dull thud. It was a middle-aged woman, her chestnut-colored hair fanning out across the base of her skull. Jason clutched her wrists and stepped back, dragging her away from the side of the car until he flopped her down onto the sidewalk, out of their path.

As Samantha checked a second vehicle, Jason slipped into the driver's seat, eyeing the key that was still in the ignition. The woman had put the vehicle in park and the auto-off function had killed the engine to save fuel. With a twist of the key, Jason fired the SUV back up, keeping the door open. Tapping the gas, he eased the car forward a bit, guiding it out of the intersection and up onto the nearby sidewalk.

He returned to Samantha's side as she was dragging another corpse across the stretch of road from a white colored SUV. Coming in to help her, the two of them worked together, wrestling the large woman across the pavement and dumping her face-first on the sidewalk.

"I don't know if she was the driver or not. I couldn't see a key in the ignition and there were no keys in her pockets." Samantha stood and wiped more sweat from her forehead.

Together, they returned to the SUV and peered into the driver's side door, which had been left open. There was no key, as Samantha had said, and it was old enough to not have a push-button start, either. Jason lowered both visors, looking for a set that might come tumbling out, but with zero luck. He checked the floorboards and under the seat but found no joy there either. Moving a bit further into the car, Jason studied the gear shift and located a small, square shaped plastic cover embedded in the housing near the lever.

"I don't suppose you have a screwdriver?"

"Nope. We have that toolkit back in the RV, I can run and grab it if you want."

"Not yet." Jason reached into his pockets and fished out his set of keys.

Using one of the longer keys, he jabbed its angled teeth into the square shaped cover and dug at it, working it into the seam of the cover. It took some work, but he was able to crack the square cover and pop it open, exposing a narrow hole beneath. He flipped through the rest of the keys on his chain and found one that was even thinner, then poked it into the hole, until the shift lock release depressed with a click. Keeping pressure applied to the shift lock release, he moved the gear from park to neutral.

"Here, let's swap. You steer, I'll push." He backed out of the driver's side and walked toward the rear while Samantha walked past him and stepped up into the driver's seat.

Jason positioned himself behind the SUV and leaned forward, wedging his shoulder into the trunk as he pressed his palm to its rear quarter panel. Bending his legs, he pushed forward, the SUV slowly rolling as he grunted and strained against its weight. Inside the front seat, Samantha twisted hard on the wheel, turning it to the left, the SUV slowly moving at an angle, swinging gradually out of the intersection it had been blocking. It took a few minutes of extra effort, but they were able to roll it free and open up a narrow space for the RV to fit through.

Samantha left the car, the two of them walking back toward the RV, wiping the sweat from their necks and faces, still enveloped by the almost preternatural silence throughout the entire city. Their footfalls scuffed on the pavement, all that much louder with the silent void of a backdrop. Jason's own pace quickened as they made their way back to the RV, the penetrating silence of the world around them almost more horrific than if it had been teeming with monsters or some sort of an angry mob. Moments later, they were back inside and settling into their seats, their masks and gloves disposed of in one of their small trash receptacles.

"That's some spooky stuff," Jason said, just sitting in his seat, fingers gripping the wheel as he stared through the wide expanse of window before them.

"The quiet?"

"Exactly."

"Agreed. Those were the worst times back when—" Samantha's voice faltered. "If you heard something...

"That meant you knew what direction the threat was coming from."

"Yep. And that's what you wanted. The worst moments were the silent ones, that's when you had no idea what to expect."

Jason nodded, patting his wife's hand. "You two doing okay?" He turned and called back over his shoulder.

Eli and Sarah were huddled around the small kitchen table, their own silence almost as disturbing as that in the city outside.

"We're okay." Sarah shrugged softly.

"I don't like this one bit." Eli gripped his phone with both hands, staring intently at the screen. "Music's not helping anymore."

"I'm sorry, dude. We'll be out of it soon, though." Jason accelerated, driving forward, squeezing between the gap they'd made in vehicles at the intersection.

They crossed onto the next section of road, once more slowing to steer around a vehicle parked askew along the sidewalk, looking as though it was in the process of pulling out into traffic when the attack had come. Jason angled around a pair of bodies, twisted into an eternal entanglement, though it was impossible to tell if it was one of love or anger. They passed through a few blocks, able to maneuver the RV through and around the traffic and bodies. The smaller side streets were emptier than the ones where they'd started, the stretches of pavement opening up into longer and wider passages requiring less evasive maneuvers. However, while the streets were better, their surroundings trended in the opposite direction.

They'd left immaculate high-rises far behind them, the stretches of well-manicured storefronts and neatly parked vehicles giving way to staggered apartment buildings, fenced-in abandoned lots, and a litany of spray paint scrawling unique characters and murals along stretches of otherwise empty pavement and walls. To their right, a loose cluster of three-story brickwork apartments flanked each other, an old, burned-out sedan broken and forlorn in a section of gravel and dirt out to the side of the buildings. More spray paint had been etched on the side of the blackened vehicle, elaborate scrawl coloring the triangle of brick walls behind it. Overflowing dumpsters stood every couple hundred feet along with overturned trash cans disgorging full bags of refuse, some of which had torn open and were strewn across sidewalks and roadways.

Jason's gaze swept across their surroundings, his hands tightening around the wheel as they continued moving through a dirtier, more run-down section of L.A. The smoke that had been plaguing them ever since the chaos had started was thicker, and the surrounding streets were cast in a deeper darkness, existing in the shadows of the sprawling city that attracted all the tourists and celebrities. It was a stark, darker reflection of the other areas broadcast on television and in movies, a section of veritable slums all the darker in contrast to the city's other brilliance.

"Hold on," Samantha warned, gesturing through the windshield ahead. "Ugh, more blockages ahead."

Several tall spires of other apartments rose to their left, the tallest buildings within the last several city blocks they'd traveled. For the first time in several minutes, more cars blocked the roadway ahead, narrowing the gaps between them, too slim for the RV to squeeze through.

"We're going to have to move those, too." Jason tapped on the brakes, scanning the sidewalks, vacant lots, and buildings that surrounded them. "As fun as it is to play bumper cars with your Dad's RV, I want to minimize the damage for the sake of keeping it running."

A scattering of dead bodies were in view, the numbers significantly less than the other neighborhoods, but still at least a dozen or more they could see. Three of them were directly to their left, all three young men with two in tank tops and one wearing no shirt at all, his chest littered with an array of dark inked tattoos. There were two women to the right, one of them lying motionless near a capsized stroller, its contents mercifully hidden from sight. Samantha swallowed hard and turned her attention back to the RV's console, scrolling through the map and checking surrounding roads.

"I don't think we can easily go around. Best to just move the cars and go through like we did before."

Jason leaned forward, looking at the area around them. "Okay." He turned and lowered his voice. "Should we bring the kids this time? There aren't as many bodies out there."

"I don't know..."

"There are a lot of cars. It would go a lot faster if the kids helped."

Samantha nodded her approval. "We'll bring Kale, too."

"Absolutely. Keep her close and use her as a lookout." Jason leaned back in the driver's seat, cut the engine and unclasped his seat belt. He stood and stretched as Samantha did the same, Kale immediately launching to her feet and inching excitedly forward. "We've got some more cars to move. We could use some help."

"Really?" Eli shot to his feet, dropping his phone down onto the table.

"Sure!" Sarah pushed herself up from the table alongside Elijah, the two of them moving in unison.

Kale skittered back and to the right, tail sweeping back and forth eagerly, then she darted forward, weaving between the twins and pushing her way toward the door.

"Okay, okay," Samantha said, crouching and stroking the dog's head. "Take it easy. You can come out, too." She nodded toward Eli. "Can you reach into that alcove and grab the tool kit that's in there? It'll help things go more quickly."

Eli did as asked and came out with a compact case, its lid firmly secured. He handed it to Samantha, who unclasped the lid and opened it, revealing screwdrivers, a ratchet set, and a few other miscellaneous tools that could be used for general repairs. She tucked it underneath her arm, passed out gloves and masks to everyone, then eased open the door and stepped out into the silent street. Samantha took a step backwards, turning and eyeing the nearby sidewalk as Eli and Sarah came out next.

"Don't look under the RV, okay?" Jason came out last and Kale bounded out alongside him, immediately sniffing the ground. "Kale. Heel." Jason gestured toward the dog, and she peeled herself away from where she was sniffing and trotted along after him.

Eli's gaze remained fixed on the pair of dead women on the other sidewalk, lingering for an extra few seconds on the over-turned stroller. Jason edged around the front of the RV and eyed the three dead men, then as a group they moved forward. None of them spoke, the thick, dead weight of silence settling upon their already weary shoulders. Jason led the way, with Eli and Sarah behind him and Samantha pulling up the rear. Kale moved along as well, enveloped within the group. Reaching the cars a moment later, Jason and Samantha handled dragging a few dead bodies out from around the clutch of vehicles. They worked quickly and efficiently, dragging three bodies off to the side, ensuring they were out of the way.

Samantha returned first and opened the door of an ancient green sedan with more rust than intact paint. She opened the door and found the vehicle had a standard transmission and was stuck in second, where it had been when the driver died and the vehicle crashed and stalled out. Balancing between the clutch and the gear shift, she moved the stick into neutral, then worked with Elijah and Sarah to steer the vehicle out of the road and onto the sidewalk. Jason took the screwdriver from the tool kit and activated the shift lock on the second vehicle, a black Volkswagen, several years newer than the green vehicle. He worked the gear into neutral, then got out and pushed, the car inching slowly forward.

Elijah jogged over from helping his mother and sister, then took up position next to his father, the two of them pressing on the trunk and moving the mid-sized vehicle out of the intersection. As the vehicle slowly rolled forward, Eli stopped abruptly and stared to the left, gaze rising toward the top of the nearby apartment building.

"Did you see that?"

"See what?"

"I thought I saw something move up there. On one of the top floors."

Jason stopped pushing, standing up, leaning against the trunk with one hand. "I don't see anything."

"It was up there, somewhere. I'm sure I saw it."

The two of them stood side by side, staring at the building as Samantha and Sarah finished what they were doing as well.

"What are you two looking at?"

"Do you see anything moving up there?" Jason pointed toward the top of the apartment and all four of them watched in silence.

A short time later, they all agreed that they saw nothing moving, shaking off the unsettling feeling that they were being watched. Jason and Elijah continued pushing their car forward while Samantha and Sarah focused their attention on the third vehicle. It took about five more minutes for the other vehicles to be pushed aside and to open up the intersection wide enough for the RV to fit through. The O'Brian family gathered together, Kale sticking tight to Jason as he'd asked. Eli kept glancing toward the top of the nearby building, though he shook off his concerns and joined his mother, father, sister and dog on their slow approach back to their vehicle.

Jason opened the door, stepping aside to make room for the kids to enter while Samantha lingered behind. Kale drew back as well, seemingly understanding that the priority was getting the kids inside first, then held her place next to Samantha's leg. Suddenly, as Elijah approached the open door, Kale stiffened, and a throaty, guttural growl emanated from the German Shepherd's throat.

"Kale?" Samantha asked, looking down at the dog, who was facing directly toward the nearby apartment building, hackles raised.

Samantha focused her attention on the front door of the brickwork building, taking Kale's collar in hand. Doors at the front of the building that had been closed moments before now stood ajar and several people were emerging from within the building, walking slowly toward the O'Brians. One of them raised an arm and shouted something incoherent, too far away to be understood, or speaking in a foreign language that she couldn't recognize.

"Jason!"

Samantha shouted and Kale began to bark furiously, jerking forward, throaty and angry, a sound she had rarely made in the time Samantha and Jason had owned her. Jason came back alongside Samantha so he could see past the front of the RV and toward the building across the street. A crowd had formed just outside, not huge, but big enough to pose a threat. The young men continued walking forward, all wearing red hats and patterned jackets that all resembled each other. As one of them separated from the other, Samantha could make out an elaborate number five stitched into the fabric of the young man's vest, right above his heart. As the group came closer, the same number became visible on all of their jackets. Another man shouted, then a third, though the words were almost unintelligible. Samantha and Jason shot each other a look as Samantha clutched tight to Kale's collar to keep the angrily barking dog from launching forward.

"Kids!" Samantha hissed. "Get in the RV. Right now!"

CHAPTER TEN

The Tills Family
Silverpine, Oregon

Sheila continued staring across the rolling green hills of the Oregon wilderness, her attention fixated on the twisting spirals of smoke in the distance. Low, charcoal clouds lingered in the sky, fed by the columns of black and gray, the smoke so dense that it was difficult to make out where it ended and the cloud cover at the edge of the horizon began. It was a roiling, churning creature moving in slow motion, but still seeming as alive as a serpent winding its way from the ground up into the sky and spreading slowly, inexorably outward.

"Try not to worry, Brandi," she said softly. "We have no idea what's going on. That almost seems to close to be Portland, though." Sheila reached toward her belt at the small of her back, but the walkie talkie she expected to be there was absent. She angled her neck back and looked toward the sky, her eyes pressed tightly closed.

"Give me a break."

"What's wrong?"

"I forgot the walkie-talkie back at the main building." Sheila shook her head incredulously. "Doug always has to remind me to bring it." She lowered her head and gave Brandi a sideways glance. "Don't tell him, okay?"

Brandi smiled and nodded, though the worry never left her narrowed eyes. Sheila took a few more steps forward, near to where the sharp slope of the hill rolled down into the valley and removed her phone from her pocket, holding it aloft with two hands, framing the columns of smoke within its rectangular screen. Sparing a brief look at the battery indicator, she centered the viewfinder on the smoke and tapped the shutter button, clicking a picture of the burning city. She adjusted slightly, zooming in, and took a few more pictures, then returned the phone to her pocket.

"What should we do?" Brandi asked.

"I think we've done all we can do right now. We checked all the tasting stations and there was nobody there. Last I knew, Doug and the others were checking the outbuildings and other areas. I feel pretty comfortable saying we're the only ones here at the moment, so I'm thinking we should head on back." Together, they stepped away from the edge of the grass-covered hill and walked back toward the side-by-side.

Brandi slipped silently into the passenger seat and Sheila walked around the vehicle, climbing up into the driver's seat. She keyed the ignition, then slowly backed up the vehicle. Moments later, she'd steered it back to the gravel-covered roadway and they were making their way back to the main building.

"Who would even do something like that?" Brandi stared at the vineyards as they passed, heading back in the other direction.

Twisting coils of green vines encircled clusters of ripe, shining fruit, the lingering scent refreshingly familiar in Sheila's nostrils. Whatever else was going on in the world, her favorite place on earth— the vineyards— were still right where they belonged, unspoiled and unsullied by whatever was going on around them.

"I have no idea." Sheila shook her head as she gripped the steering wheel, moving more quickly on the way back since they didn't have to check for lingering guests or employees. "I just hope—" she cut her statement short and Brandi didn't press the issue, the pair of them continuing on in uneasy silence.

They bumped and jostled along the gravel roadway, passing by the tasting stations once more, angling past the side road leading toward the diesel tank. Sheila went faster than she typically preferred and soon the looming structure of the main building came into view ahead. From the ground it rose two stories, the base level where the loading dock and storage warehouse were while the restaurant, administrative offices and living area for her and Doug were on the upper levels.

Sheila steered to the right, following the upward slope of road through the employee parking lot and back up to the main entrance of the rest of the building. She cut the engine of the utility vehicle and stepped out while Brandi slid from the passenger seat, the two of them walking toward the front door. Sheila unlocked it with her keys, and they went inside, pausing for a moment in the entryway. To the left of the main entrance was the hosting station and the restaurant, while the right path led to the office spaces. They both looked up at the ceiling as the fluorescent light, motion activated when they came in, flickered. Its pale glow wavered somewhat as they stared at it, drifting dim, then brightening again, then jittering in between a state of on and off.

"Is that the power flickering?" Brandi's voice was a sheepish whisper. "Or does that bulb need to be fixed?"

"I'm not sure," Sheila replied, trying to keep her voice steady, but a touch of anxiety put a slight tremor in her words. "Let's check Doug's office, okay? We can see if it's just this light or if the others are doing the same thing."

Sheila opened the door leading into a squat hallway, walked down a few strides, then opened an office door to the right. A moment later she was inside Doug's personal office, lined with filing cabinets pressed up against oak walls, framed posters and photographs set in even spaces throughout the office's perimeter. A thick layer of dust lay upon the entire place, and there were haphazard stacks of paper, old cardboard boxes and knick-knacks scattered around the room, making a maze to navigate through to actually get to the little-used desk. On the wall across from his desk was a large photo of the entire family, Sheila and Doug with Samantha, Jason, Eli and Sarah. Kale, their German Shepherd, sat on the grass in front of them all, looking quite a bit smaller than she had when last Sheila saw her.

The photograph wasn't much more than three or four years old, but so much had already changed. Where the twins had been no more than ten in the photo, they were both teenagers, going through some of the most dramatic changes of their young lives. Sheila lost herself for a moment, staring at the photograph, hypnotized by the faces that stared back at her and the sprawling vineyards at their back. So much was the same, yet so much else had changed. Another staccato flicker of overhead lights snapped her out of her momentary haze, and she stared at the ceiling. They'd turned the lights on when they'd entered the office, but clearly something was going on with the power.

"Mrs. Tills?"

"Sheila, remember?" She gave Brandi a lift of her eyebrow and a smile.

Brandi didn't respond, staying near the doorway as she stared at the flickering lights.

"We should probably get some of your stuff out of your car." Sheila changed the subject. "If you're going to stay for a while, anyway."

"Oh. Right. Okay." Brandi nodded, her attention momentarily diverted from the lights. "Are you sure everything is okay?

Shouldn't the power, like, be on or off, not... doing whatever it's doing?"

"Doug'll take care of it. Don't worry about things we can't control, okay?"

Brandi nodded warily as Sheila side-stepped through the maze in Doug's office and approached a section of shelves along the far wall, which were mounted just above a set of cabinets on the floor. A charging cradle for portable radios rested on top of the lower cabinets and she removed one of them, clicking it on. Static hissed from the speakers and she checked the power indicator lights, verifying that they were all illuminated.

"Remember what you promised," Sheila said, gesturing toward Brandi and giving her a wink, "me forgetting the walkie talkie is our little secret."

"I've got you covered." A hint of a smile appeared which soothed a little of Sheila's own anxiety.

Standing near the exit to Doug's office, Sheila pressed the call button and less than two seconds later, a thrumming vibrato sounded from within the office. Sheila whipped her head around and stared at the charging cradle sitting on the cabinets a few feet away. There was another radio in the charging cradle, and it vibrated loudly with the chime of the call she was making.

"Well, I'll be—" Sheila shook her head, lowering the radio and releasing the call button. "Doug forgot his radio, too." She chuckled and turned back to Brandi. "I'm never going to let him live *this one* down." They shared some snickers as they shut off the lights and left the office, heading back toward the front door of the main building.

A minute later they were back outside, the doors to the main building locked back up behind them. Sheila gestured toward the utility vehicle, the two of them once more climbing inside, then she turned the key in the ignition and set back off toward the employee parking lot. They traversed the section of pavement and passed Darryl's camper van, then crunched down onto the gravel road on the other side. Sheila followed the same path they'd taken previously, though she turned onto a narrow stretch of crushed stone which branched off to the right, moving toward a section of trees.

That winding path brought them to another small, out-of-the-way parking lot east of the main vineyards. An old, beat-up Dodge sedan rested in the lot, parked in the shadows of a row of trees along the far edge. Sheila angled the utility vehicle toward it, pulling up alongside and gently slowing, then stopping. The sedan looked to be twenty or maybe even thirty years old, peppered with a few dings and dents along the passenger side of the vehicle. Running along the base of the vehicle were the first signs of rust, the normal color fading into a coppery crust. The body sagged slightly, as if weary from years of hard miles and neglect. There were a few scattered pits in the windshield, and the tarnished chrome trim reflected the sun in dull smears of light. The tires, half-bald, looked as though they hadn't been rotated in years.

"That's your car, I assume?" Sheila asked.

Brandi nodded. "It's an old beater, but it's bought and paid for. I couldn't really afford anything better.

"Doesn't look very comfortable to sleep in."

"Not in the least. I'm pretty tiny and even *I* was cramped in there." Brandi lowered her head and wiped absently at her eyes. "I'm sorry, Mrs. T—Sheila. I really am. This is all so embarrassing." Brandi shook her head repeatedly as they stepped out of the side-by-side.

"Nonsense. It's not embarrassing in the slightest, I promise. It's okay, Brandi."

The younger woman fumbled in her pocket and drew out her keys, then made her way to the driver's side, unlocked the car manually, opened the door and reached inside to unlock the others. Sheila stood nearby, trying not to crowd the girl as she came back and opened the back passenger door. Inside the vehicle, the worn cloth seats were stained and torn, with the stuffing poking through like old battle wounds. A faint smell of mildew and gasoline clung to the air, lingering like the car's last breath of life.

"I don't know what to say," Brandi whispered, pulling out a backpack that was on the back seat and carrying it over to the utility vehicle.

"The only apology I'll accept is apologizing for not coming to us sooner. We would have been happy to help."

"I've only been here for a month or so. I didn't feel right asking for that sort of thing."

"We would have helped you with the repairs. Advanced your paycheck, done something. Once you come to work for us, you're a part of our family." Sheila walked to the car as Brandi pulled out another bag, hoisting it onto her shoulder. "And I mean family like, well, *family*. Not like how you hear big corporations use the word."

"Rocky gave me a ride home one night after work, helped me pick up some of my stuff. He offered to float me some money to repair the car, too, but I told him it was fine." Brandi's cheeks flushed a deep crimson as she loaded another bag onto the rear bed of the utility vehicle.

"There's nothing wrong with asking for help if you need it." Sheila placed her hands on Brandi's arms and then gave her a gentle embrace, the younger girl almost falling into it. "We're all in this together, and you've been such a huge help in the month you've been here. You've been invaluable to us, Brandi; of course we'd be willing to help you, and we still are."

Brandi sniffed loudly, jerking her head into a nod.

"Let's get the rest of your stuff."

There were two more tote bags in the car that they unloaded and placed into the utility vehicle. The driver's seat had been extended backwards to turn it into a makeshift bed and Sheila shook her head, picturing the young woman sleeping there every night. They didn't speak any more as they finished loading up the side-by-side, then Brandi used her keys to lock up the car, and together they began to make their way back to the restaurant. Winding back up through the two parking lots, they stopped outside the front entrance as they had moments before.

Killing the engine of the UTV, they exited the vehicle, and Sheila unlocked the front door again, ushering Brandi inside. Each of them took one bag to start, moving through the entryway past the hosting station and into the broad expanse of the restaurant's dining area. Sheila gestured for Brandi to follow her, and they walked the perimeter of the larger dining area and toward a smaller room near the rear, which was a secondary dining room that was available for parties or other events.

Stepping through the door, Sheila used her elbow to turn on the lights, and after a brief, heart-slowing moment of unsteady flickering, they finally came on. The pale glow undulated as the power flickered, though they supplied enough light to guide Sheila and Brandi to a far corner of the private dining room. They set her bags down and then walked back out to retrieve the others, returning moments later with most of Brandi's worldly possessions.

"Follow me." Sheila guided Brandi back through the dining area, then took a shortcut through the kitchen, back to the administrative office spaces.

They approached a door about midway down the hall and Sheila opened it, revealing a cavernous storage room, lined with shelves of various supplies. She edged sideways into the room, angling her neck and standing on tiptoes as she scanned the various boxes of items within. Finally, she reached up and grabbed a box, grunting softly as she hoisted it from its upper shelf, hugging it tight to her chest. Brandi stepped away, giving Sheila room, then followed behind her as they walked back toward the dining area.

"Is that an inflatable mattress?"

"Sure is. Doug and I bought it for the RV, just in case we needed an extra bed."

"That RV is pretty nice," Brandi said quietly as they cut back through the kitchen and into the dining area.

They walked along the near wall and into the separate room, then Sheila placed the box down on the floor.

"Doug and I saved up for several years for that RV. One of our life's ambitions."

"That's nice," Brandi replied, her voice somewhat quiet, almost dreamlike.

"Help me move these tables." Sheila pointed toward a scatter of round tables that had been set up inside the dining room.

They were solidly built but had wheels and folded up so that the room could be arranged in several different ways, based on the requestor's needs. Together, they tilted the tabletops up, then rolled them to the side, stacking them along the walls where the chairs were already placed.

"Doug hated this furniture. Said it made the dining room look more like a conference room." Sheila chuckled, staring at the furniture, all folded and stacked along the far walls.

"I think it looks fine. You've got the fancier stuff in the main dining room still, and this is supposed to be for parties or events, right?"

"Exactly." Sheila gave Brandi a wink. "You get it."

Brandi flushed again and smiled, turning her attention to the inflatable mattress. She crouched by the box and opened it, pulling out the deflated and folded bed. Step by step, she began to unfold it, spreading it out on the floor in the corner of the dining area. Sheila dug into the box and retrieved a power cable, plugging it in, then slotting the extra end into a nearby wall outlet. She spared another glance toward the ceiling to make sure the power was on, then flipped a switch. There was a vibrating thrum from inside the mattress as it began to self-inflate, growing larger and thicker by the moment. As it blew up to full size and thickness, Sheila hit the switch again, then coiled up the power cable and put it back in the box.

"There we go." She stood, folded her arms and looked down at the inflatable bed. "We've got plenty spare sets of sheets and blankets in the upstairs living area. We'll make sure we get the bed made up for you before it's time to use it."

"Mrs. Tills, I don't know how to thank you. This is just... it might be the nicest thing anyone has ever done for me."

"What did I tell you? Call me Sheila, sweetheart." Sheila reached out and squeezed Brandi's arm gently.

"Is there anything I can do to help? There has to be something."

"As a matter of fact, I think there is."

"Just name it."

"You've spent plenty of time in and around the kitchen since you've been here. I'd love it if you could take stock of everything we've got in the refrigerators and walk-in freezer. Get a good, thorough inventory of all of our food. Just try and be quick and careful and don't leave the doors open for too long. The power could go out at any moment by the looks of things, and we'll need Doug to help out when or if that happens."

Together the two of them walked back out into the main dining room, then approached the kitchen. Brandi made a detour, separating from Sheila and walked toward the nearby hosting station, then returned with an order pad and a small pencil. She held them up, earning an appreciative nod from Sheila before she continued on into the kitchen to start the inventory. Sheila watched her go, sighing quietly as the events of the day caught up with her. She turned away from the kitchen and stared out through the wall of nearby windows overlooking the vineyard. Removing her phone from her pocket, she used it to check the time.

"All right, Doug, where are you off to?" She stared through the windows at the sprawling carpet of green coiled leaves, seeing nothing but the rolling hills and lines of trees to the north.

Doug took the lead with Benjamin and Darryl walking a few paces behind him on either side as they made their way slowly across the sprawling meadow that separated the trees from the housing development before them. Doug hadn't spent much time in the area, and most of his interactions with the people were on his own property. In fact, if he hadn't met a few of them, he might have had a similar opinion of the place that Benjamin did, that they were transplants from other states living in luxury houses.

Three evenly spaced homes stood before them on equal sized lots, squared off and even. It was all far too artificial, everything closely measured and cordoned off, people living in their own little isolated rectangle of personal space, wedged up tight against their neighbors. It was nothing he would have ever wanted for himself or his family, and he'd spent his whole life working hard to make sure they didn't have to experience the constant noise and buzz that came from living in such close proximity to other people.

They stopped walking partway toward the first row of houses and Doug tilted his head, listening for any sign of activity. "It's so quiet," Darryl said, reading Doug's mind. "Is it always this quiet?"

"Nope." Doug shook his head. "There's always activity back here, no matter the time of day. If kids are in school then moms are at home or dads have the day off or *something*. This is weird. I'd think someone would be around." Doug stared at the houses. "Here, let's check the Chancellors' place first." He gestured toward the house he'd pointed at earlier.

They crossed the meadow at an angle, making their way

toward the single-story structure on its own evenly sectioned off plot of land. There was a grill perched on the corner of a neatly angled patio, a pair of steps leading to a squat deck with a few chairs set out in orderly fashion. Sliding glass doors led to the inside of the house and Doug crossed the wooden deck, trying to peer into the home beyond. Closing his fist, he rapped his knuckles on the glass and listened for signs of voices within but heard nothing. Together they walked around the house and he repeated the knocking at the front door, but once again there was no response from inside.

"Maybe they're at work?" Benjamin asked, taking a step back to survey the home, as if that might indicate where its inhabitants had gone.

"Marcus is retired and he's been resting an injured hip. His wife still has a job, but I would have thought he'd be here." Doug shrugged and looked for a moment at the garage, considering what to do next.

While they huddled around the front door to the Chancellors' house, an abrupt slam of a car door echoed from behind them. All at once, the three men wheeled around in the direction of the noise and immediately began walking toward it. Another row of houses ran along the opposite side of the street, each one with the same pattern siding, the same overall design and even the same exact width driveway and two-car garage. It looked like each house had come off a conveyor belt exactly the same, simply dropped into each lot fully assembled.

To their right, in the driveway of the house across the street, a man stood alongside a mid-sized sedan, its trunk pulled open with several bags of items jammed inside it, peeking out from within. Through the windows, more stuff was visible inside the car itself, and a cargo box was attached to the top of the vehicle. It was closed, but a stray sleeve poked out through the lid, the box apparently filled with clothing of some kind. A woman was bent over near the rear of the car, reaching inside, buckling a small child into a car seat. As they watched, she stepped back, closed the door, then walked back into the house, leaving her husband to continue loading and securing the car. Doug gave Benjamin a passing glance, the older man shaking his head slightly in response. Doug chose to ignore Benjamin's concerns and stepped off the grass and onto the rounded road, lifting a hand in greeting.

"Hey!" He raised his voice from where they walked, looking to announce their presence before they scared anyone.

The man jerked his head up and stared at them over the slope of the windshield, his brow knitting into deep furrows.

"How are you all doing?" Doug shouted as they came a bit closer.

The man stepped behind the opened driver's side door, his eyes still fixed on them as he fidgeted with something on the other side of the vehicle that Doug couldn't see. Benjamin rested a hand on Doug's arm, holding him back.

"Let's keep our distance," he whispered, his own piercing gaze fixed on the fidgeting man in the driveway.

The man stood rigid on the other side of his sedan, the driver's side door open, his arms moving gently as if holding or lifting something.

"We're fine!" he shouted back, jerking his chin toward them. "Who are you and what are you doing over here? I don't recognize you."

"My name is Doug Tills!" Doug lifted his hand again, though didn't take another step closer. Turning slightly, he gestured back toward the trees. "We're from the Tills Vineyard just on the other side of those trees."

"Okay," the man replied, caution edging his voice.

"We saw some pretty hairy stuff on the television back at the vineyard and wanted to check on our neighbors. See if everyone is okay. I tried to track down Marcus, but he's not answering his door." Doug pointed toward the Chancellor house.

The man standing behind the car visibly relaxed, his shoulders drawing slightly down as he seemed to set something back in its place behind the car. Closing the driver's side door, he made his way around the vehicle and toward the street, his empty hands visible. Benjamin relaxed as the man approached the street, glancing back momentarily at the vehicle still parked in the driveway.

"We didn't mean to startle you," Doug said as he came closer.

The man looked up and down the rows of houses on both sides of the street, his head shaking at their darkened windows and empty driveways. "You just missed them. Anybody who was still here lit out a short time after the reports came on the television. It was a bit of a madhouse around here first thing. Everyone packed up and took off running." He nodded toward the house across the street from his. "Those folks have family just outside Eugene and they said they were going to go see if they were okay. I told them they were idiots, man. Last place I want to go is anywhere near a city right now, big or small."

"Took the words out of my mouth," Doug replied.

"Well, that's where a bunch of them went. They mostly wanted to get back with their families. The folks in the house behind mine have a kid in college up at UW, just outside Seattle." The man shook his head. "Believe it or not, they packed their two younger kids in the car and drove straight in that direction. Talk about going into the mouth of the beast."

"We saw some footage of Seattle on the news." Doug stuffed his hands in his pockets. "It didn't look pretty."

"I saw the same thing. Tried to warn them, but they weren't having it. Said they had to get to their kid. I suppose I get it, I just don't know about risking your entire family to get to one of them."

"Parents will do crazy things when it comes to their children." His mind, as it so often did, drifted to Samantha.

"What have you heard? Anything about which cities were hit?" The man nodded back toward Doug.

Doug blew out a breath, trying to piece back together the scatter of news footage that had come through that morning. "Los Angeles, Seattle and Chicago were three of them. New York City, too. The grisliest footage came from Chicago, though. They had some sort of cell phone footage of dead people in Millenium Park; those were some images I'm not sure I'll ever get out of my mind."

"It's bad," the man said, once more glancing back at his car. "I got a couple of alerts pushed through to my phone. Looks like Boston was hit, too. Miami, Denver, a dozen different locations throughout Texas."

"A dozen?"

The man nodded. "I have a cousin who lives in Oklahoma, and he shot me a few texts until he couldn't anymore. Obviously the big places like Dallas, Houston, Austin and others. Fort Worth, Galveston were also hit, even a few different areas I hadn't really heard of before."

"So, it's not just big cities?"

"Started that way from the sounds of it, but then some smaller cities started getting hit, too. So far it's just cities, but not just the big metropolitan areas. I tried to get some more information, but since the networks went down I can't even send a regular text or make a phone call. It's like the stone ages again."

"Makes me wonder if the attacks aren't even done yet," Benjamin chimed in. "Maybe there are more coming."

"Well, that's a lovely thought. Wonder how widespread they'll get." The man shifted his stance and again stared back at the car, taking a short step back toward the driveway.

"Looks like you're heading out?"

"Planning on it. My dad has a place up near Tillamook. We're not heading toward the cities like these other crazies, we're heading as far from the cities as we can get. I figure if anyone wants to target Tillamook, things are already too far gone."

"If you ask me, that's the right idea," Benjamin said. "Nature is your friend in times like this. Sure, as hell isn't other people." He stared around them, a clenched look of anticipation on his face despite the empty neighborhood that surrounded them.

"Is there anything you need?" Doug asked, nodding toward the man. "I mean, before you go?"

"Kind of you to ask, neighbor, but I don't think so. We're just going to be—"

"Denton!" A female voice shouted from the direction of the house, and the man twisted toward the sound of the shrill scream.

"The power just went out!" She stabbed a thumb back toward the house, her other hand holding the door open. "What do we do?"

"Son of a—" Benjamin shook his head and turned back toward the trees they'd come through. "We ought to get back."

The man shook his head, grumbling something under his breath. He took a few steps back toward the car and the house, then peered over his shoulder.

"You stay safe."

"Same to you," Doug replied, watching for a moment as the man rejoined his wife in the driveway, engaging in some heated, but inaudible conversation.

Benjamin had halted as he approached the far side of the road, giving Doug and Darryl a moment to catch up. The three of them converged, then stepped onto the lawn and headed back, between the nearby houses.

"With the issues with the power," Benjamin said in a low voice as they passed between two of the houses, "I assume you're going to want some help with the panels?"

"You read my mind." Doug glanced back toward Benjamin for a moment. "We're mostly ready, but I could use a hand checking everything. Talk about validation of what we were thinking, huh?"

"Count me in, too," Darryl said with a nod. "Happy to keep helping however I can."

"It's a deal." Doug picked up his pace, walking more quickly forward. "First, though, let's head back to the main building, see if the girls have finished their rounds yet. I want to let them know what we found out."

As a trio, they moved deeper into the trees, winding their way back to the vineyard's walking path.

CHAPTER ELEVEN

The O'Brian Family
Los Angeles, California

Jason dashed for the door, ushering everyone up and into the RV ahead of him. Stubbornly, he refused to go ahead of Samantha, waiting for the twins, Kale and her to go in before he went in himself. Slamming the door behind him, he swept around the passenger seat and nearly threw himself behind the steering wheel. The group was still heading toward the RV, not altering their speed, still slowly walking toward the O'Brians as they raised their arms and shouted.

"Buckle up, kids!" He yelled over his shoulder, shoving the key into the ignition and gunning the engine to snarling life.

It revved and roared around them, the RV shuddering with the force of initial engine turn over. Eli slung his harness across his waist and Sarah did the same, the two of them strapping into the seats by the kitchen. Kale continued to bark, sensing the danger outside, her fur standing up on end as she howled. Inside the RV, her aggression was deafening and palpable, her righteous fury unleashed at strangers approaching her family.

"Get her under control!" Jason cranked the gear shift into reverse, fighting it a bit. "I can't hear myself think!"

"Got her!" Elijah yelled as he grabbed for Kale, pulling the dog close and shushing her.

The group advanced, moving across the parking lot, starting to spread out along the sidewalk. They stayed away from the corpses that the O'Brian's had moved to the side of the road, stepping over or around them, but they closed, still shouting words Jason couldn't understand. Battling with the gear shift, he managed to move it into reverse, then leaned left, looking in the rear-view mirror.

"You can't do that!" Samantha shouted, searching her own mirror. "We've only gone a short distance; you start moving backwards now and we're going to end up back where we were!"

"Good point!" Jason slammed the gear shift forward again, ramming back into drive.

Up ahead, the group began to jog toward them. The man in the center, wearing a bright red bandanna and a jacket with the Roman numeral V stitched into it, waved his arms up and down, frantically shouting, his face contorted with the force of his screams. Kale resumed her barking, her mouth gyrating wildly as her aggression drowned out almost everything else inside the RV's cabin.

"Everyone hold on!" Jason hammered on the gas, the RV lunging forward, its engine revved to a shrill pitch.

It lumbered at first, then lurched, then sped forward, sending the group of men scattering away as it screamed down the road. Jason pointed the blunt face of the vehicle toward the gap between the cars they'd cleared moments before, pressing the gas all the way to the floorboards. Buildings along each side of the road smeared into colored blurs, whipping past as the RV picked up speed. They rode ahead, navigating a gradual bend in the road, and suddenly more vehicles appeared before them, loosely gathered in the path of traffic.

"No time to move them by hand!" He leaned into the acceleration, the RV slamming headlong into a pair of stalled vehicles.

A sudden bang of impact crushed metal on metal, one of the small vehicles spinning wildly to the left, the force of the RV knocking it aside. Just beyond the first, they clipped the front corner of a van, sending that vehicle spinning away as well, the opposite side of the boxy RV hammering into a light post with a crunch of metal. Jason angled left and bumped up onto the center divider between the two blocked lanes of travel, the middle separation not nearly wide enough for the full width of the RV.

He rode the central divider, the accelerator still pressed all the way down, the large vehicle plowing into stopped cars and trucks on each side. Clipping the vehicles sent them lurching right and left, creating a gap for the RV to fit through, the large, box-shaped vehicle hammering its way down both lanes. Jason checked the rearview mirror, angling his neck so he could see the twins. They both clutched their seats, eyes wide with shock as the vehicle thundered its way down the Los Angeles street, carving a ragged, crumpled path through the tangles of traffic. Kale had ceased her barking, focused on staying upright as Elijah clung to her. Jason gripped the steering wheel tightly, still pushing the gas down, his arms vibrating as the vehicle shuddered through the gap between stopped cars and trucks.

"Intersection ahead! Watch out!" Samantha braced herself with a palm on the dash as she pointed through the windshield.

A delivery truck had started to turn through the intersection when it had stopped, its bulk blocking the center divider, its doors open. On the street a short distance from the front of the truck was a dead man, face-down dressed in brown, evidently the truck's driver. Jason steered left, accelerating further, pointing the RV at the rear box of the delivery truck.

"Are you sure about this?"

"Not even a little." After slowing a bit on approach, he hammered the gas again, the RV leaping toward the rear of the truck.

At the last second Jason turned the wheel sharply in the opposite direction and hit the brakes, the RV's wheels screeching as the heavy rear end slid out to the side, parallel with the box truck. The RV shuddered as it collided with the full length of the box truck, the impact spreading out across the entirety of the vehicle and preventing any serious damage to any part of it. Turning the wheel straight again, Jason hammered down on the accelerator, gunning the engine and taking them forward before they had a chance to slow more than a few miles an hour.

"There! Up there!" Samantha jabbed her finger even more, poking at the windshield. "The drain system is that way, I can see it from here, off to the right!" To reinforce what she was seeing, she bent down toward the satellite navigation system, the drain system indeed appearing ahead of them.

"We've got more traffic up here," Jason hissed as they approached yet another intersection.

"You need to get over there! Try and make that turn." Samantha gestured toward the right of the street.

As they neared the intersection, Jason leaned to the right, cranking the wheel sharply in the same direction. The RV bucked, its tires skidding slightly as it tried to maintain purchase. All around them, the vehicle leaned precariously, dangerously close to toppling over without another object to brace them like the box truck had. Guiding the wheel left again, Jason corrected the over-steer, crossing the intersection at a diagonal.

"Oh no, not again." Samantha shook her head as the sidewalk came into view before them.

Once more, corpses littered the sidewalk, a nearby hotel having been hastily evacuated, the guests all sprinting out to their own deaths. The five-story building loomed before them along the right side of the road, but Jason was more focused on the dead bodies sprawled across the sidewalk.

"Kids! Cover your ears!" Samantha shouted.

"What?" Elijah asked. "Why?"

"Just plug your ears!" Jason yelled back. "And hold on tight!"

Eli and Sarah shoved their fingers in their ears, bending over and tensing as if anticipating a crash. The RV continued at speed, clipping a light post and knocking it over as it transitioned to the sidewalk, barely wide enough for them to travel. Almost at once, the RV started its familiar jostling and jerking, rolling over the uneven terrain of death. Jason gritted his teeth at the sounds the bodies made as the tires crunched over bone and burst organs. They rocked across the sidewalk, tires slipping on gathered gore before he was able to steer around a clutch of vehicles and move back onto a stretch of somewhat empty pavement.

They sped up, then he angled right, heading toward the sprawling expanse of what used to be the Los Angeles River stretching out before them. It stretched just beyond a length of chain-link fence that separated the population center from the drainage system. Jason eyed a section of the fence, spotting a gate built within the diamond-shaped pattern of metal. Pavement ran alongside them just on the other side of the fence, the service road running the length of the drainage system.

"Hold on!" Jason steered sharply to the right again, bouncing across a section of sidewalk, onto a narrow road which led directly to the chain-link gate and a ramp beyond.

Gripping the wheel tightly, he plowed directly into the gate, the momentum of the RV splintering the chain that held it closed, tearing the gate from its hinges and sending it scattering inward, tumbling into the drainage system itself. Jason bumped the brake and cranked the wheel, fighting the RV into a sharp right-hand turn. Just ahead, the service road dropped off into a downward angled slope of concrete running along the drainage system.

"Jason—" Samantha braced herself against the dashboard as he leaned into the steer, forcing the RV to swing right.

One tire thudded on the raised edge of the service road as they came around, then skipped over, hanging in mid-air for a fraction of a second. Jason stomped on the gas and finished his steer, and the RV lurched back onto the service road and continued forward, the chain-link fence now on their right. The interior of the vehicle was silent except for the ragged, uneven breathing of its occupants, everyone tensed and bracing until they slowly, hesitantly began to relax, riding the service road along the edge of the Los Angeles River. He leaned and glanced into his rearview mirror as Sarah unbuckled her seat belt and navigated her way along the center aisle.

"Whoever they were, I'm pretty sure we lost them a long time ago," she shouted from the rear of the RV. "Nobody's following us."

"Yeah, well, I wasn't about to take any chances." Jason turned to Samantha. "Who do you think they were?"

"Get back in your seat, Sarah." Samantha twisted around. "Buckle up, okay? We don't know what else to expect." She turned back around to face front. "I have no idea. Gang members, maybe?"

"They all wore the same colors." Jason shrugged. "That seemed like it was about to go bad. Glad we got out of there."

"Hey, I think I've seen movies that were filmed in here." Eli sat up straighter in his seat, looking through the window.

Sarah joined him in huddling close to the glass, looking up and down the ditch on the driver's side of the RV. The drainage system followed along the service road, a broad swath of pale-colored concrete with two slanted walls leading up both sides. Every now and again a thick pillar stood in the center, a bridge spanning the concrete with the vague shapes of cars stranded along each overpass. The path remained clear for the RV, though, and for a silent span of time they continued to drive on in relative peace.

After a while, the RV jostled, the steering wheel shuddering slightly in Jason's tight grip. On the instrument panel, the temperature gauge had inched a bit higher than earlier. Samantha reached over and placed her hand on Jason's leg.

"Hey. That was good driving back there."

"Thanks. Unless that was sarcasm." His eyes darted toward her. "Was that sarcasm?"

"When have I ever been sarcastic?"

"See. Right there. More sarcasm."

Samantha's mouth flickered into a smile. "Not sarcasm. You did well."

"Sorry. I'm coping with stress with bad jokes again." He glanced at the instrument panel again as the RV rattled along the service road. "Engine's getting a bit hot. Feel's like it's running a little rough around the edges. I hope we didn't do too much damage."

"You saved us from those guys," Samantha said, "whatever you did to the RV, I'm sure Dad will forgive you."

"I'm more worried about actually being able to make it out of the city than I am about your father."

Samantha cocked her head, listening to the steady thrum of the engine. "It sounds okay. Is it running that rough?"

"Considering what we just did, no. But we still need to stop for gas, at a minimum."

"Yep. I'll start looking in a sec." Samantha nodded out her window at the sprawling city to their right, separated by a thin layer of chain-link fence. Her shoulders were taut, bunched with tension, her narrowed eyes scanning the nearby buildings.

"You okay?" She called back to the kids. "Elijah? Sarah? How you two doing?"

"This sucks, mom." Eli called back, still holding Kale, who was remaining quiet, pressed against the teen, her tail slung across the floor unmoving.

"I'll take that as a 'I'm alive' then. Sarah, how about you? You alive?"

"Yep." Sarah's reply was curt, shorter than Eli's. "Fine."

"None of us are fine, Sarah."

"Yeah, well... I'm fine."

"Got it." Samantha turned back, exchanging a wide-eyed look with Jason.

Jason kept his attention focused on the fence to his left while Samantha started scrolling through the satnav console, zooming in as far as she could. The intersecting grid roads to their right continued on as they made their way along through the artificial, dry riverbed, the frequent outlines of buildings spaced on either side of the paved roads.

A stretch of highway rose tall to their left, a mass of stalled vehicles glittering in the sun, reflections gleaming off metal and glass. Their low vantage point prevented Jason from seeing the surface of the highway itself, just the tops of the stopped vehicles. Judging by the number of cars, trucks and SUVs that were unmoving, though, the number of dead was almost unthinkable. Samantha leaned over in the same direction, the shadows cast across the service road drawing her gaze.

"Awful," she whispered. "Where's it gonna end?"

"You still leaning away from biological?" Jason spoke quietly.

"If this is biological, I'm the queen of England. No, it's gotta be something else."

"Lovely. Hopefully whatever it is, there's none left in this direction."

Frequent pockets of black birds crouched on various vehicle roofs before flitting out of sight to the ground, scavengers feasting on the dead. A series of sharp brays of crow calls filtered in through the RV, another cluster of descending avians landing on an eighteen-wheeler caught in the throng above them and to the left. A sign rose tall to their right a short distance ahead, its square metallic shape crusted with muddy rust. It advertised exorbitant prices but was close enough to the service road to be accessible.

"I think we should stop at that gas station. Judging by where that sign is, it should be just on the other side of the fence." Samantha pointed. "It's our best bet without crossing over another block or two."

Jason focused on the instrument panel. "Okay, good. The engine is still heating up so I want to peek under the hood as soon as possible."

"Okay. Hopefully they'll have gas so we don't have to go too deep into the city. I've had my fill of L.A. for a while. This," she gestured out the window, "is *much* nicer than all that stuff before."

"Yup." Jason turned toward the twins. "Did you guys hear that? We're going to stop at that gas station up there. Where that sign is."

"Sure, Dad." Sarah nodded, while Eli remained transfixed by the wide, impossibly long concrete riverbed just outside his window.

Jason steered toward the fence, accelerating slightly as he eyed a parallel road just on the other side. A few more scattered vehicles were stranded in various places along the road, but there were wide gaps between them. He ground the RV against the fence as he steered, then once an access road appeared, he cranked the wheel more sharply, pushing the RV through the fence and tearing a section of it apart. Ripping away from the rest, the section of metal dropped down beneath the rolling tires of the RV and they crushed over it, continuing on to the road beyond.

Steering around a collision in the middle of an intersection, Jason accelerated lightly again, the gas station spread out before them, perched just under the sign they'd seen from the service road. It was a relatively small station with a handful of old pumps and a squat, square-shaped building along the left side of its parking lot. Two cars sat at the pumps, both doors opened, their corresponding drivers slumped on the concrete next to their vehicles. Both vehicles were on the interior side of the pumps and Jason drove the RV along the exterior side, finding a section of empty parking lot to ease the RV to a stop.

The crowded city surrounded them on all sides and the moment the RV came to a rest, the tension returned to Samantha's shoulders. She once more pressed tight to her window, staring out into the cavernous clusters of buildings, looking for signs of movement or life, and finding neither. Jason killed the engine, and the inside of the RV became instantly draped in a solemn, contemplative silence as everyone considered the situation and absorbed the reality of what they'd just experienced.

Jason was the first to let out a sigh of relief, leaning back into his seat, stretching his arms behind his back, ligaments snapping as he stretched noisily. His action was the breaking of the dam the others needed, as they all began to move around, unbuckling their seatbelts, stretching and standing to their feet. Wordlessly, Samantha got out of her seat and walked back to the twins, embracing them, tears falling from all of their eyes before she squeezed them tight and let them go, patting their backs and giving them a half-hearted smile.

Jason repeated her action, then Sarah quietly excused herself to go to the bathroom while Elijah sat back down, and Jason and Samantha returned to their seats up front, staring out the windshield and side windows. The streets around them were devoid of life, cars and trucks spread about like discarded toys, bodies splayed next to nearly every one of them. An acrid tang of gasoline smell carried into the cabin, the sunlight reflecting in pools of fuel gathered beneath a few of the vehicles at the pumps.

"The attack swept through so quick it looks like it killed these people while they were pumping gas."

"Maybe that's for the best. Better than knowing it was

coming." Samantha pinched the bridge of her nose and slowly massaged it, eyes squinted shut.

"Y'know, in some way, it's good to know there are people still alive, at least." He turned to his wife. "How do you think they survived?"

"Who knows. The height of the buildings, maybe?" Samantha looked back in the RV to the kitchen area. "Hey, that movement you saw, you said it was an upper floor, right?"

"At those apartments?"

"Yeah."

"Oh yeah, it was right near the top."

Samantha nodded at Jason. "We were able to ride it out on that overpass and it was almost the same height as the upper floors of that apartment building they came out of. I'm betting those who were on the top floors survived the same way." Once again, she turned her attention to the surrounding buildings. "So there could be a *lot* more people alive out there."

"I wonder why we haven't seen them."

"Maybe they ran down to ground level when they saw what was happening and got caught up in it? There was that pile of bodies we had to go around, remember?"

"Ugh. Don't remind me." Jason shuddered. "Or they could just be hiding out. If I saw something like *this* happen, I wouldn't want to get down to ground level anytime soon."

"Same here." Samantha paused. "And once they do start coming down, who knows what we'll be dealing with."

Jason reached out and squeezed her hand. "We'll burn that bridge when we come to it."

"Yeah."

It was Jason's turn to scan their surroundings through the various windows, knuckles white as he gripped the steering wheel. Darkened glass lined the gas station's exterior with no signs of movement within. Buildings rose all around them, most of them only a story or two tall, though rising spires of skyscrapers were visible further in the distance. The world was still and quiet, save for the occasional bray of crows, and the already darkened sky was continuing to grow bleaker as more smoke swirled high overhead.

"Sarah, Eli? Are you up for a little breather? Taking a bit of a break while we check the RV and get some gas?"

"Sure." Eli nodded and unclicked his safety belt, letting it retract into the seat.

Sarah did the same, the two kids standing and stretching their arms and shaking their legs. Jason stood as well, watching them going through their motions.

"The way you're acting it's as if we've been in this thing for eight hours! Get a grip, you monkeys." Jason strode toward them and playfully punched Eli in the shoulder, winking at Sarah.

"Nobody says get a grip anymore, Dad." Sarah rolled her eyes. "You're so old."

"I'm... old?" He turned toward Samantha and gestured toward himself. "Do I look old?"

"Now that you mention it, you are getting a little gray in your hair." Samantha took a few steps forward and placed a hand on his face, studying his hair with a penetrating stare. "It looks— distinguished." She leaned in and gave him a kiss on the cheek.

"Oh, come on!" Eli rolled his eyes and turned away in disgust.

Kale bolted to her feet, ears twitching and tail wagging, excited that her family was up and moving again. Jason paused for a moment to give Kale a quick scratch on her head, then moved further down the RV's center aisle and into the kitchen. He opened one of the built-in cabinets and studied its contents, scowling. There was a single box of crackers, a plastic container of coffee grounds, and a few stacks of paper dishes. He moved things aside, looking deeper into the cabinet, then he crouched and opened a lower cabinet where there were some bottles of water, a few camping supplies and two larger bottles, one of store-bought lemonade, the other of iced tea. He checked a few other cabinets, taking a mental inventory of what he could find there. A bag of potato chips, a half-eaten package of cookies and an untouched box of granola bars were most of what he found. Eventually, he moved to the refrigerator and went through it as well. Standing by the opened door, he sighed before closing it, his foot tapping restlessly on the floor.

"Do we have any other food here anywhere? Anything stashed away?" His eyes fixed on the twins. "Now's not the time to be holding out on me."

Eli sighed and rolled his eyes, then stood and walked back into the bedroom. He returned a moment later with his backpack and fished out a few candy bars that were concealed inside and held them out to his father while looking at his sister. "I only grabbed them so she wouldn't hog them all."

"Uh huh. You can keep them. I just need to know what we've got stocked. What about you?" He turned toward Sarah.

"I'm the good one, remember? I don't stash away any candy I'm not supposed to have."

"Only because *I* took it first!"

"Calm down for a second," Jason continued, "you two can argue once we're back on the road. Let's talk food for a minute."

"We were supposed to hit up a grocery store this evening before we headed out for camping," Samantha interjected.

"Yeah, and plans have unfortunately changed, and not for the better. Let's talk reality for a minute." Elijah and Sarah stopped poking each other as Jason eased into a seat at the small kitchen table. "It's like we were saying before. The supply chain has likely ground to a halt, at least for the city if not for wider areas."

"We need to stock up." Sarah said pointedly.

"Yep. We've only got a few snacks and drinks." Jason gestured toward the cabinets and the mini-fridge. "Given how long things have taken so far in the last, what, mile or three, we have to plan for an extended trip back home."

"Agreed." Samantha walked toward the front of the RV and leaned down a bit to get a better view of the gas station building they were parked near. Still leaning over, she turned her head and stared back over her shoulder. "This looks like a good place to stock up."

"I agree." Jason gave a glance toward the kitchen sink. "I know we've got a water supply built-in, but even that won't last forever, so we need to prioritize water and non-perishable food, or whatever the closest equivalent is in gas station terms."

Samantha considered his response, crossing her arms over her chest, brow furrowed in thought, nodding slowly.

"Any more thoughts about the nature of the attack?" Jason asked. "That might affect what kind of food we can or can't get. I know I keep asking you the same question but you're the best expert of the four of us."

"It's definitely chemical." Samantha nodded slowly. "It has to be. Biological attacks are fatal, but they take too long. People won't just start dropping dead like we saw."

"Makes sense. So it's chemical. Any guesses as to what?"

Samantha looked at the twins, who were watching, wide-eyed. "This isn't anything you two haven't heard before, but you can always put your earbuds in if it bothers you."

"Nope," Sarah shook her head. "I'm good."

"Same," Elijah chimed in.

"Anyway," Samantha continued. "The thing with chemical weapons is, they're so widely varied that it'd be tough to narrow something specific down without testing. Plus, they're *really* sensitive to heat, water, even exposure to oxygen in some cases. But that makes sense given what we saw – they killed *fast* and then... they were gone, probably rendered inert by the environment. But if it was sarin or mustard gas, the bodies would show visible reactions to contact, but all we've seen is that people were universally bleeding from their mouths and noses."

"Their eyes, too." Elijah chimed in quietly.

"Eyes, too?" Samantha asked.

"Yep. Not everyone, but a lot of them."

"That potentially helps." Samantha smiled at him. "Thank you."

"Alright, so we're going to operate off of the assumption that this was a chemical attack." Jason let out a deep breath, leaning back in his seat at the weight of the words. "Jeez, that feels weird to say. If this is true, though, how contaminated do you think the food will be? I'd guess it's out of the air given we're, y'know... still alive, but...."

"We should definitely stay away from anything opened. No fresh fruit or vegetables, nothing without a wrapper or package of some sort. It's unlikely that a chemical agent would have bonded with organic material, but it's possible, so it's best if we err on the side of caution. Canned goods or anything still sealed in plastic are fair game, in my opinion."

"Then I suppose that's what we're looking for."

"I agree with you, by the way," Samantha continued. "We need to stock up with as much as we can, and we need to do it now." She gestured toward the gas station through the windshield of the RV. "Things look relatively untouched at the moment, but if there *are* a number of survivors in the city, that's not going to last long. Once people understand the real scope of what they're dealing with, things will get chaotic and the first thing they'll be after is food and water, especially if the power goes out. Maybe it already has?"

"I don't know," Jason replied. "But either way, we know what we're looking for and what we need to do." Jason turned toward the twins and Kale, giving a sharp whistle and patting his leg. Instantly, the dog darted forward, nails clicking across the hard floor of the RV until she was stuck tight to Jason's leg. "Kale and I will go check out the gas station. We'll see what sorts of supplies they've got and focus our attention on food and water."

"While you're doing that, I'm going to pop the hood and take a look at the engine. See if we can figure out why it's overheating and make sure things are all running okay."

"What about us?" Eli asked, taking a step forward. "What can we do?"

"You're not going to like this." Jason held up a hand. "We need the two of you to stay in the RV. Hold down the fort, station yourselves at the windows and keep a look out."

"Come on," Eli replied. "We want to help."

"You will be helping." Samantha gripped her son's shoulder gently. "You'll be our lookouts. I don't want us to get caught with our pants down like we almost did back at those apartments."

"Fine." Eli sighed.

"You, too, Sarah, okay?"

"Yeah, Mom, I've got it. We'll watch your back."

"Yeah," Eli chimed in. "We'll rotate through the windows and keep an eye on things."

"Good man," Jason smiled. "Honk the horn if you guys see anything. We'll be back in a jiffy." Jason made his way toward the front door of the RV with Kale clinging close to his side, Samantha close behind, the three of them heading out into the unknown.

CHAPTER TWELVE

Jane Simmons
An Undisclosed Location in New England

Jane Simmons is ready for the whirlwind to stop spinning, for the dream to end and to wake up back in her bed. All it took was a single evening to turn her life upside-down. She stands by a window overlooking the backyard, the rear perimeter lined by thick clusters of pine, birch and maple trees. Her location is a mystery even to her, and as the world is consumed by fire and smoke, only one thing is clear. She is no longer the Speaker of the House. She is the President of the United States of America, and the disaster the nation finds itself in is now her problem to deal with.

Jane is no stranger to challenge, though. Her road to Speaker of the House was neither smooth nor easy, her path to ascension mired in conflict and difficult decisions. She's also a mother and a wife and has spent years juggling her priorities accordingly. That's been difficult enough as the Speaker, but as President of the United States, it seems almost impossible.

Throughout the hardest moments of her political journey, her family has stood by her side, stalwart and unwavering, supporting her in everything she does. She recalls a particularly hard conversation with her husband, Charles, before her latest term as Speaker of the House, a frank and solemn discussion about her needs and her wants, a conversation that feels a lifetime away.

Jane's elbow rests along the side frame of the window as she leans toward the glass. Figures stand along the tree line, a cadre of Secret Service who stand to protect her. Not just Secret Service, but active duty military as well, a full platoon of armed operatives who stand at the ready, guarding her from a threat she's unsure of. All she knows is that her nation is under attack, that nearly two dozen cities have already fallen and more are in the process of toppling. The response from the government has been fractured and desperate, their infrastructure already failing, the most powerful nation in the world brought to its knees in a matter of hours. As if that isn't bad enough, the weight of that broken nation rests on her already weary shoulders, her rigid spine bearing the brunt of its heft.

She sighs as her gaze lifts upward, tracking the silhouetted movement of yet another helicopter moving across the sky. It isn't one of the Ospreys that delivered her here, it's another kind entirely, one whose name stands on the tip of her tongue, but she can't quite recall. There is so much she doesn't know about doing the job of president, so much she doesn't understand. In her position as Speaker of the House, she'd been exposed to much of that knowledge, but nothing except actually holding the office could properly prepare her.

During a normal transfer of power, there would be dozens – hundreds – of people available to offer advice, answer questions and ensure things operate properly. Jane has virtually none of those resources, though. The attacks that decimated the nation have equally decimated its political structure. Only a few of the Joint Chiefs of Staff are still alive, and both the President and Vice-President are presumed dead. Staff members have been trying to reach members of the Senate and House for hours, desperate to piece together the fragments of a political hierarchy, but the results have so far not been encouraging. Words and conversations blur in Jane's ears, her static-laced briefing from the Joint Chiefs of Staff tangled with the mix of instructions and directions from the Secret Service, staff members and local military. At the heart of the chaos, though, is Colonel Drake, looming over her, somehow subservient and authoritative both at the same time, gently giving her orders while deferring to her newly minted leadership.

The air smells stale within the strange building that holds her, the faint tang of cleaning supplies accented by the mothball scent of disuse. She stares through the window at the Secret Service and military personnel walking the grounds. Certainly they have their own lives, their own families and their own priorities, yet there they are, standing watch over her as their nation burns all around them. If they're willing to do that, she must be willing to do her part as well, she owes these people nothing less.

"Jane?"

The voice jabs her like a pointed stick, though she does her best to suppress the effect it has on her. It's only her husband, after all.

"Hi, Charles." She turns away from the window and takes a step toward him.

"They're looking for you."

Jane nods, lingering in the middle of the rectangular-shaped room, a quiet sitting room by the looks of it. Its walls are lined with tightly stacked bookshelves, with a reading nook in one corner near a window that would normally be facing the sunrise. It's a comfortable room - or would be if she hadn't been thrust into her new position so suddenly and without warning. Charles steps back into the hallway and Jane follows, the two of them moving down the corridor and into a larger conference room a few strides ahead. The rest of Jane's family waits in the room, her daughters Ramona, Lucille and Pearl joining her husband. Her two dogs lie nearby on a pair of cushioned dog beds she's never seen before. One of their cats slinks across the long conference table in the center of the room, tail twitching, curiously examining its new surroundings. At the rear of the room, Colonel Drake stands with his wrists crossed at the small of his back, a Secret Service agent standing on each side. There are a few other well-dressed men and women inside the conference room, all standing along the far walls, staying out of the middle of things. Softly, Colonel Drake clears his throat, gently tilting his head toward a door at the end of the room.

"I know," Jane says. She takes a few steps forward and swings her arms around her husband's shoulders, pulling him tight. "These people are here to help," she says, pulling back, looking Charles in the eyes as she gestures toward a few of the well-dressed handlers standing around the table, a young woman with waves of blonde hair nodding her acknowledgement.

"You tell them if you need anything." She steps around her husband and looks at her three children. "You, too. Anything at all." Stepping forward, she gives Ramona a hug, her eldest daughter taller than she is. Moving down the line, she does the same with Lucille and finally with Pearl, letting her hand linger on Pearl's glistening cheek. "This is going to be hard for all of us. It's going to get rough, but we will get through it." Jane takes a step toward Colonel Drake as Charles fills the void where she'd been.

"Everything is going to be okay," he says softly, fixing his warm gaze on his trio of daughters. "Your mom is tough. She's going to rise to the occasion and she's going to get things done. Our primary responsibility right now is to let her. She's going to be busy, but you'll still see her, just not as much at first. Understand?"

All three girls nod their heads in unison, saying nothing, their emotions painted on their expressive faces. A fist closes its fingers around Jane's beating heart, a gentle squeeze and application of pressure in her chest.

"I love you all," Jane says, somehow managing to keep her voice steady despite the cascade of emotions that boil inside of her. "See you all soon."

Charles nods and draws his two youngest daughters close as Ramona positions herself on the other side of them, almost as a surrogate mother. Jane looks at her eldest daughter long and hard, gives her the slightest of an affirming nod, then steps out of the conference room ahead of Drake. All at once, a crowd swarms from all directions, appearing as if from nowhere and everywhere.

"President Simmons, follow us." A member of Secret Service is suddenly at her left arm, gripping it lightly, leading her down the hallway.

"We've got reports coming in from Fort Meade, Madame President—" a voice speaks from her left.

"Intel from overseas is trickling in. Secure communications from MI6 have been received by Langley, and—"

"Passengers on a plane over Los Angeles have landed safely at a small airport east of Sacramento and are being debriefed by boots on the ground—"

The crowd surges behind and around her, a cascading chorus of voices singing from all directions. Jane grits her teeth to keep from shouting at them to be quiet and organize their thoughts better, focusing all of her energy on a swift forward stride in the direction they're leading her.

"We've set up a situation room just ahead. The remaining Joint Chiefs of Staff are already dialed in and on the screens, though the connections are struggling to hold—"

"Power has already failed across the west coast, which has spiraled into rolling brown outs throughout the remaining interconnects—"

"—supply chain is at a standstill with the Port of Los Angeles and New York City both devastated by the attacks—"

The Secret Service agent to Jane's left goes before her as another appears from the opposite side, both of them working together to launch a set of double oak doors open. Beyond the doors, a state-of-the-art situation room stands exposed. As Jane steps into the room alongside her cadre of Secret Service and advisors, the heavy, soundproof doors close behind her with a soft hiss.

The room is a fusion of sleek modern design and hardened security, its walls lined with dark, matte panels that absorb light, creating a somber atmosphere. A large, oval table dominates the center, crafted from polished steel and smooth black granite, its surface reflecting the low ambient light from recessed ceiling panels. Embedded in the table are touchscreens and digital control panels, their soft glow flickering momentarily—perhaps a sign of power fluctuations outside—but the flicker quickly stops and everything holds steady.

The far wall is taken up by a massive, wall-length digital display, which flickers ominously as a pair of staffers work on the cables attached to the rear of it. A section of the wall is broken up into four separate panels, each one featuring a static-laced image of the Joint Chiefs of Staff, the same four men Jane had spoken to in the Osprey on her way to the undisclosed location. The rest of the display shows live satellite feeds, intelligence data streams, and an ever-shifting map of the United States, marked with red zones of attack. Smaller, independent screens hover around the room's perimeter, displaying secure communication lines, surveillance footage, and a series of encrypted data flows that occasionally stutter as the network compensates for external interference. Not all the screens have images; some of them sit in dormant, solemn darkness, a sign that many avenues of intelligence and information are offline or struggling to connect.

Despite the flickers of instability in the systems, the room is secure and built for resilience. Reinforced steel beams form a visible grid pattern in the ceiling, hinting at the layered defenses surrounding the undisclosed location. Hidden speakers emit a low hum, keeping communication channels open, while microphones embedded discreetly in the walls and ceiling ensure every word spoken is captured for analysis. When more than a pair of people walk in unison, there's a gentle, almost imperceptible swaying in the floor, a sign of the isolation springs that the room sits upon, all part of the design to keep the place separate from the outside world in every way possible.

Around the table, sleek, high-backed chairs are positioned in perfect symmetry. Each seat has its own small monitor and biometric access panel, ensuring that only authorized personnel can interact with the secure systems. The air smells faintly of sterilized metal and ozone, a byproduct of the backup generators working to keep the technology online amid the chaos outside. A low hum of voices rises as the Joint Chiefs and intelligence officers exchange clipped updates. Despite the modernity of the room, tension hangs in the air—everyone is aware that at any moment, the next wave of attacks could ripple throughout the network and provide yet more chaos that they are meant to wrestle down and control.

In the corner, a discreet vent releases a cool stream of air, keeping the room at a steady temperature despite the surrounding crisis. But the light dimming slightly in one corner of the room is a reminder: even here, beneath layers of concrete and steel, the outside world is creeping in. For a moment, Jane is frozen in place, standing before the vast array of intelligence at her disposal, frozen and momentarily unsure about what to do next.

"Are those lines secure?" They're the first words she speaks inside the situation room, her attention focused on the Joint Chiefs of Staff.

"Point to point ISDN," Colonel Drake replies. "End-to-end

AES 256-bit encryption. We've danced this jig before. This room's as secure as you can get."

Jane stands in the situation room, taking it all in, bracing herself for what is to come.

"Have a seat, Madame President," Colonel Drake advises, gesturing toward one of the high-backed chairs at the head of the table.

Jane moves toward it, spotting a nameplate perched on the oval-shaped table near where she's been instructed to sit. It reads President Simmons, and her eyes fixate on the words for a time, trying to figure out how such a nameplate could have already been manufactured in such a short period of time. Deciding she'd rather not know the answer, she pulls the chair out and settles in, facing the quartet of cordoned off screens where the Joint Chiefs stare back from a distance.

"Before we get started," she says, and the men and women around her positioned to sit instead freeze in mid-motion, hovering almost comically.

"I need to know everything you know, and I need it broken down for me. Talk to me like a child if you have to – just give me everything I need to make decisions, understand?" She rests her elbow on the curve of the table, her eyes fixed intently on the screens featuring the Joint Chiefs.

Everyone around her nods and says "Yes, Madame President" and then finishes sitting.

"Let's start internationally. What do we have from the Five Eyes? Admiral Austin?"

Admiral Austin shifts a bit on the screen, glancing down at some papers on the desk before him.

"We've reached out to the other four members of the Five Eyes, Madame President. Communication has been spotty, but from what we're hearing, America is not alone in this struggle. Our early data suggests we've been hit much harder than some others, but London has been victimized as well. Montreal,

Toronto and Vancouver have all reported a fresh wave of attacks, though our messages to Ottawa have gone unanswered."

"What about Australia and New Zealand?" Jane folds her hands together on the table, pressing them together to keep them from trembling.

"We've been unable to reach New Zealand, though Sydney has confirmed our fears of a wide-scale attack there as well. Early estimates are saying as many as five hundred thousand dead, but we strongly believe those numbers are being underestimated." Admiral Austin lifts the paper from his desk, his fingers tightening, crumpling the gathered sheets.

"Do we have a total death toll? Worldwide, I mean?" Jane draws her eyes from the admiral and scans the room.

"It's been impossible to quantify." Drake sits at the head of the table across from her. "Early estimates put it in the millions, but we hesitate to guess just how many millions."

"Well, stop hesitating. If we're going to make any sort of educated projections about what the future looks like, we need hard facts. If we're going to put together a recovery plan we need to know how many survivors to plan for. Understand?"

"We understand, Madame President and we appreciate your insistence."

"Do we even know what did this?" Jane asks, not even bothering to look at the Joint Chiefs of Staff.

"There's been some very early analysis. We were able to gather samples of some residue off of one of the bodies and there were definitely foreign agents on the skin cells - some sort of chemical agent - though we don't have confirmation of exactly what agent or how it was dispersed."

The conference room door opens, another trio of figures filling the doorway. The man in front stands tall, though disheveled, his hair roughened up, a shirt that should have been neatly pressed untucked and wrinkled. His tie has been removed, his top few buttons are unfastened, a thin, pale, upside-down triangle of skin visible.

"Madame President, if you could come with us."

"I just got here."

Behind President Simmons, two Secret Service agents move forward, closing in on each side, preparing their escort. Jane glances at Colonel Drake and he nods for her to go.

"We'll continue our strategy session," he says. "I'll make sure we have a cohesive briefing for you ASAP."

"Madame President, this is important."

"Everything is important."

"Colonel Drake mentioned a chemical agent," the man whispers in her ear, "we have a little more information on that."

"Can you share it with the rest of the class?" Jane looks around the room.

"Not at this time, Madame President."

Jane very nearly stands to her feet then pauses and sits back down. "No," she speaks forcefully. "If you have pertinent information, you'll disclose it here and now. I need all my best people in the loop on anything about what's going on."

The man flanked by the Secret Service agents flexes his jaw as he stares her down for a few seconds before finally sighing and acquiescing. "Yes, Madame President."

"Who are you, anyway?" Jane asks him as he slides into a chair next to her, placing a folder on the table in front of him.

"My name is Provost. Colonel Drake can vouch for me." Jane glances at Drake, who nods.

"And what department are you with?"

"My position is... fluid."

"I see." Jane points to the folder. "So what do you have for me?"

"The samples that Colonel Drake referenced that we pulled from one of the dead bodies." Provost opens the folder and begins rifling through the papers. "We've been able to confirm that this is a nerve agent. It's very reminiscent of an old project by the Soviet Union that—"

"Wait - are you saying Russia is behind this?" Colonel Drake interrupts.

"That's not what we're saying at all." Provost sighs. "This is exactly why I wanted this information compartmentalized. If you people are going to go off all half-cocked before I can even finish a sentence, then what's the point of any of this?"

"Take it easy, Provost," Jane holds up her hands. "Nobody's doing anything until I give the go-ahead." She looks at the people assembled around the table and on the screens. "Everyone's going to keep quiet until I say otherwise. Now, please, continue. What are you telling me?"

The man slides the folder across the table, and Jane slaps her hand down upon it to stop it from careening off. "The chemical has markers that match ones developed during Russia's FOLIANT program. Computer analysis couldn't even figure out what it was, it's rare enough; we had a lab tech who's been around long enough that he recognized the pattern." The man nods toward the folder that now rests before President Simmons. "FOLIANT was the MOAB for chemical weapons back in the day. It's what led to another, more familiar nerve agent you'll probably have heard of."

Jane flips the folder open and stares at the contents. Along the top and bottom of each sheet of paper, bright red words are stamped in clear, bold text.

TOP SECRET//RSEN//ORCON//SCI

Jane stares at the bold-faced red words, then her eyes drift down the paper. Some details are blocked out with black high-lighter, but others are not, one of the body paragraphs containing a set of words in their own dark, bold print. Following her finger down the sheet, her eyes stop short at a key word that stands out against the rest. She swallows hard, her clenched jaw nearly dropping open.

"This is Novichok?" She can barely bring herself to lift her eyes back toward the man.

"Not exactly."

"What does that mean, 'not exactly'?"

"It means it bears some similarities to it, but it's not Novichok. Russia has used Novichok quite a bit in recent years, mostly to silence state enemies. We've had plenty of opportunities to analyze it and the chemical composition of this is not quite the same."

"But it's built upon a similar foundation? From this... FOLIANT program?"

"We believe so."

"What does Moscow have to say about this?" Jane speaks through clenched teeth.

Colonel Drake replies. "We've been unable to reach them. Sat imagery shows that Moscow was hit by the same attacks we were, though. Or else they have a *lot* of people taking impromptu naps in Red Square."

Jane's brow furrows thick and deep above the narrow slant of her eyes. "That makes no sense."

Provost speaks again. "Our intel capabilities are crippled at the moment, and we're working hard to get things back on their feet." He looks at Drake. "Assuming the military doesn't go off half-cocked, I do think we can make progress on this. But I need time."

Jane Simmons sits quietly for a moment, gaze fixated on the pages in front of her, slowly flipping through them before she stacks them into a neat pile and slides them back into their folder and slides it back over to Provost.

"I need a drink."

A nearby staffer opens a cabinet and removes a bottle of water, cracking the lid open and handing it to Jane. Gratefully, she accepts the offering, then takes several long swallows before even taking a breath.

"Got anything stronger?" She sets the empty bottle on the desk, giving Colonel Drake a wink.

"Not at the moment," Drake replies. "But we—"

"Relax, Colonel. It was a joke." Jane takes a deep breath. "Okay, people. You've been quiet long enough. Opinions?"

Colonel Drake is the first to speak. "Russia is behind this."

Immediately a chorus of voices rises again. Heads spin toward each other, the Joint Chiefs of Staff all begin speaking at once, chaos bubbles, though it isn't quite boiling yet.

"Colonel, you just told me that they've been hit." Jane raises her voice. "How does it make any sense for their capital city to be hit if *they* did it?"

"It could be a feint. They could have staged an attack in Moscow to divert attention from themselves. This is the opening salvo in a war, Madame President, and we cannot afford to—"

"What we cannot afford to do is make any rash judgements, Colonel. What we cannot afford to do is run off half-cocked and make things worse than they already are - and I can tell you, they're already pretty damn bad." A sudden authoritative tone drops the octaves of the words she speaks, the rise in volume quieting the rest of the suddenly vocal room. "I need someone here to track down Roman Kukilov. We need to know the exact nature of Russia's involvement in this, if there is one."

"If there is one?" Admiral Austin shakes his head from the monitor. "I'd say their involvement is more or less confirmed by what Agent Provost just said."

"Admiral, you do realize that the Soviet Union is not Russia, correct? We need a measured response, Admiral. These attacks appear to be worldwide. We've had our disagreements with Russia in the past. Other nations have as well. But what would be their end goal here? Why launch attacks throughout their own nation? We need to become more informed before we start making decisions we cannot walk back."

"Look, Madame President," Admiral Austin replies, inching

closer to the camera. "Things move fast around here and we need to be prepared to move just as fast. I understand you're conflicted. You're new to this, and that's okay. But you cannot tie our hands on this. We need a show of strength, now more than ever, and we need to be prepared to retaliate."

"Admiral Austin!" Jane stands from the head of the conference room table, slamming her hands on its polished surface. "I will not be rushed into decisions that could cost millions more lives than have already been lost without more solid evidence! We are teetering on the edge, and I will *not* condone a course of action that could lead to millions of more lives lost simply because someone thinks that a decades-old Soviet program might have a connection to what's happening here and now!"

"President Simmons, if—"

"No, Admiral, there are no 'ifs' here. My decision has been made. Is that clear?"

The situation room draws silent. People sit around the table in uncomfortable postures, eyes shifting to look anywhere but at either Jane or the Admiral. Nobody speaks for several seconds until, finally, the Admiral sighs, closes his eyes and nods.

"Yes. My apologies, Madame President."

"None necessary." Jane smiles at him. "We're all struggling with this. Now, how about we pick up where we left off?" She focuses her attention on one of the other advisors who sits next to Colonel Drake. "What information do we have on the severity of the attacks? Anything?"

The young advisor clears her throat, then sweeps a shock of hair from her eyes. "Our initial estimates run around thirty million lives lost. Most of those numbers are focused on urban areas, but we're starting to receive reports of deaths spreading throughout smaller communities as well."

"Thirty million dead? In one day?" Jane struggles to process the information.

"The day is still young, Madame President," Colonel Drake

interjects. "Our estimates are that we'll be closer to fifty million by day's end. Perhaps even more – as we talked about earlier, it's hard to get accurate information still."

Jane blows out a breath, unfolding her arms and easing back down into her seat, the tension in the room slowly easing.

"Is there any good news?"

"For what it's worth," Drake replies, "the chemical agent used seems to dissipate almost as quickly as it kills. The satellite imagery we've been able to piece together shows some movement throughout even the larger attack vectors. We know there are survivors out there, but they may be a bit few and far between and they'd be dealing with a figurative hell on earth."

"What about the President? McDouglas, I mean." She shakes her head. "You know what I mean. He was supposed to be at the Los Angeles Convention Center at a political rally. Was he there when the city was attacked?"

"Yes, Madame President, he was. Washington got hit shortly before Los Angeles and the moment word came that it had happened, we tried to move him. But the attack in Los Angeles came quickly, much more quickly than any of us envisioned. The convoys that were headed toward the convention center to rescue him were taken out."

Jane rubs the bridge of her nose with pinched fingers.

"Everyone who was on site at the convention center is presumed dead based on the drone reconnaissance we've been able to perform. We've got more teams ready to move in, but the city is a charnel house, to put it mildly."

"We need to prioritize survivors. I understand the value of confirming the lives lost, but our survivors need us now more than ever. Whatever we need to do to protect those who are still living, you've got my authorization. Whatever documents I need to sign, whatever orders I need to give. Anyone who has survived these initial attacks must be rescued. Enough lives have been lost already."

Heads nod throughout the room, both around the table and on the monitor screens. Even Admiral Austin affirms his agreement readily and eagerly. All at once, the people seated around her begin looking through their files and folders. One of the advisors stands and walks to a nearby wall, lifting the receiver from a wall-mounted phone. Colonel Drake stands and walks to the monitors where the Joint Chiefs of Staff still broadcast and talks to them in hushed tones.

Jane remains sitting at the head of the table and watches it all unfold. She listens as best she can, absorbing the frenetic pace of the people in the room. That relative silence lasts for only a few moments. Just as she's wondering what else she can do, a figure appears beside her, leans down and gently taps her shoulder. Jane turns, lifting her ear slightly to listen to the words whispered in it.

"There are some things you need to look over, Madame President."

CHAPTER THIRTEEN

The Tills Family
Silverpine, Oregon

After leaving the housing development, Doug, Benjamin and Darryl walked through the trees and approached the familiar clearing with the tiny house situated in the center of the sprawling meadows of grass. Benjamin diverted from his course, walked to the tiny house and around its perimeter, checking windows and doors, making sure all was secure.

"Times like this," he said, "you never know who might be wandering around. Like a trio of idjits out for a stroll."

"House of that size, you ever worry someone will just load it on a truck and drive the whole thing away?" Darryl gave a crooked smile, and Doug laughed before he could stop himself.

"Is that supposed to be funny?" Benjamin scowled at Darryl, the crinkles around his eyes betraying his good humor.

"Well, yeah. Kind of."

"Don't quit your day job." Benjamin stalked past him and walked back toward the path leading toward the vineyards.

"Do I... still have a day job?" Darryl turned to Doug as he started to follow Benjamin.

"Of course you do." The words came quickly to Doug, though uncertainty immediately followed.

Every one of their guests had picked up and run earlier without even paying their bill – not a big deal, in the grand scheme, but if what was going on in the world continued unabated, the likelihood of any customers in the near or distant future was scarce, to say the least. Still, there were far more important things to worry about than cash flow.

"As far as I'm concerned," he finally said, pushing his worries aside, "anyone who's here is welcome to stay here for the duration, room and board taken care of. We can ride this thing out and figure out employment after it's all over."

"Over?" Benjamin looked back from a few strides ahead. "I doubt this is just going to be 'over' with any time soon."

"Maybe. Maybe not. All we can do is what we've always done, which is to keep our best people close and take things day by day."

Benjamin chuckled. "If Mrs. Tills heard you say that, she might throw her ledger at you. That woman plans like my mom used to talk. Non-stop and at the top of her lungs." Benjamin walked a few more strides. "No disrespect intended."

"None taken. You're only speaking the truth. Best not let her hear you, though, or else you'll find your house getting towed away by a matchbox car."

After another good-natured scowl from Benjamin, they made their way back toward the vineyards, walking faster than they had initially, hurrying to return to the main building and share the bit of new information they had with Sheila and Brandi. Doug continued to sharpen his gaze, focusing his attention on the trees and grass around them, turning and glancing into the vineyards occasionally as well. There were no signs of human movement, and the world was blanketed in a stark silence, interrupted only occasionally by the shrill call of an unseen bird.

"I pretty much know Benjamin's life story already," Doug finally said, if only to break the silence. "What's yours?" He turned toward Darryl, who kept his eyes facing forward and simply shrugged.

"Not much to tell. Been bouncing around for a while and I like working for you better than most so... yeah."

"You got anyone you're worried about anywhere?"

"I've got family back east. No clue what's going on with them. We don't really keep in touch these days."

"Sorry to hear."

"Eh, don't be."

"What do you mean?"

"My family's who I choose to surround myself with." Darryl shrugged nonchalantly.

"Sorry. Didn't mean to be a downer."

"Nah, not a downer." Darryl smiled. "I'm the luckiest SOB on the planet. I've got everything I need in my van, I work outside in the sun all day, my bosses are awesome people and I have plenty of time to myself. Who could ask for more?"

"Well, when you put it that way...."

"Y'know, in a way," Darryl continued, nodding toward Benjamin, who still strolled a few paces ahead, "he reminds me of my dad, just a bit."

"Benjamin?" Doug chuckled softly. "I can't picture him as anyone's dad."

"My dad was an ornery old cuss, too. Wanted me to come out of the womb with a wrench in my hand. Wanted me to be the same sort of man he was, but didn't have the patience to teach me. Benjamin at least takes the time. Helps me learn what to do. Him and Avery both."

"He's a good man. Don't let him hear you say that, though." Doug whispered.

"You two do realize that I'm old, not deaf, right?" Benjamin groused, still continuing on ahead of the other two.

They walked for a few more silent moments, then Darryl spoke again to Doug. "Avery took off, did he?"

"He did."

"I kind of thought he'd be one to stick around."

"Oh I'm sure he would, but he's got a sick wife at home, plus children and a young grandchild. He's got bigger things to worry about than the vineyard; it's tough to blame him for that."

"I wonder how they're all doing."

"I'm sure they're fine."

"I sure hope so."

Blue sky spread out above them as they continued on toward the main building, only a few scattered white clouds showing, the sun beaming through. Whatever destruction was happening in the world, they saw no sign of it from where they were. Separated from the masses of civilization, a few hundred acres of rural farm-land in a quiet section of the Oregon wilderness. He'd been just as upset as Benjamin when the word had first come about the housing development being built next door, but the trees had been a suitable barricade, and their large and sprawling property was more a home than a business.

The large barn they'd searched a short time before loomed to their right, standing tall and broad against the backdrop of trees. "Batteries still in there?" Benjamin shouted back from a few strides ahead.

"I think so. Good question, though. You want to go check? I can't remember if I saw them in there or not."

Benjamin nodded and stepped off the walking path.

"Hey. You got a flashlight?"

Benjamin shook his head, and Doug slipped his light from his pocket and tossed it through the air. The other man fumbled with it for a moment, but finally wrestled it under control, then returned to approaching the barn, stabbing the light on as he went inside.

"Those batteries for the panel project?" Darryl asked.

"Yeah. The panels are good to go but half a day with power is gonna suck. They'll be a pain to get hooked up, but they'll be worth it." They stood side by side, slowing their pace as they awaited Benjamin's return. "Tell me about this campground you've been staying at. Sheila and I like to go camping from time to time."

"It's a little place, about ten miles south, near the beach. Off the beaten path a little bit. Only reason I even know about it is because one of my buddies runs it. Gives me a good deal on using the facilities and carves out a small space for me near the back. It can get a little tricky during the summer months when it's a lot more popular, but he looks out for me. One of those chosen family I was talking about."

"Fair enough. And you're sure you're not worried about your folks back east?"

"Nah. They'll be fine. They always land on their feet somehow. I'm the one who always seems to stumble."

"You seem to be doing okay for us."

"Appreciate you saying so. Liking the people I work with is important and I like all of you. Haven't been many folks as kind as y'all have been."

Benjamin left the barn, holding a single thumbs-up as he approached, flashlight in hand.

"Even people like Benjamin?"

Darryl shrugged. "Maybe for some folks 'tolerate' is a better word than 'like'."

The two shared a chuckle as Benjamin reached them, handing the flashlight back to Doug, who slipped it back in his pocket.

They continued following the path as it wound along the far edge of the vineyards and bent left. It angled back toward the employee parking lot, and they followed its lead. Doug shaded his eyes and peered toward the front of the building, up on the sloped section of pavement.

"I think I see the side-by-side up there. They must be back from their tour of the property." He lowered his hand.

"You didn't bring your radio? I was wondering why you hadn't just called her." Benjamin glanced back, nodding toward Doug's belt.

"I forgot it on the charger." Doug shook his head. "With everything going on, it just slipped my mind. Hopefully she didn't see it. I always give her a hard time about forgetting hers."

"She's a woman," Benjamin replied sardonically. "I guarantee you she saw it, and I double guarantee you she'll be giving you a hard time about it. Rightfully so."

"Yep, you're probably right."

They crossed from the walking path onto the pavement and Doug picked up his pace, coming up alongside Benjamin, the steeper slope slowing the other man's progress. Doug reached the front door first, then took a moment to let Darryl and Benjamin catch up. Opening the door, the three men filed inside.

"Sheila? You in here?" Doug cupped a hand to his mouth and shouted into the restaurant.

"We're in the restaurant!" A familiar voice carried back to them from deeper inside the building.

Doug angled left past the hosting station and into the cavernous main dining room. As they entered, Sheila and Brandi exited the kitchen, walking directly toward them. Before they even reached each other, the overhead lights flickered, dimming then brightening, then dimming again, more sporadically than they had earlier. There was a rapid lightning flash of brightness, then they settled into darkness. Doug kept one eye on the lights as they came on again, but more faded and muted than they had before. As he started to talk to Sheila, they faded out and then remained dark for the next several seconds. Eventually, after another tentative flicker, they illuminated again.

"They've been doing that." Sheila shook her head. "Making me a bit nervous."

"You and me both. We'll have to get a move-on with the panels. County inspector'll be fit to be tied but oh well."

Brandi held an order pad in her hand, a pencil clenched between the fingers of her other. Her hair had been tugged back into a ponytail and the paper was dotted with scrawls of words. Sheila was standing next to her, arms around herself as she stared up at the lights, then over at the order pad before motioning to it as she spoke to Doug.

"We've been taking inventory of our supplies. I've spent the last few minutes down in the basement and that shipment we just received is pretty big. Brandi's been checking out the kitchens and cold storage, just to take stock of things."

Doug was about to ask a follow-up question when the lights flickered again. There was a warble of light and darkness, as if electricity itself had stopped to take a breath, and then the lights blinked out completely. They tensed, waiting for the light to return, but overhead, the chandeliers remained dark with no sign of easing their way back to life. Within the main dining room, the hum of the kitchen appliances had been a constant and expected backdrop, but as the lights faded, those sounds did as well. A deeper silence settled throughout the restaurant's interior, all the more stark and solemn because of the sudden ceasing of kitchen equipment. Doug lifted his gaze toward the lights, then the television screen, then back toward the kitchen. For a few minutes they all stood there doing the same thing, as if anticipating a return to normalcy. Normalcy did not return, and if anything the silence grew thicker and stronger, a solid wall in contrast to the fluttering of unsettled heartbeats in the Tills' chests.

"You going to want my help flipping the panels on, boss?" Benjamin turned partially toward Doug, his voice low.

"Absolutely." Doug continued staring at the lights. "In fact, I think we all need to head to the panels together. It's been our little pet project, but if the power is going to stay out, we'll all need to know how to deal with it."

"I assume you didn't find anyone hanging around either?" Sheila asked. "The tasting stations were all empty."

"Same for us. The outbuildings were all empty; everyone seems to have moved along." Doug turned away from the group, gesturing back toward them. "Come on, everyone, let's head back outside."

Everyone converged, following Doug as he swiftly made his way toward the front door. "All the refrigerator doors are closed, I hope?" He didn't turn as he spoke, pushing open the door and leading everyone through.

"All closed," Sheila confirmed.

For a moment, Doug hesitated at the front door, his gaze darting to the right, where an adjoining hallway led deeper into the building.

"Go get your radio," Sheila said, tilting her head slightly. "It's on the charger."

Doug cleared his throat, said nothing, then hastily navigated the hallways, dipped into his office, grabbed his radio and his bag of tools that rested on the floor just inside the office door. He hooked the radio on his belt and slung the tool bag over his shoulder before returning to the group, who had already gathered outside.

"Had to get my tools," he said sheepishly, rotating his shoulder to show her the bag.

"Just between you and me," Sheila whispered, leaning close, "I forgot mine, too. I'll let you off the hook if you let me off the hook."

"Deal." Doug smiled and planted a gentle kiss on his wife's

cheek before everyone made their way back toward the parking lot.

"Wish we could all pile in the side-by-side, might be quicker." Sheila walked past the utility vehicle, catching up to Doug.

"Nothing wrong with stretching our legs," Benjamin said. "You kids and your devices are too darn soft these days."

Doug and Sheila both chuckled as they reached the bottom of the employee parking lot and angled right, following the gravel road around the backside of the restaurant.

"Can I ask where we're going?" Brandi's voice was quiet and almost timid, one hand elevated from the back of the group.

Doug spun around, continuing to walk backwards, facing the group. He made the transition with ease, keeping his balance, leading with a tour guide's expertise and commanding voice.

"Have you seen the solar panels out by lot three?"

Brandi nodded. "I did when I first started, but I kind of forgot about them."

"It's been a long process," Doug acknowledged. "How long have we been working on the solar project?" He glanced toward Benjamin.

"A couple years, at least. That's what happens when you don't want to hire contractors. Anyway, things didn't start picking up until we got Darryl involved." Benjamin nodded in his direction. "He pitched in starting about a year ago and we made some decent progress."

Doug turned again so he was facing forward once more, then continued walking.

"We actually finished the final mounting and set up several weeks ago, got things just about ready to go." Doug pointed to an area alongside the gravel road. "Shielded the cable, ran it just under the ground over there. Did that at the same time as we were figuring out some of those drainage problems we were having with the back walkway."

"Wait," Sheila said, drawing back slightly as she strode alongside Doug, putting in some effort to keep up. "Are you saying everything is wired up to the main house circuit already?"

"Surprise." Doug lifted both eyebrows. Sheila's mouth gaped open as they kept walking. "Believe it or not," he continued, "all we were waiting for was the county inspector to come, which they did just this morning. "

"County inspector, my tuckus." Benjamin shook his head. "We did better work than most of those fly-by-night solar companies. Don't need no county inspector."

"Mhm." Doug waggled his eyebrows. "I tried to get you to agree to pay for any fines if we didn't call them, but you weren't game for that."

"Bah." Benjamin waved a hand dismissively.

"So yes, we're set to go for the panels, I'm happy to say." Doug smiled. "That won't help much at night, but we've got all the batteries in the barn and we'll be getting to work on that as soon as possible. Probably good we're so far along, considering...." Doug's smile faltered and he shrugged.

"That's amazing, Doug." Sheila tried to return the smile, but as she reached into her pocket and felt the weight of her phone, her face fell.

"What's wrong?" he asked.

"I'll show you when we get there. Let's just hurry."

Ahead of them, there was another narrow branch to the gravel road, and they followed it, making their way toward lot three, another overflow parking lot that rarely got used. Thick clusters of trees grew on either side of the lot, forming a narrow passage down the road, and they passed beneath the shaded canopy before emerging in the opened square of flattened gravel. It was larger than lot two, and along the rear of the empty section of gravel, a set of massive solar panels were elevated on thick, metal mounts.

All around the panels, the trees had been trimmed back to avoid blocking the light and the panels had been strategically placed so that they wouldn't cast shadows on each other as they caught light from the southern-oriented sun all year long. A few metal posts rose from the gravel at the corners, two of them with rows of powerful lights pointed down toward the lot. Electrical boxes were mounted to the racking system of the panels themselves, a series of them spaced out among the metal support posts that held the panels in place.

Having reached their destination, Doug stopped and looked at his wife. Sheila pulled out her phone, then accessed the photos app with a swipe and tap of her finger. She opened up the first image in her camera roll and held it out so Doug could see it clearly. He stared at the picture, eyes narrowed and eyebrows bunched into thick fists, the others gathering around them.

"What am I looking at?"

"Do you see that smoke in the distance? Over beyond these trees?" Sheila spread her fingers apart, zooming in on the image.

"There it is." Doug leaned in a bit more for a better look.

"That's in the direction of Portland, though we're not sure if it truly is Portland. There are other, smaller sized cities in that direction."

"Well shoot." Doug gestured toward the picture with a nod of his head. "Portland wasn't on the list we heard on the news, or got from the neighbors."

"But it tracks with what the people at the development said." Darryl nodded toward Doug in agreement.

"Indeed, it does."

"You spoke with them after all? Did you talk to Marcus?"

"He'd already left."

"Left?"

"According to the guy we talked to, most of the residents of that neighborhood took off earlier today. Those who weren't already at school or work, anyway. Even the guy we talked to was packing up."

"Where did they go?"

"Believe it or not, some of them went to the cities. I think many of them were looking for family members they were concerned about. Others were heading for the hills, trying to get even further away from civilization than they already are."

"This is all so awful." Sheila shook her head. "Every time I try to think about something else, I just keep thinking about the kids. I think about the kids and I—"

"Wait. The kids?" Brandi leaned forward.

"Our daughter Samantha. She was here with her husband and our grandchildren. They borrowed our RV for a while so they could travel the west coast on a little vacation before flying back to Michigan in a week." The sun-bleached sky shone down on Doug from above.

"Where are they? Do you know?"

"We don't know exactly where they are." Doug reached out and clutched his wife's hand, squeezing gently. "They were in Yosemite National Park yesterday and heading south from there. I just really hope they...." his voice trailed off, his grip around his wife's hand loosening.

Sheila turned toward him as he slowly released her hand. "What is it?"

"Why didn't I think of this before?" His voice was a quiet whisper.

The strap holding his tool bag aloft slowly slid down the slope of his shoulder, then rode the curve and tumbled free, sliding down the length of his arm. The tool bag struck the gravel parking lot with a thud and Doug was off at a sprint, his shoes spraying up rocks in his wake.

"Mr. Tills?" Brandi shouted, taking a hesitant step forward.

"Doug?" Sheila asked, her mouth hanging agape.

"Come on, let's go!" Darryl lunged forward, starting to take off after him.

"No!" Sheila grabbed Darryl's arm. "Please. You two stay here with Benjamin. See if you can help with the solar panels, with whatever he needs. I'll figure out what's going on." Sheila didn't give them time to argue, as she threw herself forward, legs pumping as she took off in Doug's wake.

Sheila wasn't out of shape, but she wasn't exactly a sprinter either. Doug was already crossing into the employee parking lot and banking left, racing up the slope of pavement toward the main building. Sheila continued running, pushing past her gasping of breath. At the edge of the employee lot, her foot struck pavement and caught fast, propelling her forward, the smooth, hard surface giving her more traction than the loose gravel.

The incline shot more pain through her legs and into her back, but she buckled down and ran on, leaning into the slope as she passed the camper van and angled up and around toward the main entrance. Audibly gasping for breath, she slowed as she passed the side-by-side, nearing the front doors, which Doug had left unlocked. Sucking in a breath, Sheila threw the doors open and plunged inside, stumbling toward the hosting station. Somewhere, deeper into the building, there was a crashing thud of noise, a muffled curse and the slam of what sounded like a cabinet door.

It all came from the right of the entryway, from the administrative offices of the vineyard. Still catching her breath, Sheila passed into the right-side hallway, navigated the corridor and soon arrived at the open door of Doug's office. Her husband knelt on the floor, the bottom drawer of a desk open, several items pulled out and tossed aside, a stack of papers and boxes scattered around him. As she came into the office, trying to speak through the hitching choke in her throat, Doug let out a small cry of victory. Reaching into the bottom drawer, he wrestled out a small, hand-held device and shot to his feet, slumping backwards into the office chair alongside his desk.

"Doug— what— what the devil are you after?" Sheila struggled to say.

"I found it. Sheila, I found it!" He held the item up victoriously.

Sheila step forward, her narrowed eyes staring at the device, trying to figure out exactly what Doug had found. Doug pressed a power button and a small light winked on, a square shaped screen illuminating.

"Wait. Is that the tracker?"

Doug nodded and casually waved at her to come closer, lifting the device up as he scrutinized the screen.

"Does it work? Will it still see the transponder in the RV with the cell networks down?"

Doug was still struggling to catch his own breath. "It uses pay-per-view satellites. It should work."

He held the device up as the screen continued to boot. A tiny status bar illuminated near the top of the screen, three words etched in letters so tiny that Sheila could barely see them.

Waiting for signal...

"Come on." Doug stood from the chair, pushing it back aggressively, sending it thudding against the wall behind him.

He waved the device throughout the office as he crossed the floor, walking toward one of the far windows.

"Come on!" The same three words read on the top of the screen, the LCD showing a blurred image with no clear picture of the RV's location.

"Let's go outside." Doug jerked his head back and forth in frustration and stalked from the office, fingers clenched tight around the small, cellphone sized device.

Sheila trailed behind him, following him step-by-step, her unsteady breath finally settling into some semblance of a rhythm. The aching burn in her chest faded, her body slowly recovering. *I am too old for four-hundred-meter sprints.*

They returned to the entryway of the building, then back out the front door and into the warm sun outside. Doug stopped and held the device high, staring up at it, his head shaking as it continued to wait for a signal. "Are the satellites down, too?" Sheila continued following him as they walked back down through the parking lots.

"No way. Whatever attacks these are, it shouldn't affect satellite communications. I can understand cell service. There's limited bandwidth and millions of people trying to funnel through a small pipe. The cell network is notoriously fragile and prone to collapse under strain. Don't get me started on what happens once the generators powering the cell towers run out of fuel." They took another several strides. "Satellite communications skip all that nonsense."

"So why isn't it working?"

"Could be they're under a bridge, a thick forest or... somewhere else that's blocking the signal."

They walked through the employee parking lot and back to the gravel road, Doug still staring at the screen as he adjusted the position of the device. The words on the screen flickered for a moment, vanishing for a split second before fading back into view. Sheila and Doug continued along the gravel road, heading back in the direction of lot three, Doug still clutching tight to the receiver. Shoes crunching on gravel, they continued onward, following the road as it wound around the perimeter of the vineyards to their left. They focused intently on the device and its screen, shutting out the pleasant rustling of vines, the warming heat of the sun and the appealing scent of ripened grapes.

As they neared the road leading to lot three, Doug stopped short, fingers closing more tightly around the handle of the receiver. "Wait." He held up a hand, whispering. "Look!"

Sheila peered over his shoulder, eyeing the screen, the words gone from view, a blurred image slowly coalescing into clarity. As they both stared at the image crystalizing, their chests filled with a dull, burning ache of dread. Coastal California came into view first at a high altitude, looking down from some far-off distance above. Slowly, the signal triangulated, then refocused, the imaginary camera zooming in, drawing them down, closer and closer to the coast.

"Oh no." Sheila pressed a hand to her chest, her low voice little more than a croak of noise. "Oh, please, no."

As the satellite imagery continued to zoom and clarify, it zeroed its focus, moving down, down, down, directly into the heart of the city of Los Angeles.

CHAPTER FOURTEEN

The O'Brian Family
Los Angeles, California

Jason crossed the gas station parking lot, leaving the twins inside the RV while Samantha checked the condition of the vehicle to see if she could locate any problems that could be easily remedied. Kale's claws clicked on the pavement as the German Shepherd tagged alongside him, her ears perked into rigid triangles. There was no tail wagging, just a slight backward droop, her nose twitching and head sweeping side-to-side.

Kale had, as a pup, been in a program that trained dogs for military use. Unfortunately, Kale hadn't made the cut, and after Jason and Samantha had learned of her from their friends, they'd gone to see her after promising each other that there would be no way come hell or high water that they'd come home with her. They'd left an hour after arriving, Kale in Samantha's arms with leash in hand, vet visit scheduled and six months' worth of food hoisted over Jason's shoulder. Elijah and Sarah had been ecstatic, and Kale had taken to her training remarkably well. Neither Jason nor Samantha could quite figure out why she hadn't made that final cut, as she took to her training under Samantha with gusto.

As Jason approached the gas station he slowed and Kale was fully at attention, ready to leap into action, which steadied his stride and added a level of comfort to his anticipation. The building ahead and to his right was a block of gray stone, its textured exterior showing signs of a few decades of smog and Los Angeles wear and tear. There were off-color sections where graffiti had been scrawled, then painted over with a color that didn't quite match and around the upper border of the building, dull, rust-colored brickwork ran the perimeter, gapping at the corners astride a section of thicker, reinforced concrete slabs. Tall, wall-high windows framed the glassed-in entrance, sunlight reflecting from the smooth surface, gleaming and preventing Jason from seeing whatever was inside.

A motorcycle was parked away from the two other cars, slotted into a narrow space beside a green dumpster on the other end of the building. Kale moved in front of Jason, lowering her head and sniffing eagerly at the walkway and the base of the entrance. Her tail didn't wag and her ears perked as she gave the front door a once-over, preventing Jason from entering until she'd finished. A low growl curdled in her throat, and she backed off a few steps, dark eyes staring at the door. Jason gently pushed her to the side with a sweep of his right leg, clearing the way to the tall windows flanking the entrance. He cupped his hands, pressing the sides to the glass as he peered through the shade, squinting to get a better view.

There was nobody visible at eye level. While the main section of the station wasn't huge, it was large enough to accommodate a number of free-standing store aisles, upward shelf fixtures separating the various sections. There were eight aisles total, four toward the right and four more toward the left and along the back wall, stacks of drink coolers ran the length of the small store. A leg extended beyond one of the aisles, visible from the knee down, its pant leg hiked slightly to reveal the snakeskin texture of a cowboy boot, toes pointed straight toward the ceiling. Shifting left, then right, Jason did his best to peer throughout the store but picked up no movement or sign of anyone living.

A counter along the far left held two separate cash registers and a plexiglass wall separating them from the main section of the store, a wall behind it littered with cartons of cigarettes, tins of chewing tobacco and rows of scratch-off lottery tickets. Toward the back corner of the store, a rectangular opening was built into the wall to the right of the drink coolers, the word *RESTROOMS* stenciled in the brickwork above the doorway. The leg with the snakeskin boot remained the only sign of any sort of humanity within the small store and, satisfied there wasn't anyone or anything lying in wait, Jason eased the door open, letting Kale nose her way in first, then followed behind.

The interior of the station appeared completely normal. Everything was in its place, and the air carried the lingering, fragrant smell of cleaning products and seared meat, a strange, tangled combination. To the right of the counter, which had been blocked from view by a shelf unit, was a free-standing roller grill. A rectangular box with metal exterior held two rows of darkened hot dogs on a series of rollers, a glass canopy draped over them. The hot dogs rested still, not moving, and Jason lifted his eyes toward the ceiling, spotting the darkened lights for the first time.

"Guess the power went out, huh girl?" Jason rubbed Kale's head as he walked toward the cash register and stepped around the back of it, drawing back with a sharp gasp and a reflexive turn of his head.

A dead body was wedged in the narrow space between the register counter and the wall of cigarettes behind it. The overweight man had toppled sideways, bent over his left shoulder, his broad torso filling almost the entire gap along the floor. His face was pale and glistened with sweat, his eyes closed, a thick tongue pushed out from a mouth covered in blood, several flies crawling over his exposed skin. A dark, too-tight polo shirt was stretched over his broad chest and broader belly, the logo of the gas they sold outside stitched on its fabric. Kale growled as she peered around the counter, sniffing the floor and the base of the shelves.

"Go on, girl," Jason said, ushering her away. "Check the rest of the store. Go on, find. Find!"

Kale reluctantly backed away, then continued sniffing, her claws clicking the hard tile as she moved toward the shelves. Searching the wall, Jason located a set of light switches, and slowly approached, then reached out and hit them upward. No lights came on anywhere visible, and the station remained stark and silent.

"Silent as a tomb," Jason whispered to himself, a shivered streak of goose flesh racing down the length of his spine.

On the other side of the wall beyond the dead cashier, a set of swinging doors were marked with the words Employees Only. Jason stepped over the dead man in a long, somewhat off-balance stride, then shouldered through the double doors and looked out into a back room. Several shelves of miscellaneous supplies like printer paper, batteries, a mop bucket and other things were within view, but the back room was devoid of anyone, either living or dead. Satisfied with the cursory check, Jason let the doors swing closed, then cautiously stepped over the cashier's corpse once more.

Moving back out from around the counter, he walked toward the shelf units ahead. Boxes, cans, and packages of food filled each section of shelving, the store appearing to be fully stocked. Passing by the first aisle to his right, Jason moved to the second, where Kale continued sniffing the floor, ears on alert. She kept her distance from the second dead body, a skinny man wearing a polo shirt and blue jeans, sprawled near a four-foot section of beef jerky, plastic-sealed packages dangling on a few dozen pegs.

His neck was bent back, his head upturned, a wide-brimmed

cowboy hat resting on the floor next to his narrow face. The top of his head was dusted in a thin layer of tussled hair, and a neatly trimmed western-style mustache was covered in dried blood, as was his mouth, and a good section of the floor around his head. He was the owner of the snakeskin boot that Jason had seen from the front door, and a package of beef jerky rested on the floor near his outstretched hand. Kale sniffed the shelving unit, inching her way near the body, interested, but cautious.

"Leave it." Jason's voice was quiet, but firm and Kale obediently backed away from the corpse, then followed Jason around the shelving unit to the next aisle.

There was a third dead body in the next aisle, a woman, lying face down, her neatly curled perm of gray hair covering her entire head. She wore an off-white sweater and slacks, a well put-together older woman who had died while reaching for a package of chocolate covered snack cakes. Jason stayed there for a moment, looking up and down the aisle, allowing Kale to spend some time sniffing, though remembering her master's earlier order, she kept her distance from the dead body. Jason didn't linger in the aisle; he took stock of what he saw on the shelves, then moved to the last aisle, a gap between the final free-standing shelf units and the wall of drink coolers to his left.

He pressed a palm to the glass door of one of the coolers, feeling for any sign of cold air recirculating from inside. The surface of the glass was tepid against his skin, and he cracked the door open, no rush of cold air coming out. Closing the cooler, he strode down the aisle carefully, listening for any signs of anyone else who might be inside. He'd seen nobody and he'd heard no movement anywhere, but he proceeded with caution all the same until he reached the entrance to the restrooms. Walking into the broad alcove, he opened the men's room first and took a quick glance inside. It was a typical gas station men's room, the mirror smudged, the white sink discolored with age. It smelled mostly of an over-abundance of bleach, though the stale stink of sewage was just beneath the artificially sterile surface.

Even Kale remained outside as he walked across the stained tile, took only the briefest, most casual look at the single urinal, then opened the door to the stall. After confirming it was empty, he closed the stall door and retreated quickly, moving back out into the alcove. He did a similar check of the women's room, confirming that it, too, was empty, and also discovering it was quite a bit cleaner and better-smelling than the men's. Both doors closed, he walked toward a third door at the rear of the alcove and eased it open. A small, dark room extended before him, lined with shelves containing various boxes of cleaning supplies and other items. Once he confirmed that the area was too small to be hiding any lurking strangers, Jason closed the door and headed back out into the main store.

Cases of soda and bottled water were stacked along the front-facing windows as he walked by on his way to the front door, flanking a tall rack of local maps and tourist guides of the Los Angeles area. Most of the tourist guides focused on various films or celebrity sightings and a second rack stood nearby with cellphone chargers, batteries, headphones and earpieces. Pushing the door open, he stepped back outside and waited for Kale to exit. She obediently followed him, and he shut the door behind him. For a long moment, he stood just outside, staring at the tall buildings that surrounded the gas station. They were a few blocks away from the downtown spires of skyscrapers that stretched endlessly toward the heavens, but there were still plenty of six, eight, or ten-story buildings within eyesight and he scanned the upper levels, looking for signs of movement.

Kale had already started walking back to the RV and Jason picked up his pace, approaching the large vehicle. Samantha had her back to them, the small hood lifted open at the front of the vehicle. She stood on her tiptoes, reaching into the engine compartment. A side door was opened on the RV and a toolbox rested on the pavement next to her ankles.

"Gas station's clear." Jason announced. "Power's out, though. That could make getting gas a little tricky."

Samantha shook her head. "Nothing can be easy, can it?"

"I suppose not. What do you have in there?"

"Honestly? It doesn't look terrible." She lowered back onto her heels and wiped her grease-covered palms on a rag draped over her shoulder. "A few things got knocked around a little and the radiator fluid seems unusually low. I'm wondering if there's a small leak somewhere or if one of the hoses got knocked loose. It's going to be impossible to track it down without taking some more stuff apart, though."

"Did you check the underside?" Jason stepped back and leaned a bit, looking toward the base of the RV, shivering involuntarily as he spotted the red stains.

"I didn't. One of us should." She gestured toward a section of the parking lot where a free-standing air compressor stood alongside a loop of hose. "They have a self-service car wash around the corner. If we had power we could do our best to wash the underside, but...." Kale sat alongside them both and Samantha leaned over, giving her a quick scratch on the head. Kale's tail swept over the cracked pavement of the parking lot. "How was it in there?"

"There were a few dead bodies inside. Nothing horrible. I'm thinking we should grab as much stuff as we can from in there. It might take several trips if one of us does it alone."

"What are you thinking?"

"I'm thinking you and the kids go inside, grab as much stuff as you possibly can. It's a gold mine in there, to be honest with you. I can check the belt and the fluids of the RV, make sure there aren't any other issues anywhere, then maybe we can figure out how to get some gas."

"How bad is it in there?"

"Better than anything they've seen or heard so far, trust me.

Plus, we can't shield them forever. I'd appreciate some shielding, though," Jason glanced at the nose of the RV. "I don't want to think about crawling under there."

Samantha nodded, though she pinched her lower lip between her teeth, looking back at the windshield, Sarah sitting inside and watching out the side windows.

"I'd like to spend half an hour here. No more, if at all possible." He gestured toward the taller buildings clustered around them. "If there were people in the upper levels of some of these apartments, they could still be alive and if they see us moving around down here, they know it's safe. If they start venturing out, things could get complicated fast."

"Half an hour. Got it." She patted the side of the RV with a soft shake of her head. "Good luck with this thing. They build them for our comfort, not for ease of maintenance."

"Pretty sure I can figure it out." Jason crouched next to the tool kit on the ground and opened it up, searching through it. "Make sure to grab a couple containers of radiator fluid from in there. Worst case, I can just top it up even if I can't find the leak."

"Will do. Oh, and put that back when you're done, okay? There's an open compartment on the driver's side. That's where it goes."

"Your dad really does think of everything, doesn't he?"

Samantha offered a wry smile and walked toward the door of the RV, Kale choosing to follow her instead of staying with Jason. She opened the front door and stepped up into the RV, leaving Jason staring into the opened hood in the front.

"Sarah? Eli? Everything looking okay?"

Eli drew back from the window he'd been peering out of, nodding his head. Sarah made her way forward from the rear of the vehicle, her chin bobbing in a similar motion.

"We haven't seen anyone. None of those guys with the jackets and nobody else either." Eli eased himself up from his chair.

Kale passed Samantha and eagerly approached Eli, who

crouched and scratched both sides of the dog's head with clawed fingers.

"Good girl. Who's my good girl?"

Kale pushed her head into Eli's chest, tail wagging, nearly knocking him over as Samantha addressed the twins. "We've got a job to do."

"A job?" Sarah's voice was a mixture of apprehension and eagerness. "What kind of job?"

"Dad took a walk around inside the gas station. There's nobody in there, but there's plenty of food and drinks. We need to grab whatever bags or boxes we have, empty them out, then go into the gas station and stock up."

"Gas station food?" Sarah's nose bunched up.

"Food is food. We need to focus on high calorie items, preferably with some good protein. Sugar and salt next, but water should be first and foremost on the list."

Sarah had already taken a few steps back toward the rear of the RV and was opening one of the built-in storage doors. She tugged out a backpack, rested it on the floor and unzipped it, starting to remove a few of the items she had inside. Eli followed her and opened a different door, pulling out an old, ratty-looking gym bag and doing the same. Samantha threaded her way between them and walked to the far back of the RV, then opened another storage bin and found the rolling suitcase and the large backpack that she and Jason had brought. They took a few moments to remove the items inside their bags, then dragged and carried them back toward the front of the RV. Kale whined softly, staring at them.

"You're coming, too," Samantha replied, patting her leg.

Kale's tail thrashed and she skittered along after them, everyone filing out of the RV, arms loaded with the empty bags. Jason was half-submerged in the engine, grunting softly as metal tools clattered against something Samantha could not see.

"We'll be back."

"Half an hour," Jason replied, his voice muffled by the engine compartment. "No longer. And be sure to watch the buildings every time you come out. Don't let me get snuck up on."

"Yes, sir," Samantha replied half-jokingly, but Jason stayed where he was, his head and shoulders swallowed by the darkness around the RV's engine.

"Just a warning," Samantha advised, glancing over her shoulder at the twins. "Dad says there are three dead bodies inside. You need to be prepared for that."

"Dead bodies?" Sarah swallowed hard.

"Yes. Though they should be in better shape than the ones we've seen along the road so far."

"That makes me feel *so* much better," Eli muttered, a scrunched look of disgust shaping his features.

"Just focus on your jobs. You know what we need to get – ignore everything else and focus on your task. Think you can handle that?"

The twins both nodded.

"Good; I know you can. Let's get this done." Samantha returned to the front door and eased it open, shouldering the empty backpack as she dragged the rolling suitcase in her other hand.

The twins filed past her and inside the gas station, each of them carrying their own empty bags as well. Samantha took in their surroundings, looking over the interior of the building. She spotted the double doors marked Employees Only beyond the cash register counter, then fixated on the wall of coolers across the way and the aisles to the left and to the right.

"Look for some jerky first," she said, eyeing Eli. "Beef, pork, turkey. It's dried meat, well-preserved and chock-full of protein. It's also held in sealed bags which will keep it for a long time, and it doesn't take up much room. It's almost a perfect to-go food, except that it tends to be high in salt."

Eli stepped aside and walked the length of the first aisle,

checking the contents of the shelf units. Kale followed on Eli's heels, eagerly guarding her young master as Samantha gestured for Sarah to join her. They approached the register counter, then circled around the end of the shelves and glanced down the next aisle.

"Dead body," Samantha warned. Lifting her head slightly, she called out to Eli. "There's a body here," she said, pointing to where a dead cowboy lay on his back. "But he's in front of the jerky."

"Oh," Eli shook his head. "Of course."

He braced himself at the opposite end, drew in a breath, exhaled, then circled around and advanced, his gaze darting away from the corpse.

"I see some nuts there, too," Samantha instructed, pointing toward another section of shelves. "Focus on the jerky first but grab as many nuts as you can. Check that shelf, too. Looks like a mix of protein bars, meal replacement shakes and granola bars. We're looking for food that's sealed, a good balance of protein, fat and sugar, and high calorie if possible."

"I'm on it!" Eli was already unzipping his gym bag and easing his way around the dead cowboy, taking a cautious step over the upturned toe of a snakeskin boot.

"What are we looking for?" Sarah asked.

"Let's check this aisle. Look for water first, then things like juice, lemonade, iced tea, sports drinks – anything that doesn't need to be refrigerated." They worked their way to the next aisle and immediately found what they were looking for. "Remember: water first, then everything else after." Samantha and Sarah worked together, filing through the drinks on the shelf, picking out medium-sized bottles which Samantha began loading into the rolling suitcase.

While the girls worked on drinks, Elijah filled his gym bag with virtually the entire shelf of jerky, then moved on to salted nuts and a few boxes of protein bars, energy bars and even a few meal replacement shakes. The bag was heavy, though bearable, and he wrestled through the store with it on his shoulder, making his way toward the back side of the aisle he'd been working in.

"How's it coming?" Samantha stood and peered over the shelf.

Her rolling suitcase was heavy with bottles of juice and water, though still easily rolled. Sarah had placed a few more bottles at the bottom of her backpack, but had then graduated to a few cannisters of rolled oats and some canned fruits and vegetables, though the selection in the gas station was somewhat meager. Samantha had moved on to a section of soup and canned stew, continuing to load up the rolling suitcase with the heavy items.

"Doing okay. What about dried fruits? They have cranberries, raisins, even some dried mango and pineapple over here."

"Grab it all, or as much as you can carry. They'll last a long time and have a lot of calories."

Eli nodded and crouched behind the shelving unit, starting to pull packages off of pegs.

"Watch out for her," Samantha warned, nodding toward the dead woman with the gray-haired perm, lying face down on the floor.

Sarah had already seen her, nodding solemnly, then stepped over her to join her mother in looking through the soups and stews. They worked together, focusing their attention on the selections with plenty of protein-rich meat. A few moments later Eli stood again, grunting as he hoisted his gym bag.

"This is getting sorta heavy."

"Okay, good, you're doing great. Can you run into that employees only room behind the counter? See if they've got any leftover stock out there that looks useful? I need to grab some coolant still."

"Sure." Eli labored a bit as he walked down the aisle, the gym bag sagging along his narrow shoulder.

He reached the end of the aisle, then circled around the counter with Kale at his heels. Stopping short, he drew back with a little croak, staring down at the floor. "Another body." His voice came through clenched teeth, his bunched eyebrows forcing both eyes into a tight squint.

"Sorry, kiddo."

"It's okay." He shook it off and swallowed hard, then made an exaggerated step forward as he stepped over the larger-sized corpse.

Samantha kept her eyes on him as he disappeared through the double doors, both of them thumping closed in his wake. Kale stood by the end of the counter, whining softly as her tail drooped.

"He'll be okay," Samantha promised.

She focused her attention back on Sarah, moving alongside her to finish checking the last few shelves. To her surprise, some small canned hams were wedged on the counter alongside the stews and she immediately grabbed them and stashed them away in her suitcase.

"Mom!" Eli's voice came from the back room, a hint of excitement in it.

"Stay here, okay? Let me see what he needs." Samantha left her rolling suitcase where it was next to Sarah, then called Kale over.

The dog trotted toward her and Samantha gave her a stay and guard order, gesturing toward Sarah. Kale obeyed eagerly, perching herself near Sarah, ears on alert. Samantha exited the aisle and veered left, making her way toward the cash register counter. Moving quickly, she stepped over the corpse of an over-weight man wedged behind the counter and was already pushing through the double doors when Eli shouted her name again. He stood near the back of the storage room where a chest freezer was wedged against a far wall, partially hidden from view from the doorway.

"What is it, bud?"

Eli lifted the lid of the freezer, a rush of cooled air sweeping up from inside, dropping the temperature surrounding the box-shaped appliance.

"There's still some ice in here. We've got that cooler still out in the RV, right? Would it make sense to get this ice out and put it in our cooler?"

Samantha stood next to him, placing a firm grip on his shoulder as she looked into the freezer herself. There were scattered tubs of ice cream and popsicles inside, thick clusters of ice layering the interior of the freezer walls.

"That's a great idea, Eli." She nodded her approval, then jerked her head toward another small cooler that stood next to the freezer as well, and he popped the top.

There wasn't much in the cooler, just a couple quarts of milk, some containers of yogurt and some blocks of cheese, but when he opened the door, more cooled air wafted out.

"The stuff in here is still pretty cold, too." She touched the plastic exterior of a milk quart with her fingers, then immediately slammed the cooler shut again. "Go out in the main store and hang out with your sister and Kale, okay? Help her pack up some more cans of pasta and soup. I'm going to run out to the RV and grab the cooler, I'll be right back."

"Okay."

Samantha darted out of the back room and Eli followed, the two of them lunging across the large corpse on the floor ahead of them. Together, they swept around the counter, with Eli diverting to go join his sister and the dog while Samantha headed for the front door.

"I'm going to grab the cooler, Sarah. Eli is here with you, I'll be right back!"

"I don't need a babysitter, Mom! And anyway, technically I was born first, I should be babysitting him!"

Samantha chuckled and rolled her eyes as she headed for the front of the store, grabbing four containers of coolant before pushing the front door open and walking out into the parking lot.

She stopped and stared at Jason, who was standing over the open engine bay.

"You doing good?"

"Yep!" Jason gave her a thumbs up. "One of the radiator hoses nearly came off. Had to wrestle the stupid hose clamp off, but thankfully it's the one near the top, so we didn't lose much radiator fluid and I've just about got it back on."

"You need a hand?"

"Not unless you've got a pair of little baby hands somewhere. I swear, none of these things are designed for adults to actually work on. I can barely jam my hands in between anything in there."

"No kidding. Let me know if you need anything." Samantha dropped the four bottles of radiator fluid on the ground near the RV. "You need more than this?"

"Heavens no. One's plenty, thank you. How's the food collection going?"

"Not bad, actually. This place is more like a supermarket than a stop n' rob. Oh, and Eli found a small stockpile of ice, so I'm grabbing the cooler."

"They doing okay in there with the bodies?"

"Surprisingly well. I'm not sure if that's a good thing or a bad thing." Samantha took the steps up into the RV. "Anything else broken that you can see?"

"I'll check as soon as I get this radiator finished!" Jason called to her, then took a step back to grab one of the containers of radiator fluid.

She found the cooler in the kitchen where they'd left it and picked it up by its handles, moving it toward the aisle nearby. Pausing for a moment, she opened the built-in mini-fridge and held her hand inside, testing the interior temperature. The battery backup was still powering the chiller, and she closed the door, then carried the cooler through the RV and back outside, navigating the steps carefully as she descended. Jason was pouring coolant into the radiator, looking around as he did so, eying the tops of the buildings that surrounded them.

"Keep your eyes open, okay?" Jason called out to Samantha as she went by. "We've already blown past that half hour limit."

"I know," Samantha replied. "But we've gotta do what we've gotta do, I suppose."

"I'll wrap up as soon as I can."

The two of them separated and Jason finished filling the radiator before glancing back, watching Samantha head back into the station. Once she was out of sight, Jason leaned in to once again inspect the gas-powered V10 engine. He scanned the serpentine belt, checking for any signs of wear, and ran his hand along the hoses, feeling for cracks or softness. The alternator, power steering pump, and water pump appeared intact despite the rough ride through the city. He glanced at the fluid levels—engine oil, coolant, and transmission fluid—and everything was within normal ranges.

With overheating being the only real issue the engine had faced, Jason grabbed a short breaker bar and a set of sockets, testing a few of them against the lug nuts on the front driver's side tire before finding the one that would fit. He tightened them down on each tire, discovering along the way that a few of them were nearly loose enough to spin freely, no doubt a side effect of the 'off-roading' they'd been forced to do in the RV. After finishing up, he packed up the tools and was about to head back to the gas station when he knelt down, double-checking the underside of the radiator. After watching for a few seconds, he saw a drip of something fall to the ground, then another followed a few seconds later, then again and again. Reaching out, he caught one of the drops on his hand and drew it near his nose, inhaling.

"Son of a…" Jason groaned, then laid down on the ground, looking up at the underside of the radiator. "Yep. Figures."

He stood, wiping his hand on his pants leg before he headed to the gas station and entered, finding his family gathered together near the front door, the cooler and their array of bags all piled around it as they did a quick inventory of the supplies they'd gathered.

"We did good, Dad," Eli announced happily.

"You sure did, buddy. Nice work." Jason gave both Eli and Sarah approving nods, then turned his eyes toward Samantha. "Looks like I'm not as good as I thought. There's a leak from the underside of the radiator. Pinhole, but if we don't patch it, we'll be dry again in a day or less."

"You think they've got something here to fix it?" Samantha looked around the store.

"When I was in here before, I checked a storage closet by the bathrooms. There was definitely some car stuff in there, more than was on the shelves." Jason separated from them and walked down the length of the aisle, then cut left and entered the alcove where he'd been earlier.

He removed the flashlight from his pocket that he still carried from checking the engine and shone it into the dimly lit storage room, walking his beam of light across the shelves. There were several bottles of motor oil, and a few more containers of anti-freeze, and he took a few of the 10W-30 quarts of oil, stacking them on the floor near the door. Probing the darkness with the light, he located a small pegboard within the storage room, where a few packages of JB-Weld were hanging. Jason grabbed all of them along with a couple of quarts of oil and backed out of the storage room, calling to Samantha and the twins who were coming back inside from the RV.

"Hey, somebody grab the rest of this oil. If we get a chance down the road, it'd be good to change that out."

Eli and Sarah each grabbed a couple of quarts of oil and they all made their way outside and back to the RV. "If you can get some light underneath the front there for me," he said, pointing toward the nose of the RV, "I should be able to get this done pretty quickly."

Samantha held the flashlight while Jason went into the RV and grabbed a paper plate, dishcloth and a plastic butter knife from one of the cabinets, then came back out. Putting the plate on the ground, he opened both tubes of JB Weld, squeezed equal parts from each tube onto the plate, then used the plastic knife to mix them together into a single compound. Using a bottle of water, he moistened the dishcloth, then got down on his side near the front of the RV.

"I'm going to clean around the leak first, try and get as much of the gunk off as possible. If you could keep the light pointed there, then hand me that paper plate and plastic knife when I ask you for it, that would be great."

"On it."

Samantha did as Jason asked, positioning herself out of his way and pointing a narrow beam of light underneath the RV, in the general direction that he had requested. Jason laid down and shimmied under the vehicle, wincing as the light revealed the gory, dark red horrors that coated the entirety of the undercarriage. Blood covered virtually every surface, most of it dried and congealed, though some of it was slowly oozing out of small cracks and crevices. Bits of flesh and the odd splinter of bone were stuck as well, and Jason flinched as he brushed against one and knocked it to the ground.

After a moment of moving and adjusting, he finally caught a glimpse of the pinhole, illuminated by a backsplash of light from Samantha's flashlight. Using the damp dishcloth, he scrubbed the section of the radiator around the hole, wiping away some layers of blood and gore, the cloth catching every time it passed over it.

"Hand me the flashlight?" Jason called out, and it appeared next to him. Holding the light up to the hole, he groaned and shimmied off to the side, holding the light back out for Samantha to take back. "Figured out how the hole got there...."

"Do I want to know?"

"Nope."

"Can you fix it?"

"As long as this stuff will harden while it's being leaked on. Give me a sec."

Using the dishcloth to protect his fingers and for better grip strength, Jason grabbed onto the sliver of bone that was embedded into the bottom of the radiator with his thumb and forefinger. Wiggling it back and forth as he pulled on it, he finally got it to pop out, and the slow leak became faster, the drips coming a couple of times a second.

"Paper plate?"

Samantha slid the paper plate next to his head, the plastic knife still on it, and Jason brought it up next to him and turned on his side. Using the plastic knife, Jason scraped the two-part epoxy from the plate and spread it across the pinhole, going back and forth several times, layering it in place. It was already starting to cure as he extracted himself, grunting at a stabbing pain in his lower back. Folding the paper plate, he stuffed it in a nearby trashcan and dropped the knife alongside it, then slowly stretched, trying to work the feeling back into his muscles.

"As good as we're going to get, I think." He grabbed the dishcloth he'd discarded and used the cleaner side to wipe the grease from his hands, then dropped it on the ground before kneeling down to check on his handiwork. "Yep, I'm not seeing any leaks. Fingers crossed it stays like that."

"Nice work. We'll start cleaning up?"

"Sounds great, thanks."

Gesturing for one of the gallons of anti-freeze, Eli handed it to him, and he topped off the radiator again. As he did so, Samantha, Elijah and Sarah took the other containers of coolant and motor oil and stashed them in one of the side compartments. Above them, the sky grew dark as a cloud of smoke drifted across the sun, blotting out the sky. Jason rubbed the sweat from his forehead with the back of his hand and stared at the gas pumps a short distance away.

"I hate how long we've been here, but we need to fill the tanks up before we get going."

"How are we going to do that without power?" Samantha asked.

"Wait!" Eli took a step forward. "I forgot to tell you!"

"Tell us what?" Samantha and Jason both faced him simultaneously.

"In the back room— we got so caught up with the freezer, I forgot that I saw a generator on the far wall!"

"They have a generator inside? Seriously?"

"It was inside the back room, resting against the wall. Come on, I'll show you!" Eli was already halfway to the gas station before Jason caught up to him.

Samantha and Sarah dashed after them, Kale sticking close, and Jason following Eli as he stepped over the man behind the counter and shouldered through the double doors into the backroom.

"I checked this room out when I first came in." Jason shook his head, looking throughout the cavernous interior.

"Not closely enough, I guess." Eli shrugged and gestured toward the far wall.

There was a desk with a computer on top, a swivel office chair resting on the floor nearby. A narrow door leading to a restroom was set into the back wall while on the left, a square-shaped box of brushed metal was nestled up against the sheet rock. It was surrounded by a red metal cage, mounted on a set of wheels with a tall handle that could be used to move it outside. Next to the wheeled cart was another door, a square sign above it labeling it as an exit.

"Well shoot, you weren't kidding." Jason strode forward and unlocked the deadbolt to the exit, swinging the door open so he could venture outside. "I'm guessing they'd put it out back here, through this door."

Turning immediately to the left, he located a power box on

the rear of the gas station exterior and smiled, then lifted the black latch and swung open the metal cover. Inside the electrical box was a series of breakers and a corresponding diagram on the inside door, identifying which items inside the gas station each breaker was associated with. Jason started by turning all of the breakers into the off positions, snapping them to the right. Alongside the breakers themselves was a larger main power breaker, as well as a clearly marked transfer switch and he switched off the main power breaker, on the off chance that it happened to come back on while they were working.

Just beneath the transfer switch was a circular receptacle with a round cover and Jason unscrewed and removed the cover, revealing a 240 volt inlet. Samantha and the twins were already wheeling the generator cart closer to the electrical box, and he knelt down and peered around the generator until he found what he was looking for. Coiled against the rear of it was a power cable with a 240 volt plug and he unraveled it and plugged it into the building's inlet. It took him a moment to find the power switches on the generator and he first clicked the safety off then depressed the start button, holding it down as the starter motor turned over slowly at first, then faster until finally the main generator's engine started, the metal box in the red cage suddenly snarling to life. It growled into an angry, chattering roar, eagerly feeding off its fuel source.

Standing again, he gripped the transfer switch and twisted it, then examined the breaker diagram on the inside of the power panel cover. It took a few seconds to locate gas pumps one through six, and he switched those breakers on, then he took another moment to find a breaker marked front counter and he switched that one on as well. Jason was just about to leave, when he re-examined the diagram and located two sets of breakers labeled "car wash" and "tire fill", then turned those on as well.

"I thought we were in a hurry?" Samantha asked, squinting at him.

"It's only been forty-five minutes," Jason shrugged, pushing his way past his family and into the back room. "If you saw what I saw underneath there, you'd want to rinse it out, too."

He headed straight for the register counter, stepped over the corpse and crouched down, examining a recessed set of switches partially concealed by the countertop.

"What are those?"

"Bypass switches. Manual controls to activate the pumps that work around the credit card processing equipment." Jason flipped a few of the switches.

"Since when did you learn about that sort of thing?" Samantha asked, smiling crookedly. "You been out stealing gas on the sly?"

"Gas Station Simulator!" Elijah called out, pumping his fist and mouthing 'yes' to his sister.

"He's not wrong," Jason shrugged. "I watch way too much of Eli's games."

"I don't want to know any more details." Samantha put up her hands. "But it means free gas, I assume?"

"Yep. Free gas," Jason confirmed.

Together, the O'Brians walked back out across the parking lot and to the RV. They were close enough to one of the pumps that Jason unhooked the nozzle and stretched the hose a bit before inserting it into the gas tank after removing the cap. Motioning for Sarah to hold onto it, he nodded toward the RV.

"You guys might want to step back or head inside," he advised.

"Why?" Eli asked.

"I'm going to use the hose over there to clean the underside, and you probably don't want to get any backsplash of what's under there."

Eli scrunched up his eyebrows in confusion, then realization settled in and his clenched face relaxed. Saying nothing else, he, Sarah and Samantha headed toward the door of the RV, swiftly climbing up inside. By the time Jason retrieved the hose that was hanging near the nearby air compressor and walked it over, everyone was in the RV. Directing the hose toward the base of the RV, he squeezed the trigger, a thick jet of water hurtling out. He played the spray beneath the RV and grimaced as swirls of rust-colored water seeped out from beneath the vehicle, working their way toward a nearby drain.

For some time, he sprayed back and forth, rinsing the underside diligently, pelting it with a powerful jet of water until the rest of the liquid washing free was clearer than red. Once he was relatively satisfied that the undercarriage was clean, he sprayed off the sides of the RV as well, then placed the hose back where he'd picked it up. He climbed up into the RV, turned it on and glanced in the rearview mirror, gently touching the accelerator while in reverse to ease the large vehicle closer to the air compressor. Steering tightly, he swept the back side around and reversed further until the driver's side front tire was even with the compressor.

"Last thing, I promise." Standing again, he left the RV, unhooked the hose from the tire fill station, then pressed it into the valve of each of the tires, filling them until they were within a couple of pounds of spec.

Hooking the hose back where it belonged, he made his way behind the RV and back toward the gas station, then went around the back side where he killed the generator, switched the transfer switch back, and activated all the breakers again, just in case the power came back on. Grunting as he wheeled the enormous generator into the backroom, he left it where he'd found it, then closed the door and returned to the RV.

By the time he was done and back inside, the sky had darkened further from the smoke, the surrounding buildings taller and more imposing with each passing moment. "Well then," Jason sighed as he gripped the wheel. "That doesn't quite beat seeing the redwood forest, but it was definitely an adventure."

"I want the redwoods. *Please*." Eli settled into his seat, his safety harness buckling as his shoulders slumped slightly against the seat back.

Kale sat on the floor next to Sarah, cocking her head slightly as Sarah stroked the dog's ears. "So, what's our plan? Back to the concrete river?"

"That's my vote," replied Samantha. "Back to the service road, then we get out of the city. I've had more of Los Angeles than I ever wanted."

"Agreed," Jason said, turning the key in the ignition, putting the RV into Drive and slowly pulling out of the gas station parking lot.

CHAPTER FIFTEEN

The Tills Family
Silverpine, Oregon

Sheila choked as she drew in a breath, staring at the screen of the tracking device in Doug's hand. All around her, time slowed, from the call of birds on distant grapevines to the wind turning the leaves as it flowed up and over the hill, the tracker's blinking light the only thing moving at regular speed. At her right shoulder, Doug stared at the screen as well, slack jawed, his lower lip trembling slightly. His jaw flexed as he pressed his teeth together, desperate to keep his unsteady composure.

"Mr. and Mrs. Tills?" Benjamin called over from the rack where the solar panels were mounted. The tool bag rested at his feet, a ratchet held in his left hand, resting still on a bolt. His normally gruff demeanor had been washed aside by a look of legitimate concern. "Everything okay?"

Sheila did her best to clear her throat, though there was a ragged scrape to the sound, a wet gurgle underlying the makeshift cough. Benjamin tossed the ratchet into the tool bag and strode forward, Darryl and Brandi giving each other curious looks.

"What's that you have?" Benjamin approached, nodding toward the tracking receiver that Doug held firmly in one hand.

"It's a tracking device," Doug replied, his voice barely audible. "Part of a security package we bought for the RV."

"According to this, Samantha, Jason and the twins... they're..." Sheila's voice came dangerously close to fracturing. "They're in the middle of Los Angeles." Tears squirmed loose from her eyes and tumbled down, rolling their way across her cheeks. "There's no way they're still alive. There's just no way."

"Here," Benjamin spoke in a surprisingly calm, quiet demeanor, a gentle warmth to his words as he held his hand out. "Let me take a look."

Doug placed the tracker in Benjamin's palm, moving almost only by muscle memory, his eyes vacantly fixated on something in the far distance. Benjamin took the tracker, turning it over to study it with a pensive glare, his thick eyebrows knitting above his eyes. He tapped the screen, using his fingers to adjust some of the settings. Zooming in on a specific location, one bushy eyebrow lifted, his eyes widening.

"What is it?" Sheila wiped the tears from her eyes and dried her cheek with the back of her hand. "Benjamin, what do you see?"

"You're right," Benjamin replied with a nod, "they are in the middle of Los Angeles."

Sheila sniffed, taking a step closer. On the other side of Benjamin's broad shoulders, Doug closed in as well, twisting to stare at the screen.

"But this dot's moving."

"What?" Doug's voice lifted and sharpened as he moved forward for a better look.

He fought the urge to yank the device from Benjamin's hand, instead focusing his attention on the small LED screen. Sure, enough as he stared, a few seconds later the screen refreshed, and the signal from the RV had indeed moved. It crawled, bit by bit, upwards across the screen, moving slowly but steadily.

"It is." Sheila expelled a breath of air. "It's moving."

"That doesn't seem possible." Doug swallowed, almost not daring to believe it. "But it is. Look, Sheila! Look!" He pointed toward the screen and again, the small dot representing the RV crawled upward, moving along a narrow, grid-work passage.

"They're near that big empty section there." Benjamin pointed toward a broad, dark line that traversed the screen at an angle. "I don't know much about your family," Benjamin said, still staring at the screen, "but what little I know of your daughter, if anyone's alive in Los Angeles, it's them." He handed off the tracker again, setting it in Doug's palm. He gripped it with both hands, still staring at the screen.

"Do you think?" Sheila asked, her voice almost silent. "Do you think they're actually alive?"

"They have to be." Doug wrapped an arm around Sheila and squeezed her tight.

"Not that I want to interrupt this happy realization," Benjamin interjected, then softly cleared his throat. "But can we wrap up this project real quick, then figure out what to do with your family? No offense, Mr. and Mrs. Tills, but there ain't a whole lot we can do for them from here, and we just need a little bit of time here with this."

"You're right." Doug powered down the tracker and slid it into his back pocket. "Let's try and focus on getting the solar panels up and going, then we can figure out what's happening with Samantha and Jason." Clearing his throat, Doug spoke to the group. "Let's help Benjamin get these panels checked over one last time. County inspector already checked them over, but we're going to do a final look-see before we switch everything on."

Darryl and Brandi stood a short distance away and as Darryl

took a step toward the panels to help, Brandi reached out, touching his arm with a gentle poke.

"What's up?" Darryl's head turned over his shoulder.

"What did Benjamin mean?" Brandi asked, her voice an almost silent whisper. "About the Tills' daughter?"

"Who? Samantha?" Darryl glanced toward the panels, the three others several strides away, gathered around the rack where the electrical boxes were mounted. His gaze lingered there for a moment, then he turned back toward Brandi. "You haven't heard about Samantha?"

Brandi shook her head. "I've only been here for a month, Darryl. Nobody tells me anything."

"Fair. I don't know much about her, just what I've picked up here or there, mostly by overhearing comments that the Tills or Benjamin make. But from what I understand, she's former military. Her and her husband Jason both. I think he was mostly in logistics? He didn't see a whole lot of combat, but he's got a pretty sharp mind, knows his stuff. Helped them get a lot of stuff set up here."

"What about her? Has she seen combat?"

Darryl's eyes widened slightly, and he nodded his head slowly up and down. "She was a combat medic. Did a few tours in the thick of the worst of those sandboxes. And from what Mr. Tills has said a few times, she wasn't behind a desk or running with safe convoys. She was in the thick of it, getting shot at left, right and center."

"Seriously?"

"She's good at her job, too. Scary good. So good that she set up a survival school out here that she runs a few times a year. I can't believe you didn't meet her during their last one, before her family went on their trip in the Tills' RV."

"I remember something going on, but I was inside most of the time." Brandi shrugged.

"Well, it's hardcore stuff. Wilderness survival, medical training, she puts her students through the wringer for two solid weeks. They come out of that training with skills they didn't even know they had. She is a certifiable badass."

"Wow. I had no idea."

"They don't talk about it much. Like I said, I've just mostly overheard stuff. But I agree with Benjamin, if anyone is going to survive what's going on in the cities right now, it's Samantha and her family."

"I really hope they're okay. The way Mr. and Mrs. Tills were looking at that screen, I've never seen that look on their faces before. They always have their stuff together, they're on top of everything. Their faces... they just looked lost."

"They love their family. Every time Samantha plans one of her sessions out here, that's all we hear about in the weeks leading up to it. I hate to say it, but it made me feel a bit bitter sometimes. Thinking about my own family, I just—"

"Darryl! Brandi. Come on over here. We've got something to show you both." Benjamin waved a thick hand in their direction.

"Yeah! Sure." Darryl nodded, he and Brandi separating and walking toward the rest, moving quickly.

Darryl and Brandi arrived at the rack upon which the solar panels were mounted. Benjamin and Doug stood a few feet apart, flanking the main electrical box that was bolted to the intersecting slats of metal holding up the panels.

"You see those boxes on the rear of each panel?" Doug pointed toward the upward facing panels, rectangular metal shapes bolted to the underside of each one. "Those are the individual junction boxes that wire the panels to the main electrical system. They're all wired back to a combiner box right here." Doug pointed toward a rectangular box which was mounted just above the main electrical cabinet.

"The combiner box is where you'll find some of the fuses or circuit breakers. We don't need to get into the nitty gritty of what makes them work, but if we tell you that we have to swap out a fuse, this is where you'll find it." Benjamin smacked the side of the combiner box.

"You follow?" Darryl asked, turning to Brandi, grinning. "I've been through this rigamarole already."

"Sure, I follow."

"Good," Benjamin replied curtly. "We all need to get really familiar with how this works. It's great tech, but like all tech, it breaks. The more people who know how to fix it, the better." Reaching to a box below the combiner box, he slid up the latch and opened the door.

"This is the electrical box. We rerouted the mains into here and this manual transfer switch is what you need to pull in order to disconnect grid power and transfer to solar."

"You wired this all up yourselves?" Brandi shifted her attention from Benjamin to Doug and back again.

"Sure. It's just electricity, right?" Doug replied with a wink. "No, it's all good and up to code, if that's what you mean. That's why we had the inspector come out and take a look."

"Inspector. Right." Benjamin rolled his eyes. "I was fourteen years old when I helped my cousin tap into his neighbor's power. To this day I don't think that guy ever figured out why his bill went up so much. Couldn't have happened to a nicer dirtbag."

The group shared a chorus of quiet laughter, and Doug held his hands up for attention.

"Now this isn't perfect. We got the solar panels all racked up and wired, but we didn't get the batteries installed yet. They're still sitting out in the barn, Benjamin made sure they were there on our way back from the neighbors. Without those batteries, we're only going to have power when the sun is shining. Not perfect, but better than nothing. In the next few days or weeks, depending on how this whole situation plays out, we'll have to figure out how to get the batteries installed and wired to the local grid. We'll also need to figure out where to mount them and wire them where the weather won't get to them."

"Don't forget, we don't have all the supplies we need to do that, Mr. Tills." Benjamin added.

"We'll burn that bridge when we come to it." Doug took a step toward the electrical box. "Everyone ready?" Doug positioned his hand near the manual transfer switch.

Before anyone could respond, he slapped it down, killing access to the grid. Stepping back slightly he pressed two fingers to a secondary transfer switch and jerked them up, turning the second switch on. Throughout the rack of panels, on all of the individual junction boxes, tiny green lights illuminated, each one winking on and staying steady.

"All green," Benjamin confirmed with a satisfied nod.

"All green." Doug took a step toward Benjamin, his hand extended and they shook vigorously, then Doug turned to Darryl. "Get over here!"

"Yes, Mr. Tills?"

Doug clasped a hand on Darryl's shoulder, then shook with his other. "You were a huge help with this project."

"Thank you, sir."

"For the last time, stop calling me sir." Doug raised his voice, looking to Brandi, Darryl and Benjamin. "Stop calling me Mr. Tills. All of you, my name is Doug and from now on, that's all I'll respond to, you hear me?" Brandi and Darryl both nodded, but Benjamin simply stood stoic and unresponsive. "All right, so this takes care of the outside power. We've still got some work to do inside. Let's head on back to the main building and tackle that next, shall we?" Doug lifted his tool bag and slung it back over his shoulder.

Together, the group gathered and walked along the gravel path, back to the main road. They angled left, gravel and crushed stone crunching under the shifting weight of their footfalls. Somehow, the day had gotten away from them. The sky had changed color, the clouds churning thick and gray, the sun slowly retreating toward the West. Though the tracker was stashed away in his back pocket, he kept seeing its small screen in his mind, the tiny dot representing the RV trapped within the desolate city of Los Angeles. He tried hard not to imagine what Samantha, Jason and the twins were going through, but the harder he tried not to imagine it, the more vivid his imagination became. Towering buildings, smoldering from unseen fires, grid-locked traffic in streets teeming with the dead. An entire city boiling with rot and decay, the skies choking black from smoke and desiccation. Horrific, startling imagery crept in his mind, though he tried hard to blink it away.

"Doug?"

He turned, blinking quickly, the death and destruction scattering beneath the rapid flutter of his eyelids.

"Are you still with me?" Sheila touched his fingers with hers.

"Yeah."

"What's wrong?"

"I keep seeing those videos play in my head over and over and over again. Those dead bodies in that park in Chicago. New York City with so many cars people can't even walk through. I keep... I keep picturing the kids in that mess. Not just our kids but our grandkids."

"I know. But I don't know what to do."

Doug pulled the tracker from his back pocket. They were still outside, crossing the employee parking lot and he turned the device on again, the screen wavering into illumination and for a moment it gave that same warning about waiting for a connection. Then the words vanished, and the Los Angeles roadways faded into clarity. The small dot was even farther than it had been back at the solar panels, though not a great distance further. It was moving, but it was moving slowly.

"Still going?"

"Like the little engine that could."

They walked up the remaining slope of upward pavement, crossing onto the customer parking lot and approaching the side-by-side still parked by the front door. Continuing past it, Doug picked up his pace a bit, walking briskly toward the front door. Fumbling for his keys, he unlocked the door and opened it, then stood, framed in its doorway, staring up at the ceiling mounted lights. A soft, white glow emanated from the circular shape, the interior of the restaurant clad in pale illumination.

"Let there be light!" Doug pumped a fist and stormed past the host station, jogging into the larger main dining room.

He stood in the center of the room, all of the chandeliers glowing bright with illumination. Turning in a lazy, circular motion, he stared up, the lights shining back down on him.

"You did good, Mr.—" Darryl's words broke off. "You did good, Doug!"

"*We* did good. All of us." Benjamin harumphed at Doug's words, though the slightest hint of a grin creased his wrinkled face.

Within the large dining room, the familiar background hum of power running throughout the kitchen appliances was back, one small slice of the old world returning. "Imagine that," Sheila smiled broadly. "You weren't kidding that they would run everything, Doug."

"I hadn't quite finished taking inventory of our food supplies," Brandi said softly, leaning close to Sheila. "Should I do that now, since we've got power back?"

"Yes, absolutely. Darryl, can you help her?" Sheila gave Darryl a slight nod.

"Sure thing." He joined Brandi. "Just point me in the right direction." The two of them disappeared into the kitchen, the double doors swinging through in their wake, thumping softly.

"Now that we've got the power figured out," she said, gently plucking the tracker from Doug's hand. "We need to figure out what we do about them." She held it up and pointed to the dot on the screen.

Doug nodded without hesitation. "I already know what we need to do."

Light shone down from the overhead chandeliers, the expansive dining room brightened in a yellow glow from the lights. Tables had been cleared, chairs upended and set upon the tops, the booths along the far wall swept clear and washed to remove the remains of abandoned lunches left by customers who'd all run out of the restaurant in a blind panic. One of the long tables in the center of the dining room had been left alone, a cluster of chairs around it as Doug, Sheila and the others strategized.

"I don't know." Doug shook his head and leaned back in his chair, dropping a pen on the table. "This doesn't look like it'll work."

Sheila sat next to him, twisting to look as he pushed himself backwards. Benjamin was seated across from them both, his broad arms crossed over his equally broad chest, bunched eyebrows tilted inward, his jaw clenched in an expression that bordered on annoyance. The table between them was buried beneath a small pile of paper maps, one of them unfolded enough to cover nearly the entire table's surface. To the right of Doug, resting near the wall was the tracker they'd been using to follow the RV's movements. A pad of paper, a few other pens, a high-lighter and calculator were all scattered about, signs of a brain-storming session.

"I understand the freeway is our best and quickest option," Doug continued with a firm shake of his head, "but it's going to be way too congested. If what our neighbor said is true and his whole housing development picked up stakes to head toward the cities, there's no way the road is going to be passable."

"So what other options are there?" Sheila placed a comforting hand on her husband's leg.

"Interstate 5 is the straightest shot through the state and down into California." Benjamin leaned forward and stabbed his finger to where I-5 was marked. "Problem is, you'd have to travel close to Portland to get on it. Then taking it south goes right through Salem and Eugene both." He traced his fingers along the projected path.

"We don't know for sure if Portland, Salem or Eugene were hit. None of those cities were mentioned on the news." Sheila leaned forward as well, studying the map through narrowed eyes.

"You saw smoke rising from the east. I'm still not convinced that was Portland itself, but Oregon hasn't escaped this thing." Doug waved a dismissive hand toward the map. "If that smoke is coming from anywhere, it's likely at least one of those three cities, and most probably Portland."

"So, you just want to stick with back roads?" Benjamin picked up the highlighter from the table and leaned over the map.

Studying it for a few moments, he placed the chiseled tip against the paper and drew a ragged, winding, uneven line throughout rural Oregon, heading south toward California.

"If you follow the back roads all the way, it's going to take you three times longer. Look at all this real estate you need to travel."

"So, if the highways are too blocked and the back roads will take too long, what are our options?" Doug sighed, total exasperation forcing the breath from his lips.

"Simple." Benjamin shrugged his wide shoulders, his gaze still focused on the unfolded map before them. "You split the difference." Leaning forward, he swapped out the highlighter for a pen and circled a point south of Portland where tiny veins of narrowed roads twisted into a tangled knot with a thicker, darker line continuing south. "Pick up the highway south of Portland right here. Take it as far as you can. Hopefully you can make it past Salem. It's the capital, but I don't see a reason why it might be a primary target. Portland is much more likely."

"So, take I-5 south through here?" Doug paid more attention, a single eyebrow arching above his left eye.

"If you can make it through Salem, great. I suspect you might need to jump off the highway south of there to try and avoid Eugene. Move through some of the back roads just east of the national forest. Once you clear the California border, you might be able to make your way back to the interstate. Sure, I-5 goes straight through Sacramento, but it avoids both San Francisco and San Jose." As he rattled off the instructions, Benjamin traced the route he was discussing, navigating a meandering southward trek toward California.

Benjamin dropped the pen down on the table as Doug reached over and lifted the tracker from where it rested against the wall. "All of this is dependent on just how bad the roads are and how many other people have similar ideas. We already know that an entire neighborhood next door vacated to do something similar. If there are thousands or even hundreds of those people trying to get south at the same time you are, using the same strategy, it doesn't really matter what lines we draw on a map. You'll just have to wing it and roll with whatever punches come your way."

"I think we have to try." Sheila leaned in close, studying the patchwork of veins and arteries winding their way through the state.

Next to her, Doug turned on the tracker again, studying it as he angled it close to the window, holding it near the translucent glass. Slowly, the screen faded into view, the beacon shining against the roadway of Los Angeles.

"They're still moving, but they haven't gotten very far."

"We have to try this, Doug. We have to. We know where they are, we know they're alive, we have to try to get to them so we can help them. I know Samantha and Jason can hold their own, but —" A shadow passed over Benjamin's face for the briefest of moments as Sheila spoke.

"You'll get no argument from me." Doug set down the tracker and stabbed the power button, the screen winking into blackness. "Why don't you go see how Brandi and Darryl are doing with the inventory?" Doug nodded toward the kitchen. "I'll come get you when Benjamin and I sort some of this stuff out." Sheila hesitated for a moment, but finally nodded and slid from the booth and, a moment later, she'd disappeared from view, going into the kitchen.

"What is it?" Doug leaned over, his voice quiet.

"What?" Benjamin wouldn't meet his eyes.

"You had a look. When Sheila was talking about how we knew the kids were alive."

"I don't want to—"

"Spill it, Benjamin."

"That tracker." Benjamin nodded his head toward the dormant device resting on the table.

"What about it?"

"All it's telling you is that the RV is moving."

"Right?"

"It doesn't tell you who's driving it."

Doug sat still in the booth, slightly leaned over, resting his arms on the map covering the table.

"I didn't want to say that to Mrs. Tills, but... you guys are going to have to be careful. *Very* careful. I know Samantha is about the best person to be in the situation she's in, but still."

Doug's hands curled into fists for a few seconds before he let out a breath and nodded, fingers slowly uncurling. "You're right," he said softly. "I've been thinking it myself, but hearing it out loud is tough."

"I don't want to rain on anyone's parade."

"You're not. It's a hard truth, but one we need to hear."

"If you're up for hearing another one...."

"Of course."

Benjamin leaned back, shifting uncomfortably. "You and Mrs. Tills aren't exactly spring chickens anymore."

Doug smirked, raising an eyebrow. "Are you the pot or the kettle?"

"I'm just saying, if you end up not being able to make it down there, you need to come back, and not just push forward until the two of you end up getting yourselves killed." Benjamin spoke matter-of-factly. "Just don't be stupid. Stay alive so that you can help others stay alive. Get my drift?"

"I get you," Doug nodded. "I promise we'll be smart. We've got to try this though, y'know?"

"Of course you do. I'd expect nothing else."

The kitchen doors thumped open, and Sheila emerged.

"They have it under control." She slowed as she approached, studying Doug's expression. "Is everything okay?"

Doug smiled and slid from the booth, using the table to push himself upright. "Everything's fine."

Benjamin followed suit and exited the booth as well, stretching his back as he stood upright. "I'll go start getting some things ready for you, and we'll hold down the fort until you get back. Whether you take back roads or the highway, it's close to a thousand miles between here and L.A. so we'll get as much gas as possible for you."

"We're taking the Jeep?" Sheila asked.

"Makes the most sense to me," Doug affirmed. "Just in case we have to go off-roading. I know we've got plenty of diesel fuel in the tank out by the access road. I'm not sure how much gas we have." Doug stood next to Sheila, putting his hand at the small of her back.

"We've got plenty." Benjamin looked out the window. "Nothing that's going to last us years or anything, but plenty enough so I can hook you up with some jerry cans to get you down to California and back."

"Thanks, Benjamin."

"I'll need to talk to Brandi, too, take stock of what we've got in the kitchen. You'll need food and water, stuff you can eat on the go."

"If Brandi's inventory is even partially correct, that shouldn't be an issue. Between the kitchen and what we've got down in the storage rooms in the basement, I think we'll be fine for a few days of food and water." Sheila nodded.

"And don't forget to take protection." Benjamin gave Doug a pointed look.

"I understand."

"Like I said, we'll take care of things here. Focus your mental energy on getting to your kids. Don't spend one second worrying about us."

"I don't think that's possible. We'll worry about you plenty." Sheila stepped forward and rested a hand on Benjamin's arm.

"Thank you, Benjamin." Doug said. "Hopefully it'll just be a couple of days. We'll be down there and back lickity split, with a lot more help in tow."

Benjamin nodded, an uncertain expression carved in the rigid stone of his face. Doug turned and embraced Sheila, pulling her tightly to himself, then together they strode off, heading toward their residence on the upper level to start packing for their trip.

CHAPTER SIXTEEN

The O'Brian Family
Los Angeles, California

The RV rolled along the service road, moving at a steady clip, the urban sprawl of downtown Los Angeles passing by block by block. Jason was hesitant to push the lumbering vehicle too fast on the narrow stretch of pavement alongside the drainage system as there were sections of the service road so narrow that he feared the driver's side tires might slip off the edge. When they reached a wider section, he spared a moment to twist and look over his shoulder, toward the rear of the RV. Eli rested on a seat within view, his head turned to one side while Sarah was hunched over the table, fingers gripping her phone which was still tethered to the charger. Kale lifted her head from where she lay, sighing heavily as her tail darted left-to-right. She huffed forlornly at her empty food dish, then rested her chin on her paws, looking up with as much guilt as she could muster. Jason chuckled, and Samantha cleared her throat from next to him.

"Eyes on the road, Mister." Samantha's own eyes were closed, as if asleep, her head resting back on her headrest.

"I thought you were sleeping."

"In the middle of this?" She gestured out the windows at the desolate, broken city that surrounded them.

"I thought you knew how to sleep anywhere."

"True enough. You, too, though."

"Nah, I need a comfy bunk and two pillows to really get some solid sack time."

"Let's not get into that right now." Samantha opened her other eye, rolling them both dramatically at him. "Desk jockey."

Jason laughed again and turned his attention back to the road. Up ahead, the service road bent slightly to the left, following the curve of the empty Los Angeles River basin and he steered along its angles. As they navigated the curve, Jason tapped the brakes, a sudden jolt jostling the RV, yanking Samantha from her half-sleep into a fully awake state. She lurched forward and braced herself on the dashboard.

Up ahead, sprawled across the service road was a California Department of Transportation truck. It had overturned, toppling onto its side and three men in Caltrans uniforms lay on the pavement, two of them face down, the other with arms spread and empty eyes staring toward the sky above. The RV shuddered to a halt about thirty yards from where the truck had overturned and Jason's fingers gripped the wheel with a tighter intensity, his arms rigid.

"What are we supposed to do now?" Samantha angled her neck, staring to the right and to the left, trying to see a way around.

Chain-link fencing barricaded them from the main road just beyond, and a sharp drop-off led to the drainage system to their left. There were no immediate gaps to navigate the R.V. through.

"Can you break through that fence?" Samantha pointed

toward the chain-link. "Like how you did to get in here in the first place?"

"The angle's not great from here. I don't think I can hit it straight-on."

"Dad? What's going on?" Eli rubbed his eyes as he sat upright.

"There's a truck blocking the way. We need to figure out how to keep going." Looking in his rearview, Jason shifted the RV into reverse and slowly started to back around the corner they'd just turned.

It was slow, methodical work, navigating the slender slip of service road with an oversized vehicle. Jason handled it with relative ease as Samantha continued watching for an alternate route. For a long time, Jason inched backwards, traversing the service road until he finally saw what he'd been looking for.

"Over here," he said, nodding toward the driver's side. "There's a ramp going down into the drainage system. It looks wide enough for the RV." He continued backing up, pushing the RV into reverse until the ramp fell into view and then stood before them, just on the left.

"If we got a bit farther back there's an access road there, too. Should allow us to get a better angle to knock down the fence." Samantha peered through the window she'd opened, leaning out to get a better look.

"So, do we go back out onto the main roads, or do we try to drive along the base of the river basin?"

Samantha leaned over and accessed the touch screen navigation system in the RV dashboard again. She pinched her fingers together to scroll out, drawing the visibility to a higher altitude. Moving to the east, she scrolled through a network of intersecting roads.

"If we move back to the main streets, we're just going to end up running into the same problem that drove us here to begin with. Traffic, dead bodies, or we might even risk people venturing out from the upper levels of their apartments and office buildings."

"Whereas if we head into the drainage system?" Jason leaned a bit, staring through his own window.

"It'll probably be slow going. We'll have to watch out for anything that might pop the tires and getting back out might be tricky depending on how many of these ramps there are going in and out. It's got my vote, though." Her voice lowered. "I've had enough driving over bodies to last several lifetimes over."

"Works for me," Jason said, glancing back at the twins. "Any objections?"

"Nope," they both said in unison.

"Let's get this party started, then."

Jason slowly accelerated, steering the RV left toward the ramp. They crested the top and began heading down as he applied the brakes, letting the RV coast down its slope. It hit the base of the ramp and evened out, pulling onto the wide, concrete layered base of the drainage system. Eli turned and stared through his window, eyes wide as they continued on, the sloped walls of the basin rising up sharply on each side.

"This is so cool. So many movies were filmed down here." He stared out for a few moments, his alert eyes probing their surroundings. "Remember The Core, with the shuttle? Oh, what about Terminator 2?! He crashed that big tractor trailer truck right down onto the concrete! That kid was riding his dirt bike right through here."

"Did you just call that an old movie? It was a sequel, young man! I'm pretty sure your mom and I might have seen the original on VHS together."

"VHS?" Sarah scrunched up her nose. "What's VHS?"

"Never mind." Jason shot a sideways glance toward Samantha who was doing a bad job muffling a chuckle.

On the flattened surface of the concrete, Jason accelerated slightly, picking up some speed, but keeping it manageable while they kept an eye open for obstacles they might find in the old Los Angeles River basin. Up ahead, an overpass crossed the basin, tall enough that two RVs stacked on top of each other could have passed beneath its concrete base and Jason continued onward, Eli and Sarah still hypnotized by their surroundings. A shallow layer of water darkened the passage ahead, the RV plowing through it, dark green liquid spraying in an outward arc on either side of them.

"How far will this take us? Do we even know?" Sarah asked from the back.

"I looked on the satnav before," Samantha answered, "and it extends a decent way north and then eventually bends west and heads toward the Pacific. Whether it'll be navigable that entire way for us, though, is anyone's guess."

"We'll just keep moving until we can't." Jason said.

They continued following the serpentine path of the drainage system, their speed faster than it had been on the surface streets, but significantly slower than would have been preferred. Above them, the sun continued to drift westward as the day wound on, the shadows cast by the skyscrapers and smaller buildings subtly shifting around them. Every once in a while they came upon the burned out wreck of an abandoned vehicle, large piles of trash or other obstacles he navigated around, but the passage was far clearer than it would have been on the surface roads. They passed a few different ramps leading back to the service road, but ignored them all, winding along the bent, concrete-lined river until they came to another overpass which stretched across the wide gap between streets on each side.

Jason slowed as they passed by more garbage, shopping carts and abandoned vehicles, finally letting out a sigh of relief when they were through the overpass and the road cleared, but Samantha shouted, slamming a hand on the dashboard.

"Hold up!"

Jason had been staring up at the overpass and off to the sides while driving, but her exclamation drew his attention forward again and he hit the brake, halting the RV with a lurching jolt.

"What's going on?" Sarah dropped her phone and tugged against her safety belt, craning around for a better look.

A few hundred feet ahead, stretched across the wide breadth of the concrete riverbed was a litter of various tents and makeshift shelters. Some were actual camping tents, while others were shelters constructed of sheets stretched across supports, the tightly clustered village clogging the entire passage before them. Each tent was pressed so tightly against the next that the combined surface area of their sides and roofs concealed whatever was beneath, a favela of cloth instead of sheet metal. There was no sign of movement from within the encampment, though seeing inside was impossible due to the density of the place.

"Should have known it was too good to be true." Jason's hands curled tight against the steering wheel, the leather groaning and creaking in response. "We passed a ramp back up to the service road a short ways back. Should we double back and go back up?"

"We've been making great time. I'd hate to change that up now." Samantha pointed toward the right edge of the tent city. "There's a bit of a gap through there, do you think we could make it?"

"I don't know if we should try. What if there are people in there?"

"If they've been down here on the surface, they're probably all dead." Samantha kept her voice to a low whisper.

"I don't know if we can even fit through that gap... maybe?"

"I'm not sure what to do, then."

"The ramp isn't that far behind us." Jason shifted the RV into reverse and began watching the mirrors to navigate through the debris. "I'll take the ramp to the service road, and we'll go around."

"Don't." Samantha shook her head, pressing her palm over his hand gripping the gear shift. "Let me check it out. See if there's anyone alive in there."

"Why?"

"If we can go through, we'll go through. It'll save us tons of time over backtracking and risking coming across another blocked passage on the service road. And if nobody's alive, we can just take down anything that might snag on the RV."

"Okay, makes sense. I'll go with you."

"I'll be careful." Samantha unclasped her seatbelt.

"Samantha." Jason shifted back into park. "I don't like this. You shouldn't do this alone."

"Someone needs to stay with the kids."

"I'll go."

"No. I need to do this, Jason. I'm just as capable of it as you are. Besides, you're a better driver than I am. If we need to get out of dodge, it's *you* I want behind the wheel."

Jason ran his tongue across his teeth, turning slightly in the driver's seat. He glanced through the windshield, drumming his fingers on the steering wheel.

"If it'll make you feel better, I'll bring Kale."

"That... helps, yes. Thank you."

Samantha stood and stepped between their seats, slapping her thigh while looking at Kale. The German Shepherd sensed her desire and stood, collar jingling, ears perked, her dark eyes following Samantha's movements, back rigid, clearly on attention.

"Mom? Are you sure about this?" Elijah clicked his belt free and stood, stepping forward to get a better view out the windshield, Sarah doing the same next to him.

"It'll be fine, buddy. Kale and I will check things out and we'll be back before anyone knows it." Samantha looked at Jason and smiled.

Jason's thin-lipped grimace shifted for a moment, finally easing into a slightly slanted smile. "All right," he said. "I know better than to push by now." Turning in the driver's seat, he turned the wheel and put the RV back into drive. "Hold on, I'm going to at least pull you a little closer."

Eli and Sarah settled into their seats, though Samantha stayed standing. She gripped the seatback as Jason gently accelerated, driving slowly forward, the tent city growing larger with each passing second. He never moved faster than a few miles per hour, inching the RV along, closer and closer until he tapped the brakes about thirty feet from the first row of tightly pressed tents. He shoved the gearshift into park, killed the engine and sat in the front seat, staring at the tent city.

As Jason leaned over the steering wheel, a silhouetted shadow shifted among the draped fabric of the tents. Figures shuffled throughout the darkness, the tents blowing gently, revealing a brief snatch of movement before being obscured from view once more.

"Something's moving in there."

"Looks more like someone than something." Elijah bent over his father's chair and stared past him, through the windshield.

Samantha stood again and took another step toward the door.

"Can I just reiterate how much I don't like this idea?" Jason slipped off his seat as well and fixed his wife with an unwavering gaze.

"Point taken."

"You're still going."

"I'm still going."

Fabric shifted throughout the tent village ahead, a figure ducking beneath a section of sheet as a man emerged. He stood, a narrow scarecrow of a man, clothes hanging loose from his narrow shoulders. Thick, twisting tangles of facial hair dropped from his narrow jowls, a blanket of thin strands of white hair down near his steeply sloped shoulders. Another man appeared behind him, a third figure pushing free, a woman, long, black hair framing her slender face. Jason took a step toward Samantha, but she'd already opened the door, a cool slice of air coming in from the outside.

"Kale. Here, girl." Samantha stood on the concrete and patted her thigh.

Kale bounded down the stairs and landed next to her master, staring at the people gathered just outside the tent city. The dog didn't growl as she clung tight to Samantha's leg, showing no sign of intimidation or fear over the strangers in front of her. Elijah and Sarah gathered close to Jason, all three of them at the dashboard, silently evaluating the landscape before them. Without hesitation, Samantha walked forward, Kale at her heels, the three inhabitants of the tent city watching her every single step of the way.

"Kale's not barking," Elijah whispered. "But I still don't like this."

"Neither do I," Jason whispered back.

Samantha spent a moment talking to the three people just outside the sprawling expanse of the makeshift city. Moments later, she vanished beyond the fabric with them and disappeared from view, leaving behind an empty expanse of pavement.

Jason stood near the driver's seat, no longer capable of sitting. He crossed his arms, staring through the front windshield at the tent city before turning his arm, glancing down at his watch, arms crossed tightly, muscles flexed.

"Dad, you checked your watch, like, ten seconds ago." Eli sat in the passenger's seat, hunched over, his arms resting on his bent legs. Staring up from his hunched-over posture, his gaze lingered on the tents, staring at the spot where his mother had vanished into their canvas and cloth walls. "You always tell us that a watched pot never boils."

"It's been half an hour." Jason stepped back from the driver's seat and into the narrow space between the front seats and the RV's kitchen. "What is going on in there?"

"I'm sure everything is fine." Sarah still sat on one of the kitchen chairs, though she was at a quarter angle with a clear view of the windshield. "Kale hasn't barked once. You saw how she was with that group at the apartments."

Jason paced back toward the front seats. "I never should have let her go."

Elijah chuckled. "Nobody ever lets mom do anything. She does what she wants, Dad, you know that better than anyone."

"What she wants to do doesn't typically put her in harm's way. Not anymore, at least."

"Those people who came out didn't look so scary. Kale didn't mind them"

"Looks can be deceiving."

He leaned on the back of the driver's seat, fixated on the tent city. For a moment, movement shifted from within, dark figures just beyond the exterior row of cloth. Jason kept focused on the movement, following the shadows. They paused momentarily, then moved again, finally pushing their way through the tightly gathered tents.

"There!" He pushed himself bolt upright and ran to the front door of the RV as Samantha and Kale emerged from the makeshift neighborhood.

Two of the same three people who had greeted her trailed behind her, the man with the loose-fitting clothing and the long bush of gray beard turning toward her. He gestured wildly with his hands, as if trying to explain something exceptionally complex. As Jason reached the front door, Samantha lifted a hand in greeting, waving it above her head at the RV.

"Stay inside, kids." Jason pushed the door open and stepped outside, pausing near the door as Samantha and the two strangers walked up.

"Jason! Can you grab us two six-packs of soda from the RV? And some of that jerky Eli found in the gas station?"

Jason didn't move, studying his wife as she approached. The

bearded man beside her had stopped his frantic gesturing, his attention fixed on Jason instead of Samantha.

"Jason. Please?" Samantha's left eye twitched as she asked, winking twice.

Jason's rigid posture slackened as he stood there, his clenched fists slowly loosening. Jason hesitated for another brief second, then opened the door and made his way back into the RV.

"Dad? What's going on?" Eli turned toward him and started to stand.

Jason gestured for him to keep sitting. He peered through the windshield as he paused behind the front seats. Samantha stood by the front hood, talking in quiet whispers to the two people from the tent city. The woman with long strands of fragile hair reached into an inner pocket of her threadbare jacket and removed folded papers, showing them to Samantha, who nodded in acknowledgement. Walking down the short space to the kitchen, Jason opened one of the cabinet doors and removed a few packs of the jerky Eli had recovered.

"What are you doing?" Sarah asked. "What's going on?"

"I have no clue." Jason moved to another cabinet and lifted out two six-packs of soda, placing them on the counter.

"Are we giving them our food?" Eli's smooth brow thickened.

"Just doing what mom is asking me to do." Jason stuffed the jerky in an outside pocket, then hooked his fingers into the plastic rings of the 6-packs and lifted them. "The two of you need to stay in here."

"Dad, come on. You might need help."

"Against two people? I think Mom and I have it covered." Jason navigated the steps to the front door of the RV and muscled it open while holding the six packs in his fingers.

The previously folded clutch of paper had been unfolded and spread across the hood of the RV and the woman with stringy hair held a thick, green highlighter pinched between her fingers. She and her bearded friend scrutinized Jason with unfiltered suspicion as he approached, bearing gifts. Still looking intently at Jason, the woman handed the highlighter to Samantha, who lifted it from between clenched fingers and pushed it into her pants pocket.

"Thank you," Samantha said quietly, putting a hand on the woman's shoulder.

A smile flickered on the woman's face and her gaze turned hungrily to what Jason was carrying. Samantha folded up the makeshift map as Jason took another step forward, holding out one of the six-packs. The bearded man took them both, his smile visible even from within the tangle of gray, untamed facial hair. With the soda out of his hands, Jason reached into his pockets and pulled out the packets of jerky, a mixture of beef and turkey, and held them out. The woman nodded her hesitant gratitude, then took them from his hands, tucking them into the same pocket she'd retrieved the maps from.

"Thank you both again," Samantha called after them, Kale standing by her side, wagging her tail furiously.

They both nodded, smiled, and waved as best they could, then continued making their way back toward the tent city.

"Are you going to tell me what just happened?" Jason stared at the people leaving, then turned back to Samantha. "How are they even alive?"

"That attack, whatever it was, clearly wasn't evenly distributed throughout the city. I'm not sure why; it could have just been wind currents or the method of dispersal the attackers used. These folks managed to make it through somewhat unscathed, though apparently about half their neighbors in another tent city did end up dying just a block or two away."

"So, what exactly were you doing in there with them for thirty minutes?"

"Honestly? Just listening to them, mostly. Helping them with a few minor wounds, too. Mostly scrapes and scratches and a couple twisted ankles. They were a little scared of me at first.

Usually when people come down here it's to knock down their tents and chase them off. But I just talked to them."

"And offered to give them our food."

"We had to pay them something." She lifted the folded map and shook it. "What they gave us is a lot more valuable than two six-packs of soda, some gas station beef jerky and a bit of my time."

"Are they not capable of going into stores and grabbing it like we did with this?"

"They've been too scared to, after seeing what's happened. They probably will now, after talking to me, though. Let's go inside before the kids start bouncing off the walls." Samantha turned toward the dog. "Come on, Kale."

They walked together back into the RV and Jason followed along, still staring in the direction of the tent city. The two people who had followed his wife out had vanished back inside, leaving no trace of them ever being there.

"Mom! What happened?" Sarah was waiting by the front seat next to Elijah, and they both followed their parents into the kitchen area.

"Sorry if I worried you," Samantha said, placing the folded map on the small table, then slowly spreading it out across the small surface. "The people in that camp were very helpful. I think they might have helped even if I hadn't promised them something to eat and drink."

Jason stared down at the map. A thick, green, neon line wound its way from the bottom of the map to the top, an angled and meandering trail written by the green highlighter.

"Bottom line: they know the city better than anyone. They walk its streets and they know the safe parts and the dangerous parts. Based on what they've seen and heard throughout their little network of survivors so far, this is as clear as we're going to get for the next few miles." She leaned down, resting on one hand, the finger of her other hand dragging its way along the green line.

"So, we go back?"

"We go back to this ramp here." Samantha circled a space along the drain. "That leads us back to the service road like we'd talked about doing. According to them, the way should be clear all the way to here." She moved her finger along the green line, then tapped it a few times. " It branches off here a bit, and we need to take the left fork up to here." She moved her finger again to a spot where the green line ended abruptly.

She stood upright and sighed, looking down at the paper.

"What happens then? The line just sort of ends." Jason angled his neck to look over at his wife.

"What happens then is we're on our own and we'll have to figure it out from there. This still gets us a pretty long way and we should be able to move a little faster than we have been. They told me the streets are pretty clear. Not completely, but better than what I told them we've run into so far."

Jason contemplated the map, standing upright as he continued staring at it. They stood in silence for a few seconds before he shifted his gaze to Samantha again. "We were worried about you. You were in there for over thirty minutes. I was just about to go in looking for you."

Samantha chuckled and rolled her eyes a bit. "You should know better." She turned and placed a hand on his shoulder, squeezing as she fixed him with a long, silent stare. "I appreciate the concern, though, truly." She turned and leaned down on the table again. "To be honest, they were very kind people. Remarkably relaxed, considering everything that's happening. In reality, they probably didn't need anything from us. In a way, what happened has been almost a blessing for them. There're countless places for them to find food or water now, and hardly anybody alive to fight them for it or to have them arrested. I know it sounds morbid, but..." She stood again and turned, not just toward Jason, but toward the twins as well. "Anyway. I'm very sorry for worrying you all."

"It's okay," Jason replied, studying the map a bit more closely, trying to keep a grin suppressed. "You did great and, loathe as I may be to admit it, you were right. I gotta remember to let you do your thing more often."

"Hold on. Let me go get my phone and take a voice memo of that. I think I might want to keep that for later use."

The twins shared a laugh and Jason lifted an eyebrow, fighting a grin of his own. He studied the green line, paying close attention to the surrounding landmarks, committing them to memory as best he could, then he folded up the map again and tucked it under his arm.

"Let's get moving again. We'll backtrack to the ramp we passed a short while ago and get back on the service road. We'll continue on that road for as long as we can. Do the best we can to put this city in the rearview mirror. I don't know about anyone else, but I've had just about all I can stand of Los Angeles."

There were nods of agreement around the small kitchen table, then Jason and Samantha made their way toward the front seats as the kids buckled themselves in preparation for getting back on the road.

CHAPTER SEVENTEEN

The Tills Family
Silverpine, Oregon

Benjamin knelt by the rear passenger tire of the Jeep, examining the pressure gauge. Nodding to himself, he stood, slipping the tire gauge into his pocket and dusting his hands off on the thighs of his pants. The Jeep was parked along the edge of the road leading out of the customer parking lot and toward the street that edged the vineyard property. He slowly made his way around the Jeep, pausing for a moment to stare into the open rear hatch, which was shielded by a hardtop cover. Two oversized camping backpacks were stashed in the rear compartment, tucked to one side. Both were full to bursting, the fabric pulled taut and bulging with their contents.

The backpacks mostly contained changes of clothes, though Benjamin had located a couple of tarps and placed them inside as well. A sleeping bag was bound tightly to the top of each pack and a box of calorie-rich protein bars sat wedged within a side pouch as well. A separate duffle bag was also in the back with some more provisions. Bottles of water, some rolled oats, crackers, mixed nuts as well as a jar of peanut butter were carefully stacked in the duffle bag, along with two loaves of bread and an assortment of other food that could either be eaten as-is or prepared without much effort.

Several narrow jerry cans of gasoline Benjamin had gathered from the property were tied down to the sides and rear of the Jeep, secured by canvas straps so there would be more room inside the vehicle. It was a four-seater, so Benjamin hadn't quite figured out how they might bring their family home in just the Jeep, but there was room in the back as well, and Doug was resourceful enough to figure out what to do. He continued walking around the vehicle, eyeing its exterior, mentally cycling through all the items he'd prepared, still anxious that there was something he might have forgotten. When it came to taking care of himself, Benjamin didn't worry, even a little. But when the Tills' lives were in his hands, he couldn't help but second and triple guess every last decision he'd made over the past few hours.

"I'm sure we'll be fine." Doug seemed to read his mind, placing a hand on the man's broad shoulder.

"You've got five days' worth of clean clothes in there in addition to everything else." Benjamin nodded toward the Jeep. "A thousand miles there and back would be a long trip in normal circumstances. I don't know what to expect what with all the mess going on." Benjamin cleared his throat. "Should be plenty of bottled water. Protein bars in the backpacks, stew, veggies, crackers and stuff to make peanut butter sandwiches in the duffle."

Doug walked toward the hood of the Jeep and once more removed the map from a pocket, spreading it out along the flat surface. He leaned in and traced the decided-upon trajectory with his finger, taking a few last scrutinizing looks at their plan.

"I won't lie, Mr. Tills," Benjamin said, "still not crazy about how close to the cities you're getting. But it's like we said before, there aren't exactly a lot of options."

Doug traced his finger down the long, straight path of I-5 as it headed toward California.

"If you do get off the highway, try to stick west." Benjamin tapped his finger in a large section of green wilderness between I-5 and the Pacific Ocean. "Better to stay off the beaten path. Crater Lake is over this way, which is a pretty big tourist attraction. Might be a huge influx of people heading toward the interstate from that direction."

"Duly noted." Doug studied the long, winding line that connected central Oregon to Los Angeles, his head shaking.

"You both still sure about this?"

"Sure, about what? Trying to find our family? Never been surer of anything in our lives." He looked over his shoulder as Sheila approached, dropping his voice to a whisper. "And yes, if things get bad, we've already discussed what we'll do. I'm not going to get us killed."

"Good man," Benjamin nodded. "I think I did the best I could to get you ready. Also, if you look at this line—" he stepped forward and pointed at the map spread across their hood. "I did my best to mark the locations of the rest areas, far as I know, anyway. It's not exact, but it might help. Just in case you need to pull over."

Doug nodded, then turned toward Benjamin, extending a hand. Benjamin pressed his own palm into Doug's, the two men shaking.

"I appreciate everything you've done for us, Benjamin."

"Don't say it like you're saying good-bye, Mr. Tills. You'll be back in a couple of days."

"And you're okay to hold down the fort?"

"Been doing it for a long time. No offense to you or the missus, but we all know who really runs the show around here." The corners of his mouth tilted upward, and Doug chuckled.

"You couldn't be more right." Sheila grasped Benjamin's shoulders and leaned in for a gentle embrace, the older man's cheeks flushing a deep, boiling crimson.

"We'll be back, like you said." Doug opened the driver's side door. "Sooner than you think."

Sheila made her way around to the passenger's side of the Jeep and opened her door as well. "Thanks for keeping things together while we go."

"We'll make sure it's just the same as you left it." Benjamin nodded back toward the building.

Brandi and Darryl stood just outside, keeping their distance. "Stay safe!" Sheila lifted a hand, waving toward Brandi and Darryl, the two of them waving back.

"You, too!" Brandi called, then hugged her arms around herself.

Doug and Sheila climbed into the Jeep and shut both doors, then Doug rolled down his window.

"I'd tell you to call us if you need anything, except, well—"

"We'll be fine," Benjamin replied. "We'll be just fine."

Doug and Sheila both nodded, then the Jeep's engine growled to life and it pulled away, easing up the gradual slope of the driveway to the adjoining road. Braking slightly, it angled left, merged onto the road, then vanished behind the trees. For a time, Benjamin remained where he was, waiting as the engine faded, the Jeep driving further into the distance. Brandi approached from behind, walking forward slowly, Darryl lingering farther behind.

"Darryl told me that their daughter is ex-military. Is that true?"

"Yeah." Benjamin barely nodded. "What else did Darryl tell you?" There was a sharpened edge of annoyance in his words.

Brandi cleared her throat self-consciously as she searched for an answer. "Not much, really. Just that Samantha holds week-long training courses up here a few times a year. Teaches wilderness first aid. Some basic survival skills, that sort of thing."

"Yeah. That's true."

"So why are they doing it?"

"Doing what?"

"Why are Doug and Sheila racing off to their rescue? Seems like their daughter and her family can take care of themselves."

The hard edges of Benjamin's expression relaxed, one eyebrow elevating. He fixed Brandi with a sympathetic look, showing no sign of the rigid exterior he'd maintained moments earlier.

"Once you have kids, you'll understand."

"I don't follow."

"If you have kids, once you have them, you'll realize that no matter how old they grow or how capable they might get, you'd do pretty much anything in your power to help them. Even if they don't necessarily need it."

Brandi nodded, staring off in the direction where the Jeep had left a few minutes before.

"I only hope it's as easy as they seem to think it is." Benjamin stuffed his hands in his pockets and listened to the vast, silent world that surrounded them.

Doug gripped the wheel as the Jeep hurtled down the narrow road, thick, green walls of trees blurring past them on each side. The trip had been almost relaxing, a calm and easy Sunday drive through the narrow back roads of rural Oregon. Sheila pressed herself up against the passenger window, staring at the sprawling wilderness. Up ahead, a green sign warned them of the upcoming junction of Interstate 5, the merging lane opening up on the left. Moments later they rounded the bend, and fluttering specks of pale gray drifted along the slope of the windshield. Doug leaned a bit, studying the sparse flecks, squinting through the glass.

"Is that—" Sheila hesitated as Doug hit the windshield wipers.

They swept across the windshield, smearing the gray pieces into charcoal smudges across the glass. More flakes dusted the air ahead, floating and falling, filling the area before them like aimless insects. Mixed within the flakes were tiny, pinprick lights, coasting and fluttering to the ground.

"It's ash. Ash and embers." Doug followed the bend of the road, the trees separating slightly to their left.

Smoke boiled across the horizon, a thickened, churning blemish that coated the sky. Within the Jeep, the temperature rose a few degrees, and the flakes of ash grew in intensity. Doug accelerated, pulling to the left and joining the merge lane, following the signs toward I-5 that promised to be a mile ahead. The entire horizon had darkened with a gray charcoal smoke, spreading far and wide beyond the trees.

"That *is* Portland." Sheila gripped the interior handle of the Jeep's car door and Doug only nodded his agreement.

They completed the merge from the access road to the interstate and Doug was about to accelerate when he instead slammed on the brakes, swerving around a glut of traffic in and around the onramp to I-5. He steered sharply left, rolling along in the grass for a moment before he corrected, bumping loudly across the ridged shoulder before he got back on the highway itself. Across the median, cars and trucks had created a second bottleneck attempting to get off the interstate toward Portland. Vehicles sat side by side, clotting both lanes of northbound traffic, and one multi-vehicle accident was tangled near the rear of the traffic jam, a handful of cars and SUVs jumbled together into a bent and buckled mass of metal.

Although the offramp was bad, the northbound lane cleared as they continued south, the numbers of cars lessening, the space between them growing wider and wider with each passing moment. Doug accelerated further, increasing his speed, whipping past rows of trees and the occasional stopped vehicle.

Smoke-filled skies drew further to the east, then backed away, thinning to reveal the gray-hued horizon. Doug stared in the rearview mirror as they headed south, thick columns of black smoke twisting up toward the sky, smaller and further away behind them. A downward ditch separated the southbound and northbound lanes of travel and, up ahead along the right shoulder, an eighteen-wheeler had pulled off, half on the grass and half on the pavement and Doug angled around it, crossing between the northbound and southbound lanes using the median as necessary, the Jeep handling the transitions with ease.

The northbound lane was dotted with traffic, though not enough to block travel further south of Portland. Several cars had pulled over, a few of them with their doors still open, though none of the vehicles appeared to have anyone in them, the drivers having all evacuated. There were many other tracks down the median that criss-crossed in the same manner as Doug was driving, though how long ago they'd been made was impossible to tell.

With their path relatively clear again, Doug relaxed, his shoulders loosening, his body settling into the driver's seat. Sheila fished out the tracking device, powered it on and studied the screen carefully, squinting at it.

"They're still moving. Slowly, but still moving."

"Can you tell where they are?"

"Still in the city. Still in Los Angeles." Sheila shook her head in disbelief. "They've barely moved at all. It's been so long, how are they still stuck in more or less the same place?"

"L.A. traffic was legendarily bad even before all this happened. If a lot of people have died, that's going to be a lot of traffic that's going nowhere fast."

"If we keep up this pace, we could be in Los Angeles by midnight."

Doug smiled, patting her on the leg. "Let's focus on getting out of Oregon first, then we'll talk about what it'll take to get to

L.A. I'm in just as much of a hurry as you are, though, trust me."

"Sorry. I know Samantha and Jason can take care of themselves. I know they can handle almost anything that's thrown at them. But...."

"I know. That's why we're here." Doug smiled at her. "We'll get to them, I promise. We'll get to them, and we'll get back to the vineyard and things will be just fine."

They continued in silence for a stretch of time, following I-5 south, moving through the Oregon wilderness. Along both sides of the road, trees came and went, occasionally spreading far enough apart to reveal quiet, residential neighborhoods throughout the smaller Oregon communities. Single family houses peered out at them from between gaps in various trees, and from time to time, people were standing outside the homes, huddled in groups, talking amongst themselves. Just south of one of those neighborhoods, a stretch of grass covered a wide section of the right shoulder, just beyond an SUV that was pulled up against the guardrail. Three deer stood in the meadow near the SUV, a buck, a doe, and a baby fawn. The doe and the fawn were bent low eating grass while the buck held his head high, a broad rack of antlers extending from just behind each twitching ear, watching the Jeep intently as they drove by.

"What is it?"

"The deer," Doug pointed. "Some beauty amidst all of this nonsense."

They passed the field with the three deer and crossed over into another sprawling, residential neighborhood. Trees separated and revealed a look at a stark, white church in the near distance. Though it was far from the road, a man in a black robe stood visible at the top of the steps, arms outstretched, a gathering congregation forming on the grass. The man's voice didn't carry, but he gestured with a calming authority, communicating with a captive audience. Trees filled in the empty spaces again and the congregation was gone, ethereal as the wind.

As they continued, several silhouettes darkened the north-bound lane, drawing closer at a fast clip. Moments later, the throaty snarl of engines carried, a line of vehicles coming into view. A caravan of armored vehicles filled the slow lane coming northbound, led by a pair of Humvees. Two military transports followed, with a half-dozen supply trucks afterwards, then another handful of Humvees filled out the rest of the line. They roared past, showing no signs of interest in the Tills' southbound travelling Jeep and, moments later, the military caravan had vanished into the distance, heading toward the smoldering cities to the north.

They passed another neighborhood, clusters of one and two-story homes gathered around a common road which circled throughout cookie cutter neighborhoods. Two children played in one of the roads, though as Doug passed, a front door opened and an angry woman demanded that they come back inside, gesturing wildly with her hand. A few moments later, they passed by a glass-encased car dealership set amidst a frontage of trees. Even from the road, the shattered windows were visible, smoke trailing from the large building, a gathered mass of people huddled around luxury vehicles in the parking lot and showroom. One of the men struck at a vehicle's window with a crowbar, repeatedly trying to force his way inside and a chill passed up Doug's spine.

"Did you see that?" He asked, and Sheila nodded.

To the left, more businesses came into view, and more people on the streets outside them gathered in groups, their angst and anger on full display even from the highway. Doug pressed the gas further to the floor, driving more quickly, his knuckles growing white as he gripped the steering wheel tighter.

"Do you think it's like that in Los Angeles?" Sheila asked.

"I suppose that all depends on how many people are even still

—" He bit off the words just a second too late, though Sheila didn't repond. "Sorry, I didn't mean...."

Moments later they passed a sign telling them they were within ten miles of the Salem city limits. Doug took a steadying breath and scanned the road ahead, which bent sharply to the left, a thicket of trees separating the two lanes of the freeway for a brief moment. With Salem approaching, Doug leaned forward, still pressing the gas to the floor, a sense of anticipation hurrying them onward. The Jeep navigated the turn with a clean, wide sweep, working its way around another stopped tractor trailer truck on the left, and an SUV on the right. Doug swerved around the final portion of the bend and swore loudly as his foot jumped from the gas to the brake.

"Doug! Look out!" Sheila drew back, pushing against the floor and dashboard, eyes growing wide in horror.

Across both lanes of southbound traffic, a twisted tangle of a collision stretched from shoulder-to-shoulder. An eighteen-wheeler had jackknifed, twisting to the right with enough momentum to topple the trailer over. Three other vehicles had plowed into the capsized trailer at speed, pummeling themselves into little more than twisted wreckage. Shattered glass and spilled fluids spread across the entirety of I-5 south, the air rich with the stink of gas and smoke. Shredded strips of torn metal and other debris littered the roadway as well, spread in a wide arc from the point of impact. Doug slammed on the brakes and hauled the wheel sharply to the left, his teeth grinding, bone scraping bone.

"Hold on!" He swerved hard, his arms and wrists in sudden pain from the exertion, the Jeep lurching wildly toward the median between south and north.

The Jeep's tires squealed and thumped from the force of the ABS, crunching across a scattered layer of debris in the street, the vehicle jostling wildly as they plowed through a narrow gap between crumpled vehicles. A muffled bang echoed from the front passenger tire, the wheel yanking in Doug's grip, threatening to tear itself loose from his fists. The Jeep thundered through in a shuddering barrage of forward movement, the entire vehicle shaking furiously around them. All at once, as they passed through the debris field, the Jeep wrenched to the left, a second tire exploding, the sudden jolting thunder of rolling on rims jostling the vehicle.

"Doug!"

"Hold on, Sheila!"

The rear of the Jeep kicked out, sliding at an angle toward the crumpled mass of a small car that had bounced off the trailer. Doug tapped the brake, then stomped the gas, steering through the fishtail that dragged them sideways. He steered into it, coaxing the Jeep forward and through. There was a moment of over-correction, the vehicle lurching slightly, tipping toward the driver's side as Doug gritted his teeth and torqued the other way. He hit the gas again, pulling the Jeep through its near turnover, then shot forward, rolling awkwardly over the ridged shoulder. Ahead of them, the center median dipped down into a grass-covered ditch and Doug hit the brakes again, steering right. His evasive maneuvering could only carry them so far, though, and the front tires slammed through the grass and carried them over the edge of the median down a sharply angled slope.

The Jeep skidded and slid, then hammered suddenly into the bottom of the ditch, coming to a sudden, shocking halt. The scream of adrenaline and jolting momentum whip-lashed through Doug and Sheila, jerking them forward, their safety belts tugging them tightly back, both heads snapping with the abrupt change in direction as the airbags inflated. The echoing, almost deafening chorus of the accident ceased all at once, a sudden silence settling into the Jeep's cabin. A soft and steady tick from the engine was the only lingering sign that the vehicle had ever been functional as husband and wife sat strapped into their seats, willing the world to stop spinning.

Breathing came in strangled, haggard inhalations, frantic at first, before settling into a more even rhythm. Doug's leg ached, his back was coated in knives of pain and his neck was clamped in a too-tight vice. He sat in his seat, staring through the windshield, his entire left leg awash in an acid bath of pain.

"Sheila? You... you okay?"

"I... think so?" Sheila nodded, though the movement of her neck caused her to wince.

Doug reached across his body and unclasped his seat belt, slowly drawing it back over his stomach and chest. Every breath he took shot pain through his back and into his left leg, a lingering agony permeating in his skull. Sheila unbuckled her belt as well, reaching over to slowly open her door, pushing the remnants of her airbag out of the way. They moved cautiously, testing each of the smallest motions to make sure they didn't cause more pain. Doug slid to the left, carefully stepping out, favoring his left leg.

As he cleared himself from the Jeep, he tested the leg a bit, putting some extra weight on it, rotating his pained ankle and rubbing the bone-deep throb on his left thigh. Pressing a hand to the hood of the Jeep, he grimaced as he made his way from the driver's seat, slowly massaging the pain away. His heart hammered in his chest, the rapid-fire, adrenaline-fueled beat fluttering against his ribs, a nauseous pit forming in his stomach. The passenger door slammed as Sheila exited, moving more comfortably and less gingerly than he was.

"You're limping." She made her way around the Jeep and over to where he leaned against it.

"It's fine. Just feels like a bone bruise or something." He rubbed his palm into the dull, aching muscle of his thigh and moved his toes within his boot. "Everything is still attached."

"Are you bleeding?" Sheila touched his pant leg.

"I don't think so, but I don't exactly want to take my pants off right here to double check." Doug massaged his temples and stared up at the sky.

Clouds slowly tracked their way above him, meandering across the horizon. His children and grandchildren were trapped within a dead city and his attempt at a rescue had utterly failed practically before it had begun. He tore his eyes from the clouds and limped away from the Jeep, turning to get a better look at it. Both front tires were popped, rubber flattened against the rounded, metal rims. Doug took a slow walk around the front, taking in the grille.

"Relatively unscathed up here," he said, making his way toward the passenger side and taking a look down the length of the vehicle. "Things don't look awful, all things considered. Some scrapes and dings, but besides the flat tires, she still looks roadworthy."

"Besides the flat tires." Sheila followed him around, walking a bit faster so she could catch up with him, just in case his leg went out from underneath him. "Is there anything we can do?"

Doug groaned softly as he lifted his left leg again and rotated his ankle. He opened the passenger's side door and took out the tracking device, holding it in his hand. Turning it on, he studied the screen as it brightened, though the same message about not getting a signal appeared instead of an image.

"I swear, the satellites that this thing's connected to must be the cheapest ones they could throw into orbit. Let's head back up to the road, see if we get a better signal."

Sheila clung to his side, allowing him to lean on her slightly to ease the strain on his leg. Together, they navigated the shallow slope of the hill, walking up to the shoulder of I-5. Doug's attention was focused on the screen of the tracking device, his eyes narrowed as the static faded slightly and the words *Waiting for Signal...* winked away. They reached the shoulder, stepping up to the crest of where the road met the grass and the RV's beacon became clearer. It was still swarmed by an interminable gathering of intersections, crossroads, and thick, obscure shapes, trapped within the confines of a concrete, steel, and glass prison. Doug was absorbed by the screen, watching as the beacon made an ever-subtle shift forward, traveling at an eternally slow pace. He shook his head, momentarily captivated, and barely reacted to Sheila stopping short. She was no longer next to him, but standing stock still.

"Sheila?" Doug was a few steps ahead and turned to look back at his wife, then back in the direction she was staring unblinking.

An almost endless stretch of pavement lay before them, Interstate 5 moving farther south, traveling a seemingly eternal distance, but wrecked cars dotted the landscape, twisted collisions along each side of the interstate, across all lanes and shoulders, both northbound and southbound. Pale smoke rose in narrow trails from various crumpled heaps of crashed vehicles, and the still forms of bodies were visible in more than a few of the wrecks. The buildings of a small town peered through the trees along each side of the road, even more dark smoke rising from within the fists of residences and small businesses. The sky darkened with the rising smoke, a swirling, charcoal smog that blocked the floating clouds and accented the horizon in shades of dull, gunmetal gray.

"What do we do?" Sheila asked, quiet and thready, words barely held together by narrow strands of her voice.

For the first time that Doug could remember, he didn't have an answer to her question. Almost absently, he stared down at the tracker again then moved close to his wife, his arm dropping to his side, the tracker slipping from suddenly slack fingers and clattering to the pavement at his feet.

CHAPTER EIGHTEEN

The O'Brian Family
Los Angeles, California

The continued trek along the service road had proven the
residents of the tent city correct and Jason was allowing himself
just the briefest sense of optimism. They followed the mostly
empty service road, moving as fast as the narrow ribbon of pavement would afford until Samantha leaned into the unfolded paper
on the dashboard, tracing through an imaginary section of it as
she bit her lip.

"There should be a way through to the right up here. Hopefully it'll be gradual enough that you can maintain speed and
break through the fence."

"Break through the fence?"

Samantha nodded. "They told me that was the most direct
way to get back to the main roads."

"Okay," Jason let out a breath. "If you're sure."

"Not much choice. Service road ends about a half mile north

based on this map, and if we get back into the river proper then it'll become much more river-like, at least according to what Jerry and Caitlyn told me. We won't be able to travel through here much longer."

"Got it. Divert to the right, you say?"

Samantha nodded and looked up from the map, squinting at the service road that stretched before them, drowning in surrounding shadows. Jason kept a close eye on the fence to their right as it drew further away from the road, the pavement stretching on straight as the fence bent gradually to the right.

"There." Samantha stabbed a finger toward the windshield.

"Yep, got it."

The pavement bent at a forty-five-degree angle, moving toward the city beyond and Jason maintained his speed as he steered right, guiding the RV along the diverging stretch of concrete. Seconds later the fence stretched before them, and rather than slow, he pressed the accelerator further, increasing their speed as the grille of the RV buried itself in the chain-link, ripping it from its moorings, twisting it and dragging it beneath the rolling wheels of the RV.

"Left!"

Jason steered the wheel and tapped the brakes, merging onto another road just beyond the fence. Tires squawked with an abrupt peel of rubber on road as the RV jostled with the speed of the turn. Jason straightened out and continued driving. To the right, on a parallel road, cars were scattered, several of them parked in oblong angles, their doors open with bodies slumped over steering wheels or lying on the ground.

"Where are all the cars here?" Samantha nodded at the road ahead, which disappeared into the creeping darkness of taller buildings on either side.

"Good question. Not that I really care... long may the clear roads last."

Jason swerved left, avoiding a clutch of three corpses, but the driver's side tire rolled over the sprawled legs of another. A muffled crunch jostled the front wheel, and he guided the RV back, trying desperately to navigate through the obstacle course of dead bodies. He narrowly missed a piled group of a half dozen or more — impossible to tell how many within the tangle of arms and legs— but as he did so, he crunched over a pair of what looked like teenagers, tangled in a final embrace, their bodies bursting beneath his tires. Samantha winced visibly as she turned backwards in her seat and Jason checked the rearview mirror. Sarah and Eli were both awake, watching out the windows, their bodies rigid as they braced for the bumps and jostles.

"You two good?"

"Good is relative, mom," Sarah called back.

"Agreed," Elijah nodded. "We're alive."

"Good enough." Samantha turned back. "Hold on—" Samantha yanked the map from the dashboard. "We're supposed to take a right up here."

"Seriously?" Jason gestured to an intersection of wide cobblestone that crossed the smooth asphalt ahead.

"That's what it says."

"Is that stone? Is this even a road?" Jason eyed a diamond-shaped sign mounted to a post, falling into view as they neared the intersection.

Pedestrian Walkway – No Motor Vehicles Allowed

"Do you see that?" Jason nodded toward the sign, tilted at an angle, but still visible as they approached.

"I don't think the police are going to stop us."

Jason sighed and drove around the sprawled form of three young men wearing local sports team jerseys, then braked and twisted the wheel to the right, navigating the turn. They crunched over another sprawl of lifeless limbs, the RV jostling as it rolled across more bodies and then continued bouncing as they traversed the cobblestone path, the steering wheel bucking in Jason's tight grip.

"Whoa!" He slammed the brakes suddenly as they approached another intersection.

The RV lurched to a sudden halt, all of them pulled tight against their seatbelts by the stop. Kale lifted her head, ears perked, looking around curiously as she slid a few feet across the slick kitchen floor, stopping when her body reached the carpeted section. Just ahead of the RV was a series of bollards, cylindrical-shaped posts that rose from the cobblestone, spread across the path near the intersection. They blocked off another section of the pedestrian walkway beyond where restaurants had set up outside dining areas and where racks of goods stood just outside the front-facing windows of various shops.

"What happened?" Eli turned slightly, inching forward on his seat.

"Our way is blocked." Jason drummed his fingers on the steering wheel. "Are you sure this is the right way?"

Samantha lifted the map and leaned in to check it more closely. She touched the marked passage with her finger and then lifted her eyes to look at the surrounding landmarks.

"Definitely matches what we're seeing here."

"Is there a way around?"

"Not that I can tell. I mean, besides backing all the way out of here and finding an alternate route. But look at that stretch of cobblestone ahead. There aren't even any dead bodies there. If we can get past these barricades, it might be clear sailing for a bit."

Samantha stood and turned toward the twins. "You guys stay in here, okay? Dad and I need to run outside for a second."

"You guys can't leave us in here again." Eli started to stand, Sarah mimicking his motions and nodding in agreement.

Samantha and Jason shared a look and shrugged. "Okay. Fine. Put a leash on Kale, too, would you? She probably has to do her business."

Eli nodded and retrieved Kale's leash from a nearby hook and Samantha led the five of them outside through the opened front door of the RV. Once again she was stunned by the vast silence that surrounded them, a penetrating, bleak nothingness in all directions. Somewhere in the city, outside of view, more birds called from several different directions, but there were no other signs of life outside of their family.

"What's on your mind?" Jason stepped up next to Samantha as they walked toward the bollards. "I see that look in your eyes."

"When I was teaching this one time— it might have been last year, I don't remember. I had some downtime for a few days."

"I think I remember that. There was some scheduling SNAFU."

"Yeah, that was when you guys were at home and I was at the coast." Samantha's eyes narrowed in recollection. " I stopped at this tiny little snorkel shop that was taking beginners out for lessons."

"I don't think you ever told me this before."

Samantha shrugged. "It wasn't all that important. I just remember going beneath the surface of the water, sinking down and there was this vast ocean of silence all around me. The instructors were taking the beginners out a ways and I was by myself and... it was like the world itself had retreated, leaving me isolated in this strange alien world beneath the sea." She wrapped her arms around herself. Nearby, the kids threaded their way through the bollards, letting Kale lead them around on the leash. "I've spent plenty of time in the water, but that was different."

"What made you think of that?"

"Listen." All around them, the void of noise was draped like a thick cloak across the shoulders of all of Los Angeles. "Just— silence." Jason nodded his understanding. "Only this silence isn't comforting." Samantha lowered her voice, leaning in close. "This silence feels ominous, Jason. Like the gap between giant's footfalls and it's just a matter of time before the next step comes down."

"Easy, there. We're still alive, and we're making good time. We're gonna be fine."

"I know we'll be fine getting out of the city. I just wonder what's going to happen after that." Samantha cleared her throat and forced a smile as she called to the twins. "Don't go too far, kids."

"You gotta come check this out, mom." Elijah called. "There's a booth over there." He pointed a narrow finger toward a nearby building.

Samantha gave Jason's hand a squeeze and stepped past him, walking toward the narrow structure that stood nearby. Following Eli to the booth, she stepped inside and studied a small control panel by a square-shaped window.

"Will you look at that. These are retractable bollards, by the looks of it."

Jason came up behind her, confirming her suspicion. "Looks a lot like the controls at the embassy. Although," Jason poked his head out of the booth, "with the power out, getting them down's going to be an exercise in frustration. Hm... hang on a second."

Jason walked toward one of the nearby bollards and crouched down, searching it for a handle or release mechanism.

"Maybe we *will* have to double back?" Samantha called from the booth.

"Nah. There has to be some sort of redundancy in place." Jason circled the bollard, looking for anything out of place on its smooth surface.

Back inside, Samantha stared at the control panel, chewing her lip as she studied the various buttons and switches. To the right of the panel, there was a large, red, circular plunger beneath a simple rectangular plate that read 'Manual Release' in bold, red letters.

"I think I found something!" Samantha called out.

Jason looked at her from where he crouched next to one of the bollards. Samantha pressed her palm into the plunger and leaned into it, shoving the plunger flush with the console. Jason stood and stepped back, staring at the bollard, though nothing had visibly changed.

"Anything?"

Jason shook his head, then stepped toward it again, craning his neck. He crouched once more, squatting around to the rear of the post.

"Hold on! I've got something here." He reached down near the base of the bollard and flipped up a small, glass shield covering a small silver ring. "Hit that switch again!"

Samantha depressed the plunger as far as it could go as Jason reached toward the base of the bollard and pulled up on the ring. There was a quiet, prolonged hiss of hydraulics, but the post itself didn't move.

"Eli! Come over here!"

Eli swung around and jogged toward him, leaving Sarah and Kale standing together near a far bollard.

"Push down on the top of this would you?"

Eli nodded and got up on tiptoes, then pressed his palms into the rounded top of the bollard and shoved down. There was another hiss of noise as the bollard slowly retracted with the combined effort of the three of them. Working together, they finally shoved, pushed and forced the bollard to retract fully, seating itself within a rounded hole in the cobblestone, flush with street level.

"Nice work, guys!" Samantha shouted from inside the booth.

"Come on, Eli, let's take care of these others." Jason stood back, silently evaluating the width of the passage. "Three of them should be enough."

They walked to a second bollard and Samantha pressed the manual retraction button while Jason activated the release on the bollard itself and Eli helped shove it down into the ground. They repeated the process for the third, as Kale stared at them, her head cocked in curiosity.

"Excellent," Samantha stepped out of the booth. "Let's get moving."

The others had read her mind and were already on the way back to the RV. They all filed inside, and Samantha slipped into the front passenger seat while Jason took up his position behind the wheel. Starting the engine, Jason accelerated slowly, squeezing into the gap they'd created by manually retracting the bollards, then crossed the intersection and moved into the next section of the cobblestone walkway. As Samantha had already observed, the path was clearer throughout the next block; there were scattered dead bodies, but they all rested alongside the various store fronts and businesses, leaving a wide enough gap in the center for the RV to move without hindrance.

Chairs that had been positioned around restaurant tables were capsized from the people eating their meals having slumped to the ground. Food littered the ground around them, some of it still on plates on the table's surface. Squirrels huddled almost everywhere they could see, gathering around the rounded tables, picking at the various morsels of left-behind food. Several birds did the same, clutches of crows and pigeons pecking plates and tabletops with sharpened beaks, hacking at the food eagerly, though the growling engine of the RV sent them scattering as the O'Brians moved through.

To the right, several racks of clothing had been toppled over, two dead women sprawled nearby, face down, cups of spilled coffee resting on neatly pressed cobblestone. Reflections from the storefront windows prevented visibility inside, though most doors stood open, corpses visible within the shops as well as outside. It was a moment, frozen in time, the living replaced with the dead, a makeshift mausoleum in celebration of twenty-first century capitalism.

"Hold up. More barricades." Samantha pointed ahead, another series of rounded bollards blocking their path of travel.

The familiar shape of a slender booth stood to the left of the bollards and Jason eased on the brakes, bringing the RV to a stop a few feet from the series of posts that blocked their path. Jason cut the engine, and everyone gathered together, once more leaving the RV through the front door and heading out onto the pedestrian walkway. Samantha took up her spot in the booth while Jason and Sarah worked together to retract the posts, leaving Eli in charge of Kale the second time around. With the process having already been ironed out previously, it didn't take long before the way was clear.

As they started to head back to the RV, Samantha stopped momentarily and took a look at their surroundings, lifting a hand toward a nearby storefront.

"Hey, Jason. There's a pet store here. How much food did we bring for Kale?"

"Probably not enough. Should we check it out?"

"Absolutely." Samantha turned slowly, studying their surroundings. "Things are pretty quiet here, all things considered. We might want to take advantage of that and do a little shopping."

"It's not really shopping, though," Sarah quietly interjected. "Isn't it stealing?"

"I suppose that depends on how you look at it." Samantha gently squeezed her daughter's shoulder. "I can definitely see why you might say that, and to a point, you're probably right. Most of these people are dead, Sarah, including the owners of the stores. I'm not about to hurt anyone or take anything from someone who's alive who needs it, but we need to look out for ourselves and if that means doing some things that are illegal but aren't hurting anyone, then that's something I'm willing to do."

"I understand." Sarah nodded.

"I know you do." Samantha nodded toward the pet store, guiding the family toward it.

The door wasn't open, but it was unlocked, and Samantha swung it open freely, exposing the interior of the store so they could all file inside. It wasn't a large store, but the shelves were very well stocked with supplies for cats, dogs, birds and several species of reptile and rodent. A dead body rested in the furthest right aisle, on its back, wedged in a narrow space by a rack of leashes and harnesses. Samantha led them to a second aisle, which cut through the middle of the small shop and headed toward the rear where cases of canned food and stacks of bags lined various dark-colored shelves.

A permeating smell of dog food, cat food and odorous toys and treats filled the air, partially masking a richer, more acrid underlying scent. Jason held up a hand, stopping short, halfway down the center aisle, his nostrils flaring. He walked to the end of the aisle and peered into the next, where a pet owner lay on her side, leash still in her hand, leading toward a large still form a few feet away. The dog had perished along with its owner, both of their bodies starting to smell.

"Come on," Jason waved to the family. "Toward the back, there's food there."

They made their way toward the back of the store all together where Jason quickly located the familiar label of Kale's favorite canned wet food and pulled an entire case from the shelf, then turned and handed it off to Sarah.

"Can you take that?"

"Yep, got it."

Jason returned his attention to the shelves and lifted a second case, turning toward Eli. His son held out his arms in wait, though Kale was tugging her leash, nose pointing at a case of treats that bore a familiar label.

"Can you handle the food and Kale?"

"Sure, I can. She's all show." Elijah gave the leash a quick tug and Kale obeyed, returning to Eli's side, though her attention was still on the bags on the shelf.

"I'll grab some for her." Jason lifted a couple bags of treats from the shelves which he set on top of the case that Sarah held. "Last thing - we need some dried food, too. Mom and I will each take a bag." He crouched low and grunted as he hefted a fifty-pound bag of dried food and levered it up in Samantha's direction. "Can you—"

"Don't even ask." She shook him off, took the bag and dumped it over one shoulder. "I'm fine."

Jason stifled a grin and did the same, lifting a fifty-pound bag over his own shoulder.

"Okay, let's go. " They navigated back through the aisles and toward the store's front, then they made their way across the cobblestone walkway and back to the RV, opening the door and going inside, depositing the pet food on the kitchen counter and floor.

Across the street from where they were parked was a coffee shop, its modern frontage shrouded by a broad, green awning, an inviting chalk-lined logo welcoming visitors inside. Cafe seating was set up in a tight cluster within a roped-off section of cobblestone, with seven dead bodies sprawled on the ground throughout an ornate combination of round and square-shaped metal tables. The door stood ajar, a barista in a green apron lying prone on her right side, arms tangled together, a coffee pot resting on the ground just outside the reach of her fingers.

"Stay here for a minute." Jason strode forward, ignoring the questions from Elijah and Sarah, and stepped past the fallen barista and into the coffee shop.

The decor was a rich, dark, aged wood, bearing more resemblance to a small-town tavern than an upscale coffee shop. A wooden counter was polished to an almost gleaming shine, several taps along the wall marked with various blends of cold brew. Three tall coffee carafes were lined up side by side, a chalkboard mounted to the wall identifying their esoteric collection of regional and international beans. Four people were dead inside, at least within Jason's view, two of them by the counter, one sitting at a table, the other slumped on his side on a thickly cushioned couch off in the corner.

The air carried the bitter but pleasing scent of coffee beans that reminded Jason why he'd come inside in the first place. He walked toward the near side of the counter where some souvenir items with the coffee shop's logo were set out. One of them was a canvas tote bag and he lifted it from its shelf, peeling it apart to check its size. Nodding his silent approval, he walked back into the center of the shop. A small, circular island with pegboards carried several snack items and he unloaded every one of them, placing the kettle-cooked potato chips, varying flavors of dried meat, mixed nuts and trail mix into the tote bag.

After emptying the center island, he walked over to another set of shelves built into the rear wall, splitting the counter at the back where people would sit and nurse their expensive coffee drinks. Water bottles and coffee mugs were set in even rows on the shelves, but Jason immediately focused on the two rows of canned coffee drinks. They carried colorful diagrams along their curved, aluminum exteriors and promised all natural ingredients and the same caffeine as a cup of strong coffee. Jason removed every single can and put them in the canvas tote, the bag getting heavier and heavier with each one. Satisfied that there wasn't anything of value left behind, he walked back toward the door and out onto the cobblestone walkway.

When he returned to the spot his family had been, they were gone, and it took a moment to notice that Samantha, the twins and Kale had moved across the street, standing next to a large window.

"Uh huh!" Samantha waved him over. "Should have known, had to get your caffeine fix?"

"They had some cans of coffee on the shelves in there that don't require refrigeration and will keep without spoiling for a while. Figured a little extra energy boost wouldn't be a bad thing. Bonus find of some trail mix and other stuff." He lifted the bag to show her. "What did you stumble upon?"

"Sarah noticed it while we were standing there. Says it's an antiques and collectibles store, but..." she pressed her hands to the glass and stared inside. "Seems more like an upscale pawn shop to me."

"Anything good?"

"I had my eye on those." Samantha tapped the glass.

Within view of the window was a small set of shelves on the sill. Upon each of the shelves was a different knife, the blades set in various lengths and sizes.

"Knives?"

"Sure. Besides that dinky little pocketknife you have, we don't really have any. If we're going to be on the road for a while they'll always come in handy. Either for household purposes or... other things."

Jason nodded without hesitation. "I'm on board."

The family made their way to the front door and eased it open, stepping into the pawn shop. Samantha had been right – though it had framed itself as some sort of upper-class antique store, it was a glorified pawn shop, much of its contents shabby old items of little use. They all took a quick perusal around the shop but found little of interest aside from the knives Samantha had already pointed out. One of them was a thickly curved hunting knife, its blade long and built into a thick, textured hilt. A second knife had a thinner blade, slender and straight, its hilt smooth and rounded outward to fit the contours of a person's hand. Both knives were displayed with leather sheaths, and after pulling the sheaths away to examine the blades, Samantha returned them and stuffed them in her jacket pocket. There was a single jackknife and a Swiss Army knife, both of which Samantha took and stashed away along with the first two.

Moments later, after Elijah paused for a moment to look long-ingly at an abandoned video game system, they made their way to the door and stepped back outside. They spent a few more minutes window shopping past nearby stores and, finding nothing of interest, they returned to the RV, going inside and returning to their places. Both kids went back to their seats by the makeshift kitchen while Samantha and Jason settled into the front seats, the canvas bag and the knives set down nearby.

"Let's check that map again." Jason pointed to the folded paper on the dashboard and Samantha lifted it off and unfolded it, smoothing it across the dash's surface where, together, they studied the map and the route the tent city inhabitants had helped them chart.

"This area here— looks like more residential areas. Potentially even apartment buildings." Jason shook his head. "We didn't have great experience the last time."

"Tough to tell how tall the buildings are on this map."

"Even if they're five or six stories that could be a problem."

"Following their instructions got us this far; I think we need to keep going and just deal with whatever we come across."

"Good enough for me."

Jason started the RV and drove slowly over the place where the bollards had been when they'd arrived, moving onto the final stretch of cobblestone before it intersected once more with regular pavement. He managed to avoid the littered sprawl of dead bodies until he reached the road itself, but as he turned onto it, more corpses were spread across the street before him. Touching the gas, he drove the RV forward, tightening his grip on the wheel as they jostled roughly across the muscles and bones of the dead bodies.

As he'd been doing since they set off, Jason did his best to avoid the larger groups of corpses, but still couldn't help crushing limbs beneath the tires, muffled, crab shell cracks and splinters carrying into the cabin of the vehicle. Sarah and Eli both huddled in their seats, staring anywhere but out the windows, bodies tense with Kale at their feet. As the RV continued onward, a few taller buildings appeared in the distance, flanking the same road they traveled, their tall spires casting deep shadows across the pavement. Jason followed Samantha's directions, both of them keeping as alert as humanly possible, scanning the sides of the roads intently. He crossed an intersection, angling around a pile of bodies which had rushed to vacate a nearby building, all gathering on the sidewalk outside in a vomit of humanity from the mouth of the brickwork apartment.

Jason swerved right again, avoiding a similar collection of corpses on the left side, inadvertently rolling awkwardly over a fallen police officer and what appeared to be a man with his hands cuffed behind his back. Samantha gestured toward another section of road ahead where a horse lay on its side, motionless, still saddled, the logo of the L.A.P.D. stitched on its fabric. They passed the fallen horse and moved across another intersection, the darkness momentarily pierced by a strobe of blue lights, faded in the distance. Jason and Samantha shared a tentative glance, the lights flashing dimly, but still visible from almost a block away.

"Do you think someone's alive?" Samantha asked, nodding toward the flickering blue lights.

"I'm not sure."

"Should we look for a way around?"

"No. I say we keep moving forward. If it is a cop and he's still alive, he might be able to help direct us. If he's not alive, then we'll just keep driving through."

Samantha nodded and they continued driving another few moments until they came upon the scene and Jason swore under his breath. The police car was parked at an angle across one lane of traffic, though just beyond it were two others, pressed into an aggressive perpendicular embrace. One vehicle had slammed into the other broadside, likely just before the attack had come. Broken glass littered the roadway around them, the Los Angeles Police Department car parked just nearby. The tangle of the vehicular collision had blocked both lanes of travel through the intersection, creating a makeshift barricade they had no chance of squeezing through.

Jason applied the brakes, halting the RV a few yards from the point of impact, both he and Samantha staring at the twisted collision and the parked police car through their windshield. A few bodies rested on the road on the other side of the collision, shadowed by the taller buildings that surrounded them.

"Good grief," Elijah said from the back. "Even the police didn't make it."

"Are you going to check and see if anyone's still alive here?" Sarah asked.

"If anyone was alive, there'd be movement." Samantha shook her head and pointed at the map. "We should just move the cars out of the way and keep going. This is the right path."

"You sure there isn't an alternate route?" Jason stared up at the top levels of the nearby structure, rolling down his window and craning his neck to get a better look. "Those are some tall apartments."

"We'll be fine, especially if we're quick. I'm not all that keen on getting off-track. You make the call, though. I'm up for it if you are."

"Alright. Let's do it, and be fast."

"We need to move some cars." Samantha gestured through the windshield, speaking louder to the twins. " Up for giving us a hand?"

"Sure." Sarah stood first and Eli stood after.

Excitedly, Kale almost leaped to her feet, wagging her tail enthusiastically.

"You have to stay inside, girl." Jason crouched and gave the dog's head a stroke. "Sorry."

Kale's tail dipped and the O'Brians gathered together and vacated the RV, moving out onto the paved road outside. The walls of the surrounding buildings were painted in an outward strobe of dim glow from the police car's lights. An SUV had blasted into the passenger side door of a smaller sedan, metal crunching together, broken glass spilled across the surrounding pavement. The impact had been hard enough that it had pushed the sedan away from the hood of the SUV, so at least the vehicles weren't stuck fast to each other.

"Let's move that car first." Jason pointed toward the sedan, its passenger side scraped, crushed and buckled. "I'll get it in neutral, the rest of you help me push it as much as we can."

He walked around the driver's side and opened the door, leaning across the front seats. Samantha and the twins positioned themselves at the rear of the smashed car and as he shifted the vehicle into neutral, he gave them a thumbs up. Together, they maneuvered the damaged vehicle out of the intersection, pushing it inch by struggling inch toward the adjoining street. Once it had been moved, they retreated, approaching the SUV. Its hood was severely buckled, smashed up into the driver's seat and when Jason opened the door, he struggled to see how to access the gear shift.

"It's a miracle whoever was in here even survived." He brushed broken and gummy safety glass from the seat, grimacing when his hand became sticky and red from dried blood. "If they did. Hold on."

Grunting, he leaned into the vehicle, groping around until he finally found the shifter. It was an older SUV with a manual transmission, so he grabbed the stick and wrestled it out of third and into neutral. However, as they all gathered together to move it, the vehicle jerked but would not roll.

"Let's try again." The four of them worked together, leaning into their movements, desperately trying to push the vehicle out of the way, but it still wouldn't budge.

Jason blew out a breath and stood upright again, wiping sweat from his forehead.

"What should we do? I still don't think we can fit the RV through here." Samantha studied the space alongside the SUV.

"Why don't you all step over there?" Jason pointed toward the opposite sidewalk. "I'll just use the RV to push it out of the way."

"Not like it can get any more scraped up. Works for me." Samantha gave him a thumbs up.

He walked back to the vehicle and returned to his driver's seat, starting the engine as Samantha and the twins moved toward the opposite sidewalk. Kale sat on the floor next to him and whined softly, voicing her displeasure at not being included. Jason gave her an absent scratch on the head, then pressed the gas, pointing the nose of the vehicle toward the SUV. He eased it forward, tightening his grip on the wheel as the grille thudded into the rear of the SUV and ground to a halt. Jason accelerated further and the SUV began scraping across the concrete, the force of the RV's shove pushing it forward.

Jason moved slowly, trying not to cause untoward damage to the RV, but feathering the gas enough to push the vehicle across the intersection and toward the left, freeing up the central passage for them to continue driving. Once he'd scraped the SUV out of the way and pushed it up against a nearby apartment building, he shifted into reverse and backed the RV up to where it had been moments before. Standing, he walked to the door and left the RV, closing it between himself and Kale, who stared at him longingly.

"Do you think that'll do it?" Jason asked as he approached his family, gesturing toward the cleared section of road.

"I think we need to still move the police car." Samantha nodded toward the vehicle, emblazoned with the LAPD logo on its driver's side, still sitting half in the middle of the road. "It's not damaged, though, so it should go easier."

"Then let's do it."

They'd just reached the police car, bathed in the dim flicker of flashing blue lights, when a shout came from a nearby apartment. Jason froze, extending a hand, twisting toward the direction of the sharp, piercing voice from their left. The apartment building rose tall before them, at least eight stories, and the front doors were open. A trio of men walked toward them, striding across the cracked and glass-littered pavement, wearing the same colors and pattern as the men they'd run into earlier, the same Roman numeral five stitched into red fabric.

The group could have been part of the same as the one hours before, except for the fact that the newcomers carried pistols in their hands and were gesticulating wildly. From inside the RV, Kale erupted in a howling snarl of fury, barking wildly, her voice carrying through the half-open driver's side window. Jason glanced at the RV – it was too far to retreat to like they had done at the last encounter, and he and Samantha exchanged a look, both of them pushing together, standing between their children and the threat. The man in the lead lifted his pistol, pointing it at the O'Brians from across the street as he and his compatriots stopped, leering at the family.

"Well, well, well. What've we got here?"

CHAPTER NINETEEN

Los Angeles Convention Center
Los Angeles, California

The City of Los Angeles had been described to them as dirty, crime-riddled and not a place where you wanted to leave your car parked on the street. In actuality, nothing could have prepared them for what Los Angeles had become. Together, the group had watched from the upper levels of a nearby apartment building as death itself had walked through the streets, killing everyone in sight, with no survivors to speak of. While so many of their fellow coworkers had dashed down the stairs to the emergency exits, they'd stayed where they were, their fear of what was happening below being the only thing that had saved them from sharing in the morbid fate of their peers. They'd huddled in the upstairs conference room for hours, watching through the windows and waiting until they were convinced that whatever had killed so many people had cleared out.

"For the record," a skinny man with glasses said, glancing over his shoulder, "I'm still not wild about this idea."

A hulking building loomed before them, the pale glow of their flashlights splashing color across the stoic, stone exterior of the convention center.

"What's the worst that could happen?" The second man pointed his flashlight toward a darkened shadow near the side entrance to the building. He'd replaced his expensive suit coat with a canvas Army jacket that hung down to his hips. "We stumble upon more dead bodies? I've seen enough dead bodies to last me three lifetimes. A few more won't hurt."

"I should've never transferred to LA. I enjoyed my time back in Montana. It was nice, quiet, I got to work from home...."

"You and me both, man – except I was in Miami. Montana sounds like hell on earth."

"Montana's great. Way better than this craphole, that's for sure."

"Quit bickering. Door's open, let's check it out. Try to find some survivors." A third man, larger than the first two, speaking with an air of authority, pushed through them and reached the side entrance first.

He shouldered the door open, revealing an access hallway beyond, draped in darkness. The three of them directed their lights into the black, casting slices of faint illumination. Immediately, a corpse was in view, lying face down on the floor, sprawled where it had fallen.

"See? What did I tell you?" The man wearing glasses stabbed a finger at the dead body. "We're not gonna find any survivors here."

"Let's keep going," the second man said, following the lead of the larger of the three. "You never know."

"You don't need to be a brown noser anymore," the man with the glasses whispered to his friend. "He's not our boss anymore. Pretty sure the firm isn't coming back after this."

"Just be quiet. If he wants to lead the way, let him lead the way." The other man in the Army jacket rolled his eyes, then followed the first.

They made their way around the corpse and moments later entered a network of hallways leading to surrounding offices that supported the massive structure they found themselves in. Using their flashlights to navigate, they walked the perimeter, coming across a few more corpses but little else. Eventually, they came across a set of double doors which led to a staging area along the rear of the building. Dozens of bodies littered the carpeted hallway just outside the double doors, a surge of attempted escapees who hadn't made it nearly far enough before the invisible killer had claimed them.

The man with the glasses swallowed audibly as the larger man pushed against the double doors. It didn't give at first, the doors bumping into something on the other side, and the large man had to put his weight into it, grunting as he shoved them forward. The doors pushed away a heap of dead bodies just on the other side, barely creating an opening wide enough for the large man to fit through.

"I really don't like this." The man with the glasses shook his head.

"Nobody's forcing you to stick with us."

"Who else am I going to stick with?"

The man in the Army jacket stepped through the gap between the doors and over the dead bodies just inside. They entered the loading area for the building, discovering another large gathering of corpses strewn about. The floor beneath their feet was neatly polished cement, shelves standing along walls, several totes of supplies stacked nearby. They walked their flashlights throughout the large room, the glow reflecting from a pair of corrugated steel garage doors, both of them still pulled closed. A few people dressed in work uniforms lay motionless along with a few other men wearing three-piece suits of black and white, plastic earpieces in their ears and hanging out of their collars. The three exchanged puzzled looks, then understanding dawned, and their expressions grew grim.

From somewhere ahead, the muffled sound of a hammering bang echoed from the deeper recesses of the loading dock. As a group, the trio charged forward, jogging across the cement floor in the direction of the desperate banging sound. In between the slam of fist on metal, a voice called out, filtered through the barricade of double doors.

"Is someone out there?" The voice was little more than croak, faded through the doors. Almost immediately afterwards, another drumbeat of thuds battered the interior of the doors hard, a repeated blow of desperate impacts. "Please! Is someone there?"

"Hold on!" The large man shouted back, lumbering his way to the doors.

He clutched the two door handles and pulled back with all of his strength, but the doors wouldn't budge.

"Please!" A voice came from inside again. "I need... please... I need help!"

The other two men joined the first, all three of them trying everything they could to pry the doors open.

"It's not working." The large man bent over, placing his hands on his thighs.

"Hold on." The man in the Army jacket pointed toward a nearby supply closet.

He jogged off toward it and opened the door, surveying its contents. Shelves of tools lined each wall and in the narrow space between two of them, a crowbar rested against the wall. The man darted inside and grabbed the crowbar, then retreated, turning and running back toward the other two men, huddled by the double doors.

"Step aside," he gasped, lifting the crowbar. "Watch out!"

The large man and the smaller one in glasses did as requested, each of them taking a step back to give the third man access to the doors. Dropping his flashlight in his jacket pocket, the man clutched the crowbar with two fists and rammed the sharpened edge hard into the seam between the doors. It banged loudly, though didn't wedge deep.

"Come on!" the man shouted, then drew back, torquing his waist, and swung again, brutally stabbing the spear of the sharp end of the crowbar toward the two doors.

It struck home. The blade hammered into the seam, slamming between the doors with a satisfying metallic echo. Grunting, his white knuckles tightening around the other end, the man in the Army jacket pushed, then pulled, his jaw clenched. Returning his own flashlight to a pocket, the larger man perched alongside the other and together they shoved the crowbar as hard as they possibly could.

"This isn't working." The man in the Army jacket gasped for breath.

"The hinges. Try the hinges!" The man with the glasses stabbed a narrow finger at the hinges of the door.

"Maybe... you are good for something... after all," the larger man gasped and the third one immediately went to work on the hinges, striking and prying them with the crowbar.

The hinges were, indeed, weaker than the center lock on the door had been, and within moments he'd separated two of the hinges and was working on the third.

"Hey! You still there?" The large man shouted at the doors as the man in the Army jacket continued working on the third hinge. "Hey! Say something!" He turned toward the other man. "Go faster!"

"Almost there!" He wedged the blade end of the bar into the last segment of the hinge and tore it away, freeing it from its housing.

The door jolted as the hinge came free and the man in the Army jacket used the crowbar to pry it from the surrounding frame. A man appeared in the shadow beyond the door, his face pale, dressed in a rumpled, wrinkled suit. His voice was a rasping gasp of desperate dehydration, more of a breathy exhalation than an actual collection of words. His face glistened, his hair was tussled, his white-colored shirt was stained yellow with sweat and he held a gas mask in one hand, which dropped to the ground as he caught sight of his rescuers.

"Th-thank... thank you," he choked out as he stumbled free, then lurched forward.

The man in the Army jacket tossed the crowbar aside and held out his arms, barely catching the man as he collapsed, gingerly setting him down on the ground. Beyond the fallen man, the small room was filled with another sprawling crowd of corpses, bodies resting face-down or face-up, several of them wearing the same three-piece suits and earpieces as the dead bodies on the loading dock outside.

On the floor, gasping for breath was the only survivor and the man in the Army jacket stared intently at his features, his eyes drawing wide and his mouth growing dry as recognition dawned on him. He looked up to his friend, the man with the glasses, who tipped them up from his eyes, squinting at the same face.

"Is that..." his voice was a thin whisper. "Is that who I think it is?"

"Yes," The man in the Army jacket nodded slowly. "I think it is."

READ THE NEXT BOOK IN THE SERIES

Foliant Book 2

Available Here
books.to/foliant2

Made in the USA
Las Vegas, NV
28 February 2025

18823640R10204